C000285215

SORRY. NOT SORRY

EMILY JAMES

STALK EMILY JAMES:

Facebook
Goodreads
Amazon
Newsletter
Bookbub

BOOKS BY EMILY JAMES:

The Blingwood Billionaires series

Book 1—Sorry. Not Sorry

Book 2 – Chasing the Wrong Bride

Book 3 – Catch a Falling Star

The Love in Short series

Book 1—Operation My Fake Girlfriend

Book 2—Sexy With Attitude Too

Book 3—You Only Love Once

Book 4—Leaving Out Love

The Power of Ten series

Book 1—Ten Dates

Book 2—Ten Dares

Book 3—Ten Lies

CHAPTER 1

SKYLA

"*P*ut the mop down and step away from the bucket," Jessie orders.

I keep my back to her and continue to scrub the floor of my office.

"Skyla, you're going to wipe the shine from the marble."

She's wrong. Marble gets its name from the way it glistens, much like my eyes at this very moment.

"I've been overwatering my Swiss Cheese plant and now the pot's left a mark."

Jessie steps closer. "I never knew cheese grew on plants."

Her voice is too strained to carry the joke, but I play along and laugh even though it hurts my throat.

Jessie's hand grabs mine, stilling my action. "I heard what that bastard did."

I divert my gaze out of the window instead of meeting her probing stare. The sun is shining too brightly for April, like it somehow lost the memo that today is a dark day. After what happened, I'd done the first thing I always do when I'm in a mess—clean.

In the courtyard below, my boss, Mr. Blingwood, is taking a call. He's beside the elaborate fountain that marks the entrance to the finest hotel in Santa Barbara. Shouldering his cell against his ear, he pulls the sleeve of his suit jacket up to check his watch. He's always so busy. Any moment now, he'll dash inside our office building and, if I'm not careful, catch me idling.

I need to pull myself together.

Dropping the mop in the bucket, I turn to face Jessie. She's wearing her pink maid outfit with white canvas sneakers. She looks like a Hollywood starlet playing a part in a movie, instead of the best housekeeper the resort has. "I'm fine. It's not like Mike and I were exclusive." The smile I force on my lips is trembling.

"Skyla, you went out for dinner three times last week. He had flowers delivered to your desk—then he screws the new hire in the cleaning closet! I don't care if you weren't 'official,' that's not how a guy plays things casual. It's downright disrespectful. He's been playing you this whole time." Even though I wince at the brutal truth, she keeps going, "But don't you worry, I'm going to get him back. If he wants to play, then game on. I'm up to bat and my eyes are on his balls!"

I shake my head. "Let karma take care of it. No point you getting fired or landing yourself in jail." I try to reassure Jessie that there is no need to be angry on my behalf, but nothing is deterring her from her warpath.

"I'll torture him first, screw with everything he ever loved. The *Star Trek* figurines on his shelf—they're dead—and the picture of his sister, that's next. I mean, who has a picture of their sibling on their desk? It's weird! Then I'm going to—"

"Jess, it's fine. I'm fine. We wanted different things, that's all."

"You're damn right you wanted different things. You wanted and deserved respect and he wanted to screw the new girl! He is a lowlife, Skyla."

"Mike and Jenny really shouldn't be doing it during office hours. Maybe that's why he was late with the quarterly reports," I huff. "I'm really regretting hiring him. Mike performed so well in the interview, but he's turned out to be incredibly disappointing." For a second I wonder what upsets me more, him hooking up with our boss's new personal assistant and humiliating me in front of our colleagues, or him proving to be a bad hire. "I'm normally so good at my job. Mr. Blingwood says so all the time."

Jessie concentrates on me intently, then arches her brow. "You're brilliant at your job. The Blingwood Beach Resort would fall apart without you at the helm of HR. Don't let Mike have you questioning your judgment. At least you found out what he was like early on and now you won't waste another minute on that loser."

"You're right. Better to find out now that he's a cheater than to waste years of my life with the wrong person."

"Exactly, and besides, I bet the sex was awful with a man like him."

"I never—"

"You were dating nearly two months and you and he never...," Jessie's reply is casual but her mouth hangs open with shock. "Well, I guess I'm not surprised. A cheater like him probably has a micropenis and a machine-gun style," Jessie mocks. "He looks like the sort of guy who leaves his socks on. I doubt he even preheats the oven before he rams his little nugget in. You need a man capable of satisfying *all* your needs—"

"Jessie, stop." I hold out my hand. "I never...." My cheeks

warm as I wonder what's wrong with me.

"Oh honey, don't worry. I'm not surprised Mike couldn't bring his O game. He probably thinks the G-spot was developed by Google."

I chuckle halfheartedly and then clarify. "No. I mean, we didn't. I never...." I widen my eyes at her, hoping not to have to say the words.

"You never had sex with him?" Something like relief lights up her face and her tone heightens a decibel. "That's a good thing in lieu of what's happened." She's nodding her head with satisfaction until her expression turns serious. "Wait, you've got a B.O.B. until we find you someone new?"

"Just a small one someone got me for the Christmas Secret Santa. But that's not important—"

"Honey, getting your O is very important."

"I wouldn't know." There's a tightness when I try to swallow.

"You wouldn't know," Jessie repeats. "You've had an O before, right?"

I bite my lip until the slight smarting of pain distracts me from my embarrassment.

Ah yes, let's add more humiliation to my day by discussing my non-starter of a sex life.

"Mike and I tried to do it once after the office party when we'd had a few too many drinks." My stomach churns as I remember the ill-fated fumble in the passenger seat of his car. I had hoped the alcohol would give me a spring in my step and ignite something. That I'd feel the urgency and passion I'd read about in romance books, but when it came down to it, it felt unnatural and forced, and Mike couldn't "rise" to the occasion. I can't help wonder if my curvy girl status and lack of flexibility in the confined space was to blame. "I couldn't make him hard." *Maybe that's why he cheated?*

4

Jessie scrunches her nose. "He couldn't perform?"

I nod.

Her lips tip up in a smile but she fights to keep it neutral. "That's a *Mike* problem, not a *you* problem. Wait, he didn't let you think you were to blame for that, did he?"

"No," I reassure her, remembering him frustratingly palming himself and telling me this had *never* happened before, while I fumbled around like an oversized, drunk contortionist, almost kicking through the windshield as I hurried to pull on my panties.

"Your subconscious was probably screaming at you not to go all the way with him—"

"Maybe, but I never...." Jessie's my best friend and I should have told her before today. But, like everyone else, she assumed I had experience, and I didn't want to identify myself as different. I take a calming breath and admit, "I'm a twenty-four-year-old virgin, and even though I know there is no shame in that, I am starting to wonder when I'm going to get my happy ending."

"Oh." Jessie looks away momentarily shocked, her mouth puckering as she considers how to reply, and then she faces me and gives me a huge, gratified smile. "Well, then I am super proud of you for not wasting it on a schmuck like Mike."

"Do you think I'm broken? To get to this age and not have... it's weird, right?"

"No! You're not broken and it's not weird." Jessie's hand grips mine and she squeezes. "Honey, I threw my virginity at Dirk Davenport in senior year because I was stupid enough to think he loved me and that he'd ask me to prom. Two weeks later he screwed the captain of the cheer team and took her instead. Holding out for 'the one' and not rushing into anything you'll regret is admirable."

"I don't want to be admirable; I don't even care if he's not 'the one.' Mike was supposed to take my damn virginity and he couldn't, or he had too much to drink and his penis stopped working. After our failed attempt, he backed off, and I don't blame him. I couldn't excite him—"

"Don't you start with that shit, Skyla. He is the problem here, not you!"

"The problem is, I want a healthy sex life like other women my age. I want passion and fury and to feel like I'm going to spontaneously combust if I don't get some. But so far, I've never felt like that, Jessie."

She brings the palms of her hands to my shoulders, and her sparkly blue eyes pin me to the spot. "You will feel like that one day. But it won't happen right away. You've got to adjust your expectations. The first few times you have sex it's going to be pretty lackluster. Take my first time with Dirk. He thought foreplay was squeezing my boobs like he was kneading dough!"

I let out a sympathetic chuckle. "Mike and I got to second base, but his attention to my nipples felt like an algebraic equation. I even heard him counting aloud."

Jessie rolls her eyes disgustedly. "That doesn't surprise me. You need someone hot who has experience, who can teach you *all* the ways—that person is not Mike Powell. Trust me, when you meet Mr. V-Card destroyer, you won't hesitate, and he won't have any problems doing the business. And then, my friend, you'll want to do it all over again, every day, forever." Her grin is giddy, like she's remembering the best sex of her life.

"Yeah, it'll be different when I meet the right guy," I reply, replacing the hurt and disappointed tone of my voice with one of conviction.

"People rarely choose right the first few times. Look at me, I've got a two-year-old and no baby daddy in sight."

I give her a consolatory one-armed hug while still

holding the mop handle in my other hand. Jessie's the most attractive woman I know. She's loyal and her sense of humor is off the charts, yet she's been single since she got knocked up. I think that's mostly because her confidence was shattered—not that she'd ever admit it—but she reached out to the baby daddy to tell him about the pregnancy and he never got back to her.

I lean back and tell her, "Thank God Macy has your brains because Mr. One Night Stand must be a complete idiot not to come running when he heard you were pregnant. And maybe you got it exactly right. You got some mind-blowing sex and your gorgeous daughter with none of the ensuing relationship politics."

"True. I'm fine being single, and since my mom got her new job selling sex toys, I'm never short of orgasms."

I snicker uncomfortably. A while ago Jessie told me how her mom hosts adult parties and how she sometimes exchanges black-market premium hotel supplies like toilet paper, shampoo, and body soap for the latest O-inducing technology.

"You've got to stop stealing hotel supplies," I remind her.

"What's a few sheets of toilet paper when it makes me a happier, more vivacious and alert employee." She winks. "It could be worse; Mike uses company packaging to send the *Star Trek* crap he sells on eBay. Can't you get him fired? Then you'd never have to see him again."

"No, I can't do that." I sigh, even though the thought of never seeing him again is appealing. "But I do wonder how I might avoid employing such a work-shy, arrogant asshole in the future. Perhaps there are some new screening tools I've overlooked," I think aloud. "Myers-Briggs and Clifton tests are good tools for identifying employee strengths, but they don't highlight flaws like idleness, two timing, and back-sliding tendencies." I use the hand that's not holding the mop, lean over my desk and scribble a note on my to-do list—research new employee personality tests!

When I look back at Jessie, she's peering through the blinds. "Mr. Blingwood just finished his call. I better get back to work before he catches me here. I've still got a dozen rooms to turn over."

I follow her to the window, and we watch as Logan Blingwood puts his cell inside his suit jacket before opening the door to the car that pulls up beside him. Out jumps a gangly pre-teen with long blonde hair that's past her hips.

"That's our boss's niece, Callie," I say.

Logan Blingwood messes with his niece's hair to greet her—earning him a playful blow to the ribs. From the driver side, her father, Logan's brother Drew gets out of the car and joins them. Together, the two businessmen are knee-weakening hotness—forces to be reckoned with in designer suits cut perfectly to emphasize their power and perfection.

"Wow. That family has like really, really good genes, but they could at least smile now and then. If I had a bazillion dollars, a luxury resort, and a fleet of high-end cars, the grin on my face would have to be surgically removed, 'cuz you can bet your butt it wouldn't shift otherwise."

"Logan, I mean, Mr. Blingwood isn't so bad."

Jessie shrugs her agreement. "He's okay as far as billionaire bosses go—not that I would want to get on the wrong side of him, but man, his fiancée is a first-class bitch."

Logan Blingwood's fiancée, Dana Gee, is a hotel heiress famous for attending each and every swanky party she can get an invitation to. She makes Paris Hilton look like a Walmart checkout girl and seeks fame more than a curvy girl like me covets the last slice of our resident chef's filthily decadent triple chocolate fudge cake.

"What's she done now?" I probe, glad of the distraction from discussing Mike and my eternal V-card.

"The newspapers portray Dana as this socialite party girl, but they don't know the half of it. Since she moved into one of the penthouse suites after her fight with her rich daddy, and she got her claws into Logan—God knows what he sees in her—she now spends her time between her own penthouse and his. She actually runs her finger about the place after I have cleaned checking for dust. She makes me do her laundry which, okay, so it's my job, but she also gives me her 'hand wash only' underwear to wash."

I shudder. Jessie's sent me plenty of photos of Dana's suite. Whenever Logan's away on business, it's littered with vodka bottles, weed, and the odd line of coke she forgot to snort. But hand-washing other people's underwear should always be a hard pass on both sides of the equation, regardless if you are a maid or not.

"She is pretty high maintenance," I say, which is putting it nicely.

We stare at the two men for a moment, knowing that as soon as Logan turns and walks inside the building it'll be time for us to hurry back to our respective jobs.

Our boss's older brother is the slightly taller of the two. And merely standing still, wearing a suit that skims his thick, broad shoulders like it was cut to emphasize every hard muscle, he looks perfect. Perfect and powerful. Like he was sculpted rather than born. He's unnerving yet mesmerizing to watch as he removes his jacket, throwing it over his forearm and unbuttoning the sleeve of his black shirt beneath the midday California sun.

"So, that's Drew Blingwood?"

I nod while I exhale through my mouth.

"I thought he lived in New York. What's he doing here?"

Drew turns his head unknowingly toward us and I sigh heavily at his brooding good looks. Even unsmiling his distinctive cheekbones and thick-set jaw has my heart rate quickening. He's gorgeous despite his scowly expression as he and Logan discuss important billionaire brother business.

"Drew's moving into one of the penthouses. He's an architect and is staying here while his new beach house is built, according to Mr. Blingwood," I tack on in case Jessie thinks I've been snooping or looking him up online.

Callie, his daughter, who had been swooshing her hand in the fountain, stops and joins her father. He begins unloading their luggage from the trunk of his SUV. "Poor thing, her mother died and now she's living with Drew full-time."

"That's sad."

"It's heartbreaking. Growing up without a mother is so hard," I say, referring to my own personal experience.

"So, he's grieving?"

"I don't think so. Not in the conventional sense. They were co-parenting before his ex-wife died."

"So, he's single and available?" Jessie asks but doesn't give me a chance to answer. "Hot, rich, single dad moves to the Blingwood Resort. Whatever will we do with him?" She waggles her eyebrows mischievously at me.

"He's certainly cute, in a brooding, panty-destroying way," I agree, ogling the ease in which he throws the luggage onto the hotel cart. "And he probably has a size zero nanny with a killer body and an infectious smile."

Jessie turns from the window to face me. "You have a killer body and an infectious smile. You're smart. Beautiful. Maybe he's the V-Card destroyer you've been looking for?"

"No. No way," I insist. "After Mike, there's no way I am getting involved with another coworker from the resort. Gossip spreads like wildfire in this place, and I am not drawing it my way ever again."

Jessie shakes her head disgustedly like caring about what people say is a bad thing. "Screw the gossips. But you are going to have to deal with Mike since he works in the office opposite yours and Jenny is Logan's PA. I think you should get Mike's ass fired."

I chuckle. That would be one way to make sure I don't have to deal with the mortification of having been cheated on by the office jerk.

"No, I'd never do that. I was setting a poor precedent sleeping with a colleague anyway. I'm not getting him fired from his job because it didn't work out. People would lose trust in me."

"Hey, you can date whomever you please. There's no policy here against fraternizing with colleagues. Most of the resort staff are either dating or screwing. You've done nothing wrong, Mike on the other hand—"

"I know, I'm just saying. I'd rather people didn't find out I was seeing someone from work, and you can be sure him getting fired will raise questions. I'm going to have to rise above it. Move on."

"Rise above it? Honey, you might have tried to hide it, but people knew you were dating Mike. Betty from house-keeping is the one who told me that you walked right in and saw Mike and Jenny making out in the janitor's closet, and you just picked up the mop bucket and left!" Her face is incredulous. "Tell me why you didn't shove the mop right up his—"

"I was in shock...." A wave of nausea passes through me again at the thought of my colleagues knowing I was not only dating someone I worked with but got cheated on with another employee. "Jess, he was talking about us booking a flight to see my dad. I feel like such an idiot." I clamp my eyes shut so I don't have to see her reaction. "You're sure he didn't cheat because I failed to turn him on? Sex is important to guys, isn't it? If I can't get a guy to be attracted to me, I'm doomed to stay single."

"No!" she shrieks. "Sex is important to men *and* women.

This happened because he is a limp-dick moron whose pride got hurt. Skyla, please don't ever think that you had something to do with him cheating. He cheated because he is too stupid to realize how special you are. You're a beautiful, strong woman, and it'll take more than dicky-dickface to bring you down, you got me?"

A pained chuckle passes my lips. "I am so done with men. Jenny can have dicky-dickface."

"Atta girl!"

"I'm never *ever* dating a person from this resort again."

I glance through the window and see Logan directing Doug, our valet from the hotel lobby, to take care of Drew's car while his remaining luggage is loaded onto the trolley.

"I better get back to work." I sigh.

"Macy's at Betty's tonight for a sleepover. Why don't we hit the beach bar, order some nachos with extra cheese and drown our troubles? It'll cheer you up and we can plot Mike's downfall while sampling the wine list."

Jessie is grinning and nodding as though trying to make the subliminal message take root.

"I can't tonight. I have a work dinner with Mr. Blingwood to strategize the new resort. Rain check?"

"Of course, but we are getting some drinks soon—it's been too long. I'll get rid of this for you." Jessie pries the mop from my hands and scoops the bucket up by its handle, then turns to leave, casually commenting over her shoulder, "If I see Mike, now I have all I need to drown him."

Strangled laughter forces its way past my lips, and I cover it with a cough so I don't encourage her.

"Seriously don't. He's not worth the effort it'd take to jam his big head in there."

Jessie throws me a cunning smile that has me concerned she might get arrested today.

"Let me worry about that."

CHAPTER 2

DREW

"I'll take this room," my twelve—going on twenty—year old says, pointing to the master suite from its doorway.

Boasting cashmere tones with restoration hardware furnishings, doors to a private balcony overlooking ocean views, a walk-in closet and a master bath, this is one of the best suites in the entire Blingwood Resort—I should know, I designed it.

"Nice try, kiddo, this is the master. It's for grown-ups."

"Hmph," Callie grunts. "Fine. I'll take the smallest room with the en suite, and Susie can have the second largest when she comes to stay with us when she gets her vacation."

Susie was Callie's nanny, who is still back in New York. It's doubtful we'll see her again, but I can't bring myself to say that to Callie since she's already lost more relationships than is fair to a kid her age.

"Will Uncle Logan sleep in our penthouse too? There are

enough bedrooms," she says barely catching me shake my head as she glances over the hotel information sheet. She grins sweetly as her eyes flick to where it has been graffitied in *sharpie* with: *Doug loves Sally*. "Did you know there's a spa, a golf course, a yoga studio, spectacular gardens…." She rolls her eyes.

"Yes, I am aware of the amenities." I smirk. I won several awards a couple of years ago for the redesign of the resort. It's one of my finest projects. I do, however, worry that raising my daughter in a hotel resort—even temporarily, until our permanent home is built—is a bad idea, but I try not to worry I am failing her and instead think of it as an adventure of sorts.

She purses her lips. "I'll be the judge of whether anything is spectacular. You know what would be spectacular?"

I shake my head.

"A water park or a death slide." Her face lights up. "That would be cool. Maybe we can persuade Uncle Logan to install one."

"No. There's no death slide or any prospect of one." *And even if there was, my dare-devil daughter, you would not be going on it.*

"Dad! You're so grumpy," she huffs. Maybe she's right, but if being grumpy means that she stays in one piece, I'll take it. "There's a pool you can use if you want."

Callie reads from the pamphlet once again. "A 200-foot infinity pool with free cannabis."

My eyes flick to the page in horror.

"Cabanas. *Not* cannabis."

She smiles serenely. "I know, I'm screwing with you, Dad."

I inhale a long breath—my daughter screwing with me is aging me ten years at a time. I try to bring the conversation back to lighter matters.

"We'll be staying here awhile, until our new home is ready in June. You think we'll be okay?" I try to remove the concern from my expression. Moving back to my hometown was not part of my plans for world domination in the architectural field, but after the third and final nanny quit, I decided something had to give and unfortunately that was my career plans. Callie's needs trump being located in the business hub of the world and technically, as an award-winning architect, I can work anywhere. Here, we have the support of family, and that's what Callie needs. Sound connections and people she can rely on.

"Dad, stop looking so grumpy, you'll give yourself wrinkles—you're already starting to go gray. You need to take better care of yourself or you'll never bag a woman."

I cock my brow at her. "I have no plans to meet any women, let alone *bag* them."

"You'll meet someone when the time is right. Relax, we'll be fine here. Grandma is right up the road and Uncle Logan is in one of the other penthouses. Uncle Tate will be in town as soon as he finishes filming his movie—"

"You spoke to Uncle Tate?"

"I text him all the time. He's working on a really cool movie, and it's set in the future where women rule the world. Uncle Tate says they're all super-hot, so I think he must be somewhere tropical like Africa." She winks, and I shudder.

Callie probably already knows that my brother, the Hollywood superstar, is not referring to temperature when he describes his co-stars, so I move the conversation along and make a mental note to warn Tate to stay PG when he talks to my daughter.

"We've got our own state-of-the-art kitchen, and there's a world-class restaurant on-site. And best of all, Uncle Logan says we can eat for free while we're here. You want me to cook you something for dinner or shall I order you room service?"

"We should probably unpack first and then I want to check out the pool. After that, you can take me on a tour and then order room service since I'm not in the mood for food poisoning today."

"Oh, I can, huh? And hey! My cooking isn't that bad."

"It's terrible, Dad; it's a wonder I'm still alive. We should check out the gift shop, too. Don't those places sell candy and souvenirs? We can send Susie something nice. That way, she won't forget about me."

My heart sinks in my chest.

"As if anyone could forget about you."

She blinks twice. The tip of her blonde head dips down, and I feel like my chest is trapped in a vice. I crouch down and use my finger and thumb to tip her face to mine. "Honey, no one is ever going to forget about you. You're quite simply, unforgettable."

"I know, Dad. I just wish we found our people, you know?"

"We have people. You have two uncles and an aunt. You have your grandma and—"

"I don't have a mom, and Grandpa died." The very mention of my ex and my father is like a knife to my heart. Too much loss, not enough chances for redemption. From here on out, there'll be no more mistakes. No more testing fate. My relationships stay clean and uncomplicated.

Callie continues, "Dad, I won't be around forever. I'm going to go to college one day and I don't want you to be left alone."

"I won't be alone. I'm going to college with you. I've given it a lot of thought. I'll buy a house next to your campus. Hey, I could even enroll in some of your classes."

Her expression turns aghast, which has me fighting to keep my laughter from escaping.

"Just screwing with you," I tease her back, but then add, "You don't need to worry. Your old dad is fine on his own. We have family who care about us, and I'm not going anywhere. You know that don't you?"

She nods her head. "Except swimming, you're coming swimming with me, aren't you?"

I find myself smiling even though my heart is breaking for my girl who is without a mother. "Yes, Callie. We'll go to the pool, but after that you have got to eat, and then Nanna is coming to sit with you while I go to a business dinner with Uncle Logan."

"Will Nanna bring the dogs?"

"I sincerely hope not," I reply, earning me a comically cross glare from Callie.

My mother opened an animal rescue place not far from here. I personally don't care for household pets but it's helping to keep Mom busy since we lost Dad. She says it's better than therapy.

"Maybe we should get a dog. We'd be helping Nanna out. She's always looking for homes for her rescue animals. Big ones, smelly ones, hairy ones—we might find you your twin. And best of all, we'd be doing a nice thing since they all need good homes."

"Honey, we've been over this. We can't get an animal because of my allergies. You know how their fur makes me sneeze."

Which isn't an outright lie. Okay, so I haven't had an allergy attack since I was twelve, but I do have a severe lack of time, and if Callie thinks I can tolerate pets we'll wind up with a whole menagerie.

"You're right, I forgot about your allergies. I'll ask Nanna if she has any bald ones when she comes over. Now, you better get unpacked or else you're never going to find your bathing suit in time. I'll text Uncle Logan and ask him to come join us—it might cheer him up since he seemed a little distracted earlier. You think he's okay?"

At her mentioning it, when we arrived at the resort, Logan seemed distracted and not himself, but it didn't seem prudent to ask why while Callie was in earshot. I can't help wondering if it has anything to do with his high-maintenance fiancée.

"I'm sure he's fine. Probably work stress. The new resort we've been designing in Miami is almost ready to open and so Logan has a lot of work to do."

Callie, seemingly satisfied with my answer, moves toward the next biggest room and I watch her, wondering how such a small person can evoke such powerful feelings—and also how she manages to twist me around her little finger.

"Oh, and Dad?"

"Yeah?"

"I love you."

My swallow becomes painful. "I love you too, squirt."

WE MAKE it to the pool later that day to find Logan, still in his suit, seated at one of the tables. Callie and I grab a couple of luxury recliners—complete with sun canopies—near him.

"Why don't you do some laps in the pool while I talk to Uncle Logan?" I ask Callie, who is chomping at the bit to cool off from the late afternoon sun.

"Okay, Dad," Callie replies, greets Logan and then pulls her swim goggles over her eyes and dives in, quickly darting toward the deep end.

Callie swims with confidence and I try to relax. She's taken swimming lessons since she was old enough to walk.

Before that, her mother used to take her to the pool in our apartment building. A water baby, that's what Crystal used to call her. Still, I don't take my eyes off her.

"You're amazing with Callie," Logan says, moving to the lounger beside me.

"She's easy to be amazed by."

"She sure is."

"Do you think you and Dana will have kids?" I ask, even though I can't imagine my brother's fiancée risking the weight gain and stretch marks that can come with pregnancy. A surrogate is much more her style, along with a team of nannies in case lack of sleep prompts a dark shadow or heaven forbid an eye bag.

Logan is quiet, so I flick my eyes to his and then back to the pool. Callie performs a perfect turn and then heads back toward us.

"What is it?" I ask.

"She's pregnant. Dana is pregnant." My mouth falls open and my head snaps to his. He has the look of a broken man. "We were careful. I was careful. Not once without a condom. Dana was on the pill. She *said* she was on the pill. I don't…." He shakes his head and I turn back to watch Callie who has stopped swimming and is talking to a woman in the pool.

"I guess no contraception is one hundred percent." Though two methods failing, that's super unlucky—or lucky maybe? "Congratulations, bro!"

"Thanks, I guess."

"So, that's why you announced your engagement?"

"Proposing felt like the right thing to do." He shrugs like the weight of the world is on his broad shoulders. "Dana thinks she's about one month into the pregnancy. She's sending out the invitations for an engagement party right away—she wants to get married before she's showing. We're keeping the wedding date a secret so we don't get invaded by the press. So, yeah. I'm sticking by her."

"Never thought for a second you wouldn't. But, you're not happy?"

"I'm… I'm in shock. When she told me she was pregnant, I… froze. I kept thinking about when the doctor told us Dad had died and… being a dad is a big deal."

I remember that moment too, but it twists in my gut for a whole bunch of additional reasons.

"Yeah, being a father is a big deal. The biggest. But it's also worth it."

Logan nods. "Dana wants to do this photoshoot with one of the gossip magazines to announce our engagement formally. She wasn't happy about it, but she agreed to wait a while before spilling the news of the baby. You know how she is with her celebrity image. She wants to be in control of how the information gets out."

I let out a chuckle. "But you don't want to do it?"

"Normally I run a mile from her *great ideas* of photoshoots and magazine interviews, but I feel like I need to give her this. She's scared too."

"Yeah, can't say I'd want to be on the cover of magazines either, but I suppose it's a necessary evil when you date someone semi-famous. I still don't get how our little brother puts up with the attention, but you can handle one measly photoshoot. And, bigger picture—happy wife, happy life!" I try placating him since he seems unsure. I remember my own uncertainty when Crystal announced she was pregnant, but it didn't last long. As soon as I saw Callie on the screen, moving around inside her mother's swollen belly, I knew right there and then that life was about to get better. It'll be the same for Logan too. "I'm happy for you. You'll make a great dad. But I didn't even think you and Dana were that serious."

"We weren't," he admits. "I've been so busy with getting this place remodeled and planning the opening of the second resort, having a baby was not on my to-do list. But he or she will be loved, I'll make damn sure of that."

"They sure will. Has Dana had an ultrasound yet?"

"No, she's scheduling it. She wants the same doctor Rihanna had and there's a wait list." He rolls his eyes.

"I'm proud of you, man. Doing the right thing is scary as hell. When Crystal and I found out we were expecting Callie, I already knew our relationship wasn't working but we made co-parenting work. We were friends first, and somehow we managed to maintain that through the divorce. When she got sick, boy was I glad of that friendship." It still cuts me to this day that Crystal died, but I'm glad I was there with her when we said our final goodbye. She passed knowing I was as committed to our daughter as I'd been that first day seeing the ultrasound.

"How's Callie doing now?"

"I can't believe it's been almost a year since Crystal died. Callie had her last therapy session in New York before we left and the therapist said she's doing great, but I still worry. I'm barely surviving as her father; I don't know how to be her mother too."

Callie's head dips under the water and I jump to my feet just as her head pops back up. Then she does it again and I notice she's doing a backward roll. I sit back down and watch as the woman beside her does one too.

"Callie's fine. Relax. The woman in the pool with her is the head of my HR department. Skyla. She's one of my best employees and totally trustworthy."

I relax a little and watch the woman perform handstands in the water with Callie. Her shapely thighs standing up, shimmering in the sun, draw my attention. When she comes back to the surface, she flings her long, dirty blonde hair back. It's an entirely innocent action, but from where I'm sitting—*and watching*—it looks hot and my dick takes notice.

Damn, it's been so long since I got any action that innocuous, random, curvy women swinging their wet hair out of their face now turns me on.

"You thought about meeting someone new? I could ask Dana if she has any single friends."

"No."

"What do you mean, no? No, you haven't thought about meeting anyone new or no you'd rather meet someone organically?"

"I mean, no. I have no interest in meeting anyone. My hands are full with Callie, and I'm not risking another person coming in and out of her life. Stability. That's why we moved here."

"I know things didn't work out with Crystal but—"

"Logan. I'm not looking to date. I had a few hook ups in New York but I never saw anyone twice. I have no plans to meet anyone. You'll see once your kid gets here; their needs take priority over anything and everyone else." Which is something I don't mind at all. In fact, becoming a father is the best thing that ever happened to me. I squash the thought and concentrate on Callie and Logan's HR woman as they shriek while they playfully shove water in each other's faces. Skyla seems to be enjoying it as much as Callie.

"Okay, bro, but don't think you can't have it all. A successful career, a person you love, a healthy, well-balanced daughter…. You deserve all of that. Is this about Dad?"

"What? No—"

"Because I know you guys weren't talking when he died but you know he—"

"It's not about our father. I can't multitask a relationship and fatherhood, and I'm not willing to screw up my relation-ship with my kid. Now drop it and hail someone to grab us some drinks. Your niece is going to be in need of one when she finally stops trying to drown that poor woman over there."

* * *

AWHILE LATER WHEN Logan has gone back to his office, I check my emails but look up every few seconds to check that Callie's safe. She and the young woman with the dirty blonde hair and shapely thighs lark about in the pool; they're having so much fun, it takes almost all my effort to stay on task rather than join them.

I read an email from my assistant in New York letting me know that everything is running smoothly since my departure. Then I fire off a reply checking how the Dubai project is going, and when I look up from my screen, I see Logan's HR woman pulling herself out of the water and casting her toned thigh over the side. In a simple black swimsuit that accentuates a curvaceous body, she looks divine, shimmering beneath the late afternoon sun.

As she comes closer, I notice something.

She's young.

Too young for the way my body is reacting to her.

Early twenties, perhaps.

I must have ten years on her.

Her breasts are full and perky. Her hips wide but perfectly proportioned to her waist, and when she turns back to check if Callie is following, all I can see is her ass! It's big and round and fucking perfect.

Mind outta the gutter! She's too young for me!

Callie catches up beside her, and I pull my sunglasses into place and divert my gaze. I then force myself to stop staring at the young woman who has caught the attention of my daughter—but for entirely different reasons.

23

A few moments later, Callie drops herself down on the foot of my lounger and pulls a towel around her. Meanwhile, Skyla's hair drips a path right between breasts that are so firm and full I wonder if they are real.

I decide they are one hundred percent natural—not that I care, but they are a very impressive pair.

"Hi! Your daughter is quite the water baby," she says through a full-lipped smile, having no idea of the significance of her comment.

"She sure is. I hope you didn't mind your swim being invaded."

Callie rolls her eyes causing Skyla to chuckle and grin widely.

"Dad, you're so embarrassing. Skyla didn't mind having fun with me, did you?" She looks at Skyla expectantly.

"Not at all. You're more fun than most women my own age." Skyla winks at me, and it feels seductive to my overactive thoughts. "Anyway, I thought I better bring Callie back before I go change. Thanks for the fun." Skyla turns and walks away, and I lift my sunglasses an inch while I fix my gaze on the delectable curve of her ass.

"Dad! Stop staring at her butt. You should ask first, it's called consent."

There's no way Skyla didn't hear that. And as if to prove it, Skyla freezes and stops walking. I let go of my sunglasses and they drop onto the tip of my nose, but the damage is already done.

"Did you know that Skyla doesn't have a boyfriend?" Callie says. "I know because I asked her and she told me. You should get her phone number and then you could ask her out."

Skyla's shoulders stiffen.

Frozen.

"Thanks, Cal. Who's being embarrassing now?" I nudge

her playfully, but inside I want the sun lounger I am perched on to fold inward and swallow me.

Start walking again, Skyla.

Run away while you still can.

"Her dad works on an oil rig, so she had to go to boarding school because her mom left, but not in the same way Mom left," Callie says, and Skyla slowly turns around, pinning me with a full lipped, apologetic smile. Which is shocking since the poor woman has zero to apologize for. My and my daughter's behavior has reached new and uncomfortable heights.

"I... um... Callie asks a lot of questions." Skyla has taken a few steps back toward us and begins to explain, and I immediately sympathize.

"Yes, she does. I'm sorry—"

"No, I'm sorry. I probably overshared—"

"It's fine," I reply, and Skyla's shoulders relax. "Callie is quite the interrogator."

Callie elbows me. "I am not. I was making conversation. You don't talk to anyone, not women, at least. You should talk to Skyla, she's really nice—and you like her butt, I could tell because your eyes were bugging out of your head like this...." Callie pulls a ridiculous face and I wonder how this interaction could possibly get any worse. "We should all go get some cupcakes, and a milkshake—"

"No!" Skyla and I say at exactly the same time.

"I mean, I'd love to but unfortunately," Skyla immediately says, "I have a work thing I need to get ready for. Another time?"

"Me too. Definitely another time," I reply.

"Tomorrow?" Callie asks.

"We'll see," I say to my daughter, knowing she isn't about to drop this anytime soon.

"I really have to go. Nice meeting you both," Skyla says

and then gets out while she has the chance, practically running to the locker rooms.

"I think that went well," Callie says with a huge smile on her face.

"I think, squirt, we need to talk about boundaries." I'm surprised when she nods seriously.

Maybe there is hope I can prevent another situation like this.

"You're right, Dad. We should talk about boundaries and consent. We should definitely talk about consent." Callie quips her brow at me and suddenly it feels like I'm the one who's in trouble.

CHAPTER 3

SKYLA

"It was mortifying," I tell Jessie, who is sprawled on my bed, watching me through the mirror as I wind my hair around the curling iron.

I have exactly eleven minutes until she's giving me a ride to the restaurant where Logan is holding the business meeting to begin the final phase of his second luxury resort.

"But was he?"

"Was he what?"

"Checking out your butt."

I turn around to face her. "I don't know! I was walking away. It doesn't matter—"

"I beg to differ. Either he was eye fucking your peachy ass or he wasn't—but it definitely matters! If he was—damn, he's fine—good for him! If he wasn't—damn, he's fine—but what's wrong with him? That is, after all, a mighty fine ass you have."

"Maybe he's gay."

"Definitely not gay. He's got a kid."

"That doesn't mean shit. But it really doesn't matter because, like I told you—I am off men. Nadda. Nothing. No more. I am on Blingwood Resort dick hiatus!"

"Yeah, but if he likes you...."

"He does not like me. We spoke for like three minutes."

"And he checked out your ass in a bathing suit."

"He was probably thirsty and merely looking for a server —it's a lot of ass to try to look around."

Jessie shakes her head and throws a hair scrunchie at me. "Or he was hungry and looking for something juicy to feast on." She sits up cross-legged on the bed and I suddenly fear what she might say next. Alas, I don't have long to wait. "This is perfect. What better way to get back at Mike—and show him he ain't shit—than to date the billionaire boss's brother. Drew Blingwood—Skyla and Drew—ooh I like it." She pulls out her phone and scrolls while I go back to curling my hair. In the mirror I watch as her smile widens and she reads, "He has his own Wiki page. CEO of Blingwood Designs. *The revered architect, Drew Blingwood was bestowed with the Sky-High Design Award four years running—a feat no other architect has achieved. Based in New York City, Blingwood Designs is at the forefront of modern, contemporary, sustainable development and design...* this must be a little out-of-date since he just moved here. I'll skip back and see what else there is—"

"There's really no need. He's not interested and neither am—"

"Ah, here we go. Brother to Logan, Tate—" Jessie pulls a gagging face that piques my interest.

"Why do you do that?"

"Do what?"

"Make a face every time Tate Blingwood's name is mentioned. Most women drool at the mere mention of the Hollywood A-lister."

"Well, I'm not a dog. I don't drool. I hate his movies. I hate every post he puts on social media… he's so contrived. Urgh. Now, back to Mr. Hot Single Dad—Drew Blingwood…. Holy cow! He's on the Forbes rich list! I knew it!"

"You ready?" I ignore all her talk of Drew and slip in the pearl earrings that Nanna left me. "He's a Blingwood, and I am an HR Manager who lives on-site in the free staff accommodation. He is my boss's brother, which alone is enough to make him off limits. And he has a child who just lost her mother. Come on, Jessie, let it go, please."

"Is the child a jerk?"

"What? No, of course not."

"I mean, I get it. I'm a mother myself. I love Macy to bits, but I get that not all kids are as amazing and adorable as mine."

"Callie's not a jerk. She's actually really cute and so quick-witted—well beyond her years. And when she wants to know something, girl, you better run for cover 'cuz she is like a machine gun with the questions, but she shares too. We were only at the pool an hour together and she told me about her mom dying. It reminded me of when my mom left and so… I felt for her, you know." Jessie nods. "I love kids, you know that and she sure is lovable, so smart, funny and sweet. It's not her, it's—"

"Okay, so you love the kid. That's all I needed to know, why're you going on about it so much?"

"I wasn't," I defend and then notice she is joking.

"He's a possibility, that's all I'm pointing out."

I shake my head, slip my feet into my heels and stand, allowing my yellow satin dress to fall to the floor. "How do I look?"

Jessie's mouth hangs open.

"Is it too much? I know it's a work function but it's at Le Bateau—which is this really fancy place and—"

"Don't you dare change! You look... sensational."

I stare at my reflection in the mirror that hangs from my closet door. The dress was an impulse buy from a vintage online store, and thankfully it fits like a glove. I knew when I ordered it, it was a risk whether it would A) arrive in time and B) actually fit.

"My biggest pet peeve is the lack of options available for girls with a good supply of meat on their bones. I'm sure plenty of women can order a dress and have confidence it will fit just right—I am not that woman. Having to shop eons in advance of events—urgh, it adds a ton of extra stress and makes me dread weddings and parties. Like seriously, do plus size dresses go through a randomizer when the patterns are being cut? Will it be two sizes too big or six sizes too small?"

"You always nail your look, babe. You have good style, and trust me, even the small sizes are a total gamble getting the right fit. Think yourself lucky you don't have to wear a maid outfit for work!"

I nod my understanding. Her work uniform is the pits but it still looks good on her. And she's right, I guess no one, no matter their size, has it easy.

Thankfully, one thing went right today and the dress—albeit with industrial, hold-me-in underwear—has made what was a sucky day an almost bearable one. My breasts look full and perky in the V of the neckline. The waist is cinched in just the right place—giving the illusion that I do indeed have a waist, and the split in the skirt elongates my frame.

I feel—dare I say it—beautiful. Which is exactly the boost I needed after the horrific realization that I had been played by the office jerk.

"You're going to have the entire restaurant drooling over

you! I have a good feeling about tonight." She grins so widely, I catch it and smile too.

"Thanks, Jess. Let's go before I'm late."

* * *

AT THE RESTAURANT I'm shown to the table that's booked in Logan's name. There's seating for eight people, but I am the first to arrive, so I fill my glass with water. With all the commotion today, I didn't check who was on the invitation list. Now that I have time to think, I begin to worry.

My palms sweat, and it's at exactly that moment that Drew and Logan arrive.

"Mr. Blingwood," I stutter and both men—unaware whom I am talking to—inform me that I should use their first names.

"Of course," I say. "Mr. Blingwood... I mean, Logan." I smile at my boss. "Drew," I say, turning to my boss's brother. I wasn't expecting him to be here. He's wearing a tailored, dark navy suit, sans tie, and the top two buttons of his white shirt are undone, revealing a slight smattering of the rich, dark hair that I ogled at the pool.

"Skyla," Drew greets me, revealing perfect, pearly white teeth. I smile back at him through closed lips. My teeth should have been perfect, but the housemaster from my boarding school paid more attention to flirting with my orthodontist, and neither of them noticed the ever so slightly wonky incisor. I wasn't complaining. Back then, I couldn't wait to have the braces taken off, since without them I'd passed for a little older and got served at the Nine and Dime. That year at school was the most popular I have ever been.

"You guys know each other?" Logan asks curiously, his gaze fixed on his brother.

"We—" Drew and I speak at the same time. I gesture my hand for Drew to go first.

"Callie" is all Drew says, and Logan nods as though it makes sense.

Drew's chocolatey brown eyes flick up and down my body, making me feel self-conscious while also causing my pulse to gallop. But I put my increased heart rate and inability to think straight entirely down to my recollection of his sexy hot, toned body in a bathing suit.

"So, what did Callie do now?" Logan asks with inquisitive fondness.

Keeping my eyes trained on Drew's, instead of allowing them to wander to his thick-set shoulders and hard chest is not easy, and my thoughts become jumbled as I elaborate. "Callie said he looked at my butt," I blurt, and both men's mouths gape.

Why the heck did I say that?!

I'm shaking my head and laughing nervously as I try to explain. "Which, of course, he did not. That would be inappropriate and is absolutely not what happened." My voice is shaky and I sound like a complete idiot so I finish the subject with the word, "Kids."

I await their responses with my breath held, but then, Drew smiles at me and I relax while both men chuckle good-naturedly as though I have told an amusing joke while also explaining everything.

When the server returns with more guests for our table, I could kiss her for the interruption, that is until I realize the evening has veered in an even worse trajectory by delivering something detestable, distressing, and disgusting.

Mike.

Worse than that.

Mike and Jenny.

Kill me now.

* * *

I SHOULD HAVE KNOWN.

Jenny is, after all, Logan's assistant—of course she would be here—and Mike is a senior accountant at the company. But in my defense, I haven't had time to process my roller coaster of a day. My head has been flung about so wildly that I can't decide what I need more, a chiropractor or a shrink. First, finding my squeeze *squeezing* somebody else, pulling out every insecurity I have spent years pushing deep inside where it can't hurt me, and then coming face to face with single dad of the century, Drew Blingwood, who's made my skin so warm and tingly, I think I might have sunstroke.

Now, here I am, facing Mike before I am ready. Before I have had the chance to practice my *I don't give a damn if you cheated 'cuz I never liked you anyway* speech.

It's the yin and yang of discomfort. Mike to the left of me, Drew to the right.

Seeing Drew at the pool today was like a tantalizing sensory overload—like when you know it's the best damn cake of your life and you haven't even had a bite.

Drew *did* check out my ass. I felt the warmth of his stare. It made me feel good. Helped me see that there are other men out there, but it doesn't make what Mike did hurt any less. I understand that Mike and I were keeping things casual and that a spark hadn't developed yet—but did that mean it wouldn't eventually? For once I wanted someone to surprise me. Someone to be overcome by the depth of their feelings for me and powerless to hold back. Maybe what I wanted doesn't exist.

Once we've all taken our seats, we're joined at the table by Fernando Ricci, our head chef and restaurant manager and his husband, Luca. No one seems to notice, since Mike and Jenny walked in that the air has been sucked from the room

—except maybe Drew, whose brows are furrowed as he watches me from the opposite side of the table.

Small talk is stilted until the last seat is filled by Logan's fiancée, who arrives fashionably late wearing a scarlet dress held together by two pieces of loosely tied ribbon.

Logan calls over a server who takes everyone's orders. I forgo the urge to eat my feelings by ordering dessert on all three courses and instead point on the menu to the chicken dish with a name I can't pronounce.

"Dana, what'll you have?" Logan prompts. He's a fine-looking man—all the Blingwood men are—but tonight he has dark shadows beneath his eyes.

"I'll have some olives," Dana replies, making me feel glutinous for ordering a real meal, but after a stern look from Logan, she relents and orders the salmon.

"I brought you all here today since we are going to be working closely on the outlines for the Miami resort. As you all know, Drew designed the space and we've both been overseeing the construction with the developers and now, I am pleased to announce, we can start planning for the official opening in June. It's going to be tight but I think three months is ample time to recruit and train the staff. We are counting on you to pull data from our current resort and create our overall projections."

After Logan's lengthy discussion about the management, maintenance costs, and income gains comes to a close, Drew's expression lights up passionately as he transitions to giving us a detailed description of his vision for the new resort. He takes his time, enthusiastically explaining the project is larger than our current resort, that it's on an East Coast peninsula of Miami with powdery white sands and aqua-marine waters ideal for scuba diving and snorkeling. "It'll have all the sophistication of the finest European hotels but with the addition of luxury private bungalows. It'll be the individual touches that set the Blingwood Resort 2.0 apart from anything else."

Logan is nodding as he smiles at his brother, clearly delighted by the vision Drew paints. Beside Logan, Dana is checking her phone.

"Mike, you will need to compile the spreadsheets for staffing costs—and you'll need to work closely with Skyla. I trust that won't be a problem?" Logan stares at him sternly and I feel my cheeks flame.

Great. Seems like he heard how Mike did me dirty. My day of embarrassment is clearly not over.

I push away my worry since I'm sure my inner voice is overreacting. I don't know that he knows. In fact, my boss is probably the only living soul in the resort who is too busy for idle gossip.

"No problems, boss," Mike says through a putrid smile. "Skyla and I can work together fine, can't we, Sky?" The way Mike shortens my name gives me hives and a shudder rolls down my spine. He winks at me jovially and my hand wraps tightly around my fork.

While they wait for my reply, I become the focus of everyone's attention.

"I'll run the numbers on staffing projections. Two hundred and forty-six guest rooms is larger than we're used to, but it should be easy to scale based on what we have now. I can run costs. I'll have the numbers to you by tomorrow." I nod to Logan, ever the dutiful employee.

"At the meeting next week will be fine. Don't do all the work yourself. Mike should pull his weight," Logan replies, and I watch as Mike's expression sours.

It's not the first time Logan has pointed out that Mike shirks work, but now that I am no longer blinded by him, it seems glaringly obvious that Mike has gotten away with delegating work, often to me, for too long.

When dinner ends and we all stand up from the table, having wrapped up the meal and business meeting, Dana says to me from across the table, "I like your dress."

"Oh, thank-you. It's vintage," I tell her proudly.

"You do so well finding big clothes. Good for you."

My cheeks engulf in flames as everyone's heads spin my way. Mike chuckles loudly but from beside him, Jenny, at least, has the decency to look awkward.

"Yes, good for me," I repeat, still smiling. It's not like I can say to the boss' fiancée, *Thanks, and you do well too—opening your giant, inflated, stupid mouth at all the wrong times to say stupid shit!*

Suddenly Drew has walked around the table, and he pins Dana with a stare that's universally recognized as *WTF*. On the other side of Dana, Logan's jaw is twitching like he's holding his tongue.

I smile back at my boss in a *don't sweat it* kind of way, but his glare doesn't slip as he shakes his head at Dana in disgust.

"Dana, let's go. Car. Now!" Logan orders and Dana latches her arm through his. Logan whispers something in her ear as they walk away, and by her expression when she looks back at me over her shoulder, I don't think she liked whatever it was.

Mike follows Logan, with Jenny behind him, and Fernando and his husband follow behind them until it's just Drew and me trailing at the back. "You look great, Skyla. The yellow, almost gold color on you, it's understated class. You're easily the best dressed woman in the room. Ignore Dana in her bright red look-at-me dress, she's a liability."

Drew's incensed glare is gone now, and he's smiling at me; the skin of his warm brown eyes is crinkled slightly at the edges—softening his rugged good looks.

"Thank-you," I reply, squirming at the size of his compliment—I don't think I have ever been the best dressed woman in any room, but I appreciate him trying to make me feel better. "It takes a lot of effort for a plus size gal like me to compete. I mean, you saw at the pool. I thought the lifeguard was going to harpoon me," I joke, trying to lighten the mood, but it misses the mark and instead of laughing, his smile disappears.

"Don't put yourself down, Skyla, even jokingly. You're worth a dozen Dana's."

"You mean I'm the size of a dozen Dana's," I joke again out of the sheer habit of putting myself down before others can do it for me.

Drew stops walking, and his fingers gently clasp my wrist, pulling me to a stop. He smells so damn good that I find myself leaning in. "No, that's not what I meant at all. Let me clarify. You're a beautiful woman. My daughter thinks you are a beautiful person and I am certain she is right. You should take pride in your body, and certain people should have some respect. Unfortunately, my soon-to-be sister-in-law speaks so much shit it starves the oxygen from getting to her brain. Please, try not to take her comments to heart."

I'm biting my lip to contain my smile and struggling to label how a simple comment has made me feel so... beautiful? Valued? Respected? I'm not sure what the feeling is or how he managed to evoke it, but he's waiting for my reply, so I stutter, "I'll try not to let her get to me."

"You want me to escort you back to the resort? I came here tonight with Logan, but I can arrange an Uber for us, if you'd like?"

"Yeah, I'd love to ride you... I mean, ride with you." I take a step forward and then pause, shaking my head. "Thank-you, but I just remembered, my friend is picking me up and she's probably left home already."

We linger in the foyer of the restaurant a beat too long. His cologne is deep and earthy and making my mouth water.

He smiles tentatively. "I'll see you around, then."

"Yep," I reply.

And a part of me really hopes I do.

* * *

BY THE TIME I get my breathing in check, pull myself together, and make my way outside, Drew is gone. I check for Jessie, but she's not here yet, and that's when Mike approaches me.

He's got his hands in his pockets, his shoulders slung low, and a stance of sheer arrogance that immediately has me wondering what I ever saw in him.

Mike stops right before me, an arm length away beside one of the oversized potted plants. I wonder if his distance is deliberate so he has a chance to run should I suddenly decide to ram his head through the restaurant window. What he should be more afraid of is that Jessie will be here to pick me up soon, and if she sees him talking to me she is very likely to drive over him with her car.

"Thanks for not making a fuss earlier. I don't think Logan would like it." He kicks his toe at an imaginary stone on the floor instead of meeting my gaze.

"You don't think he'd like what?" I answer curtly.

"You know… the boss knowing how things went down between us. He likes you and he'd probably just use it as an excuse to fire me—you know how he's always on my back."

"Always on your back? You mean how he's always telling you to do your own damn work? Yeah, no problem. I'm so glad how *you* behaved didn't cause *you* problems." I glance down the street, looking for the red Honda Jessie has on loan from Betty.

"Come on, don't be salty. We still have to work in the same building. No hard feelings?"

"No hard feelings?" I look back at him and he meets my incredulous stare. The fake smile on his face falters and suddenly I feel sorry for him, remembering his anger with himself when he couldn't perform. "Mike, is it because you had that problem?" I don't say the words erectile dysfunction. I don't want to embarrass him, but from the way the lobes of his ears pinken, I know he gets my drift. "Were you trying to prove something to yourself?"

He looks at me disgustedly. "I don't have anything to prove, not to you or anyone. You knew we were just a casual thing, right? I never dated anyone like you before. I mean, we were never going to be a good match." He gestures with his hand at himself and then to me. "I thought you'd be easy, Skyla. Grateful. But you weren't, and it was costing me a fortune taking you out for dinner. Three courses every time."

My mouth pops open, the vileness of his comments taking me by complete and utter surprise. "You're right. We're not a good match at all—I'm a nice person, whereas you are a jerk."

He dips his head and I wonder if he feels any remorse. At least he has the decency not to deny it. "Sky—"

"Don't call me Sky!" My pitch is high with anger, my hands shaking like they want to throttle something—or someone.

"I didn't mean to hurt you, but you should have known we'd never be serious. I mean, look at the two of us…."

It's the second time he's tried to point out our supposed differences, but this time I can see exactly what he means by the way his gaze is fixed on the thick part of my thighs.

"Say it."

"I'm not going to be a dick about it."

"Well, you've been a dick about everything else so you may as well continue. Come on, I'm a big girl, I can handle it."

He narrows his eyes at me, and I tense in preparation. "You said it yourself, Sky. You're pretty but you're a *big girl*—we look weird together. People were looking at me like I was one of those... chubby chaser guys."

My insecurities fizzle to the surface like an electrical current running across my skin.

A car horn captures both of our attentions, and Logan's BMW pulls up outside the restaurant. From the other side of the oversized potted plant, Drew steps forward and raises his hand to his brother before marching up to Mike and telling him, "My ride's here but I'm not going anywhere until you are gone." He squares Mike with an angry glare, then glances at me. "You okay?"

I think I nod, but my body is so tense, I'm not sure.

"Hey, if you heard our conversation, it was nothing like she made it sound—"

"Go! Now," Drew growls. "You're about a second from getting your head ripped from your shoulders."

"Okay, man. But she started it—"

Drew takes a step forward. The look of sheer brutality in his expression is hard enough that Mike flinches and walks away.

"You okay?" Drew asks me again so sympathetically that my tear ducts squirt. "I wasn't eavesdropping. Well, I was, but only to make sure you were okay. The conversation turned nasty pretty quickly."

I look away. "I'm fine. Perfect, in fact."

Perfectly mortified.

"Get in the car. I'll take you home—"

He's drowned out by full blast rock music blaring from the car behind Logan's, and I don't have to look to know that Jessie is here.

"That's my ride." I gesture to the red Honda with the fading paint. "Thanks for...." I can't finish the sentence. I can't even bear to look in his eyes and witness the rising pity, so instead I turn and leave him on the sidewalk, sprinting to the sanctuary of the car.

"Drive," I tell Jessie, who takes one look at my face, pushes her foot down hard on the accelerator and asks, "Who do I need to kill?"

CHAPTER 4

DREW

*T*he next day I'm still reeling with anger over Mike's treatment of Skyla outside the restaurant. I have a ton of work to get through, but the image of Skyla's face, hurt and on the brink of tears consumes me.

Logan warned me I'd find Mike annoying. Fortunately he's Logan's problem not mine—at least, that's what I thought.

When I left Skyla in the restaurant, she was smiling. Logan asked me to wait outside while he took Dana to collect the car—he wanted to talk to her about being a dick to Skyla—so I held back and pulled out my phone to check my emails. I didn't even know Skyla was outside until I heard her sweet voice. The way Mike talked to her, rage pulsed through my veins and I wanted to launch myself at him and tear his head off. Could I use his face to smash one of the oversized planters outside of the restaurant until he was nothing more than a bloody mess? I suspected it wouldn't be difficult.

He belittled Skyla, put her down, and had the audacity to try to make her feel less than perfect. I wanted to kill him, but I restrained myself, knowing it was none of my business. She proved she was strong enough to fight her own battles. But Mike, waving his hand at her body like it was a problem and not a perfect fantasy, telling her he thought she'd be easy, tipped me over the edge and I lost all restraint.

Logan could tell I was angry from the moment I got in the car, and I was sorely tempted to tell him to fire Mike—he hates users and bullies as much as I do—but it wasn't my place to share Skyla's upset, nor did I want to get into a conversation with my brother and his rude fiancée about why I feel protective over his HR Manager. And, as I keep reminding myself, who my brother hires—vindictive assholes or perfectly sweet, beautiful women—has nothing to do with me. Besides, in three months, Callie and I will be in our new house and I'll likely never see Skyla or any of my brother's other employees again.

Between wondering how Skyla is and dropping Callie off for her first day at the cruel and often dangerous cesspit that is middle school, my nerves are shot, so I throw on my sneakers and pound the pavement until my head clears.

Callie's first day at a new school has me in knots. She assured me she'd be fine, but she also has a tendency to tell her old man such things to save me from worry. As it is, 3 p.m.—the universal release date from jail as she calls it—can't come quick enough.

I turn onto the coastal path and keep running, enjoying the burn in my calves and the earth beneath my feet. The sun is high in the sky but the ocean breeze and tree-lined path provides a canopy of shade that brings the temperature down enough to make midday exercise bearable.

There are other people out, too, some running, some walking their dogs and a couple in their twilight years playing frisbee on the grass. I notice a couple of volunteers I recognize from my mother's animal rescue center, and I perform the obligatory wave in greetings as I pass. But mostly I keep my head down and focus on the rock music booming from my earbuds. It helps to empty my mind but my fears still creep in. Is Callie happy? Am I doing the right thing moving her away from everything she knows in New York? Will the career I've worked so hard to build remain intact in the suburbs? Is Skyla okay following her brush with Mike? Has she seen him since, and did he heed my warning? Should I have thrown my fist in his face to make sure he knew I was serious when I told him to back off?

The fact that I have spent so much time thinking of Skyla has me unnerved and I pound my feet faster—as though I can somehow outrun my craving. Ever since I laid eyes on her at the pool, her body soaking wet and curving in and out in all the best places, she's been taunting my imagination and has become something of a fantasy. So much so, last night, after I had shown my mother out and checked Callie was sleeping soundly, I rubbed one off in the shower while thinking of all the things I'd like to do to her tight body.

I run faster and try to empty my head of such thoughts.

She works for my brother.

She's too young.

She's obviously been hurt by Mike.

Off limits.

Out of bounds.

I am not starting anything up.

I don't trust myself not to screw up.

It won't just be Skyla it'll hurt when it falls apart, it'll hurt Callie too.

And that is unacceptable.

44

I didn't have to worry about this stuff when I was co-parenting. I saw women casually on the days I didn't have Callie and she was none the wiser. There's no chance of hiding a hook-up while living at the resort—the staff here watch everyone's every move—so why am I even thinking about it?

I'm so invested in listing all the reasons Skyla is off limits, I don't feel the pressure that brushes against my calf until I am tangled in something and hurtling to the ground.

"Oh! Darn it, Beanie," a woman's voice yells.

I roll to a sitting position and look in the direction of the voice but am accosted by a lively black and white collie that seems intent on licking my damn face. I stand, pushing the dog back onto four legs.

"I'm so sorry, Drew!" the woman calls and I squint through the sun's rays so I can see better.

Perspiration has started to bead on Skyla's forehead and the sun shines on her lightly tanned skin as she runs toward me—her full breasts bouncing up and down. Her curves are accentuated beneath the tight clothes she is wearing and I notice her toned arms and abdomen as she stops. Breathless, a few tendrils of her hair have escaped her ponytail and are stuck to her cheeks. The sight of her is mesmerizing.

"Hi. I didn't know you had a dog," I say, pushing my hand through my hair since I know it'll have gotten messy on the run.

She tips up those full lips of hers and replies, "Beanie's not mine. I live over at the resort and the apartment isn't big enough for pets. He's your mother's, actually. I volunteer for her during my lunch break. Pooches got to walk, right? And it helps me get my steps in."

Of course, she does. It's not enough that she looks like a temptress sent to destroy me, she has to go and be a good person on top of it all.

Skyla pulls her honey-colored hair out of the scrunchie and shakes it loose with her fingers until it rests against the swell of her breasts. It's a sexy move and to my utter fucking horror my cock hardens, but not for long. More effective than a cold shower, Beanie leaps up in the air and I wind up taking an eye-watering paw to the balls.

"Beanie, get down!" she urges, but the dog doesn't give a shit. I notice his leash dangling from his collar and grab the handle, holding it out for her to take. I use my other hand to protect my groin from another dog attack.

Skyla reaches out and, as her hand brushes mine, heat courses through my fingers and up my arm. My hand, as though pulled by magnets, rests against hers a beat too long.

"Thanks," she says. "One minute he was running nicely beside me and then he saw you and took off. The leash slipped right out of my hand. Please don't tell your mom I let go, I'd hate her to think I don't take care of him when he's in my hands."

At her mentioning them, I'm staring at her tiny little hands and painted pink nails, imagining how good they'd look wrapped around my—I shake away the thought. "Secret's safe with me. Don't sweat it. Little scamp looks lively."

"Oh, he is! But he's so adorable. Yes, you are," she tells the dog and then proceeds to fuss and lavish attention on him.

His back leg starts to judder like he's enjoying a good petting and a spike of jealousy runs through me.

Great. I'm jealous of dogs now.

"You heading back to the resort?" I ask, hoping the answer is no. Spending time with her when I have been thinking about her like I have seems like a bad idea. I need to get the hell away. I don't trust my dick not to instruct my brain to make a move on her.

Skyla hesitates and I try not to be offended—it's probably better we don't spend time together; she must see that too.

She sucks her lower lip into her mouth, then nods. "Sure, we can walk together. That is perfectly okay."

I ignore the faint spark of joy crackling beneath my skin and gesture my hand in the direction of the resort. We set a leisurely pace, our bodies just a few inches apart.

"Oh, darn it. You scuffed your knee when you fell." She stops walking to stare at my leg. My knee's scraped and there's a line of blood running down my shin into my sock.

"It's fine—" I say, but my words are cut short when she bends down onto her knees, affording me a good look down her cleavage. My balls throb and my dick twitches in my pants—which, since Skyla is eye-level with my junk, can't go unnoticed. She pulls a tissue from her pocket and wipes the blood away.

"Don't worry, it's clean." She laughs throatily. Which is funny, because with her on her knees and looking up at me like she's about to do me dirty, my thoughts are anything but clean.

I lean down and take the tissue from her. When she stands, Skyla is more than a foot shorter than my six and a half feet.

"I think I'll live," I tell her, even though all the blood in my body has suddenly shot to my dick and I might be in danger of passing out.

"How's Callie?" Skyla asks, distracting me perfectly, and we continue to walk.

"She's good, I think. It's her first day at her new school today and I'm feeling...."

"Worried?"

I nod. "She's a great kid but she lost her mother and...." My throat tightens as I think of how Callie misses her mom.

Skyla's gaze intently examines me, those wide brown eyes

glazing as she drinks in every word. "I heard, I'm sorry. Losing a mother, it's tough on kids."

"Callie's been coping really well, but the grief's still there beneath the surface."

"I'm sure you miss her too?"

"I do, but we weren't together when she died. We were divorced." I wonder why I feel the need to clarify that Crystal and I lived apart. Skyla seems to draw the information right out of me. I clear my throat and try to wrap up the conversation. "Crystal was a good mother. We had a nanny back in New York but Callie thinks she's too old for one now, so I've moved her here to be with family. I hope it's the right decision."

"I'm sure it'll turn out for the best. I know your mother and your brother are happy you've come back. You have a lovely family."

I try not to scoff. "We're like any other family, complicated and a little crazy."

Skyla chuckles and her free hand grips my wrist with a short squeeze that makes my blood pressure spike. "I have a feeling things are going to be okay. Callie will have a dozen new friends by the time the day is out, and you'll be left wondering why you were anxious." When she lets go of my arm, I'm tempted to catch her hand in mine.

"I'm not anxious."

She cocks her head and smiles ruefully. With her mouth closed, it hides the ever-so-slightly wonky incisor that makes her look adorable and captures my attention every time her mouth is open.

"Okay, so I might be a little anxious. It's the other kids, you know? They can be such…." I pause while I decide on a word. It doesn't feel right cussing in front of Skyla since she's younger than I am.

Skyla fills the silence. "Jerks?"

My lips twitch. I was going to say assholes.

"Yeah. Kids can be jerks sometimes."

"I'm sure she'll be fine." She winds the dog leash a few more times around her hand, pulling Beanie closer as we pass a couple of dogs and their owners.

"I suppose it's not that long since you were at school?" I ask casually.

"It's been quite a few years, actually. I'm twenty-four."

Knew it, too young.

"I'm thirty-six," I supply, in case she needs reminding that I'm way too old for her.

"Twelve years," she replies, replicating my thoughts exactly. "So how long will you be staying at the resort? I hear you're having a house built."

"Not long, our house will be ready in June. The construction is already underway, and once the groundwork is complete, the rest tends to go up pretty quickly."

"All while designing the new resort, you must be exhausted."

I shrug. I like being busy.

"The new resort sounds great, by the way. The way you spoke about it at dinner, you had everyone hanging off your every word. It sounds amazing."

As though remembering the aftermath at the restaurant, she nibbles on her lip and a little furrow deepens between her delicately arched brows.

"I hope what happened last night hasn't made you feel embarrassed because you have nothing to be embarrassed about. The way Mike spoke to you…." My fists clench and I grit my teeth before speaking again. "He was wrong. You deserve someone who is going to treat you better than that asswipe." I feel better for having said my piece, even if Skyla's cheeks have plumped up to a pretty pink.

"Oh, I know." She waves her hand as though batting our conversation away.

I lightly grip her arm and pull her to a stop. My skin heats and my heartbeat quickens again. Beyond her, my mother, wearing one of her bright green tees—probably with an inappropriate slogan—heads toward us to collect Beanie. But there's something I want Skyla to know before we're interrupted.

"You are a beautiful *young* woman." I emphasize *young*—as in too young for me—for both our sakes. "A man who refers to your weight negatively is not a man, he's a weasel! Mike's a player, who'll probably end up fat and bald with no one. Piece of advice: hold out for someone who respects you. Someone who is going to take care of you, okay?"

The vulnerability in her eyes is pinning me to the spot.

"Th-th-thank-you. I know he's a jerk. It stung a bit, you know?"

Knowing she was hurt hits me straight in the heart, and I feel suddenly compelled to make her smile again. The words rush from my mouth before I have thought them through. "I *was* checking out your ass the other day at the pool. I couldn't help myself. I should probably apologize, but I can't promise I won't do it again."

She lets out a throaty chuckle that sends a hum straight to my cock. The wonky incisor bites into the fullness of her lower lip as though to try stop herself from smiling.

"I know you were looking."

"You knew?" I cock my brow at her—there's no way she could be sure, even though my daughter did her upmost to rat me out.

"Your daughter came by my office before school today. Callie said she wanted to assure me that you don't normally check women out. She said it'd been a long time, in fact. But she had Simon from security show her the CCTV footage, I think she told him she'd lost something and wanted to be sure she hadn't dropped it at the pool. She recorded the footage from the security screen on her phone and then she played it for me. I saw you *looking*, and then..."

My heart has all but stopped.

"And then?"

"She tried to give me your phone number."

Skyla's smiling but she looks as mortified as I feel.

"Don't worry, I put the square of paper—" She coughs lightly. "—that was surrounded by love hearts... in the trash. I didn't think you'd appreciate me saving your number."

My hands sink into my hair. "Callie."

Callie can't get attached to another person who won't stick around. It's not fair.

"I think she means well—"

"Who means well?" my mother asks as she catches up to us, holding out her hand for Beanie's lead. Her bright green T-shirt reads: *I love a sausage.* Beneath the slogan is a picture of a Dachshund. Her T-shirts have become a family joke. Tate and Tabitha buy her inappropriate dog T-shirts whenever they see them, and Mom pretends like she doesn't get the meaning.

"No one," I reply. "No one means well. See you at brunch on Sunday, Mom." And then I get my ass out of there before any more of the meddling women in my life can get any crazy ideas in their heads.

* * *

THE FOLLOWING week I'm sitting in Logan's office going over the blueprints.

"You look tired, old man," Logan says and I stand and stretch. I am tired. Between worrying about Callie and thinking about Skyla more often than is doing me good, sleep has become a thing of the past.

"I'm going to get coffee, you want one?"

Logan nods as he examines my plans for the state-of-the-art gymnasium that'll overlook the infinity pool.

In the break room, I head for the coffee machine like a man with a single purpose, but then I see her.

Skyla.

She's wearing a tight skirt with a white blouse that dips low enough to hint at full yet perky tits. In her hand she's got a coffee cup atop a saucer that's balancing a tower of cookies. Beyond her, Mike is sitting on one of the low-slung couches and beside him is Jenny. She's a size zero and conventionally pretty with blonde hair. Mike's making no effort to hide his hand on Jenny's knee, and it pisses me off that he has such little regard for Skyla's feelings.

I'm powerless to stop the *fuck-off* scowl I throw him when I barrel past, straight to Skyla, who's moving around quietly like she's trying to make herself smaller. Unnoticeable.

"You okay?" I ask her, flicking my eyes to the other two.

She smiles broadly but it doesn't reach her eyes.

"Fine. I'm grabbing a coffee for Betty while she takes a load off her feet. She's seventy and needs a little break between maid calls." The cup and saucer she's holding tinkle together as she holds them. She looks nervous, but I can see she's fronting confidence for Mike and Jenny's benefit. "These aren't all for me," Skyla confesses, looking down at the cookies.

"Was just about to load up myself," I reply. No way I'm making her feel like shit for enjoying a cookie—she can eat as many as she likes.

Skyla points me to the cups and I take the last cookie from the jar, eating it whole. "Shit. They're almost as good as you look," I say between crunches for the benefit of the asshole cheater in the room.

"I know, right?! Fernando gets them in specially—don't tell Logan, I don't think he signed off on a cookie budget." She opens her mouth and playfully winks, and my pants suddenly feel tighter. "How was Callie's first day at school?"

I put the coffee down and lean against the countertop, making myself comfortable. I enjoy talking to Skyla, and there's the added benefit with Mike still in the room, watching us. It'll reinforce the message she has powerful friends, so he should watch his fucking mouth.

"Callie says it went well. One of the girls in her math class adopted a kitten from Mom so there's some common ground between them."

Skyla's ensuing smile widens her full red lips.

It's nice to have someone other than my mother to talk to about my daughter smashing her first day of a new school, without boring them with my "dad talk."

"I take it Callie didn't swing by your office to tell you about it?" I check. I made it clear to Callie she's not to bother Skyla. I made the excuse that Skyla could get into trouble with her boss—though I suspect she knows Logan wouldn't mind at all.

"Oh, you didn't tell her off for coming to see me, did you?" Skyla pokes her bottom lip out, and I have the over-whelming urge to bite it.

I shrug. "Just a little. Hopefully she won't harass you with phone numbers anymore."

Mike laughs loudly at something Jenny said and my jaw stiffens. I step protectively closer to Skyla and lean closer to talk in her ear. "They bothering you?"

She shakes her head. "No. Not at all."

"You sure?"

"Yes," she says firmly. "Now, tell me how Callie's enjoying

living at the resort. I imagine she and her friends think it's pretty cool?"

"Yeah, she likes it so far. But..."

My voice stops working as Skyla leans in, affording me the perfect view of her cleavage.

Her eyes fix on mine with concern. "But?"

I cough and clear my head. What was I saying?

Note to self: Stop getting distracted by Skyla's breasts.

"It's probably nothing. She's.... Callie's taking awhile to settle into a sleep routine. She says the bed's too big, but maybe she's trying to use that as an excuse to stay up later."

"Could be a tween tactic," she agrees. "Are you managing any sleep?"

This close to her, I can smell the sweetness of her perfume, the coconut of her shampoo and it's intoxicating.

"Sleep's overrated," I say.

She grins. "Maybe you should get one of your mom's dogs. She has plenty to go around and the daily fresh air might do you and Callie good."

"Don't ever say that in front of my daughter." I nudge her playfully and the feeling is like electricity surging up my arm. Skyla's eyes widen and I know she felt it too, but then her gaze flicks to where Mike is playfully tickling Jenny like they're in the school yard. "Don't look at them," I tell her. "Look at me."

"I'm not looking at them," she whispers, diverting her eyes to mine, staring up at me through thick lashes. She looks so self-conscious it's tearing me up inside.

"Fuck them."

She purses her lips and nods though it's barely noticeable, flicking her eyes down and staring at her calves that are elongated by fiery red, sky-high heels. I tip her chin back so she has no choice but to look at me. "Beautiful, remember?"

She nods, looking unconvinced.

"It's time someone showed you how beautiful you are," I tell her, and suddenly I want to be that person.

Her cheeks lift in a smile and her lips look so luscious and full, I can't stop staring at them and thinking how they'd look wrapped around the head of my cock. This close, smelling like she does, looking like a fucking queen and with a mouth so delectable, it has stopped my heart from beating. I lean down, just a few inches, but enough to graze her lips. I don't know why I do it, but I'm powerless not to and she doesn't stop me. No, she leans into the meeting of our lips greedily, opening her mouth so I can slide my tongue gently in. The cup in her hand rattles against the saucer, so I grip the edge of the plate with my free hand and guide it down onto the counter. Then I slide both my hands into her hair, holding her so her mouth is against mine and delighting in her flavor. The kiss is slow and deep. Her mouth is so warm and accommodating, I lose my train of thought. I don't think I've enjoyed simply making out with a girl since I was in high school, and it has me thinking I should definitely do this more often.

When she pulls back, her lips part into an *O* and she swallows. Her big brown eyes slowly blink and she lets out a breath before her eyes dart back to where Mike *was* sitting. Then she chuckles. "I didn't notice them leave."

I shrug. "Me either."

Her lips spread into a smile that makes me want to lie her back on the counter and pay them some more attention.

"Guess that showed him."

The prick from accounting. I shrug. I wasn't thinking about showing him anything. I kissed her because in the moment, I couldn't not kiss her. "Guess it did," I reply. "If he hadn't noticed you moved on, then he has now." The thought makes me feel smug. Let him understand she doesn't give a shit about him. That she won't be humiliated by him and so he better stop trying to make her feel uncomfortable.

She fingers the fullness of her lower lip and then shakes her head as though she can't quite believe what just happened. I know how she feels. As innocent kisses go, that one had my knees weakening.

"I better get back," she says picking up the cup and saucer with the cookies precariously balanced. "Betty will be wanting her…." Her voice trails off.

"Me too," I reply, not having a clue how to end this.

I watch her peachy ass as she vacates the break room and am sorely tempted to drag her back.

When I get back to Logan's office he asks, "Where's the coffee?"

"Shit. Coffee. Yeah, I'll go get it." I turn around and grin.

I forgot the fucking coffee.

"Drew."

"Yeah?"

"Grab some cookies, too?"

Then I smile like a damn fool while wondering what the hell has gotten into me.

CHAPTER 5

SKYLA

*T*he cup and saucer rattle the whole way back to my office but not as much as my knees.

What was I thinking?

"I was beginning to think you'd gotten lost," Betty says from the comfy chair in the corner. She's wearing her pink maid's dress and one of her stockings has slipped down to her swollen ankles that are propped up on the upturned garbage pail. Her hair is gray but immaculate in pin curls, and beside her Jessie sits cross-legged on the floor—also wearing a pink maid's outfit.

She puts her phone down and gives me an intense stare. "Where have you been and where did you get that smile?"

I wipe the grin straight from my face.

"I've been getting Betty's coffee." I hand her the cup and grab one of the cookies from the saucer, eating it whole and thus filling my mouth with goodness—not to mention buying valuable time to think before I speak.

"You look different," Jessie says with an accusatory narrowing of her blue eyes.

"Her hair is ruffled," Betty states, pushing her spectacles up her nose to view me better.

"I swear to God if you've been fooling around with Mike after everything he's done, I'm gonna tan both your asses. He's—"

"No, I haven't seen him—well, not to speak to, anyway." I wheel my office chair over to their corner and lower my voice. The smile breaks through my carefully composed reassuring expression, and I spill. "Drew Blingwood just kissed me in the breakroom."

Both women gasp. Betty clutches my hand in hers. Soft, papery skin envelopes my fingers and calms my pulse.

"He only did it to put on a show for Mike, who was all over Jenny. After the other night, when Drew saw how Mike spoke to me, I guess he was being chivalrous... or something. It was nothing—"

"It was definitely something! You're smiling like George Clooney himself swept you off your feet and kissed the living daylights out of you," Jessie says.

I shake my head and try not to smile. "He was just looking out for me. It was a pity kiss."

It did not feel like a pity kiss.

"A pity kiss? Girl, you look like you got a pussy kiss," Jessie harrumphs and high fives Betty whose chunky cheeks are lit up with glee.

"Been a while since I got one of them," Betty says with a wink. "At least a couple of weeks. Bob's promised me it's a blip. Going to get some of those blue tablets from the doctor when he gets a day off. He's a stallion in a donkey's body, mark my words." She nods seriously.

Jessie and I stare at each other openmouthed and then hysterical laughter bursts from our mouths.

"Good for you, Betty! I never knew you and Bob still got down and dirty. I had even less idea that there's a stallion hiding beneath that donkey," Jessie replies and she's right. Bob works part-time over at the maintenance building. He's even older than Betty with a bad hip and two walking sticks. He's certainly not what one might consider a stallion—inside or out.

"My Bob might be seventy-two but we always made sure to have a healthy sex life. You kids today think you got the handle on the spicy stuff, but let me tell you, it gets better with age."

"Sounds like Skyla here is in luck then because Drew Blingwood's definitely got age on his side."

"Hey—he's not that old." I feel Betty's stare and then add, "Not that there is anything wrong at all with being in your twilight years and still doing it."

"So, what are you going to do about the kiss?" Jessie's excitement is palpable, and to prove it she squeezes my thigh and tells me, "This is the best news ever!"

"Nothing."

"Nothing?" Both women say quizzically and each take a cookie from the stash. I take another, too, because a woman must have sustenance if she is to make sound decisions.

"Mike was in the break room, all over Jenny, and so Drew kissed me to make me feel better and to show Mike I moved on. That's all it was."

I'm almost certain that was all it was.

"I already told you; I am off men who are in any way connected with this place. Blingwood Resort Man Hiatus, remember?"

The sound of a man clearing his throat from the doorway of my office has my eyes clamping shut and my heart threatening to stop. "Skyla, have you got those reports? I want to show Drew the current staff intake versus the number of staff accommodation."

I slowly turn my head and see Logan and Drew filling the doorway to my office.

I swallow loudly. "Of course, Mr. Blingwood." I walk to the filing cabinet and pull out the staff projections I have been working on.

"I was taking my break, Mr. Blingwood," Betty says. "My old feet ain't up to it like they used to be."

"Me too, Mr. Blingwood. Going right back to work this moment," Jessie adds and both women stand and dust cookie crumbs from their work outfits.

"No problem, ladies. I know you both work hard. Though, Betty, how are you not retired yet?" Logan checks, curiously narrowing his eyes on the older woman.

"I received my company pension schedule and am planning to give my notice soon. You'll need to plan who's going to replace me." She gestures her hand to Jessie and I immediately file the thought away for later. Jessie would be a perfect Head of Housekeeping since she already knows the job inside out. "Me and Bob want to make sure we quit work while we've still got the energy for other, more important things. While there's steam in my train, I shall keep firing her up."

Jessie raises her brows up at me and I'm not sure if it's a nod to Betty's sex life or the fact that a mere minute ago I told her I kissed Drew Blingwood, and now, here he is, standing in my office.

At Betty's comment, Logan grins at his brother. Though Drew's heated gaze is fixed on me, and it's making the steam in *my* train threaten to go off!

Betty and Jessie make to leave and we all congregate by the door while I hand Drew the file. "Everything you need should be in here, but if you need anything else give me a call… or email. My details are in the company address book," I add, pushing a polite work smile onto my lips.

Suddenly the room feels hotter, a heat made much worse by the knowing smiles of my friends.

"You look ever so worn out, Mr. Blingwood," Betty says to Drew and his cheeks dimple as he smiles at her and replies, "I am pretty bushed."

"You know what you need?" Betty replies and Drew shakes his head. "Pussy."

My mouth flies open and Jessie lets out a loud belly laugh.

Logan's expression looks strangled as he tries to choke down his own laughter, but Drew looks charmed by the old lady as he replies, "How would a cat solve my tiredness?"

"Good company, stress relief, and endorphins," she explains. "You could get a cat too, but mark my words, pussy, that's what you need." Betty reaches up on her toes, tapping Drew's cheek like he's been a good boy. "Pussy," she repeats in case he hasn't heard her and then Jessie follows Betty from the room.

Logan cocks a brow at me and turns to Drew. "Right, brother, you have it on good authority, pussy is what you need." Logan chuckles and Drew's thick, dark brows rise up as he lets out a strangled laugh too, but then he stops chuckling and stares at me, and my insides melt.

"If that'll be all… umm, I have a ton of work to get through," I stutter through a smile.

"Of course, thank-you, Skyla," Logan replies, turning to leave. Drew follows, but not before throwing me a panty drenching smirk.

CHAPTER 6

DREW

ad was staring at Skyla's butt, like this!" Callie bugs her eyes out of her face and I shake my head.

What is with Callie's obsession with me looking at Skyla's gorgeous ass?

My mother and Logan look at me across the table which has held practically every family dinner since the Blingwood kids were born. Mom's wearing a yellow shirt with the slogan *Trust me, I'm a dogtor.*

"I'd rather talk about why your nanna insists on wearing those goofy T-shirts," I say, nodding to my mother to try and change the subject, knowing it's futile.

"I'd rather talk about what Callie said," Logan presses and I look away, annoyed.

At the top of the carved oak table, the carver seat remains empty since no one can quite bring themselves to take Dad's seat.

Beside me Dana huffs at my mom's beagle and wrestles her off the purse she has made herself comfortable on. Purse free, Dana pouts and snaps a selfie. She'll probably hashtag it later for her bazillion followers, adding some sort of caption like: Sunday Funday Brunch with the fam, and make out like she wasn't entirely bored the whole time. I'm actually quite surprised she made it to Sunday family brunch, since she's usually jet-setting on my brother's private plane, trying to increase her socialite status. But what surprises me the most is that my brother ever hooked up with her to begin with. He's all hard work, dedication, and loyalty, and she's nothing but glitz, glamour, and prestige.

"I was not staring," I tell Callie for the hundredth time. "I noticed it, yes. I won't deny that. But I only looked, not stared."

I'd be truly fucked if they knew I kissed her in the office a few days ago. A decision I am firmly questioning now.

Logan stares at me indignantly. "You know she works for me?"

I shrug. "Callie's got something in her head—it does not mean I am going to go there."

"You took a walk with Skyla while she was out walking Beanie. Such a lovely girl, Drewy, you should definitely give her consideration. You can tell a lot about a person from how they treat animals, and she loves animals," my mother states.

"I guess that means my dad is an ogre since he hates dogs." Callie crosses her arms over her shirt that's got some YouTuber or TikTok star's face on it.

"I don't hate dogs," I defend.

"You just like my HR Manager's bottom more, isn't that right, Drewy?" Logan smirks from beside me.

I ignore him and move the conversation along. "Callie, you have unlimited access to plenty of animals. Your grandmother owns a rescue center. We don't have time for a pet. We don't even have a house yet."

Logan asks how the plans for the new house are coming along and I explain the contractors are making good progress with the roof and the windows are getting installed soon. Then my mother ushers Callie out the door with her to go check on the animal shelter she had built on the back acres of land she and Dad had invested in years ago. I'm positive my dad never had a clue it would be home to rescues.

"I guess it'll have an eight million price tag once it's finished?" Dana asks without even looking up from whatever she is scrolling on her phone.

"Something like that," I reply to Dana, noticing she hasn't touched her bagel and is still drinking regular espresso. When Crystal was pregnant with Callie, she ditched all but her morning coffee and couldn't stand the sight of food before lunch—after that she ate her weight in bananas and toast. "I suppose you guys will be needing a house now? I could design you one. I'm guessing you won't want to raise a baby at the resort."

"I keep trying to persuade Logan to move into the city. It'd be so much easier for the photoshoots, and my friend knows this producer who thinks we'd be perfect for a reality show. *The Dana and Logan Show*, it's got a ring to it, don't you think?"

She's actually looking at me now. Her eyes alight with enthusiasm, and all I can think about is how exactly she plans to do a reality show with a newborn—in addition to the constant partying and traveling she does.

Logan pushes his brunch plate away. "I like Santa Barbara," he tells her. "It's perfect for raising kids. Safer than the city. And I already told you, I'll do the engagement announcement to the press and the photoshoot, but after that I don't want to be featured. I don't want to be in a reality show and I don't want our child to be in one either. All the child stars I've ever heard of wound up notoriously troubled, mistreated, and exploited. I'm not risking that happening to our kid."

Dana huffs, and I can immediately tell it's a contentious issue so I change the subject and try to keep the conversation light. "You set a date for the wedding?"

"Next month," Dana informs me. "The last day of May. We're having it in the evening. The photographer who covered the film festival is shooting our wedding and we're going for something twilightesque. Dark and moody. Ethereal was the word he used. It'll be beautiful, backlit by the stars and the moon. It has to be before I get too fat from the baby, and we don't want to wait, do we, baby."

"No point waiting. Late May means I am freed up for the opening of the second resort in June."

"It's the engagement party first. But Logan poopoo'd having a film crew there."

Logan pulls a face. "Better we get the wedding out the way before the baby comes, that way Dana can relax leading up to the birth. We're sending e-invites that delete as soon as they're read. We're trying to keep all the details out of the press. With Tate's fame and all, we'll get bombed otherwise. Isn't that right, Dana?"

It's childish, but I can't keep the smirk from my face as Logan references our brother's celebrity A-list status, and not his wife-to-be's Z list.

"Yeah, sure. We're doing things Logan's way, as usual," Dana replies looking none too happy.

Logan doesn't take the bait for the argument. "Actually, Drew, since I have you here, want to be my best man?"

"What about Tate?" I ask. "I don't want his nose to get bent out of shape."

"I asked him too, and he's coming home once he wraps up filming."

"I hope he can. The editor of Celebrity Gossip Magazine thinks it'll really boost our profile."

"Dana, I said no magazine deals at the wedding," Logan reminds her.

"Oh, I know, but I can share our wedding shots after the wedding. Do you think he'll bring Stella Brimworth as his plus one? Rumor has it they've been dating on set."

"News to me. I thought Tate was still into that mystery girl he got the hots for."

"There's been speculation all over social media about Tate dating Stella. She's hot stuff right now so I hope he is," Dana corrects, since Logan and I are not followers of celebrity gossip. "Perhaps there'll be two shotgun weddings in the family." She grins and goes back to tapping on her phone before standing and telling us, "I'm going to head out. There's a new line dropping at Amberly's and I want to check if they have anything suitable for the engagement magazine shoot. Maybe once you've done one photo shoot, you'll get a taste for them," she tells Logan and I wonder if she knows him at all. My brother is as stubborn as they come.

Dana holds her hand out expectantly and Logan thrusts his hand into his jacket pocket and pulls out his Amex. She snatches it straight from his hand and Logan doesn't bat an eyelid.

When she's gone, I ask, "Isn't her dad like the richest man on the planet?"

"Something like that, but she told me he cut her off, which is why she's working so hard to gain an online presence; she's looking for a new career." Logan says the word career like he ate a spoonful of cat food and is trying to talk around it. Then he sighs low and deep. "Shopping makes her happy and it gets her out of my hair."

The wealthiest member of our family, Forbes claims Logan's a billionaire. He can easily afford to pay for Dana's outfits and anything else she might need, but the thankless expectation that he should has me bugged.

Not my business.

I'm back in town to build bridges not blow them up.

"Are you happy?" I ask him.

He shrugs. "I'm not unhappy." Then changes the subject, "What's going on with you and my HR Manager? You know, I don't mind if you date her. Skyla's a great girl."

Girl.

"Nah. Too young and I told you, I'm not dating anyone. It's bad enough Callie keeps going on about her without you starting." I pick up my coffee, remembering the fire as we touched and the heat of our kiss—even if she was only kissing me back to make her ex jealous, I'll take it for how good it felt. But I've resolved it cannot happen again. I can't confuse Callie like that, and I can't lead Skyla on, and certainly not when she's so recently been hurt. No, she needs someone who'll take care of her.

I am not that man.

I need to find Skyla and tell her the kiss was accidental.

Apologize.

It's probably only a matter of time before the gossip wheels turn into motion and his assistant Jenny tells Logan she saw me kissing Skyla in the break room.

"Anyway, it's good to have you back. Between Mom and Dana, I have been outnumbered by chicks. It's about time you got your fair share of shit from them."

"Except with Callie here also, we're still outnumbered and likely to get double amounts of the shit."

He chuckles deeply. "Fair point."

"So, you're doing a photo shoot?"

"Damn, Dana's got it stuck in her head and won't take no

for an answer. We compromised on one photo shoot to formally announce the engagement to the press. But after that I'm putting my foot down. No more."

"Sure you are, brother. Just like I'm putting my foot down with Callie."

Logan grins. "You're never going to put your foot down with Callie, she's got you wrapped around her finger. I bet you a hundred bucks you're dating a woman of Callie's choosing before the year is out."

"I'll take the bet! There's no way I'm dating anyone. I'm going to focus on Callie and work. Since the move, I see most clients on Zoom. It can work, but I'm putting myself at a disadvantage from the competition that's based in the city."

"You don't need to worry. Your professional reputation speaks for itself. You're a good father. I know all that stuff with Dad shook your confidence, but you're doing great—"

"Don't, Logan, I can't talk about—"

Logan leans over and grips my shoulder. "I know, but if you ever want to talk about anything, even certain hot women in my workforce, I'm here for you."

After Logan leaves the dining room, I stand up and walk over to the sideboard that is loaded down with family photos. It's impossible not to remember Dad in this house, the place we all grew up, and I realize being here doesn't sting as much as it once did. Maybe I'm healing. Maybe the cut will never fully fuse. I lean down to touch the old photo of the six of us, smiling and laughing, sitting on the back deck at one of our traditional barbeques. "I'm not sure this place will ever feel like home again to me," I confess, "but I'll endure it so Callie has everything she needs."

CHAPTER 7

SKYLA

*S*unday is the cleaning staff's busiest day since guests are checking out and new ones are checking in. It's also the day Betty goes to church, so I help Jessie out by taking little Macy for lunch at the resort beach bar while her mom works.

At just two years old, Macy is the cutest, sweetest little girl with big blue eyes and tight dark curls she probably got from her father, since Jessie's hair is straight and blonde. Macy was the result of a fling and the guy wasn't interested when Jessie reached out to tell him she was pregnant. Personally, I think she should take the guy to court for child support, but Jessie's got it in her head that she doesn't need anything from him. According to Jessie, her own mom got by without help and she can do the same. I respect and admire her independence, but it annoys me to know there's a guy out there getting away without paying support. Clothes, food on the table, a roof over your head, none of it is free. But I don't press since Jessie doesn't like to talk about the baby daddy.

When we're done with lunch, we stroll along the beach in random diagonals as Macy gets distracted by shells, the mounds in the sand, and the occasional piece of litter.

"Bot, bot," she says excitedly in her high-pitched little voice pointing out to sea until I catch up to what she means.

"Yes, boat! Clever girl!" I clap and her face lights up.

I'm an only child—so far as I know since my mother skipped out when I was six. Perhaps I have a bunch of half siblings, who knows? Throughout my childhood, I always had a sense of lack, like there wasn't enough of something, but at the time I couldn't put my finger on exactly what it was. Sure, the boarding school met my needs for education, food, and shelter. I made good friendships, and together we all felt part of something, but likewise, something was missing, and even though I was too young to label it, I knew it was something big.

Family.

In my daydreams, I sometimes flirt with the idea of a house full of kids.

Jessie is the oldest of six children, and whenever I have visited her mom's house with her, I've instantly been enthralled with the lively chaos and laughter, and their huge capacity for love even as they fight. In their house, love doesn't feel stretched to include everyone. More like there is an abundance with more love arriving as it is needed.

I remind myself I am only twenty-four. I have plenty of time to find someone who will love every part of me, flaws and all. I had fleetingly wondered if Mike could have been that person, but before I could even get comfortable with the idea, he'd gone and banged the new hire.

I hand Macy her juice box and we sink our feet into the white sand.

Mike.

Such a mistake, and looking back I see the signs. Things he would say. Some were outright rude, others subtler.

"You sure you can get away with wearing that dress?" he said one night. My cheeks burn as I remember the way he looked at me, up and down and side to side. *"Don't you think it reveals a little too much. People might stare."* I told myself he was being chivalrous. He was trying to defend my honor with his old-fashioned views—but now I realize that's not what it was at all. He was embarrassed.

"Macy, you ever meet a guy who makes you feel less than the best thing to be put on earth, you make sure to punch him hard in the nuts," I tell her and she agrees by throwing sand inside my cleavage. "You need someone strong, who knows his own mind and is prepared to stick up for you," I tell her. "Someone like...." I stop myself from outright saying it but I'm thinking about Drew. The way he stood up for me and was prepared to fight Mike. How he kissed me, slowly at first and then deep and fast like once he got a taste, he couldn't get enough. My knees trembled and I'd forgotten anyone else was in the room. "You make sure they kiss you how a girl is supposed to be kissed." My skin warms and not because of the sun. "Come on, gorgeous girl, let's go home. Your mommy will be finished up at work soon." And I take her pudgy little hand and start heading back in the direction of our apartments.

We pass the beach bar and the reception area. From here, I can see the penthouse balconies and I force myself not to stare up at the sweeping, ocean-front apartment that Drew and his daughter are staying in. "That's it, good girl," I tell Macy as she wanders the brick path in the right direction. "I need to keep him out of my thoughts and I'll be just fine. Hiatus," I tell Macy in case she didn't know.

"Hattis," Macy repeats.

"That's right, clever girl. See, it's easy."

* * *

When we get to the staff apartments at the back of the resort, I notice one of the golf carts that's used to ferry cleaning supplies around outside.

"Jessie," I call through the open door of her apartment which is above mine.

"In here," she calls and we go through the small sitting room to the bedroom at the back where Jessie is putting away laundry. Jessie grabs Macy, spinning her around and kissing her cheek. "Baby, I missed you!"

"She'll probably need a nap. We've walked half the beach and most of the resort. In fact, I think I could use a nap."

"Thank-you. It's such a help having you and Betty babysit."

"What'll you do if Betty retires and moves away?"

"I already talked to her about that. She and Bob are looking for a place nearby, so once she is retired she'll still be able to help me out with childcare. I couldn't imagine our lives without Betty and you."

"I love having Macy, too. Besides, what else would I do?" I shrug.

I swim, I walk the rescue dogs, and I read. Apart from that, I fill my time with work. When I list it out like that, I realize some people might think it's a pretty unfulfilling life, but I'm happy. Sure, one day I'd like a family but there's plenty of time for such things.

Jessie puts Macy down for her nap and pours us both an orange juice. We go and sit on the small bench outside her front door, leaving it open so we can hear Macy if she wakes.

"Guess who I saw today?" Jessie asks without leaving me

any time to guess. "Drew and his daughter. They were on their way back from brunch with his mother apparently."

"Oh."

"Yeah. Callie seemed to know we are friends and she asked me where you were."

"That's sweet," I reply keeping my eyes trained on inspecting my fingernails. "And Drew, did he say anything?"

"You mean, did he ask me if you'd like another bite of his tongue sandwich?"

My head spins to hers, my voice several octaves too high. "Did he mention it?"

Jessie chuckles. "No, but I bet he'd be glad to know you're still thinking about it."

"I'm not still thinking about it," I reply. "I mean, why would I be thinking about the kiss or him? It was just an innocent kiss to help out a friend, because that's all we are. *Friends*." I sip the icy juice, hoping it'll take the heat out of my cheeks. "Of course, he didn't mention me."

"He did as a matter of fact." Jessie leaves me hanging for approximately fourteen hours before she continues, "Well, his daughter did. Callie asked where you were, and I told her you were watching Macy and that you were probably at the beach and then Drew said, 'I was thinking of going for a beach run.' He was going to look for you."

"Really?" I hold myself in the chair to stop myself from bolting to my feet, then shake my head. "Running on the beach is quite common. I hear lots of people do it."

Jessie nudges my arm. "Yes, but he wants to run there to look for you, you giant banana. He's into you. He must be or else why would he want to come find you?"

"Giant banana?"

Jessie quickly looks over her shoulder, as though her sleeping daughter can hear her all the way from inside the apartment. "I'm trying to cuss less. You can get away with dropping a few F bombs when they're tiny, but since Macy is picking up words now, I've got to try and dial back the swearing. Anyway, no changing the subject, back to you—are you going to go find him?"

I think about it for a second and then shake my head.

"Skyla, he's rich and gorgeous. He kissed your face off and stood up for you even though he barely knows you. You're going to pursue him, right?"

"He didn't kiss me because he wanted to. He's a nice guy and he was doing a nice thing, that's all it was."

Jessie glares at me. "How do you know that's all it was?"

"I don't. But also, I don't want to find out. I don't trust myself. Since Mike—"

"Mike was a dick!" She rolls her eyes. "Don't let that dipshit dull your shine."

I wave my hand in the air. "He was a dick. But that doesn't mean I shouldn't learn lessons from it. I knew Mike was a little out of my league in the looks department. He was an eight and I'm more of a six—"

"You're an eleven and he's a minus four!"

"If you say so, but Drew's a fifteen and he's a single dad and widowed."

"He was divorced before his ex died. He's fair game."

"It's still a loss following a significant relationship that resulted in a child. He has baggage, not to mention a daughter who needs him. And, worst of all, he is my boss's brother. He's living on the resort. Can you imagine the gossip if we got together, and the fallout if it didn't work out? No, he is off limits to me. I'm serious when I say, I won't date another guy from the Blingwood Beach Resort."

"I really don't know why you're sweating that small detail. It's not like he's an actual member of staff, and he won't even be living here long. He's the perfect guy to obliterate your V-card."

"We're just friends," I say emphatically. "I need time to figure out what I'm doing in this life. If I make bad choices, if I get a reputation like my mother did... I'm worried I'll turn out like her."

"Skyla, you're nothing like her."

"I know," I lie and Jessie's hand grips mine to reassure me. "Don't worry. I'll bounce back, and when I'm ready all those elevens had better watch out."

"Okay," she relents. "But I think he likes you, which means he's got good taste."

"Maybe we should concentrate on you and your love life. You haven't dated anyone since Macy's dad."

"Is it any wonder after what that dude put me through?" Jessie throws me a look that warns me not to press.

I keep my tone gentle. "You can't judge all men based on your experience with Macy's dad."

"Touché, Skyla. And you can't judge yourself on your mother's behavior. And you definitely can't judge Drew Blingwood based on Mike Dickface."

"Looks like we're both on D hiatus, then," I say and hold my glass up to clink it against Jessie's. And even though I am insistent, deep down I'm wondering if Drew Blingwood is looking for me and what he wants to do with me when he finds me.

* * *

LATER THAT DAY, after a long walk along the beach and twenty lengths of the pool, I'm heading out of the locker rooms when I hear someone call my name. Behind me, I spot Callie and she runs to catch up to me. "Did my dad find you?"

Excitement fizzles in my gut.

"No. I haven't seen him. Was he looking for me?" I ask innocently.

"Yes, I think he ran half the coastline looking for you. I'm heading back to the penthouse now. Why don't you come with me and *we* can ask him what he wants?" she says, emphasizing the *we*.

"Oh. I should probably go home," I tell her. "My hair's soaking wet and…" *I don't have any makeup on.*

"You look perfect. He likes the natural look."

I look up at the balcony to their penthouse and feel torn. "I'll probably see him at work tomorrow. It's probably work related. Or you can suggest he email me. Yes, that's probably better. He can email me and then it'll save us the trip and…."

Callie takes my hand. "It'll only take a minute so you'd just as well come with me now. We'll just say I ran into you and—"

"Callie, that is what happened."

"Oh yeah, totally. I wasn't looking for you," she replies leading me through the door to the elevator. "Have you eaten?"

My stomach rumbles but I sense foul play, so I reply, "I'm not very hungry. I'll just pop in quick and then I'll leave you and your dad to have dinner."

"He might not even be home but you can wait with me. It'll be nice to have some company until he gets back," she tells me as we get out of the elevator that leads straight into their penthouse. "He was out on his run and I wanted to take a walk—"

"There you are! Why didn't you answer your phone?" Drew's voice is firm and it sends a shiver down my spine. He's standing near the state-of-the-art kitchen in the open-plan living area, his arms folded over the hard expanse of his chest. He looks pissed and worried at the same time as his dark brooding eyes burn a hole into Callie's.

Meanwhile, my instincts are screaming at me to run.

Callie looks unconcerned as she holds her cell up. "The battery died."

"You were supposed to be here, doing homework."

"Oh Dad, I didn't mean to worry you. You know I'll be fine on the resort. It's not even dark yet and there's security everywhere. In fact, Uncle Logan said if I have any problems to approach the staff and tell them I am his niece. He already told them all to look after me. Besides, I found Skyla for you." She grins.

As though he was too worried to notice me before, his face turns my way and he looks me up and down, his lips parted ever so slightly.

Even in my denim shorts and cami, I feel naked.

"I... Callie asked me to come see you. Apparently, you want me?"

Even as I say it, I wish I could drag the words back. I sound immature. Unsure. Pathetic. *Want me? Of course, he doesn't want me!*

Drew takes a step toward me and my heart thumps beneath my chest.

"Skyla." His dimples pop with his smile, taking years off the scowling face of moments ago. "Sorry. I... My daughter thinks it's fine to disappear when I'm not directly supervising her."

"I already told him I don't need adult supervision all the time. I'm twelve, almost thirteen and we're surrounded by staff employed directly by Uncle Logan, but do you think he'd listen?" She thumbs in her dad's direction and I nod then shake my head, caught between the crossfire.

"You should probably be careful and tell your dad where you're going. It's better to be safe," I stutter.

"I left a note," Callie replies. "On the counter."

He glances toward it.

"You've got homework to do, young lady. Now."

Callie rolls her eyes and says to me, "He gets like this when he knows he's wrong. Don't worry, you'll get used to it." She grabs a hold of her backpack that's slumped on the couch. "I'll be in my room doing homework. Just holler if you need me."

I smile as she disappears behind one of the many doors in the enormous room. When it's just me and Drew, I intake a breath and then say, "Hi."

"Hi," he replies and expels a breath. Beneath his workout shirt I can see the hard divots of a six pack. His arms are thick and muscular and, even sweaty from a work out, he looks magnificent.

He nibbles his lower lip, either searching for a way to begin or because he forgot what he was going to say.

"You were looking for me, Callie said?"

"Oh, yeah." He ruffles his hair boyishly. "I got distracted by my wayward daughter. "Shall we?" He points to the open doors of the balcony where I can see a plush outdoor sofa and coffee table.

I nod.

"Can I get you a drink?"

I shake my head and follow him outside. My heart is beating through my chest and my hands are clammy.

"You had a good day?" he asks, making small talk and gesturing for me to sit beside him.

I regale him briefly of my day so far and when I ask how his day was, he explains he had family brunch. The entire conversation feels more stilted than our previous encounters and an enormous sense of foreboding falls over me.

Drew sits forward, his elbows on his knees. His thighs, revealed by his shorts as they ride up, are tan with dark curling hairs. I resist the urge to squeeze the muscle between my finger and thumb. When I glance back to his face, I notice him looking at my thighs squashed against the seat of the sofa in my cutoff denim shorts and I tug them down an inch.

"Is it too hot for you? I have some SPF 50 if you need it? It gets quite warm out here in the sun. Or I could pull the shade down?" He points to the sun shade at the other end of the balcony.

I shake my head and chuckle nervously. "I'm fine," I say even though it feels about ninety degrees out here and, judging by the fire beneath my cheeks, my skin might actually catch fire.

Then, I wait. I keep my eyes ahead and forget to breathe. If I brace myself, whatever he has to say won't sting. I'll just bat it away, say thank-you and leave. I'm already planning my exit when he speaks.

"I'm sorry I kissed you."

I dare to meet his eyes and suddenly my heart starts to ache.

"It's fine," I tell him. "No apology necessary."

I should stand and leave since he obviously needed to tell me he does, in fact, regret kissing me, but instead I remain frozen like a masochist, wishing he would kiss me again and knowing it's never going to happen.

"I don't want you to get the wrong idea," he continues. "You're…" He gestures his hand to me and it reminds me of Mike.

"I understand," I reply.

"You're a great girl, but…"

"It's fine. You're not my type anyway."

He pauses for a moment, then his eyes narrow. "What do you mean, I'm not your type?"

I shrug, knowing I don't even have a type. "I wasn't looking to get into anything with you, that's all. " I smile and try to hold onto whatever dignity I have left. "It's honestly fine."

He measures my expression while I try to stop my lip from wobbling. Then he continues talking and my face starts to burn hot. "It's not you. You're great. It's me. I behaved like a juvenile. I'm practically old enough to be your father. Kissing you was a stupid thing for me to do."

He stares at me, waiting for me to say something but I look away, down at my thighs sweating against the water-proof fabric of the sofa.

I think I say something like, "It's fine. It's really fine. I understand...." But the voice doesn't sound like mine and I'm not even sure my lips are moving. The sun feels even hotter beaming on my thoroughly embarrassed cheeks. And my eyes, worried for my flaming cheeks, threaten to sprout water in case there is a fire in need of extinguishing.

"I'm sorry," he says.

Before I've even register that my feet are moving, I'm hitting the button on the elevator without a backward glance.

The good thing about fancy resorts is the elevators—they come quickly.

The bad thing is the doors close irrationally slowly, and when I turn around, they are mid-close and I see Drew, and his sorrowful expression completes my humiliation.

CHAPTER 8

DREW

"*H*ere!" I point to the blueprint. "It's on the design."

Logan holds his palms up and squares me with a look that says, *What the fuck is up with you?*

"Sorry," I say, running my hands through my hair, yanking it right at the roots. "I'm not sleeping."

"Callie?" he asks.

"Partly." Like, twenty-five percent perhaps. Last night after Skyla left, Callie was grilling my ass over why she left so quick. And why I didn't invite her to have dinner with us and ask her to go watch the movie I've been dying to see. I couldn't tell her I ended up hurting Skyla's feelings. I intended to clear things up. I thought she enjoyed the kiss because it showed Mike she was over him, but when I looked at her as I tried to explain my behavior, all I could see was disappointment and hurt in her puppy dog eyes. I tried to let

Skyla down gently, but instead I put my size thirteen foot right in my mouth.

I probably shouldn't tell Logan what happened, but sometimes a man needs a second opinion, so I spill. "I messed up."

"Not like you, brother. Go on."

"I, well, it was accidental." None of the words seem right. "Not accidental exactly, more like purposefully. I wanted to do it, but I didn't think through the repercussions, like always."

"Accidentally purposeful? You have me intrigued."

"I kissed Skyla."

Logan grins. "Way to go!" He lifts his hand in a high-five motion, but I square him with a don't-you-fucking-dare glare so he returns his hand to the desk. "And this is a problem, why? I already told you; half the staff here are screwing. It's just what happens when everyone lives and works together. Unless, she's not into you?"

His comment lands like a punch to a man who is already down.

Is she into me?

I'm certain she was into me during the kiss even if it started purely to show Mike. She seemed upset last night when I tried to tell her I wasn't looking for a relationship, but instead I told her pretty directly that kissing her was a mistake—correction: *a stupid thing to do.*

Worse than that, I want her to be into me—which is all kinds of screwed up when it'd be easier if she hated me.

"I'm a shitty person. She's way too young for me. Twelve years, Logan. I'm very nearly old enough to be her father!"

"Perhaps she'll call you Daddy," he jokes and my fists clench.

"Not. Fucking. Funny. Logan."

He bites his tongue and waits for my reply. I apologetically bump his shoulder with mine. It's not his fault I'm pissed with myself for going too far and kissing her. Now my daughter's confused and I still don't trust myself not to seek Skyla out and show her exactly how hard I've been thinking about her.

"It can't—no, it won't work. I have Callie to think about. We're settling into a new place. I need to give her my time, not some woman I just met."

"Way I see it, Callie wants you to start dating. We all do. The only person who can't see it'd be good for you, is you. And Skyla's plenty beyond legal and of sound mind to make good judgments. She's one of my most reliable employees who has worked her way up through the company. Hell, I'd trust her to run this place if I wasn't too much of a control freak to relinquish the role. She's a smart woman who knows her own mind, not some juvenile kid."

My hands pull at my hair again. "She's young enough that I feel like a felon thinking what I actually want to do to her."

He frowns. "She's not *that* young. You're overthinking it. Relax and see what happens."

Easy for him to say, he's not the cradle snatcher who can't stop thinking about her pretty little mouth.

"It's too late. I already told her kissing her was a stupid mistake and now…."

"Now she hates you. Well done, brother."

"It's not like I don't know I screwed up. But thanks for your support."

"Just saying it how it is. You like her, you think she likes you or else all of this would be moot, and you're acting with the maturity of someone half her age. You're going to see her again. Trust me, the resort gets smaller when there are people you don't want to bump into, and we're all going to be working together getting Blingwood 2.0 up and running. Why not go find her and tell her you're sorry?"

"I can't. She'd think I want more and I don't. I honest to

God just want to settle into my new home with my daughter."

"Okay, so don't apologize and let her continue to think you're an asshole."

I don't like that idea much either, and after talking to Logan I'm close to persuading myself to go find her and apologize.

I remind myself: I'm not dating anyone. I'm not here to start shit with a woman.

So why am I still thinking about her?

"How's Dana?" I ask, changing the subject.

"She's gone to a pregnancy yoga retreat."

"Oh yeah?"

"We did the photoshoot to publicly announce our engagement this morning and she let slip she's pregnant. They're publishing it this week." Logan doesn't look at all happy about the revelation or his pending celebrity status. "She wants to follow it with a happy, healthy momma clothing line—or some shit. I try to stay out of it."

"It's a little early to be telling the world about the pregnancy, but I guess there's not much you can do about it now. Sounds like she's got it all figured out."

He shrugs. "Dana does what Dana wants. You seen Mom?"

I shake my head. "Not since brunch last Sunday."

"Do me a favor and go see her. She's busting my ass about volunteering at the pound. She needs dog walkers and she needs them now. I've offered to hire her some people but she's not having any of it." He mimics mom's voice, "'People have to want to do it,' like anyone ever wanted to do anything that doesn't have cold, hard cash strapped to the deal."

I become annoyed with myself as I think of doing it if it means seeing more of Skyla.

I feel Logan watching me. "Suppose I could get my assistant to email the workforce, see if anyone is looking to get a new dog walking hobby." He sits back in his chair and taps his finger on his chin. "Come to think of it, the new guy I hired for security said he liked dogs. Maybe I'll ask him."

"New guy?"

Logan narrows his eyes at me curiously. "Yeah. Ripped guy on the gate. He'd probably like to join Skyla on his lunch break. I bet they'll have loads in common."

"Fuck you, Logan," I reply. Then I decide I probably should go find Skyla and apologize. Maybe I'll take her some of those cookies she likes.

CHAPTER 9

SKYLA

"*I*t's like he doesn't understand I have work to do," Sally from the reception desk complains as we sit in my office. She's in her late thirties with bottle blonde hair and wearing the hotel reception uniform of a black skirt and patterned shirt. Sally is supposed to be here for the appropriate telling off for missed duties, but after Drew's revelation last night, I'm feeling too sensitive and raw to reprimand anyone.

I was happy pretending the kiss didn't mean anything to me—even if it felt like something—and then Drew went and made a big deal about it and now I feel like an idiot. It was so embarrassing, being told like some kind of lovesick child that not only is he not interested in me, but that kissing me was a mistake! I tuck away my hurt feelings to deal with the matter in hand—not that Sally is focused either—she seems to think our meeting has taken a turn in the direction of couple's therapy.

"We should bring Doug up here. He's the one you should tell. When he's not sexting me and telling me he loves me—hourly sometimes—then he's having flowers delivered or bringing in cuddly toys. He proposed right in the hotel reception, not that we can afford to get married yet. He bought me chocolates, left them right on the reception counter while I was checking in Mr. Gibbs—they were the dark ones from that fancy store on Vine Street, the place with the blue signs out front. He knows I can't resist; they had soft centers and those little nut—"

"Orange or mint?" I interrupt like it matters—but the mint ones are my favorite.

"Mint, of course."

I nod, understanding entirely—fruit and chocolate together is like pineapple on pizza—then I try to divert our conversation back to the matter at hand, but Sally is staring at me with tears prickling her eyes. It's unnerving.

"I'm sorry, Skyla."

"Well, that's okay. We all make mistakes. What we have to do is figure out the—"

"No. I'm not sorry if Tina thinks I'm too lovesick to do my work, I am sorry for you."

I eye her quizzically and hope this conversation is not about to go down the path of pity.

"Here I am, gushing about my super intoxicating love life. Singing about the joys of being in love and feeling the butter-flies and the rainbows, and there you are, just had your heart ripped into shreds and stamped all over in front of the entire staff here. It's humiliating for you, heartbreaking to watch, and everyone feels so sorry for you. I swear, you're worth ten Mike and Jenny's, and we'd all have nothing to do with Mike if he wasn't the one in charge of making sure our paychecks hit our bank accounts." She chuckles awkwardly but my head is still reeling from the confirmation that everyone here pities me for being a complete fool—thank God they don't know about my latest humiliation with Drew. Sally's hand covers mine on the desk briefly before I pull it away. "Are you okay?"

"Yes, Sally. I am fine. Now back to—"

"Because it's okay not to be okay. Before I met Doug, I was a shadow of the person I am today. Sure, I still turned heads, but I didn't feel whole inside." She pats her chest to add emphasis to her statement.

"Sally, regarding the business with Mike, please rest assured that I am fine. Contrary to what you may have heard, I wasn't dating Mike and I am indeed quite 'whole' on the inside. Now if you'll let me get back to—"

"Are you though?" She doesn't let me answer. "You've worked here for years now. You've dated a few guys who worked here—but none of those relationships have worked out for you—"

My stomach drops a full inch. "Sally, are you saying I have a reputation?"

"No. No, of course not. We want you to be happy. Blowing through resort guys like Mike, who aren't worth your time, it's so sad to see."

"Blowing guys?"

"Well, not literally blowing. You'd need a lot of puff for that." She chuckles but I miss her joke. "We never see your family members visit and you seem so lonely...." She continues to list the concerns that have somehow made it into the Blingwood Gossip Grapevine, including my emotional eating and lack of family. I try to return to the subject of her misconduct, feeling renewed in my desire to issue a formal warning until she says, "We're like a big, happy family here at the resort and we look after our own and you are ours. We all adore you. My only wish for you is that you had more real family."

My only close family is my dad, and he works in the middle of the North Sea on an oil rig somewhere. And as for close friends, the kids from the boarding school had families scattered across the east coast—staying in touch was hard. The folks here have become my friends and my family. Sally is right, the Blingwood Resort is like a big, mostly happy family—and as dysfunctional as one too.

Sally's hands dart back to mine. "You can tell me all about it. I won't tell a soul." She pretends to lock her lips, and for an empty second I am tempted to spill. To tell her that Mike is a cheating, dim-witted bastard, but that actually, instead of feeling let down and bereft, I feel enlightened. I dodged a bullet, and I am hoping there are no more in life's chamber coming my way. But I don't. Sally, as gullible and kind-hearted as she is, is a known gossip, and working reception gives her the perfect vantage to see all the goings on around here—and to pass them on to the staff in the cafeteria during breaks.

My tone cools by about thirty degrees as I tell her, "Sally, you have got to prioritize checking in the guests and answering the phone when it rings. That's your job, and if you are not doing your job then people are going to start wondering why you're getting paid."

I hate this part of HR but when a member of staff doesn't respond to their direct manager's concerns, it's my job to try mediate the situation before it worsens.

Am I good cop or bad cop, today? I'm not sure, but my purpose is to keep everyone happy—and normally, I'm good at it. That is, when I am not worried about blowing through all the men in the resort. Like really, it was three guys over three years and I didn't even sleep with any of them. Not to mention the devastatingly gorgeous, Drew Blingwood and our "mistake" of a kiss that was so hot it has played on repeat in my mind ever since.

"I try, I really do. But Doug works right at the concierge desk. He's there, opposite me all day in his uniform, looking gorgeous." Sally fans herself. "And I'm behind the reception desk, smiling sweetly. My endorphins are off the chart." She gasps and her hand flies to her mouth. "There I go again, gushing about my serious relationship and making you feel unloved—"

"I get you're in love and full of the joy of it. I do. But if you don't keep a professional distance, you're going to get a formal warning." Sally's mouth pops open, her eyes widen. I slowly blink and try to remember the solution-focused managerial workshop I did back in December. "Would it help if I got you a transfer? They need help in laundry or perhaps I can find you a job in the restaurant?"

"No! If I didn't have Doug opposite me each day, I don't know how I'd cope… I'd never get anything done."

I exhale slowly. "Sally, I've got to lay this down straight for you. If there are further issues, you could get fired."

Sally takes a tissue from the box on my desk.

"F-fired?"

"We have guests to look after."

"I love looking after the guests."

I smile. "I know you do. That's why you are here now discussing this with me. You need to put your phone away while you're working. Instead of texting Doug, you need to answer the hotel phone within three rings when the line at reception allows. And either you tell Doug or I will that he must stop writing love notes on the hotel information packs."

"He only writes those to keep the love alive."

"It's unprofessional." Sally's gray eyes threaten tears. "Maybe it would be best if I spoke with Doug. I will remind him that both of your duties must get done."

"Oh, Skyla, I think that would help. It's not that we're lazy. We're so enormously in love. So massively in love it's like the stars fell out the sky and wrapped me and Doug right up inside of them. You know how it is?" Then she frowns and her smile falters. "Sorry. Again. But you will know that love one day. I know cupid is coming for you just like he did for me and Doug." If I wasn't the professional I am, I'd be hurling right now listening to her lovesick monologue. Instead, I write down a reminder to make an appointment with Doug regarding appropriate office relations on my to-do list, then something catches my eye through the polished glass of my office door.

It's Drew, loitering and looking through the window pane like he wants to see me and it has my stomach flip-flopping with nerves.

"No problem. Go and show Tina that you and Doug are serious professionals who won't allow your epic love to infringe on your job roles," I say with all the sarcasm that I can muster, though Sally doesn't seem to hear it.

"Thank-you, Skyla. Doug told me you'd look after me. I hate being in trouble."

"You're not in trouble, *yet*," I tell her, standing from behind my desk and preparing to usher her out. "Neither is Doug. But remember, personal phones down during your shifts." I see Sally to the door and she walks right into Drew.

"Oops. Sorry. Don't know how I didn't see you there. My, that's a big, hard chest you have. Are those cookies you have in your hands? Lovely." She looks back at me and uses her thumb to point toward Drew's chest that's wrapped in expensive cotton and seductively hinting at impressive pectoral muscles. In his hands, as Sally pointed out, is a plate filled with cookies.

Sally winks. "Isn't that nice? He's brought you cookies to help mend your broken heart. And now that you're single and in need of the love of a good man, you can accept them free of guilt."

While I cringe out of sheer embarrassment, Drew casually brushes his soft, dark hair back away from his face self-consciously.

"He'd be a nice man for you to date, Skyla. Not like Mike."

Please go away, Sally, I urge with smiling eyes.

"If that's all, Sally." I gesture my hand to encourage walking but she doesn't get the message.

"She'd make a lovely wife. My Doug says she's the gem of the office and he's right. Thought I was going to get fired in there for a moment, but Skyla let me off. She's the kindest woman on the resort. I could kiss her."

"Is that so?" Drew grins and his gaze drops to my lips.

"I'm Sally," she supplies. "You can find me in reception if you ever need."

"Noted." He taps his nose and Sally shrieks out a laugh.

"You two could come on a double date with me and Doug. We could go down to the bingo?"

"Oh, we're not—" Drew starts but I interrupt.

"Mr. Blingwood and I are just colleagues," I tell Sally flatly and Drew looks on awkwardly.

"If you'll excuse us." Drew's voice is smooth but apologetic. "I really must talk with Skyla."

"And you should probably go back to reception if you're going to impress Tina like we talked about," I tell Sally and she nods seriously.

With Sally's heels tapping along the marble of the corridor, Drew leans against the door of my office. "Can I come in?"

No. You should probably keep walking. About eleven miles should do it.

"Of course." I nod. "I'm very busy, though. I have a-a meeting soon," I stutter, my knees knocking as I walk back to my desk and seat myself behind it. My calendar is displayed right on the monitor, and if he looks he'll see I have two straight hours until my final appointment of the day.

I turn my monitor slightly to the left.

"I brought you cookies," he says, following me and placing them on the desk before me.

"I'm watching my figure. But thank-you, anyway."

He slowly looks me over and my skin tingles beneath his gaze.

"Why?"

I glance at my to-do list and try to ignore the way my stomach somersaults over how good he looks and smells.

"I don't eat them on Mondays. I have a strict eating plan."

"No cookies on Monday," he says disbelievingly and pretends to write a note on the palm of his hand with his finger. Then he sits in the chair opposite mine.

"I really am very busy."

He leans forward onto my desk while I click my pen into work mode.

"And I really am very sorry."

Now I look up. "Oh. And what might you be sorry for?"

"For telling you that kissing you was a mistake. It probably was a mistake. You work for Logan, and you're much younger than me, so I shouldn't be kissing you. We have to work together and I kissed you in your workplace. I kissed you right in the middle of the breakroom, and what I meant to say last night was that I don't want my kissing you to make you feel uncomfortable in any way. Kissing you was—"

"Please stop saying, *kissing*," I hiss, since it's making my palms sweaty and my insides warm and fuzzy. It's making me think of doing it again—a matter made worse when I look up and he licks his lips.

He looks at me sheepish. "Sorry. Can I explain? I made a mess of things last night, and I hurt your feelings but that wasn't my intention."

"It's fine," I reply.

"You say that a lot. But how I handled our conversation, it wasn't fine. It was terrible, actually."

"I wasn't expecting anything to come from the kiss," I admit even though I now recognize that I had started to hope it might lead to something. "I know you only did it to prove something to Mike."

"Last night, I made a mess of explaining. I was projecting my fears onto you. What I didn't explain was that my family wants me to meet someone—they think they know what's best for me, but they don't understand, and the whole thing is making me antsy. You see, we're here to make a fresh start. Callie's been through a lot and I'm trying to do my best to make her happy. In New York, I failed. I worked long hours and I wasn't as available to her as I should have been. We're at different stages in our lives, you and I, and right now, my priority is Callie. I'm so worried I'm sucking at fatherhood and messing everything up that it's making me a little crazy. Kissing you was… unexpected." I nod like my pulse isn't dancing to a rave beat. "I shouldn't have kissed you. I never intended to hurt you."

His face is so handsome even in sorrow, so utterly tempting to kiss away his pain, and so genuinely apologetic that I find it impossible to stay mad at him when his intentions are pure, even if his methods require work.

"You're not sucking at fatherhood. You're doing fine. You were kissing me in front of Mike and… sticking up for me, again—I know that's all it was, so thank-you."

"No. You're wrong. I wanted to kiss you. Not for Mike but for me."

My mouth pops open but no words come out.

"I thought…." He takes a deep breath. "My family. Callie told them I was looking at your butt that day at the pool, and they were going on about you and I wondered if I had led you to believe—"

"You didn't. I don't have a lot of people who are ready to stand up for me, so thank-you. And apology accepted. I get that you don't want a relationship. I don't either. I don't know if you actually heard much of the discussion that you and Logan walked in on the other day, but I am on a... D hiatus." I cross my arms over my chest and the pressure makes my nipples tingle as I stare at Drew's perfect mouth.

"I'm still reeling from Betty's comment that it's pussy that I need." He's all perfect teeth and cute dimples. "Wait... What kind of hiatus?" Drew cocks a brow at me and I feel my cheeks color.

"A... dalliance hiatus. I'm focusing on me right now and not dating anyone from my workplace. So, thank-you for coming to apologize, but it wasn't necessary. I'm not interested."

His brows furrow. "You're not interested?"

"That's right." I draw a little line on my notebook, finally feeling somewhat in control.

Drew leans back in his chair. His long legs stretch out and his foot brushes mine. I tuck my legs away and squeeze my thighs, hoping it might tame the pulse that's raging through me—it does not.

"Because of Mike?"

"No. Mike was just another jerk. I'm taking a timeout from the dating pool while I reconfigure my goals. I might get a hobby or plan a vacation. I haven't decided yet." He scoffs and I pin him with a stare. "I suppose it's not unlike what you're doing. You don't want a relationship and neither do I—at least not yet, and not with anyone who is even remotely attached to the Blingwood Resort. It's too messy. I'm making a solemn vow to myself. When I start dating again, I will make better choices. Business and pleasure, in my case, do not mix." His stare becomes heated, so I pick up my notebook, scanning through my list and pretending I can actually see straight.

"A solemn vow, huh? Well, I suppose you're young enough that taking a break won't do any harm."

"What is your obsession with my age?" I ask but he doesn't answer and so I continue, "A break isn't always harmless. My mother was sixteen when she had me. She took a break and left when I was six years old. She dated a bunch of unsuitable men, got an interesting reputation and then took off with one, and I never saw her again." I throw down my pen and lean back in my chair, unable to meet his eyes. "I must have been a crummy kid, huh? For her to take off like that." I don't know why I just told him that, only that he seems to be listening. "It's always bothered me that I was so easy to leave. I don't want to be like her, dating a bunch of guys trying to find 'the one.' I hoped I had better intuition, but finding the right relationship is starting to feel like more luck than judgment. Maybe it's time I gave up."

When I dare meet his eyes, he's looking at me so intently I might go blind from the pressure. "You're preaching to the choir, but I can tell it'll be different for you. There's someone out there who's going to be perfect for you, you'll see."

"But not for you?" I question.

"I had my shot. Only it wasn't the other person who was flawed, it was me. And with regards to your mother, there are two types of parents that choose to leave. Some aren't cut out to be parents and they make the right choice to go, and some make terrible decisions and never find the courage to come back. But I can guarantee her leaving has nothing to do with you. I bet you were all kinds of gap-teethed adorable." Drew smiles and I close my lips, him staring at my mouth is making me self-conscious.

"You think so?"

"Skyla, you're a thoroughly lovely young woman. I am certain you were an adorable child and a perfect daughter. The problem lies not with you but with your mother. Kids tend to put their parents high up on a pedestal and think they should be perfect. When you can't get the answers you need from the absent parent, it's natural to look inward. Take Callie, she once asked me if her mother would still be here if she was a better behaved kid. I told her no way; her mother wouldn't have changed a hair on her head." His throat bobs as he swallows, then he jokes, "She accepts it was out of her control now, but on a bad day, when she's really missing her mom, I'm the asshole she gets frustrated with when I make her go to school even when we can't find her math book; it's me who forces her to eat burned food—"

"Callie doesn't think you're an asshole," I insist.

"She definitely does."

His mouth quips up in a smile and I laugh.

"You make her eat burned food?"

"Not all the time, sometimes we eat out." Drew winks and I grin back at him.

"I never took my missing my mother out on my father—I suppose I was worried he'd stop picking me up from school for the holidays, so I never told him how I felt. See, he worked away on an oil rig, and so I went to a boarding school and whenever I saw him, I tried to be the perfect child just in case he abandoned me too. Lucky guy missed out on most of my teenage years."

Drew stares at me a beat too long, his expression saddened. "That must have been tough."

I felt like an orphan most of my life, even though my dad was around during the holidays. "It was okay," I say instead. "I was fine."

His smile doesn't quite reach his eyes. "It wasn't fine, you missed him. I bet he missed you too. But you're okay and you're going to be just fine."

I nod, not realizing how much I needed to hear that.

"Callie is already keeping me on my toes. She has an answer for everything."

"Wonder who she gets that from?"

He laughs, deep and throaty then admits, "Yeah, she's like me sometimes but I was way worse. It will probably shock you to hear that as a teenager, I was a real dick."

"Really? No, I don't believe it." I smirk.

"Okay, so I haven't matured much. I blamed my father for pretty much everything that went wrong in my life and I let arguments fester for years. We had the power to fix it, but we were both too stubborn and I was foolish to think we had plenty of time. We didn't."

"I'm sorry your father passed away before you made up. I'm sure he knows you forgave him."

"I forgave him, of course I did." Drew brushes an imaginary piece of lint from his pant suit. "But did he forgive me? Guess I'll never know, but since Callie has already lost one parent, I don't want to jeopardize my relationship with her by being blindsided that we'll always have more time. That's why, when my father died, I had the realization that I couldn't carry on as before. I had to be present and put her needs first. Strike while the iron was hot, so to speak, and so now we're here and starting over."

I ponder a moment and then reply, "There's no point in waiting when you know what you want. *Strike while the iron is hot,*" I repeat. "That's admirable. You saw that change was needed and you took a leap of faith. You're a good father." I glance down where I wrote, *solution focused*, on my notepad and it makes me wonder aloud if I should apply Drew's learning to my own situation. "My *dalliance* hiatus won't involve all men, just men from the resort. That way, if it goes wrong, I won't be subjected to the whispers and embarrassment of public acknowledgment."

"Makes sense. What is it they say about not shitting where you eat?"

"Disgusting," I laugh, "but you're right. I should trust myself and not waste time. After all, I still have needs. Perhaps I should try online dating—"

"No! That's not what I'm suggesting at all. I mean, you don't want to rush into anything."

"Then what?"

He opens his mouth to speak, then shrugs. "I don't have the answer to that. But you shouldn't worry you're like your mom when you're obviously not. You deserve to be happy. Don't let a bad relationship with a guy or a parent cloud your judgment."

"Touché," I counter.

Drew smirks and his voice drips sarcasm. "Yes, I should really stop allowing my previous bad choices in men to impact my future ones."

"You know what I mean. You're taking a past hurt and using it as a shield to fend off meeting women and fully looking to the future. Callie obviously would like you to meet someone."

"So, I should add you to the list of people who think I ought to start dating?"

The thought of Drew dating has my heart hurting but I can't bring myself to give him bad advice when it might stand in the way of him experiencing love. "Do what makes you happy, but don't make choices from a place of fear. You can have a great relationship with your daughter and have meaningful romantic relationships."

Drew stands. "I'll keep that in mind. Thanks for the chat; I'm glad we cleared things up and I hope we can be friends." He takes hold of the plate of cookies and I leap to my feet.

"Friends don't take back gifts." I stare at the cookies.

He puts down the plate and holds out his hands, palm-side up. Grinning in that sexy way of his, he says, "By all means. Please enjoy them, *whenever* you choose to eat them." Drew begins walking away but not before turning back to say, "Callie and I will be at the pool later."

I watch his ass as he walks away and bite into a cookie, wondering what he means. Is he warning me he will be there so I can stay away, or is it an invitation?

*　*　*

"HE SAID WHAT?" Jessie asks as we file into the staff dining room.

One of the many benefits to working at the Blingwood Resort is free food. Like three square meals a day cooked for us in the work cafeteria, and best of all no dirty dishes. Logan had decided it was a better use of the resort's budget than adding kitchens to all the staff housing—only a few complain and I'm not one of them. The chef is incredible.

"Last night he said kissing me was a mistake. He's not going to do it again which is good since we're both not interested in relationships." Over by the window, I spot Mike forking pasta into Jenny's mouth and feel the stares of the other people. I turn Jessie to the freshly made apple pie and hope she doesn't see Mike and cause a scene. Then I fill her in with what's been happening.

"That utter—"

"No. It's a good thing. I saw Drew earlier and he clarified things. He's not open to dating. Not me, not anyone. And I agree to a point. I am not dating another person who lives at the resort, so it's good we got things straight." I remember how he listened and how easy he was to talk to. "We're going to be friends. I liked talking with him, and I ended up telling him this stuff about my mom, and he didn't judge me. He was… lovely."

"Lovely?"

I chew my lip for a second, knowing exactly where Jessie is going to lead this conversation. "Lovely, as a friend. We're not going to be anything more than friends. He's still a Blingwood guy."

"But he's not actually a staff member here. He's designing the new resort, sure. But he's not a member of the regular resort workforce."

"He's my boss's brother and he's commissioned to do the design. He's staff by proxy and by blood. That is close enough to the danger zone."

"Danger zone?"

I lower my voice. "Staff relations are bad—for me, anyway." Though most of the other staff here seem to be able to make it work—I apparently can't. "Been there, done that, still have scars from the burns."

We gather up our meals, and I swipe some pie from the server who knows me well enough to have a piece saved, and we take our seats. I make sure to sit facing Mike and Jenny so Jessie has to face me.

"I am so over men who have no respect and even less in the way of common decency!" She hisses, and I wonder if part of her comment is related to her own experience with Macy's dad.

"You can relax. That chapter is finished. I'm over Mike, and Drew was a non-starter from the get-go. I'm thinking of starting a new hobby. I already walk Mrs. Blingwood's dogs at lunch time so it'll have to be something that fits in with that. What do you think, yoga or Pilates?"

Jessie rolls her eyes. "Pass. I think you need to get laid."

I chuckle through my mouthful of meatballs and shake my head. "What I need is to keep busy. Maybe I'll meet someone the organic way at Pilates, but I'm not stressing over it."

"So, let me get this straight. You want to take a hiatus from relationships until you meet someone organically, off resort, and Drew wants to avoid relationships altogether?"

I nod. "That seems to be the gist of it."

"But you like him?"

As though summoning him, he walks by the window wearing a white T-shirt, black shorts and a smile. The sun hits his almost black hair in just the right way to highlight red tones, and it looks soft enough that I'd love to push my fingers through it.

Do I like him?

That's like asking if I like chocolate or ice cream—who doesn't?

Behind him, Callie trails, swinging her swim bag.

When I turn back to Jessie, she gives me a rueful smile. "That's affirmative. You're looking at him like he's a piece of meat."

"He's easy on the eyes, that's all. You, as well as every other red-blooded female in this resort, must have noticed?"

"He looks too much like a Blingwood boy to be to my taste." She pulls a sickened face. "But that doesn't mean it should put you off. So, what exactly is stopping you from making a move?"

"Jessie—he just told me he is not open to a relationship, not to mention my hiatus. Are you even listening to me?"

"Blah. Blah. Blah. What I'm hearing is you both don't want the formal stress of a relationship. You want to get rid of your V-card. He definitely wants to get laid. You feel comfortable with him or you wouldn't have told him about your mom, and he is a red-blooded man who's got the hots for you. You'd be totally helping each other out by having hot, no-strings-attached sex with the resident bachelor."

"I can't—"

"Yes, you can—if you want to. The solution is easy peasy. Go and lay it on him. Ain't no man going to deny you. It'll be entirely on your terms and just for fun while you're waiting to find *Mr. Not Blingwood Resort.*"

"But he is a Blingwood Resort guy."

"Show me the proof he's on payroll."

"I can't. He's our boss's brother—"

"You can't, which means you totally can! Look, his house is getting built as we speak. He's going to be out of this place in no time at all. How often did you see him at the resort before now?"

I shrug. "Never."

"Exactly. He'll be long gone before you know it. And he's older, *experienced.* Why, I bet he knows a thing or two. You'd be learning from a pro! Listen, this is my two cents, but if I were you, I'd bang him before someone else does."

When Jessie puts it like that, she makes it sound easy, when in truth I've never seduced a man before. But maybe, just maybe, she's right. Losing my virginity to a man like Drew Blingwood might give me the boost to go forward with confidence. And, if he'll agree to no-strings, maybe it'll be like getting the recipe for the best double chocolate fudge cake and eating the whole thing without putting on so much as an ounce of weight. And that is something I can get on board with.

CHAPTER 10

DREW

"*W*hy do you look so grumpy today?" Callie asks as we walk past the resort salon on the way back from our afternoon swim. Skyla didn't show up at the pool, I know because I was searching for her. But I'm not grumpy—disappointed, perhaps. I was sure she'd come to hang out with us, as friends, but she must have had a better offer. "You're frowning again. You should probably stop doing that or else you'll end up with wrinkles." Callie's dripping wet hair hangs right down to her waist. Holding water like it is, it looks darker. Bone dry, it's blonde like her mother's hair was—though twice the length.

It's gotten so long because she refuses to get a trim since Crystal died.

"Have you thought about hair styles? We could schedule you an appointment at the salon after school tomorrow?"

"Dad, there's no way I'll get an appointment with this short notice. Momma always said that." If it meant Callie swallowed her fear of allowing a new stylist to touch her hair, I'd pay twenty times what it usually costs.

"So, we're looking for a salon that's too busy to see you for a couple of weeks? We could ask your grandmother where she goes?"

Callie pulls a face. "I love Nanna, she has great style, but I'm not getting my hair cut at the same place she goes to—what if it's an old lady place and the kids at school make fun of me for having a bad cut?"

I stop walking as we pass the staff cafeteria and pull Callie to a stop. "I know it's hard. Your mother was the best hairdresser in the city and she did every cut for you since you were born, but if you let it get much longer, you'll be tripping over it." I don't even know why I'm making such a big deal about it except, getting it trimmed feels like it might be part of the healing process. "Your mom would probably want you to keep up with regular trims."

"I'll think about it," she replies, gazing in the window of the cafeteria.

"That's all I ask."

Callie turns back to me. "What's been up with you today?"

"I'm fine," I reply automatically.

"You've been distracted."

"I haven't—" Callie pins me with a glare that stops me in my lie. "Work stuff," I supply which isn't exactly a lie, since Skyla works for the resort I am also completing work for. Colleagues=work stuff.

"Who were you looking for at the pool?"

"What? I wasn't—" Her stare is back so I shut up.

"Dad, your head was bobbing left and right and it had nothing to do with your front crawl stoke. Were you expecting someone?"

"My head wasn't bobbing. But if you don't believe me, we could go check with security?" I cock my brow at the exact moment her face pinkens with guilt. "Yes, I heard about that. Want to tell me why you approached Logan's HR Manager with video footage you recorded from the security guy's screen?"

She folds her arms in front of her, a picture of sheer defiance. "Because you said you weren't looking and I knew you were."

My hands tug into my hair. "Cal, some things are better left alone."

"And other things are better when you stop messing around and go after them. Did you invite her to the movies?"

"No, I didn't. Skyla and I are just friends. Talking of things that are better when you go after them. Let's talk about haircuts. Do you want me to ask around and get you booked in someplace with a waiting list?"

She rolls her eyes like I'm the one being annoying. "Urgh. I'll do some research and get back to you if it's that important to you."

"That's my girl." I attempt to pat her head but she ducks out of the way of my hand. "We can research together when we get back to the penthouse, if you like?"

She looks past me, through the window of the cafeteria. "I'm going to go in there and see if they've got any tacos left."

I gesture with my hand. "Lead the way."

"Didn't you say you needed to make some calls to the construction team about our new house?"

I nod. I did say that. There's been a hold up on some timber, and I need to make sure the project manager has made reasonable efforts to source some more or we'll be Blingwood residents for a lot longer than I anticipated.

"You go do that and I'll grab us both some dinner. Have the table set for when I get back."

She starts walking and my instincts tell me to pull her back and tell her no. She's only twelve and already she's reaching for more independence. Our penthouse suite is a two-minute walk from here and the resort staff knows she is a Blingwood. Hell, she already knows more of the staff in this place than I do, probably knows more than Logan does.

I remind myself she's safe and she'll be fine.

"You got your phone?" I ask as she opens the door to the cafeteria. She holds up her phone in the hand that isn't pushing the door and looks back over her shoulder at me. The aromatic scent of good food hits my nose and goes straight to my stomach, making my mouth water. "Get something for dessert too, and don't be long."

"I'll be as long as it takes, Dad," she calls back to me as the door swings shut behind her.

I pull out my cell and tap out a message to Callie:

Longer than ten minutes and I'm sending a search party. And after dinner, we look for hair salons.

And then, because I sound like a cranky old man, I add: Love you

She replies after a minute: Don't forget Nanna's picking me up after dinner—she's teaching me piano. Love you too.

And even though she's said it a million times before, it still makes my heart ache.

She's going to be okay. Moving here was the right decision.

* * *

THIRTY MINUTES LATER, I'm about to go look for Callie when the elevator that opens right into the penthouse pings.

Standing before me is Callie, food boxes in hand and beside her is Skyla, who's wearing a short skirt that reminds me how much I love the ass wrapped beneath it.

"Hi, Dad. Look who I ran into," Callie says breezily, strolling in and dumping dinner on the table. "And look who forgot to set the table." She folds her arms over her chest and squares me with a glare.

But two can play that game so I glare back. "And look who's twenty minutes late and didn't send a text." Then I watch as Skyla hangs back, fiddling with a button on her shirt like she can't decide if it's done up too high or too low. When she finally meets my gaze, I smile. Damn, she's pretty. Like really fucking pretty.

"Hi," I say and she draws her lower lip into her mouth before greeting me.

"Hi, Callie asked me to come up," she explains.

"Take a seat." I pull out a chair at the dining table and gesture for her to sit and then I go about searching for plates and forks. "Can I get you a drink?"

"She'll have a glass of wine. She's had a bad day," Callie says before smiling tentatively at Skyla and telling her, "I heard you telling Jessie in the cafe."

Skyla's earlobes deepen by about three shades. "Oh. What else did you…. Actually, don't answer that."

"You shouldn't eavesdrop," I tell Callie while also wondering if perhaps my name was mentioned.

"I didn't. I was standing in line, getting your dinner, and I ran into her. Skyla is going to help me find a good hair salon. She's lived here for years; she knows all the best places."

So that's what Skyla thinks she's doing here. My meddling daughter got her here under the guise of fixing her hair, when actually she's trying to set her old man up. I can't even bring myself to be annoyed since seeing Skyla has improved my mood tenfold.

"How did your telephone call go with the construction?" Callie asks, while I set the table.

"The project manager is trying her best but there's a shortage on timber. I'm going to try and pull some strings with suppliers I know. Hopefully it won't set back the build."

"I don't mind staying at the resort longer, I like it here," Callie replies.

I spread the food out and pour Skyla a glass of red even though she tells me not to go to any trouble. She seems nervous and I want her to relax. Besides, an hour or so sitting opposite her, when I have been thinking about her all day, feels too much of an opportunity to pass up.

"You want apple juice with dinner?" I ask Callie.

"Nah. I'm staying at Nanna's tonight, she's giving me piano lessons, remember? Also, Patty had a litter and I want to go see the pups."

"But you haven't eaten and you invited Skyla over to talk hair salons. I figured you would see Grandma later, Callie." My jaw tenses with a mix of frustration and embarrassment. It's now obvious, I'm sure to Skyla, that Callie has orchestrated this whole thing to get us alone, and it's awkward as hell—even if my cock throbs it's approval at being near Skyla. I'd literally just had a conversation with Skyla today apologizing for my behavior as well as my stance on not dating anyone.

Skyla stands and suddenly I want to forget about my "stance" and feel eager for her to sit back down and stay awhile.

"I know, Dad. But puppies aren't born every day! And Skyla, you understand, right?" *I didn't know my daughter could be this bad.* "Can you and Dad figure out the place for me to go? I really want to see the puppies." Callie bites her lip to hide her smile as she watches Skyla nod her head and sit back down. "I'll see you both tomorrow!" my daughter sing-songs as she walks around the table and kisses me on the forehead.

"I don't know how I feel about you sleeping at Nanna's on a school night," I grumble with a mix of humiliation and pride as I watch this child of mine take charge of the room.

"Oh, Dad, you worry too much. Me being with Grandma gives you the night off, and after all, we did move here so I could see more of Nanna and Uncle Logan. It'll be fine. I'll text you goodnight later and you can pick me up from school tomorrow. Enjoy your evening with Skyla!"

I glance at Skyla, who's looking up at me through thick lashes, her cheeks flaming.

"Nanna picking you up?" I ask Callie.

She checks her phone. "She's right outside."

I don't even have to tell her to get her toothbrush or fresh clothes—my mother took her shopping for spares to keep at her place "just in case."

Callie grabs her backpack from the counter, throws it over her shoulder, and dashes out the door like the room is on fire. Maybe it is, but I wouldn't know because the only heat I can feel is from the stare Skyla has trained on me.

"Ever feel like your daughter set you up?"

I grow uncomfortably hot. "Yes. I'll speak to her, *again*," I reply. "You mind?"

"Not at all," she replies, licking her lips.

CHAPTER 11

SKYLA

"*Y*ou have a pen and paper? I'll jot down the number of the salon. It might not be as fancy as the places Callie's used to, but I like it there. If you say my name and ask for Nadia, she might give you a discount. I fixed her up with one of your mom's rescue kittens, and ever since she hasn't stopped gushing about how much she owes me." I'm babbling and judging by the helpless smile he throws me, Drew can tell.

But instead of taking the offer to get rid of me, he asks, "Taco?"

"I already ate with Jessie," I reply and then kick myself.

In a moment of sheer bravado, I told Jessie I would seduce Drew, and when I said it, I meant it. I want him. Though now that I'm here, my nerves are shot to pieces. The way he's looking at me, like I am his taco, it's making my heart beat inside my chest like a pinball.

He moves around the table, opening the boxes of food

until he gets to one that contains pie. "You'll have some pie, though, right? Everybody loves pie." He perches his muscular ass against the table and my breathing hitches. His hair, still damp from his swim, frames his face in dark, adorable curls. His cologne is deep and woodsy. It's making my mouth water for more than the warm pie he slides across the table.

The sleeves of his T-shirt are rolled up, displaying impressive muscular forearms. He towers over me in an almost standing position, while I sit at the table. The tense feeling in the air has my stomach tightening, which spreads to the rest of my core. His eyes drop to my lips and he picks up a spoon, bringing a piece of the pie to my mouth.

He's going to feed me. Nobody ever fed me food before, except my mom when I was two perhaps.

It takes concerted effort to pull myself together and part my lips enough so he can slide the tip of the spoon into my mouth, until just a taste of sweet apples coats my tongue.

"Delicious," I breathe and then, using the same spoon, he takes a piece for himself and my gaze is pinned to his mouth, watching his full lips close over the spoon and imagining his mouth in other places.

Drew's eyes are fixed on mine as he swallows, then he puts the spoon back in the dish and his finger reaches out to lightly push aside a stray strand of my hair. My knees quiver and I'm so tightly wound, I'm about to implode.

His stare is intent, his expression an equal mix of apprehension and anticipation. Even though I'm nervous, fear that I might leave the penthouse never having tried to get what I want overtakes me.

"Skyla," he says my name slowly, seductively, but also with uncertainty. Intuition warns me that even though he seems to want me too, he's about to back off. There's a war raging inside of his mind between what he believes is right and wrong, and I can't, no I won't let him talk himself out of this.

Adrenaline and fear flood my veins. I stand, pushing the chair away, and step closer until our thighs touch.

Drew's eyes are drinking me in. Curiously waiting for what I might do next. I edge closer until our lips are inches apart and place my palm on his chest. Beneath the fancy material is smooth, hard muscle and I bite my lip to hide the pleasure coursing through me.

"Skyla," he warns, he leans back half an inch, his fingers gripping the edge of the table.

"Drew," I counter, inching closer, sliding my palm up his chest until I am gripping his shoulder. I've never seduced a man before and don't know how to do this right, so I am going with what is making me feel good and terrified in equal measures—touching him while watching his eyes burn darker.

"You should stop."

"Why?" I slide my hand up until it cups the back of his neck. His mouth inches closer.

"If we start this, I'm not going to want to stop. You don't know what you do to me or what I want to do to you."

"What if I don't want you to stop. Maybe I've been having thoughts about you too?"

"Fuck," Drew hisses and his mouth crashes down on mine. His hands are suddenly gripping my hips, pulling me in deeper until every part of our bodies align. My nipples graze his shirt and it feels incredible. His lips are hot against mine and a need stirs inside of me.

Within seconds my skirt is hitched up and Drew's gripping my ass, pulling me in an upward motion until I have no choice but to lock my legs around his waist.

I should worry I'm too heavy, but he shows no sign of strain, the way he carries me is effortless. When I look in his eyes, I see passion, my own lust mirrored, and by the time he has carried me into the master suite and lowered me down at the foot of his bed, I am pushing myself against him, desperate to feel the friction promised by his touch.

Drew undoes the top two buttons of my shirt and then impatiently rips it over my head while I fumble at the button on his pants. When I push them down, suddenly his cock is free and the nerves I had pushed aside stir inside me.

He's rock hard and it's huge and thick!

Relief floods me. After Mike's issue, I was scared history would repeat itself. Now I'm nervous for a different reason.

There's no way it will fit.

How can it?

I give myself the briefest of pep talks. *Be brave, Skyla and touch it!* And then I grasp his cock tightly—WHOA—thank-you romance books. He's too busy pushing my bra aside and placing my nipple in his mouth to notice I lack experience. In fact, he lets out an encouraging moan as I stroke him. His other hand edges inside of my underwear and I melt against him as his fingers graze my clit. "Oh God."

It's not like I haven't been to third base before. I have. But it never felt like this. I'm moving against his hand, he's moving against mine, and the urge to finally come is threatening to tear me apart.

"I've dreamed about being inside you," he admits, his eyes wildly searching mine as he inserts a second finger. "So fucking tight." He swirls with his thumb while pushing his fingers back and forth, stretching me in a way that creates a delicious burn. "You going to come for me, sugar?"

My affirmative answer is incoherent but he seems to understand.

Drew's watching me teeter on the edge. I let go of his cock, and my fingernails grip into his shoulders with such a ferocity that he'll probably need stitches. "Don't stop—" I choke out and his fingers slide in and out faster. I don't get the chance to finish my sentence because my orgasm rips through me and my fingernails dig further into his shoulders. My head falls into the crook of his neck and he continues to coax every last climactic shudder from me. It's the first time I've ever orgasmed outside of my own hand and my B.O.B., and holy cotton balls, I'm not sure if it's the joy of having come by someone else, or if it is Drew's particular expertise—I suspect the latter—but had I known this was what it was like, I would've been beating down Drew's door the day I first laid eyes on him.

By the time I regain a coherent thought and look up at him, his face is flush and his eyes are lust drenched.

"That was fucking sexy. I need you, sugar."

Drew's fingers skim my breasts as he unfastens my bra and it falls to the floor. He takes a step back and says, "Skyla. You're beautiful."

Drew closes in on me and lowers me on the bed, sliding down my panties and throwing them to the floor. He kisses my inner thigh before spreading me wide open. "Fuck, you're beautiful everywhere." He leans down and flicks his tongue over my clit. "So pink and wet. I bet you taste sweeter than pie." His eyes twinkle with mischief before he winks and then lowers his head.

My back ripples at the feel of Drew's mouth on me. I can hear how wet I am and almost tell him to stop, but from the sound of his growl he likes it. His teeth graze my clit and I try to stop myself from bucking against him. His finger teases my entrance before two fingers enter me, and my whole body heats to melting. The pressure keeps building and building. Exhilarating pleasure has me desperate to get him inside me, but he holds me in place, teasing my core with his fingers, tempting me with what he must know I need.

"That's it, baby. You're going to come again. I can't get enough of seeing you like this for me." The combination of his words, the feeling of him taking me with his mouth and the thrusts of his fingers is too much. It's sensation overload and my fingers sink into his hair, gripping it at the roots and gasping out in pleasure. My fingers curl into fists, my cries of pleasure fill the room as my release nears. I beg for more, for mercy and for him not to stop. The nonsensical mewls force their way from my lips like I am a mere instrument of his touch. For the first time in my life, I've lost control. I no longer care that before tonight I had never achieved an orgasm with a partner, because here I am, about to come for the second time, only on Drew Blingwood's mouth this time. He tightens his hold on me and I am bucking against him, needily begging him for more until the climax roars. Rippling and shuddering, my limbs take on a life of their own as explosions are let off. I can't be certain, since I am on another plane, but I think my knee jerks and hits him in the eye. If it did, he doesn't stop, not until every judder has evaporated from my body and every last gasp I make is swallowed into the air.

When I'm finally still and looking down at him, wondering if this is the foreplay, can my heart actually survive full penetrative sex, I hear, "Housekeeping. I've come to change your towels."

CHAPTER 12

DREW

"*D*on't move an inch; I'll get rid of her," I say, quickly finding and pulling my boxers over my erection and then my pants into place before stalking from the room. I don't bother with a shirt since I intend to be naked and inside of Skyla within a minute— sooner if I can.

"Sally, isn't it?" I say, remembering her from the time I went to apologize to Skyla. *What was I apologizing for?* Oh, that's right, kissing her. And now, here I am preparing to fuck her. But I can't think about the rights and wrongs while my cock is engorged to the point of exploding.

The woman, who is probably about my age and looking at me like she knows exactly what I have been up to, steps toward my bedroom. In her arms are a pile of white bath towels.

"I'll take them. It's kind of you to bring them but—"

"It's no bother. Betty mentioned she'd forgotten to

117

restock your room and with the shift change I thought I'd help out—that's just the kind of employee I am!—so I offered to bring them right up for you, Mr. Blingwood—or should I call you Drew?"

"Drew's fine." I snatch the cotton from her arms, wanting this busybody of a receptionist to get a hint. "I'm very busy. But thank-you." I square my eyes pointedly at the exit. Next time Skyla comes over, I must remember to lock the elevator.

Sally doesn't take the hint. "Oh, Drew! There's a mark on your face. It's red, like you got punched. Are you all right?"

I press my temple with my index finger and smirk.

Boy, when she comes, she is out of control.

Badge of honor.

"Um. Yeah, I'm fine. Hit myself on the door frame. Now if you'll…"

"I thought I saw Skyla head this way. I wondered if she might be up here. She's always working! Takes her work home with her," Sally says, gazing around the room like she's partaking in an elaborate game of hide and seek.

I follow her gaze to where it has fixed on my wallet, so I grab it and pull out a bunch of twenties. It's way too much to tip, but at this point I'm so desperate to get back inside the bedroom and inside Skyla that I'd be willing to sign over a kidney. "No, just me." My expression has become a scowly *fuck off.* I hold out the cash and her hand lurches out and takes the bills.

"I'll be going then," she replies, her eyes grazing up and down my body, making my stiffy shrink.

"I'll see you out."

"Oh, no need. I know the way. You get back to whatever you were doing." The wink she throws me has me immediately realizing my mistake.

Dammit!

She couldn't see Skyla here and now she probably thinks I was jacking off. From what Logan has said about his staff, by the end of the day, everyone will know.

Screw it. I don't care. There is a beautiful, buxom woman in my bed, waiting for me to make her come some more.

"Fine. Thanks. Bye." I walk toward the bedroom door, but before opening it I turn to make sure Sally gets into the elevator. The moment the elevator door shuts, I bound into the bedroom.

"Right. Where were we—"

Skyla is staring out the window, fully dressed. When she turns, her cheeks are an even darker shade of pink than when she orgasmed.

"You got dressed," I say.

Way to go, Captain Obvious.

She nibbles on her lip. "I better go. Sally has a big mouth. If anyone finds out I was here, doing that… and after what happened with Mike…" She looks down at her dainty little feet, her shoes lost somewhere in the carnage. "I'll be a laughing stock." Her voice hitches on her last word.

I close the distance between us. "What? No, you won't."

Her chin tips up. "I'm going to find my shoes and go. Thank-you for the… um…."

"Mind-blowing orgasms?"

Her sad expression lightens as she lets out a strangled chuckle and nods. "They were mind blowing, thank-you." She takes a step and then looks down at my dick. "Want me to give you a hand job before I go?"

Her incisor grips her lower lip, and I'm reminded of her face when she was in the middle of the hottest, most explosive orgasm I think I've ever seen. I loop my fingers around her wrist, desperate to see her smile again. "I gave you two orgasms and you gave me a black eye. I think the least you can do is…" I leave the words hanging, watching her gorgeous brown eyes become wide and full, "have dinner with me tomorrow night?"

Her smile fades and it hits me like a punch to the gut. She loosens her arm from my grip and I lean into her hand as it reaches up to stroke my jaw, her finger trailing all the way to my temple and her expression becoming embarrassed as she fingers the bruise that's smarting on my face. "That's kind of you to offer, but we both know this was about getting it out of our systems. Probably best we heed the warning."

I'm searching for the right thing to say, but we both knew all along this wasn't the start of a forever something. I should be pleased she's not asking for more. Even though I didn't get the happy ending I was expecting tonight, meeting her needs still felt like getting to the gates of heaven.

I follow as she walks into the living room and bends to retrieve her shoes from where they were tossed.

"I can feel you checking out my ass," she says playfully, her heart not in it.

"I can't help it, it's a great ass," I reply and it feels good to see her smile. It's not until her finger touches the elevator button that I realize I don't want her to go like this and I rush toward her. "Screw everyone else," I tell her, standing between her and the elevator. "Do what makes you happy."

The doors open with a ping and I want to blow the damn thing up.

Skyla looks over my shoulder at the empty space, not meeting my eyes.

"You're right, but screwing my boss's brother, on the resort... it's short-term happiness—"

"It'd be really fucking good."

She grins, and this time it's an honest to God, shit-eating grin. "Oh yes, it would be. But life goes on outside of this room, and I don't want to feel like...."

I lean down and press my lips against hers, not to

persuade her to stay but because I can't stop myself, and then I take a step back. I understand her reasons, even if I don't like them.

"If you change your mind—"

"You'll be the first guy I call."

And within a second, the elevator doors are closing and then she is gone.

CHAPTER 13

SKYLA

"*L*et me get this straight, he gave you two orgasms, you punched him in the face, gave him a black eye, and then you just waltzed out of there like the Queen of Sheba?"

I'm not sure if I've ever seen a person guffaw, but now I know I have.

"It was my knee that gave him the black eye, not my fist. It was a complete accident—I was out of control." I blush, remembering how good feeling out of control was. "I didn't know it could feel like that. And, I didn't go to his place seeking wisdom and wealth, like Sheba did to Solomon, I—"

"Then what did you go there for?" Her eyebrows are positively dancing with glee.

"I went with Callie to give him some advice on hair salons and then Callie left us. Alone. Together. And then, I realized I had the opportunity for a side hustle and I made a move."

Beside us, Macy is playing on the carpet of Jessie's staff

apartment and so I lower my voice. "I wasn't expecting the evening to take that turn. I liked the idea of seducing him, but when I went to his penthouse with Callie I had no idea she would leave and... I was unprepared, I hadn't even thought about what I was going to do or how I was going to do it—"

"I'm giving you an A for your performance! It sounds like you nailed the seducing. How does it feel to have a broken hymen?"

"It's not." I sigh and drop my head back on the couch for a minute. "Sally came up to the penthouse, so I got dressed faster than you can say 'room service,' and when she left I got the heck out of there. She didn't see me, but if she found out I was having casual sex with our boss's brother, then the whole resort would find out—"

"*If* Sally finds out. *If* anyone finds out," Jessie scoffs. "Fuck. Them!" She lowers her voice and swears with her hand over her mouth. "A reputation? That's what stopped you? Have we time traveled back to the 1920s while I wasn't paying attention?"

"You know what I mean. After Mike and before that Brad, the contractor who was working on the irrigation system, and then Barry from the bar... people are going to start to think—"

"People need to shut their mouths and mind their own damn business! You didn't even sleep with those guys, not that anyone should care if you did. You can date as many Brad, Barry, and Mike's as you like and anyone who's got an opinion can go frickin' screw themselves. Show them the middle finger. No one is slut shaming you on my watch, and if they even try, heads are going to roll! Seriously, Skyla, no one at this resort is worried what you get up to, most of them are screwing one another anyway. Just do you, boo, and while you're at it, do Drew too."

I sit up a little straighter and the stirring in my gut is back. "You're right. No s.l.u.t shaming," I spell out then admit, "I sabotaged it."

"Weren't you enjoying it?"

"On a scale of one to ten, it was a thirty-six."

Jessie grins. "I thought he'd be good. Sometimes you can just tell. But then why leave?"

I shrug, feeling foolish but Jessie doesn't judge me at all. Her voice is soft and sensitive as she asks, "Do you think you fear intimacy?"

"I didn't think I did. I was enjoying the hell out of my orgasms, but as soon as an excuse to leave presented itself, I was out of there, which is crazy because he's been kind, and he's made me feel safe and cherished. Even before he was trying to sleep with me, he told me I was beautiful and I believed him. Maybe it was nerves."

"What is it you're afraid of?"

I shrug. I've never given the subject much thought but the answers soon come to me. "Abandonment. Judgment. That he won't like me or I won't like myself afterward."

"And do you think Drew would make you feel like that?"

"No," I answer emphatically. "I mean, I know we're not about to enter a relationship, and I'm okay with that. I understand his reasons are not about me. Unless..." I recall a memory and it triggers something. "Jessie, did I ever tell you what my dad said when my mom left?" She shakes her head. "He said my mom wouldn't be back because she'd run off with a guy and now everyone would be calling her *The Town Tart.*"

"What? That's a terrible thing to say."

"I know. He only said it once, but he seemed so worried about what everyone would think. It was right after she left, and he was angry and hurt. I remember him crying and he wasn't the sort to cry. After that he refused to talk about her.

It was like she died. In Drew's penthouse, while he was out of the room speaking to Sally, I guess I panicked that people would find out I was having casual sex and judge me."

Jessie pulls me in for a hug. "Skyla, you can't go through the rest of your life avoiding intimacy. What your dad said was wrong. Who knows why your mother left, but I'm sure she had her reasons." She leans back and looks at me sincerely. "You need to draw on your courage and conquer this fear. Drew's perfect to practice on. He's older, wiser, and you already said he makes you feel cherished."

"But it might sour—neither of us want a relationship with the other. And I still have to work here. What if everyone thinks I'm fat Skyla from HR, the loose woman who can't keep a man interested?"

"Stop overthinking and stop putting down my best friend. Drew is perfect because you have no expectation for a future. All relationships are a gamble, but with him it's certain to end. Maybe knowing there's a time limit will help you focus on the moment instead of all the other drama. Meanwhile, work on reframing the intrusive thoughts because the people who matter know that Skyla Manning is a smart, modern woman, taking care of her needs. Who also has a mighty fine ass!"

"Ass. Ass. Ass," Macy croons from the carpet and I raise my brows at Jessie.

"Seriously, that's the word Mommy's clever girl chooses to repeat?" Jessie shakes her head at Macy. "Dog-gee, doggie, remember, that's the word we've been practicing." She looks at Macy hopefully, but Macy crinkles her little nose and goes back to knocking down her building blocks.

"The *big banana* talk is going great, I see." I'm trying hard not to laugh.

Jessie smiles wryly. "Well, as you know, *big banana's* take work. Oh, that's right, you don't know because you left the big banana on the table. Now, you need to get your *peach* back over there, draw on your courage, and go finish what you started."

I shake my head. "I can't. I'm so embarrassed. The poor man probably has the biggest case of blue-grapes in history. I feel like I need to apologize. Maybe I should send flowers or plums—"

"Nah, I think he wants melons or maybe a taco? While you're there, you could get yourself a nice healthy portion of eggplant!"

It's me that's guffawing this time. "I probably won't see him again. He's building a house, and if I'm careful there's no reason that I…" I palm my face. "Pickles!"

"What is it?"

"His daughter still needs the phone number for my hair salon."

"Oh, you better go over. If you go right now, Callie won't be there." Jessie winks encouragingly.

"You're right. I should pop by tomorrow when Callie is home and give her the number."

"You know, with your reluctance, it's a wonder you got to feel the big banana in the first place. Are you sure you want to get rid of your V?"

"Of course, I do. I'm ready."

"Was he big?"

My cheeks burst into flames and a smile takes over my face.

"I knew it! Those Blingwood boys all got big ding-a-lings!"

"You sound like you're talking from experience—" I press but she cuts me off.

"Total guess," she replies, turning her cell in her hands and checking the screen.

"So, you wouldn't sleep with Tate Blingwood if you got the chance?"

"Yuk. No. Besides, from what I know about Tate Blingwood, he thinks with his banana, the big doop."

"Why do you hate him so much? He's America's Golden Boy."

"Well, he isn't mine." She scrolls her phone. "Look at this: Tate Blingwood caught with co-star. Tate Blingwood gets down and dirty with server. Is Tate Blingwood dating his assistant?" She throws her phone on the coffee table with disgust. "Giant zucchini head."

"Jessie, you hardly know him. Those stories could all be lies."

"I know enough to know he isn't what he seems. Golden Boy? Ha! More like piece of shitake mushroom! Now, enough about the evil brother, tell me what you're going to do with the saintly Blingwood."

Jessie is so enthusiastic, it'd be easy to think it's as simple as dialing up a no-strings, amazing sex buddy-via *Just Fuck.* Hell, if that worked, maybe they could bring pizza for afterward too. But there's no such thing. No good can come from entertaining Drew as a sex buddy—except amazing, mind and soul shattering orgasms. I need to stop focusing on the big O, otherwise I'll never forget Drew Blingwood and his masterful, multiple skills.

"I'm not doing Drew, I'm doing Pilates. You in?"

"You're no fun!" Jessie huffs. "When do we start?"

"Yay! You'll love it," I reply. "There's a class at the community center on Tuesdays at 7 p.m."

"I'll ask Betty if she can watch Macy. Meanwhile, if you see him again, go for it! Like really, Go. For. It. There's nothing stopping you—except yourself. And I can tell you want a bite of banana!"

I stand to leave, ignoring her comment. "See you in the cafeteria tomorrow at lunch?"

"You got it." Jessie walks to Macy and picks her up, cupping her pudgy hand in hers and helping her to wave. "Aunt Skyla needs to go now. Say bub-bye."

"Ass," Macy says and shrieks with laughter.

* * *

I'M in the shower when my phone rings and I manage to fling a towel around me and answer it right before it stops.

"Hey Dad," I answer, noting the years-old profile pic I assigned him.

"Hey sweetie, I'm back on dry land and realized it's been three weeks since we last spoke. You good?" he checks.

I sit on the counter and fill the quiet. "I'm good. I signed up for Pilates with Jessie—"

"How is she? Did she get the gift card I sent for her daughter?"

"Yes, Dad. She said she's going to call you to thank you. Things have been crazy busy here."

"She's a great girl. I'm glad you have nice friends; I worry I leave you alone too much. I wondered if you'd met a nice boy to take care of you while I'm away at sea, but I guess I should be glad I don't need to worry about that yet. Last thing I need is to worry about some punk I'd need to go pummel if he hurt my little girl." He lets out a deep laugh, and even though I think he's trying to be protective, it occurs to me that I have never introduced a boyfriend to him. Dad's probably starting to wonder if I'm into women.

"No. No boyfriend at the moment. You have nothing to worry about." The chuckle that leaves my lips sounds strangled. Just another reminder that I have no prospects of love anytime soon. Drew's face flashes in front of my eyes and my heart thuds in my chest. So gorgeous. And that mouth of his still has my body quivering. I shake my head to try to clear all thoughts of Drew Blingwood and listen as my dad explains he is using his leave to come visit me soon.

"Is everything okay, Dad? You don't normally take vacations."

"Everything is dandy. We thought it was time we explored a little. And—"

"We?"

Dad let's out a long exhale and my body stiffens. "Claire. I met her on the rig. She's a health and safety officer. Told me off for wearing the wrong boots and... turns out, her kids are all grown up too, and she had some vacation time to use up and so we thought, 'why the hell not come introduce her to my little girl.'"

My dad is dating.

He has never dated—not that I'm aware of, anyway. It's perfectly okay for my dad to date.

So why do I feel so weird about it?

My dad was able to find a girlfriend in the middle of the ocean and here I am, surrounded by people with no hope of love.

I swallow the painful lump in my throat and try to be happy for my dad.

"Tell me about her," I say brightly and, in his aloof dad way, he does. I know what car she drives and that he's fixing her breaks. He also tells me the university she graduated from with honors. I know she got mono and he had to bring her food. It's the most my dad has said to me in years and I feel a sense of longing for the kind of relationship he has found, but I push that down and tell him, "I'm happy for you."

"We're going to fly in and rent a car. We'll stay at the resort for a night, and take you to lunch while we're here."

"I'd like that," I say, curious to meet the woman that broke my dad's "never again" rule. "Great, sweetie. I'll text you when we land. I love you—" The line drops right as there is a knock at the door, so I put my phone on the counter, tuck my towel in tighter to ensure the girls don't escape, and make the short walk through the two-room apartment.

I'm not expecting anyone, especially not *him*.

"Hi," Drew says, leaning against the door frame and looking unbelievably gorgeous despite the angry red mark on his temple, reminding me of what we did. Tucked against him is a paper bag smelling of goodness. "I forgot to get the phone number."

"Oh." I pause. "The salon number?"

"Yeah. I brought you some donuts to say thank-you but…" His eyes graze up and down my body, making the towel feel minuscule, and I'm not sure whether to tug it up or down. "Now might not be a good time?" His tongue darts out to wet his lip and the muscles in my lower belly tighten at the sight.

"Come in. I'll grab my phone and get you the number." I walk away and hear him shut the front door. When I return with my phone in hand, he's put the bag of donuts down and is leaning against the counter.

"You ready to dial it in," I ask, approaching him, but he doesn't move to pull out his phone, instead he brushes his hand to the back of his neck self-consciously.

"I didn't come for the number." His mind seems elsewhere.

"Ah, you changed your mind about the hand job," I joke.

His mouth widens and he faintly nods. An energy passes between us and I close the gap between us.

"I couldn't stop thinking about you. You left so abruptly and…"

"You weren't done?"

"No." He blinks slowly, his mouth creeping up at the

edges. "I took care of myself after you left." His gaze turns serious. "I'm here because I wanted to check on you...."

I inch forward until I am looking straight up at him. "As you can see, I'm fine."

"Yes, you are fine." His hand reaches out slowly and he clutches the corner of the towel tightly in his fist. "I should probably go then, if you're fine." He lingers for a moment, unclenching his fist and letting go of the towel. "I'll go then."

Tension tightens my muscles.

I'm nervous, but I don't want him to go.

"Stay," I breathe and reach my hands out to hold his biceps. My heart rate quickens as he slowly slants his head until his mouth is level with mine. Time stills like it's reminding me I can still back out, but instead of feeling trapped, I feel relieved when he closes the gap and grazes his lips against mine in a slow dance of a kiss that has my legs trembling.

I pull Drew closer and deepen the kiss. He's soft with my lips but my body is tightly wound and I need more so I kiss him harder, responding to my body's demands. My fingers begin exploring, first creeping up to his thick shoulders, then along to the back of his neck, holding him in place. His hand gathers up my wet hair against the nape of my neck and he exerts just the right amount of pressure to hold me in place while he kisses me breathless.

I'm aching for his touch and it's torture waiting for him to bring me the release I crave, so I channel my courage and guide his hand to where I need it.

There is only a thin piece of Egyptian cotton towel covering the important parts, so when it falls to the floor I gasp as I am left naked while Drew is fully clothed, though his impressive hardness presses against me.

Drew growls into my mouth, "I've wanted you ever since I first laid eyes on you." He's staring at me with so much arousal that it beats in my chest. My nipples ache and my breasts are heavy and sensitive pressed against him. I whimper as his hand travels down my belly. "I can't think straight. Since you left, I haven't been able to concentrate. All I see when I close my eyes is your face as you came, and all I can think about is how much I want to see you come again." My heart is pounding as his fingers probe and I'm trembling but not from the cold, as every nerve ending burns at his touch. "But I can still stop… if you want me to." His voice is hoarse, his eyes intense and one of his hands is still tangled in my hair, holding me still.

"Don't you dare," I pant, edging closer and his fingers drive into me.

Drew smirks mischievously and wraps his arms around me, pulling me closer. His knee parts my legs, opening me up to him as he devours my mouth. I moan and wrap my left leg around his waist, melting into him as his fingers work me. Eager and desperate, I'm clinging to him for release. I'm close, so close, but he pulls away and my hand grabs his forearm, begging him not to stop. Drew grins wickedly before dropping to his knees and finishing me by lapping my desire with his tongue until I am gripping his hair and quivering with pleasure. "Ohmygod. Drew," I gasp, letting the ripples pulse through me, but before I get the chance to take a breath, he stands and lifts me onto the counter. I claw at his shirt, then at his jeans and try not to smile as he hops on one foot to liberate himself from his pants and boxers. When his cock is unleashed, I'm awestruck watching it while he reaches down to the pocket of his jeans and pulls out a condom from his wallet. Drew's gloriously sheathed in seconds, probing my entrance while he looks in my eyes.

"This could complicate things," he says and I'm suddenly more fearful he's going to stop than I am about what comes next. I'm so eager, I'd resort to begging if I had to. I want him and I'm not ashamed to admit I have never wanted anything this bad.

I kiss his jaw then say, "Screaming your name and coming against your mouth already complicated things. I don't care, I need you inside me, now."

He kisses my mouth and in one fluid motion, he plunges into me and my hands grip his ripped biceps as I scream. I feel like I'm splitting in two.

"Fuck, you're so tight," he says but I'm too busy trying to breathe through the pain to respond.

His thrusts are slow, in and out and filling every part of me. It's pleasure mixed with pain but other sensations distract me from the ache. Drew draws my nipple into his mouth. He begins to circle my clit with his thumb. I never thought I'd be a screamer, but it turns out I am. My moans become louder with every stroke. Sensations envelope me, his thumb on my clit, his mouth on my breast, his other hand gripping my hair as his thrusts gain pace. My insides clenching as he drives me to the edge. My body arches against him, pleading for him to take me higher.

He releases a primal growl against my neck. "I've never felt anything better."

I think I reply something coherent but I can't be sure. I'm lost to primal need.

"I'm going to—"

"Not yet. You'll come when I say you can come."

Something I didn't know about myself is that I like being told not to come, and my body responds instantaneously like a very bad girl. There's no containing the sensation and absolutely no stopping it. The orgasm rips through my body like an explosion.

"Sorry. Not sorry," I try to explain against his shoulder as ripples ride through me. Zings of pleasure start at my core but soon overtakes all conscious movement, right to the tips of my fingers.

Drew watches me the whole time, his expression a mix of pride and fury. "Fuck! Hold onto me, sugar. I'm going to—"

We clutch one another, me grinding and riding the waves of hot pleasure, him holding me, stiffening and jerking, staring heatedly into my eyes, until we crash and splinter into a thousand tiny pieces. Shocks ripple through me, Drew is watching me with fierce intent. He shudders, and fists my hair, his expression ethereal as he lets out a string of cusses that turn me on.

Once our breathing evens out and we're both coated in a sheen of sweat, while I can still feel him inside me, and his steady breathing is against the crook of my neck, I'm already thinking about how soon I'll be able to do it again.

"That was…" he leans back and expels a breath, kissing my neck, "incredible."

I nod, a filthy smile creeping onto my face. "I didn't expect it to be so…"

"You thought I'd be an inadequate lover?" he asks, a grin toying on his lips.

"No. I thought you'd be excellent. I just didn't think we'd fit together so well."

"I'm not going to lie, baby. I wasn't sure I was going to fit." He trails his finger between my breasts and gazes down at where we're still joined. His erection is still semi-hard and his grin widens to a satisfied smile. "But you are perfect."

A joyful, contented feeling settles in my body and I wonder what happens now. Will he want to do it again? Will he leave?

Drew kisses the tip of my head, his lips lingering. "I'm going to go take care of this," he says as he holds onto the condom and begins to pull out. I bite my lip to keep from wincing out loud. He leans down, picks up the towel I was wearing when he arrived, and wraps it around me, his gaze lingering at my breasts as he tucks them away. He smirks as he catches me looking. "I can't help looking, they're fantastic. Best I ever saw." My grin widens and he kisses the tip of my head again. "I'll be back in a second."

While Drew disposes of the condom, I stretch out my legs and then slowly lower myself down from the counter. I don't know how I expected to feel after no-strings sex, but I hadn't expected it to be this good. This special. Or this sore.

My insides ache deeply but in a good, freeing way. I feel strangely accomplished, like I smashed a hurdle I had been putting off, and man, I never thought I'd enjoy it so damn much. Clinging to him, in desperate need for release, I never felt so vulnerable, but also so cherished. Despite my uncomfortable core, I'm still smiling when I lower myself to sit in the small armchair in the living room.

Drew hangs back in the doorway but I can feel him watching me, and I try to neutralize my goofy smile. He watches me, while pulling his clothes on.

"I really did come over tonight to check you were okay, not to..."

I throw him a small, mischievous smile. "It's okay, I know you didn't come for a booty call. And I'm glad you came... finally." I wink and put my statement down to the endorphins running wild through my body. I feel crazy confident and absurdly happy.

"You want me to stay? Callie is at her Nanna's."

My instinct is to say yes, because it would feel good, but that isn't what this is. And what will happen when the post-sex hormones dissipate and suddenly we both feel awkward? I shake my head. "I have a long day tomorrow."

He nods, looking uncertain. "So, should I go?"

"Yes." I stand to see him to the door. "Thank-you for the...

donuts," I say, pushing a big fake smile on my face and walking him out.

Thank-you for the donuts.

"You're welcome." Drew grins filthily, and as we near the door, he pauses and says, "Before I go, I noticed some blood on the condom when I took it off."

A flash of embarrassment seizes my body.

Drew's hand loosely grips my arm. "Hey, it's fine. You're a woman, you get periods. It's nothing to get worked up over. I shouldn't have mentioned—" He studies me closely, probably remembering there was no sign of menstruation when his mouth and hands were at my core.

I turn away as he frowns. I can't look in his eyes.

"You weren't..." I can feel him shaking his head. "You were a..." His tone is lifeless. Robotic. Shocked.

He can't even say the word.

Like icy water is being dumped over me, my confidence and good mood washes away. "I'm sorry. I should've told you... I didn't plan to keep it from you. I got carried away and..."

The hurt look in his eyes is too much, but I don't have to endure it long. Drew turns his back and leaves.

CHAPTER 14

DREW

"What are they asking us to change?" Logan says from the end chair of the boardroom table. It's just me and him, and the blueprints are splayed out before us.

"Logan, I already told you." I jab my thumb at the front elevation. "It needs taking down here by about fifteen feet. The historical commission doesn't want a modern development visible from further up the coast, and so now we need to reposition the restaurant or rethink the design entirely."

I'm barking at him, but I can't help myself. Ever since I left Skyla's place last week, I've been cranky as hell.

I know she's younger than me, but it didn't occur to me she'd be a virgin.

Why would she give something so special to an asshole like me? I'm so damn angry she didn't trust me enough to tell me before I rammed my cock into her.

Okay, so my anger is offset somewhat by how honored I

feel, and my ego is doing somersaults at her blessing me with it, but still, nobody forgets their first time, and I don't deserve to be remembered by her.

I should have figured it out sooner. She was so gloriously tight; I was terrified I'd blow my load as soon as I entered her. And worst of all, I don't even know if she enjoyed it. Okay, so she was grinning pretty wildly after, and she called me God, and yelled my name, but maybe that's what she thought she should do?

No. She fucking enjoyed it.

So did I.

But I didn't get the chance to make it special—I just screwed her on the counter because I was too eager that I couldn't wait to get her to the bedroom or light some candles. Had I known it was her first time, I'd have done it different. Taken things slower.

But it's too late now. Her virginity can't be undone and I'll never be able to erase the memory of her face as she came apart on my cock.

I was already struggling with messing around with a woman who is years younger than me, and now this! Skyla is friends with my daughter. She lives and works in my brother's resort, and I will no doubt see her everywhere I go the next month at least.

And I have not been able to stop thinking about her.

"Okay," Logan says slowly, examining my expression, "I get that it's an inconvenience, but you've overcome these kinds of problems before?"

"I've never had this particular problem," I say, dropping down into one of the leather chairs.

"This isn't about planning. Why don't you tell me what the real problem is? Has it got something to do with the bruise on your face?"

I shoot Logan a mind-your-own-damn-business glare

before pushing my hands into my hair and tugging hard enough to feel pain.

"Did you apologize to Skyla?" Logan presses. "Is that why you've got the bruise?"

I stare up at him, scowling. "Yes, I apologized and no, she didn't punch me."

"Did she accept your apology?"

"I think so." *I mean, she was on board with me ripping away her virginity, so I think she forgave me for telling her the kiss was a mistake.*

"Callie okay?"

"Callie's fine. Up my ass as usual. She wants me to find her clubs and hobbies and a hair—shit! I forgot to get the damn salon number."

"So, you're busting my balls today because you don't have a salon number? I'll ask my assistant to look one up if that's your problem?"

"No. It's... I think I screwed up again. But worse this time."

Logan smirks.

"What?"

He bites the inside of his cheek to try to contain his smile. "Nothing, I'm just not used to my older brother screwing up. You're normally the one who has it all nailed down tightly. What's got you screwing up—I know you can handle the resort planning. So, what, or rather *who,* is it?"

At that moment, Skyla, dressed in some kind of silk blouse that falls over her perfect tits like it would slide off at the merest touch, passes the windowed wall of the board-room. She's flanked by some guy in a maintenance uniform, and when she sees me, she looks stunned. The bow of her lips straightens as her mouth pops open and then she darts her eyes away, sweeping her hair to one side so I can't see her face.

"That's weird. My HR manager seems to be avoiding eye contact with you, brother. Care to explain why?"

Logan temples his fingers on the desk and waits.

"Fine, I'll tell you. I screwed her. I don't know what came over me. One minute we're making out at the penthouse, the next I'm standing on her doorstep with a bag of donuts because get this, I wanted to see if she was okay, and then next thing my cock is...." I don't finish the sentence. Logan can see exactly where this is going and I don't want anyone imagining her like that. That image is just for me. And no way I am sharing with him that I was her first—something I am still in awe of.

"And the problem with that is?"

"The problem is, she's practically illegal. She says she's not looking for anything solid, which is good because I am not in a place to take on more, got my hands full with Callie."

Logan sits back in his chair, tapping his pen annoyingly against the mahogany.

"She's not a minor or illegal. You're looking for excuses not to get involved and I understand why, but Skyla's a grown-ass, adult woman who can make her own mind up—"

"She's closer to Callie's age than mine!"

"Wow, is she really?" The fucker smirks. "You've obviously run the math. Been drawing up the pros and cons, have we?"

I shake my head bitterly even though the answer is yes. "The numbers run to no."

"If you say so," Logan replies. "So, how did you guys leave it? Couldn't have been pretty if she's not even willing to look at you today."

"She told me to go. I asked her if she wanted me to stay and spoon or whatever, it felt like the right thing to do, but she said go."

Logan's brow furrows. "She told you to go? Did you kiss her goodbye or... I don't know, hug?"

"No. She walked me out and said, 'thank-you for the donuts.'"

"Thank-you for the donuts?" Logan erupts into laughter and my anger threatens to boil over.

"Fuck off, Logan. I already feel like a jerk."

When he's finished laughing, he holds his palm out by some way of apology. "So let me get this straight, you made out with her, chased her to her place—with donuts—screwed her, then left with barely any discussion of whether you'd see her again?"

I nod. It sounds even worse aloud than it does in my head. Add to that, I stormed off when I found out I took her virginity, and I'm pretty sure it makes me worse than the devil himself. "I'm an asshole. I didn't go over there with the intention of screwing her, it just happened."

"But she wanted to, right?"

"Yes, she fucking wanted to. I didn't make her...."

"I know you wouldn't. So, it's the ending you screwed up. That's fixable. Just go explain, you're not sure you want a relationship."

"She knows. I already told her. I told myself we were getting it out of our systems, but maybe she does want more." A woman as gorgeous as her, who saves her V-card, why else would she waste it on an asshole like me if she wasn't looking for something long-term?

"Yes. You're that irresistible." Logan rolls his eyes. "You know, Skyla is loved by pretty much everyone here. Even the delivery guy who brings the toilet paper stops by her office each week to lay it on her. It's not like you're her only option."

A bitter taste like bile coats my throat. "Logan, you're not helping." The thought of some other punk's hands on her makes me feel murderous.

"I'm just saying, there would be worse things than dating her, and if you decide not to, then she'll move on because she has other options."

Better options.

"I'm not dating anyone and I'm trying not to think about her other options. Now, if you're finished, we could move the restaurant here, overlooking the golf course." I point, still thinking about the possibility of Skyla having other options. "Or, we could put it here, beside the Japanese garden. Actually, yes, that's what we'll do. It's going next to the garden, then you've got a nice distance between the clubhouse and the restaurant." I roll up the blueprints and tuck them beneath my arm.

"I love working with you, brother." Logan grins. "You all set for Saturday?"

"Saturday?"

"The engagement party." He pulls a face like he's about to puke.

"Oh yeah, I got the email yesterday. We'll be there."

"When you say we?"

"Callie and me. You did say kids could come?"

"Of course, Callie's invited. Talking of kids, Dana and I invited Skyla."

I throw him a furious glare and Logan chuckles, then stands and claps me on the back good-naturedly.

"Just screwing with you, man. She's an adult. But she is invited. Skyla's worked for me since I took over this place, so it seems right."

I shrug. "Up to you and Dana who you invite—"

"You could ask her to go with you. Skyla won't know many people, and it'll be nice for her to have some friendly faces to hang out with."

"No. No. No," I say, shaking my head for added emphasis. "It's better I leave her alone. Done. Finito. Kaput."

"Well, if you're sure. But Dana's invited a bunch of the swim team from that fancy private school she went to. There's going to be other options for Skyla to mingle with at the party."

I pinch the bridge of my nose to stem the pending headache.

"I'm going to work from the penthouse until it's time to go pick Callie up from school. I'll adjust the resort plans and resubmit to the city. If you need me in the meanwhile, go fuck yourself." I pull my lips into a flat smile and stalk from the room.

Other fucking options.

* * *

THE AFTERNOON PASSES LABORIOUSLY SLOWLY and I find myself heading out the door early to get Callie just so I have a distraction from thinking about Skyla when my phone lights up with a message from Callie:

> Don't bother picking me up. I'm going to do homework with Ruby. Her mom said she'll drive me home. I'll grab us dinner from the cafe before I come up to the apartment.

I begin an immediate reply and then delete it. I have to give her a little more freedom. She will be fine.

> Okay, honey. Don't get into any mischief.

Unable to focus on work, and with Callie not due home for a couple of hours, I go for a run and then shower. But nothing I do gets rid of the antsy agitated feeling. Then I go through my emails. Again. But this time, there's a new one. It captures my attention right away and forces a goofy smile onto my face that makes my cheeks hurt.

- -

To: Drew Blingwood

From: Skyla Manning

Subject: Salon Deetz

Hi. Please find below salon details for Callie.

- -

That's it? That's all she has to say. After looking away when she saw me in the boardroom this morning, now I'm the one feeling used and… hurt. Why didn't she tell me she was a virgin? I would never have… or I'd at least have been gentle, made her feel special.

I reply right away.

- -

To: Skyla Manning

From: Drew Blingwood

Subject: Did you look away when you saw me earlier?

I hope you didn't. I don't want things to be weird between us.

- -

. . .

EMAILING Skyla sends a strange thrill through me and I press Send before I overthink it. I'm so eager, in fact, that I've sent it before I've truly thought the message through or even checked for typos. What if she takes it the wrong way or I screw up even worse? I'm no good at talking to women anymore and every time I spend time with her, I seem to put my size thirteens right in my mouth. The five minutes it takes her to reply is agonizing.

● -

To: Drew Blingwood

From: Skyla Manning

Subject: No

Were you in the boardroom? I didn't see you.

● -

Oh no, no, no. She's not leaving it there. She looked away; I know she did.

● -

To: Skyla Manning

From: Drew Blingwood

Subject: I know you saw me

- -

To: Drew Blingwood

From: Skyla Manning

Subject: Nope. You sure it was me?

- -

AM I sure it was her? I couldn't take my eyes off her. She smiled at the guy beside her and my chest still fucking hurts from the way it made me feel.

- -

To: Skyla Manning

From: Drew Blingwood

Subject: It was you. Who was the guy?

- -

IT'S A DICK MOVE. He was obviously a colleague, but since Logan started talking about options, I've been going crazy.

- -

To: Drew Blingwood

From: Skyla Manning

Subject: Drew, did you want something? I'm kind of busy.

• -

To: Skyla Manning

From: Drew Blingwood

Subject: Yes

Have dinner with me and Callie tonight?
She's bringing food in from the cafeteria, but
we can make it stretch.

• -

To: Drew Blingwood

From: Skyla Manning

Subject: Can't tonight

Sorry, I'm busy.

• -

To: Skyla Manning

From: Drew Blingwood

Subject: Did I upset you?

• -

WELL DONE, you idiot!

EVEN AS I TYPED IT, I knew I upset her. I should've stayed. Kissed her. Wrapped my arms around her and told her that even though I didn't want a relationship, it meant something. And that being her first, means something to me because it fucking does. I will never forget it. I remember it better than my own first time.

• -

To: Drew Blingwood

From: Skyla Manning

Subject: No

• -

I'M AN ASSHOLE. I shouldn't have left like I did.

I'm such a dick! Inviting her for dinner with me and my kid, offering free food from the cafe, that probably hasn't gone far to getting her into her good graces.

• -

To: Skyla Manning

From: Drew Blingwood

Subject: I'm sorry

I was shocked. I didn't realize you... I didn't leave things how I should have. I didn't want you to get the wrong idea and well, I screwed up. I'm sorry.

• -

To: Drew Blingwood

From: Skyla Manning

Subject: It's fine.

I'm sorry too. I should have told you.

I know it was just for fun. Honestly, no apology needed.

• -

To: Skyla Manning

From: Drew Blingwood

Subject: So, you'll have dinner with me tonight?

I could try get a babysitter and we could go out? I'll tell Callie I have a business meeting.

• -

To: Drew Blingwood

From: Skyla Manning

Subject: I'm still busy

• -

I THROW the damn phone down right as Callie walks out from the elevator.

"You look happy," she greets me sarcastically and dumps her backpack down on the floor, rolling her eyes as she passes me.

"What? I'm fine," I reply, even though I feel wildly annoyed. Skyla says she isn't mad at me, that she knows the score. But she ignored me, and then she declined dinner with me—twice!

Unless she has a date?

My stomach twists.

"Quit scrunching your face up," Callie says with a disapproving glare. "You've still got that bruise on your face. You look like you got punched."

"Yeah, like I said…. door frame got in my way. How was school?"

"School was good. Ben Bartlett is going to ask his mom if he can have one of Nanna's puppies when they're ready to go to new homes. I showed him pictures and everything. I'm pretty much the coolest kid in school right now."

The smile on her face almost has me forgetting how I got the bruise on my face. *Almost.*

"Who's Ben Bartlett and where does he live?"

"Just a kid in school. Relax." She studies me closer. "You've got a weird look on your face again, Dad."

"Just thinking about hormonal boys and puppies and how they break me out in hives," I lie.

"I brought lasagna, that should cheer you up. But you're going to have to eat fast. I need you to give me a ride to the community center."

"And what is going on at the community center on a school night?"

"Pilates. Me and Ruby, and… some others. There's a class and we think it'd be good for our physical and mental health. Since you haven't found me any clubs to join yet, I thought you'd agree?" She's smiling at me now and I can't object since I haven't gotten around to finding out what's going on in the area for pre-teens.

"I got you the salon number from Skyla," I reply in my defense.

"Oh, I know. I saw Skyla in the cafe. Her face is as grumpy as yours."

"You saw her, huh?" I ask casually and Callie nods. "And, did she say anything?"

Callie looks pointedly at me and scowls. "Of course, she did, Dad. She's not mute."

I nod. No way I can find out if she has a date tonight from my daughter. I doubt she'd even mention that kind of thing to Callie. "You want me to make you an appointment at the salon?" I ask, changing the subject.

She picks a lock of her hair up and inspects the tip. "Nah. I need to go get ready for Pilates. I'll reheat my lasagna when we get home."

I can't bring myself to push the haircut when I know what a big deal it is to her so I just say, "Okay, kiddo." And then she goes into her room while I pick up my phone and check if Skyla has sent any more emails. She hasn't, and I wonder if maybe she is on a date tonight—and then suddenly I can't face the lasagna either.

CHAPTER 15

SKYLA

"*Y*ou okay?" Jessie asks on the walk to the community center.

"Fine," I reply.

"You're not fine. You've checked your phone about thirty times in the last ten minutes. Spill."

"I hadn't realized it had been that many times. Thank-you so much for keeping count." I throw the device in my purse.

"Ooh. Someone is a Miss Snarky-pants today."

"I think I preferred it when you used actual swear words," I deadpan.

Jessie throws her arm over my shoulder. "Come on, what is it?"

When I don't answer, Jessie hesitates a few guesses. "Did you finally fire Mike's ass and now you feel bad?"

"Did you give your number to the FedEx guy and now you're worried he's married?"

I force out a laugh. "No, and no. The FedEx guy is cute, but remember, I am going off resort."

Jessie smiles wryly.

"So, you didn't eat a big banana and enjoy the heck out of it?" she asks, and I feel my cheeks warm.

"You did! I knew it!"

"How did you—" Jessie has crazy detective skills, but I'm still bowled over with shock that she guessed.

"I saw him leaving your place. And let's just say the walls between our apartments are thin." She widens her eyes knowingly and my cheeks flush even more.

"Dammit, Jessie. Do you think anyone else saw or heard?"

"Who cares. Girl, even if anyone did see him leave or hear you, they're just going to be jealous you got some nice banana from the eldest Blingwood. Ain't no one going to care who you're banging, unless he hurts you, then we'll all hurt him!"

"Guess it doesn't matter now anyway. It's over already."

"Over?"

"Yes. We had an email exchange and now it's finished. We were just getting it out of our systems, now we can move on."

Jessie pulls me to a stop. "You gave him your V-card and he left you with an email exchange?"

"Yes. Well, no, he figured out I hadn't done it before and…"

"You didn't tell him you were a virgin?"

"I know, I feel bad. But I honestly wasn't thinking much about that, it was so… So…"

"Good?"

I nod manically. "I never knew it could be so good."

She grins. "What happened after?"

"He was shocked and then he left."

"Oh crap! No wonder you're pissed. I mean, I get he was

shocked. But an email? A Zoom meeting would've been more personal. So, what did he say?"

"It's what he already said. He doesn't want a relationship and he left right after. It was just sex."

"Just amazing, orgasmic sex—that you don't want to endure again. Got it."

"I got mine; he got his—this time. It's. Done. Sex," I clarify.

"So, you're definitely not seeing him again?"

"No."

"He hasn't asked to see you again?" Jessie looks affronted on my behalf.

"Well, he asked me to go for dinner but I said no."

"Why?"

"Because we're doing Pilates," I reply firmly. "No good can come of pursuing a no-strings relationship with him. It's over."

"You gave up hot Blingwood sex for Pilates?" She checks and I nod. "Girl, this class better be the best damn class in the history of classes."

We carry on walking, passing the oceanside construction site where Drew and Callie's house is being built. Even though it's not finished yet, I can see it's going to be spectacular.

"How the other half live, eh?" Jessie remarks as she catches me looking, and I agree that it may as well be a million miles from the free, staff accommodation where I currently reside. And suddenly I'm hit by a moment of perfect clarity, Drew Blingwood was never going to want me. He probably has friends with benefits agreements with size zero models and Hollywood starlets. It was ridiculous for me to get caught up in the idea he'd be interested in a plus-sized girl from his brother's HR department.

"Hey, I thought you said you weren't seeing Drew again?" Jessie asks.

"I'm not."

"Isn't that his car up ahead, parked outside the community center?"

I gawk straight ahead and see that it is indeed Drew's luxury SUV, with him leaning against it, looking like a dark and brooding male model posing against the backdrop of the last embers of the setting sun.

"Damn," I reply, but it sounds more like, "Dayummmmmmmm."

"Uh-huh," Jessie replies. "You think he's here because he isn't taking no for an answer?"

My heart rate spikes at the suggestion, and then I remember this is the real world, and not some make-believe, fantasy world. It's then I see Callie and another girl who looks to be her age, sitting on the pavement beside the line of people waiting to go inside.

"I didn't think she was planning to come," I say and Jessie looks at me curiously. "When I told Callie in the cafeteria earlier that this is where I was coming tonight, I didn't think she would come too. Not that I mind, but warning me that I would see her father might've helped me prevent an almost heart attack."

Jessie grips my arm. "You've got this!"

* * *

"I should sue the instructor for false advertising. No way that class was introductory. It wasn't even intermediate; advanced torture 101—that's what this was! The instructor was trying to turn us into human pretzels!" Jessie complains with a hushed voice from the back of the hall, before taking a sip of her water.

I force a chuckle as I, too, down half my bottle of water, still feeling the effects of the stretches. "It wasn't so bad. You coming next week?"

"I think the question that most needs answering is, is Drew Blingwood coming next week?" She nods her head to the back of the room. He's been sitting there throughout the whole class waiting for Callie. Whenever I looked over at Drew, he was staring at his phone, pushing his finger at it like he was sending emails, yet it felt like he was watching me. My skin was on fire, my thoughts consumed by him being in the very same room as me, while I tried to bend my body into positions that strongly resembled outrageous sex positions.

"Hey, Skyla and Jessie, come over here!" Callie calls from beside her father, who is still sitting on one of the plastic chairs with one leg casually crossed over the other.

"This should be interesting," Jessie says beneath her hand and we walk to the back of the room to join them.

"My dad said we did really well for beginners, didn't you, Dad?"

Drew runs a hand through his hair before returning it to his lap. "Ladies, you did great." He turns to me and his eyes skim over my flushed skin. "That was really... something."

The sound of my swallow is louder than the instructor bellowing not to be late for next week's class.

"You guys need a ride home? My dad can drive you, if you want?"

"Oh, um—" I start but am interrupted by Jessie.

"We'd love a ride home, wouldn't we, Skyla? Ya'll are so kind." She takes Callie's arm and leads her and her friend outside under the pretense of getting some fresh air, even though it is hotter outside than it is in the darkly lit room.

"Can I get a sip of your water please?" he asks, and I hand him the bottle. He squeezes his eyes shut as he drinks and then stands, handing me back the bottle. Then his hands pull against the waist of his pants and my eyes fix on his junk. It looks enormous, like he has a… my mouth pops open. By the time I meet his gaze, he looks bashful. "It was an impressive class. Shall we?" Drew gestures his hand for me to follow and I can't help but let out a chuckle.

"Keep your laughter down, sugar," he whispers. "I'm trying very hard to make it go down."

"Did you get that—"

"I wasn't prepared for your ass in Lycra. I'll wear looser pants next week."

My cheeks are aching from smiling and I walk just a half a step ahead of him, loving that my body is making him hard. He speeds up and holds the door to the outside open for me.

"I thought when you denied dinner with me tonight, you might have a date," he says. Despite the bright light, his eyes look dark and probing.

"Just a date with Jessie," I reply. "I didn't realize Callie was coming or I would have offered to walk with her." I train my gaze on the ground as we walk across the parking lot, away from his too handsome face that renders intelligent conversation impossible.

"If you'd walked Callie here, you wouldn't have had to see me at all."

I stop walking and dare to look at him. "I'm not avoiding you."

He cocks one of his thick, dark brows. He still has the bruise on his face and I find myself smiling while I rephrase. "Okay, so it's a little awkward. I never had a… thing before."

His face turns deadly serious. "Yes. So, I discovered."

"I'm sorry, I should have told you about the V-card. I suppose, I didn't get a chance." I laugh. "But I meant, I never had a no strings… thing." Suddenly I don't know what to do with my hands. This is too embarrassing. "I mean, Mike said that's what we had. Maybe I'm naive. I just mean—"

"I understand. Did I make you think—"

"No. I knew you only wanted one thing…." I check we are not about to be overheard by anyone but thankfully the rest of the class has disappeared back to their cars, and Jessie, Callie, and her friend, are waiting over by Drew's car. "You didn't make me think anything. You don't want a relationship and truly, I'm fine with that. It was just fun, right? No need to make a big deal about it."

The way he's watching me, all wide-open eyes, drinking me in, has my stomach somersaulting.

"It was fun," he replies with a heated stare. "At least, I enjoyed it."

"I did too," I answer much too quickly. And then we're both standing there, not knowing what to say next, and me with the urge to reach up on my toes to kiss him.

"I better go. We can't accept the ride. I need to…" I'm turning away to leave before I have even thought of an excuse but his hand reaches out to stop me.

"You're going to Logan's engagement party Saturday night, right?"

I turn back and nod. He's so handsome it hurts my eyes to look at him so I squint like it's the sun that's blinding me.

"It's at that fancy new bar in the city. Dana thought it'd seem cheap if they had it at the resort. Like anyone cares where it is. Most people just want a free bar, right?" I chuckle at his joke nervously. "So, I'll pick you up at seven." He's nodding and I find myself nodding too.

"I haven't even bought a dress. I wasn't sure I was going to go," I stutter, not sure if he's asking me out on a date or saving me the cost of an Uber.

His lips quip up in a smile. "You look beautiful whatever you wear."

I look down at my yoga pants and sleeveless workout top. My sweaty hair is sticking to my neck, and without even checking, I know my face is tomato red, so I raise my brows at him questioningly.

"Skyla, it doesn't matter what you wear. You'd still be the best-looking woman in the room… or outside, or wherever the hell you find yourself."

I'm waging a war against my cheeks which seem to want to tuck themselves into my hairline. *Best-looking woman?*

"I think your erection is clouding your judgment," I reply.

"You might be right. I almost passed out from it in there."

I let out a shriek of laughter and bat his arm with my hand. Thick, hard muscle twitches beneath my palm and I am reminded of the way I gripped him on the counter in my apartment. I quickly let go.

"Seven. Saturday," I reply coolly and try to remain calm. And then I call out goodbye to Callie, tell Jessie to get her butt over here since we still need to get our steps in. And then I freak out the whole way home since Drew Blingwood is picking me up at seven on Saturday.

CHAPTER 16

DREW

*F*uck! I have never seen a woman bend quite like Skyla. Yes, she's a strong, full-figured women and yes, I knew she was fit, but man! I had to pull my phone out and pretend I was typing a message, or else I'd have gotten arrested—and if the chief of police knew what was running through my mind, I'd surely be serving jail time right now.

Okay, so I didn't mean to ask Skyla to attend the party with us. Hell, I don't even want to go, but I needed to know I was seeing her again.

"Drew, you still there?" Lisa from the New York office asks. I'd forgotten I was even on Zoom. I glance at the clock on the screen, Callie will be home soon with my mother.

"Yeah, still here. Update me when you've sent the proposals."

"Sure thing, Drew." I prepare to close down my laptop when Lisa says, "You sure you're okay? You seem distant."

"I'm fine. Callie's due back soon and—"

"Wow. The move must be doing you good. I have never known you to leave a meeting early."

"That was the whole point of moving here," I explain. "To be present." Though right now, I don't feel present at all.

"Good for you, Drew. I'll call you when I hear back."

I end the call right as Callie and my mother walk into the penthouse.

"How was school?" I ask.

"Good. Me and Ruby are going to do homework together, if that's okay?" She points to her phone. "On FaceTime so you can't complain about me being out late."

My mother greets me and then sets to pouring a coffee, pointing to the cups and asking if I want one. "You look tired," she says.

"What? I'm fine."

"He's not sleeping and he's been really weird," Callie explains, like I'm not even in the room.

I start to protest but my mother takes Callie's word for it. "Oh, honey. You should volunteer at the rescue center. I always need people to help walk the dogs, and the fresh air would soon have you sleeping better."

"Logan asked me the other day, but I can't, Mom, you know… my allergies."

She looks at me over the rim of her glasses. "Allergies?"

"You know, the fur. It makes me break out in hives." I nod my head to Callie who is getting her school work out and dialing Ruby.

"Oh. Your allergies. You know, I have some breeds that are non-allergenic." She smirks and I vehemently shake my head.

"No pets, Mom."

When Callie vacates to go to her bedroom under the guise of homework, though probably to talk about lipstick or boys or some shit, Mom says, "Callie's making friends already. That's a good sign."

"It is. I'm proud of her. Starting a new school is a big deal, but so far she's nailing it."

"And what about you, son. Are you making friends?"

Mom busies herself sliding the coffee to me and then wiping the counter of the kitchen. "Friends? What am I, twelve now?"

She sits on the bar stool and I join her. "Going on thirteen, so I hear." She lifts the coffee to her mouth but doesn't take her eyes off me.

"What else did you hear?"

"That you asked a certain favorite dog walker of mine to attend the engagement party with you." She's got a shifty look in her eyes that I don't like one bit.

"Just as a friend, Mom. That's all. Don't read anything into it and certainly don't make a big deal about it in front of Callie. You know how she gets attached to people."

"Oh son, it's human nature to get attached. You and Callie have more in common than you realize, but where she is looking for healthy attachments, you are avoiding them entirely. Callie's coping so well since Crystal died, and it's credit to you, but I still can't help worry you are not healed."

"Mom, you know Crystal and I were over long before she died. I miss her terribly, but as a co-parent and friend. Callie and I both attended the bereavement sessions. I'm... not exactly at peace with it, but I'm okay."

Mom's hand reaches out and cups mine. I feel the weight of her concern more than I do the slender weight of her tiny bone structure. "Your wound isn't about Crystal's death. She had a long illness and you had time to prepare yourself. I'm talking about your father."

The mention of him is like having an IV full of ice water inserted straight into my veins.

I pull my hand away. "I don't want to talk about it, Mom."

She smiles glibly and takes another sip of her coffee. "I know you don't want to talk about it, Drew. But that doesn't mean you shouldn't talk about it. Your father's been gone a year almost. Did you read the letter?"

"Letter?"

"Drew Blingwood, don't you feign surprise with me." She pierces me with eyes so pale, they're almost translucent.

"Mom, it's water under the bridge—"

"It is unfinished business. You and your father were both stubborn and pigheaded. But I implore you to listen, he would not have wanted you to dwell. Families are complicated, but all said and done, your father loved you. Would you want Callie to carry around this much baggage?"

I shudder at the thought.

"I thought not," Mom says. "You thought you had time to make up and then that time was ripped away, but mark my words, your father loved you—"

"Mom. I've got some stuff I need to do. Are you okay here with Callie for a while," I interrupt her and am out of my seat and sliding my feet into my shoes before she has even agreed. My chest feels compressed and all I can think about is getting out of this room and finding some air.

"Of course, take as long as you need. But please," she takes down her glasses and wipes her eyes with her fingers, "think about what I said. It's time you made your peace."

I nod, but my jaw is so firmly clamped shut, I don't know if I convey the message. Instead, I call out to Callie that I need to head to Logan's office and I'm in the elevator by the time she answers, "Whatever, Dad. I'm busy!"

* * *

I NEEDED A DISTRACTION. I'd planned to head to Logan's office to see if he wanted to grab a drink at the beach bar, but with the mood I am in, I don't trust myself to stop at one beer, and a shitload of booze in my system, with my emotions the way they are would not do any good.

Normally I work out when the anger inside of me rears its head, but since I don't have my gym gear with me, I walk the resort aimlessly.

I'm a way up the sidewalk from the cafe when I see Skyla leaving, hand in hand with a small kid of about two or three. Her friend Jessie has hold of the kid's other hand. I hang back near the resort shopping center and watch as she walks in the direction of her apartment. Still in her work blouse and skirt, with sky-high heels and her golden hair hanging lose, she looks carefree and easy, enjoying time with her friend. I can instantly imagine the smile she gives to the kid, all warm and bubbly. *That smile of hers.* So expressive with the potential to stop hearts.

As she disappears around a corner and I lose sight of her, suddenly all I want is to see more of her. It's not exactly long until Saturday, I tell myself, and so far, she hasn't canceled the arrangement we made but maybe she will. It's not like I gave her much choice as she stood before me, cheeks flushed from a zealous Pilates session with her hair all wild. She looked like she did right after I made her come.

I made her come.

I grin at the memory, feeling victorious.

She looked like that for me, and damn did it make me feel good.

I want to go to her, to do it all over again but take my time this time. But there's no way I can just walk up to her place again.

A woman barges into me right as the doors to the store make a chiming sound.

"I'm sorry, I didn't see you there," the woman says as she pulls one of her many shopping bags up her arms. "I think I overdid it in there. They have so many nice dresses." Her cheeks pinken as though she is embarrassed at the quantity of purchases she has dangling from her wrists.

"No worries. You need a hand with those?" I offer.

"Oh no. It's okay, my vehicle is right there." She thanks me and walks away, and I stand outside staring at the designer woman's store. Then I think of exactly the right reason to visit Skyla.

CHAPTER 17

SKYLA

I pause the TV right as Samantha is about to indelicately explain the purpose of her latest sex toy. It's probably Jessie who's banging on the door wanting to borrow some potato chips, but still, I fasten the button on the skirt I had undone to make myself comfortable lounging in the chair and pad across the tile.

When I open the door, the person is obscured by a raft of resort logo'd shopping bags and boxes, but I would know the cologne anywhere.

Dark and deep, my mouth starts to water.

"Drew?"

He pops his head out from the long dress bag that's hitched over his shoulder and his full lips lift to greet me. It's only a smile, but the physical effect it has on me is jarring. My heart gallops wildly beneath my chest and my stomach fizzles with excitement.

"What are you doing here?" I ask. "Come in."

I move out the way of the door and in he strides. "I hope you don't mind me showing up unannounced, but you had me thinking, and since I invited you, I thought it fair I supply you with what you'll need," he says over his shoulder as he continues a path to the chair in the living room where he deposits the piles of dresses and shoes. Then he looks at me, an excited smile toying on the bow of his lips, his hands swinging by his sides like he doesn't know quite what to do with them while he waits for my reaction.

"What is all this?"

"Clothes, shoes. The lady threw in a matching lipstick for one of the dresses and some clutch purses. I think there might be some jewelry...."

I count the dress bags. Five. Four boxes of shoes, and a store bag spilling out with purses.

"I..." I'm completely lost for words.

"I still maintain you would look just fine in your yoga pants, but I thought it only fair I give you options."

I finger the fabric that pokes from the bottom of one of the dress bags. It's a deep red satin and the material glides through my fingers.

"I can't accept these. It's too much...."

Drew bites on his lip, hands now moved to his hips. "That's a shame. The lady at the store said no returns." He shakes his head and his mouth twists into a playful line.

"No returns?" I ask suspiciously and pull out my phone to search for consumer rights information.

He scratches his head. "Sale items. Some might be faulty. They were practically giving them away, but if you don't want them, I suppose I'll have to take them to Goodwill." He bends to pick up the box with the Fendi emblem and my hand lurches out to stop him.

"Wait!"

He pauses and gives me a sidelong look.

"No need to be hasty." I'm trying to keep the grin from taking over my face, while also demonstrating some decorum—which I am failing miserably at. There is not a sale sticker in sight, and as I gently sort through the dresses in their protective slips, none of them appear anything less than sheer perfection. "I suppose I could take them." I nod seriously and his mouth twitches. "I mean, obviously I'll find some good quality items to take to Goodwill, to restore... balance."

"Obviously," he counters. His grin lights up his face and a feeling so close to happiness envelopes me that I almost break into a dance.

I unzip one of the dress bags nearest the top. It's knee length and ivory. So beautiful it could easily pass for a wedding dress. The deep, almost blood red one has a zip all the way down the back, and I flush as I imagine Drew stripping the dress from me. "They're so beautiful."

He shrugs bashfully, gnawing his lip like a kid caught in a lie. "The lady in the store piled them up."

I hold another one up, wondering how I'll decide which one to wear. "You got a yellow one."

Drew looks away, embarrassed. "You look good in yellow."

"What an amazing store assistant to have picked so perfectly." My heart fills with warmth. No guy has ever told me I look good in anything, let alone chosen items that I instantly adore. Beside me, Drew's squirming uncomfortably, so I let him off the hook and change the subject. "You want a coffee?"

His eyes light up with his smile. "I think I need one. Some of those dresses weigh a ton."

I pour two cups from my one and only luxury item—a barista coffee maker, and Drew smiles at me approvingly. "I didn't notice you had one of the good coffee machines last time I was here."

"There is much you don't know about me, Drew," I say teasingly. "Like my dress size."

He smirks. "I know your dress size."

My cheeks warm. *How could he know my size?* My dress size is double digits and probably treble in actual number compared to the women he usually dates.

"I did a little digging…," he says wryly.

"Oh?" I reply. I'm too embarrassed to admit I've done some digging of my own. His ex, Crystal, was a renowned hair stylist and salon owner who styled the hair of the rich and famous. She was a size zero and looked just as glamorous as her A-List customers. Though, I couldn't find any other exes mentioned online.

"You have a Blingwood Resort raincoat?"

"All the employees do. Mine is hanging on the coatrack in my office."

Drew bows his head and sheepishly twists his coffee cup from side to side.

"You went to my office?"

He roughly cups the back of his neck, making him look adorable. "I had to go into the office anyway, and while I was there, I happened to notice it."

I narrow my eyes, feigning annoyance, but beneath that I am strangely enjoying the way he plotted to do something kind for me.

"You're sweet under your gruff exterior, you know that?"

He takes a step toward me and nerves shoot through me like rockets.

"You're adorable when you're being ungrateful."

The good girl in me immediately spurts, "Thank-you. I love the dresses. You didn't have to do this!"

He steps closer. His smile lighting up the room and doing funny things to my pulse. "You're welcome." He lifts his hand and his finger trails down my shoulder and along my neck. "You know, in some cultures it is customary to offer a kiss when one feels gratitude."

"I didn't know that," I reply. "Is that why you bought me so many dresses, so I'd feel obligated to kiss you lots of times?"

"No." He shakes his head and his hair falls out of its usual impeccably placed style. "I bought you the stuff so you'd give me one of your eleven-star hand jobs." He waggles his brows seriously but can't keep his lips from twitching mischievously.

I exaggerate a disappointed tut and trail my finger down his neck and along his shoulder, relishing seeing him lean into my touch. "Drew." I pout. "I wish you'd have mentioned that sooner, I already gave out all my hand jobs today." His mouth pops open seriously as my comment registers. "Just kidding," I reply and am about to giggle when he captures my mouth with his and I am totally silenced. My body responds to his, melting against him and becoming alight with desire as I feel him harden against my waist.

"Fuck!" He growls, grabbing my hair in his fist before letting it go. "I didn't come here to seduce you."

I take a step back. My legs suddenly feel like jelly and I'm breathless after his kiss. There's no way I'm letting him leave now, so I sarcastically reply, "Oh, that's a shame. I was looking forward to being seduced and you got off to such an excellent start. Should I see you out?"

His eyes darken, his face becomes serious. "Just because I didn't plan it, doesn't mean I don't want to seduce you."

"Then how about I show you to my bedroom, instead of the front door?" I walk toward the room and then check over my shoulder to ensure he is following. "You can bring my new stuff with you." Then I wink, like a woman in control, and Drew eagerly follows.

CHAPTER 18

DREW

I visit Skyla's place twice in the days that follow and even found her in an office supply closet during work time, narrowly managing to avoid getting caught by one of her coworkers by using my expert skills in looking grumpy while also playing the boss's brother card and ordering people to get back to work.

But it only occurs to me to get nervous for tonight's date to my brother's engagement party, when I am standing outside her place with my daughter beside me.

Blingwood family events have a tendency to bring up the past and I have felt an overwhelming sense of dread all day. Bringing Skyla to meet my family all together is probably a mistake, and they'll all assume she's my date. A fact made worse by my daughter insisting I bring flowers to give to Skyla before we go and my mother texting me to remind me to use my "good manners."

Shit.

"I'll knock," Callie tells me, walking up the steps to her door. "You stand beside the car and try not to do anything embarrassing," she adds before taking the steps two at a time and performing a rat-a-tat-tat on the door. Then Callie glances back at me and says, "Don't look so worried. You clean up nice." It's probably the nicest compliment my daughter has ever paid me and so I accept it, gracefully bowing.

When Skyla opens the door, the blood leaves my head entirely and goes immediately to my cock. After using my best detective skills to find out Skyla's dress size, I picked a half a dozen dresses but none of them seemed good enough, and I had no idea if she'd like them or even approve of me buying them. I guessed her shoe size based on the fact she was average height—which is the one and only thing about her that could be described as average.

I wasn't prepared for how breathtakingly gorgeous she would look in the dress that is the exact color of a buttercup beneath a twilight sky.

It didn't occur to me to pick a gown that would show the exact amount of thick, toned thigh, or the perfect ratio of breast to imagination, but somehow that's what I've done. Neither did I consciously choose the most exquisite silky fabric, precariously cut in just the right way to slide from her shoulders with the merest flick of my fingers, yet here I am, imagining doing exactly that.

She looks *too good*, and I wonder how I will get through the evening resisting touching her. Kissing her. And thus, notifying my nosey, eager family that I am screwing this gorgeous woman. Couple that with the prospect of Dana's pretentious private school's men's swim team being there to gawk and make a move on her if I let her stray too far, and I feel a renewed sense of stress.

It's already getting complicated.

"Do I look okay?" she asks, scrutinizing my expression.

"Go on, Dad. Tell her she looks beautiful," Callie says as they near me.

"You look beautiful," I say but it sounds robotic.

Skyla's smile is minimal and I feel like a jerk because she looks better than beautiful. Twelve years my junior with a smile that makes Vegas look dim and an energy that constantly amazes me... the woman can screw all night and still get up early and go for a swim. She walks Mom's dogs on her lunch break, then puts in a shift helping her friend look after her kid. She's upbeat, even though her mother abandoned her and she's been hurt in the past. I love all of these things about her, but I also hate how they make me feel, like I wield the power to blow her happiness to shit. It scares the crap out of me because I already have one person relying on me to keep things happy, and as it turns out, it's frickin' easy to screw it up.

Callie's stuck with me, but Skyla could walk away now and find someone better—in fact, that's what she'll do, as soon as this thing we have going on between us comes to an end.

"You'll have to excuse him," Callie says, poking her thumb in my direction. "He's dumb—I mean—*dumbfounded* because you look so nice. You really do. I love your hair, where did you get it done? Was it that place? Will you take me there?" Callie fills the silence while they get in the car, and suddenly we're on our way to the party.

And all I can think about is what a dumb idea it was to ask Skyla to attend something that strongly resembles a date with me and my dysfunctional family.

* * *

THE VENUE IS DECORATED with all kinds of pink shit. Balloons, flowers, streamers, little pink and gold butterflies and glitter everywhere. It looks like someone set a bomb off inside a party store.

"It's a bit girly for my taste," Skyla replies to Callie when she asks if she thinks the decorations are dumb. Then she tacks on, "But it's very pretty."

"Nah, it looks like crap. This is all Dana. Uncle Logan won't have had a say in any of it." Callie laughs. "Knowing Uncle Logan, he handed her his credit card and let her have at it."

"He's very busy," Skyla says with a sympathetic head tilt.

"Or very uninterested. I give them two years," Callie replies and a look of sheer, amused shock falls on Skyla's face.

"Callie, you're not supposed to say that stuff." I throw her my warning glare but she just shrugs.

"You know it's true. I know it's true. The only person who doesn't know it's true has his head so far buried in the sand that he's practically in Australia."

"We'll be talking about this when we get home, young lady," I warn Callie. There are servers carrying silver trays all around us, but so far, no sign of my family or the happy couple. "Who wants a drink? Pink wine?"

Callie rolls her eyes. "It's pink champagne, Dad."

"Whatever. Sounds gross. You'll be having an apple juice or an orange juice. Which is it?"

"Apple."

While I wait at the bar, I watch the place fill up with a bunch of people I never saw before. There's only four years between Logan, me, and Tate, so we've got a bunch of friends in common, but so far, none of them have arrived.

The DJ is playing some kind of electro music that Skyla and Callie seem to like enough to move and sing the words to. They look like they're enjoying the dancing, which makes me feel even older, so I hang back with my beer until it's announced that the happy couple have arrived. Beyond Logan and Dana is my mom and brother Tate. My sister is probably beyond them, but it's difficult to see with the camera flashes making everyone's movements seem captured in the blink of a strobe. But when I catch Logan's face, he looks furious. Tate, on the other hand, who is an A-list movie star and quite used to the attention, shrugs it off and grins his signature Blingwood smile at the imposing herd of photographers. The second they are barely inside, Logan pushes the heavy wooden doors closed and then gives orders to the security team—probably that they keep the paparazzi out.

Then Logan pulls Dana into a side room, looking massively pissed, while Tate comes to join me at the bar, stopping to high five Callie and introduce himself to Skyla.

"What was that all about?" I ask when he gets to me.

"Photographers?"

I nod.

"Don't know. They weren't there for me. My social media manager tagged me at a concert in Denver so as far as the world's press knows, that's where I am."

The early twinges of a headache presses against my temple.

"You think it was—"

"Dana?" Tate grins. "I reckon so. Her assistant sent mine a list of public wedding events she wants to me to go to in an "effort to support" my brother. Like he gives a shit if I go try on suits in Armani or attend a joint his and her bachelor party at the Sky Bar. Lately, every time I go anywhere near Logan, Dana is there, somehow catching me in the background of her social media posts. It's fucked up, man."

"They having a joint bachelor/bachelorette party? What

does that even mean? Logan told me he wanted a few of the guys for beers at his place."

"Yeah, that was the original plan but Queen Dana will likely get her way. I don't think she's ever compromised in her life."

"Logan said she's hungry for media attention. You spoke to him about her using you to get it?"

"Nah. I'm used to it. But using our family to get attention, that's starting to piss me off. No matter where the paps follow me, I always try to leave you guys out of it. After all, you've got Callie and she doesn't need those fucks following her around." He's damn right. I turn back to watch Callie and Skyla on the dance floor while Tate orders a beer with a chaser and I cock a brow at him. "What? I've been on set for two months solid, and I still have a way to go on this movie. I'm entitled to let loose, give me some slack."

Tate looks good. The dark curls he hates are hanging longer than usual, but that's probably because he's been working long hours. The exhaustion is showing less on his face than the last time I saw him when he was hungover and straight off a redeye from Vegas.

"True. It's been a long time since I got to party," I admit, though in all honesty I don't miss it. Sure, it'd be nice to get more time to hang out with my brothers and kick back with a beer, but I don't miss the hangovers or waking up next to a stranger and having to make small talk—not that it's been like that with Skyla. In fact, I've started to hang around after the sex because I enjoy the pillow talk.

My mom and sister join Callie and Skyla, and Tate waves them over to join us.

"You know any of the people here?" Tate asks, bobbing his head toward a group of strangers, and we all look over then shake our heads.

"I thought Logan was inviting Uncle Ted. It would have

really cheered him up. Since the operation, he's been a bit isolated." Mom's voice has more than an edge of disappointment. Uncle Ted is my dad's brother and recently had his foot amputated following an issue with his diabetes.

"I doubt princess Dana would want the overweight and infirm uncle screwing with her party posts on Insta, Mom," my sister Tabitha says, telling it like it is—like always. "Though I'm surprised she didn't invite Matt, he is, after all, passable in the looks department."

Matt is a good buddy of ours. We all know Tabs has a crush on him, not that he'd ever act on it since me, Tate and Logan would kill him. It's the cardinal rule of friendship: Never screw your buddy's little sister. "Matt's working in Africa doing some pro bono work. He won't be back for a while yet," I tell her, so she can relax and stop searching the room for him.

Tabitha inspects her fingernails like they hold the answer to third world hunger, then nods. "Oh. I didn't know that."

"Well, now you do," I reply curtly; I have enough on my mind without thinking about my sister and Matt. The thought alone sends a shudder down my spine. "Where are Logan and Dana anyway?"

Mom holds her wine glass up to her mouth so no one can see her lips move. "I think Logan wanted to talk to her in private."

"It'll be about the photographers. Logan likes his privacy and Dana likes to run her mouth her minions," Callie supplies and I throw her another glare.

"What has gotten into you tonight?" My comment earns me a sour face.

Beside her, Skyla clamps her incisor over her bottom lip and stress radiates through me. She's not enjoying herself, and why would she be, surrounded by strangers and a Blingwood bunch that don't know when or how to keep quiet.

Callie's stare burns right into me before she leans up onto her tippy toes and hisses in my ear. "Are you going to introduce her to everyone?" She nods her head to Skyla and it occurs to me—not for the first time—that I'm a rude asshole. I make the perfunctory introductions and hand Skyla a glass. Maybe a drink will help her relax since she looks as tightly wound as I feel.

"So, I was thinking we should all get together and do something for Dad's anniversary," Tabitha says and my chest tightens.

"Oh, darling, I think that'll be lovely. What do you have in mind?" Mom asks.

Skyla moves closer until the side of her body is nestled into mine and I can taste the sweet scent of her perfume. I can feel her looking at me with sorrow in her big brown eyes and it's more than I can take, so I put my glass down on the bar and take a step back, plunging my hands down into the pockets of my pants, effectively shaking off her closeness.

"Remember when it was too wet to play outside and Dad used to make us watch *Top Gun* and we'd all moan because we'd seen it a thousand times, but then he'd show up with a shit load of candy and every time we'd wind up having the best afternoon?"

I remember. I remember how the sofa facing the TV wasn't big enough for all of us and so me, being the oldest, and Dad would sit on the floor and he'd say the lines from the movie at the same time as Maverick while I said Goose's lines.

"Dad loved going to the movies, and IMAX is showing *Top Gun*. We could all go watch it. Maybe get some food after, and well, I think it'd be nice to get together. Skyla, you could come too?" she asks, smiling at Skyla like they've known each other for years.

"Actually, I'll be at the new resort that week," I interject before Skyla feels obliged to accept the invitation.

Callie glares at me like my sole purpose in life is to destroy any semblance of happiness, and so I embellish on the facts, "There are shots of the resort getting taken for the website. I should be there to make sure they get the best features."

Every member of my family looks at me incredulously. Skyla's eyes are filled with concern and it makes her look about five years younger—not to mention makes me feel more of a world-class asshole for basically uninviting her to the family event.

"Yeah, but you can spare one day—" Tabs starts and I can tell she wants to battle me on this.

"No. I can't. Would you rather I let Logan down? He's sunk every bit of spare cash he has on the new resort. I don't give a shit about his investors, but do you want our brother to go under so publicly?"

It's a dumb call. Logan would survive it, and there's no likelihood of the new resort failing, but my insinuation is enough to silence them all.

"Welcome to Blingwood family gatherings," Tate says to Skyla, pouring the chaser down his throat. "They're a shit show of love and happiness."

"Ain't that the truth," Callie replies.

* * *

WE ENDURE the rest of the party. Skyla mostly dancing with Callie and Tabs. Me growling at anyone who gets close to them, while also watching Logan getting paraded around the bar to meet people Dana invited, and Tate seemingly as pissed at the world as me.

Skyla's dress fits her like it was made to caress every inch, and the disco lights illuminate every perfect curve. She's got serious moves on the dance floor, and if I were here without my family I'd be moving with her, and probably dragging her into the bathroom to see what she put on beneath the dress—but instead I stay at the bar and scowl at any of the fucks who look her way.

"She's not going to disappear if you take your eyes off her," Tate says and I look away.

"What?"

"Skyla. You haven't taken your eyes off her."

"That's bullshit. I'm keeping watch on Callie, who is beside Skyla. She's a minor in an adult venue. Logan really should have put his foot down on a safer engagement party location for Callie."

"I doubt Logan had any say in it, and it's not like Dana is maternal enough to give a shit. Besides, we're all here and the place is crammed with security. Callie will be fine, but it wasn't her you were watching. I know that look, brother. You've got it bad."

"The only bad thing I have is a headache and a serious case of wanting to get out of here. How long you think it'll be until I've done the brotherly duty long enough so I can escape?"

"I was wondering that myself." Then Tate looks over my shoulder and announces, "Logan, I was beginning to think you'd never make it over to say hello."

Tate claps Logan on the back as he joins us at the bar and then he orders three whiskeys. I decline mine on account of being the designated driver, so Tate slugs the extra one back.

"I told you I could have a car pick you up," Logan reminds me.

"I can't stay late."

"You invited Skyla, I see." Logan nods his head approvingly at her and my temperature raises by about ten degrees.

"Yeah, but he's not into her," Tate says. "So, I think I'm going to go dance with her. Maybe I'll see if her moves are as good in my hotel room as they are on the dance floor. Man, she has a sweet ass and a nice pair of—"

"Don't you dare!" My hand has lurched out and I've got Tate by the lapel of his jacket. The fucker just grins knowingly at me and I let go, roughly smoothing the fabric back in place.

"Leave it, Tate. Don't say a word," I warn.

"So, she's off limits, I get it," Tate replies. Logan is watching the whole time, but whereas normally he'd split us up, this time his attention is caught elsewhere so I follow his gaze. Along the bar, Dana is surrounded by a bunch of guys, which wouldn't usually be a problem since Logan is not the jealous type, but then I see the row of shots stacked on the bar. Logan's expression is thunderous as she downs one, two, three shots of hard liquor before whooping like she's at a frat party. Logan storms off, and two seconds later he's leading Dana into a side room.

"Rock, paper, scissors for who goes to check on him?" Tate says.

"I'll go," I reply and follow Dana and Logan.

* * *

IT's a small room lit by sconces, like a private booth at a lap dancing bar, with a red velvet sofa and a low-slung coffee table. I hang back by the door, wondering if I should have come to check on them after all.

"What the hell, Dana. You're pregnant!" Logan yells.

"Yeah, but I'm only a couple of months along. It was a few tiny shots, Logan. It's all right for you. Your body doesn't change. You don't have the same responsibility. Seven more months is going to feel like torture if I stop everything too soon. I'll stop drinking when I'm showing."

"You'll stop right away! I've had one sip of beer all night. I'll gladly give up booze with you. It's for the health of our baby."

She crosses her arms over her chest and pouts like a child. "Logan, I'm only twenty-four." *Skyla's twenty-four and she would never pull this shit.* "You're taking all the fun out of this pregnancy and our engagement. You only agreed to one photoshoot. It's like you don't even care about my career and now you want me to give up all the fun things. You're so selfish sometimes."

I stand back, filled with rage. I knew Dana could be a bitch, but gaslighting Logan over her own selfish ways is beyond what I thought her capable of.

"Fine. You're a grown-ass woman, but if you're going to jeopardize the health of our kid, then I am not standing around to watch. I'll leave now and we'll call it quits."

"What is it you expect from me?" she screams.

"I expect you to take care of yourself like you are carrying the most precious thing in the entire fucking world. I expect you to put the baby before impressing a bunch of nobodies. I don't know, Dana, maybe behave like you pretend you do in your Instagram posts!"

"That's a low blow, Logan. You know I have to present myself in a certain way to maintain my followers. Everyone knows it's not sustainable. All mothers have a tiny drink. It's self-care!"

"I'm leaving." He turns toward me. I'm standing by the door, feeling gutted for him that he has to deal with this shit but also proud of him for trying to make a stand.

"Okay," she calls after him. "I'll dial it down. It's social and peer pressure, that's all. No more drinking. I can totally do without it."

He turns back to face her. "You better, Dana. Because I won't stand by and watch you hurt our child."

She grabs his hands and tells him. "It's nice to see you care. I worry you don't care enough."

"I do. Dana, this baby, it deserves both our undivided attention. You can't be pulling this shit."

"I know. I know. I'm sorry. Sometimes I feel like you care more about the baby than you do me."

Logan sighs. He runs his hands through his hair, torn. "I care about you both. But I mean it, if you're not putting the baby first then I'm gone. I was reading this book about parenting and... so much can go wrong."

"You've been reading about it?" she asks.

"A few chapters here and there. I want to do this right."

"I'll cut out the drinking. I wanted you to show me you actually care." She closes in on him, stroking his shoulder and making out like she's realized the error of her ways. "I love you, baby."

"I love you too," he replies but it sounds strained.

"I better get back out there and work the room. There's talk of a makeup line for babies and I don't want to miss talking to Delia Clark."

Dana passes me on the way out, wrinkling her nose and proving she likes me about as much as I like her. "Might have known you'd follow."

"Enjoy your orange juice," I say through a smile. Then I go to Logan who has sunk down onto the sofa.

"I don't know what to do with her half the time."

"She's a wild one, that's for sure." I sink down beside him. "How long until the wedding?"

"Four weeks."

"You don't have to do it."

Logan's head swings my way and he pierces me with his most pissed-off glare.

"What the fuck, man? Yes, I have to. It's been announced. We have a baby on the way."

"Don't get all pissy with me. You're not happy, Logan. It's not like co-parenting isn't an option."

"And watch Dana go on a drinking binge while she's getting over it? Sit back while she spills every minute of our private life on social media. It won't just be me she talks about. It'll be Tate. Tabs. Mom. You. Callie…."

"She wouldn't dare. Why are you with someone who'd even think about that shit?"

He huffs into the air. "She's not all bad."

"She's pretty fucking bad."

His face turns angry and he leaps to standing. I do the same.

"She might not be perfect, but at least I am committing to something. Unlike you. What's going on with you and Skyla? You haven't been anywhere near her all night."

"You're the one who told me to invite her so she wouldn't be standing there on her own like a loner!"

"And you're going to screw it up like you always do."

I see red. I can't feel my fingers and my fists ball. "Leave Skyla out of this. She's just someone I'm screwing and she has nothing to do with all this. I don't even know why I invited her to this shit show."

Logan's eyes dart beyond me and suddenly his face softens and his anger evaporates.

I don't need to look to know Skyla is standing there and that she heard me, but I look anyway and her expression crushes me. Then the door slams and Logan says, "You better go after her."

CHAPTER 19

SKYLA

*D*ays pass and I don't reach out to Drew and he doesn't turn up at my door.

It's my own fault. I should have known better than to think a bunch of really great sex and a haphazard invitation to a family event would cement something—like mutual respect and common decency.

He said it himself, out loud: *She's just someone I'm screwing.*

It's not like I didn't know it, but still, hearing him say it stings like a bitch. Drew only invited me to the party so I'd have people to stand with. It makes me feel like such a loser when just a few days ago I felt on top of the world.

I stare out the window of the boardroom and gaze at the crystal-clear ocean. Working and living in a luxury resort, it screws with your emotions and makes it easy to delude yourself that you're in paradise when you aren't—not even close.

"Are you okay, Skyla?" Logan asks from across the boardroom table.

"Yes, I'm sorry, I was miles away. What were you saying?"

Logan looks about as tired as I feel with dark shadows beneath his eyes and his hair in complete disarray—far from the polished billionaire that was recently pictured in an engagement photoshoot with his fiancée. In fact, he looks worse than he did in the furious pictures of him in the papers trying to block the paparazzi when they showed up at his engagement party uninvited.

"You're doing a full recruitment job fair." He looks at me, then pointedly to Mike. "I want the best of the best. No mistakes." His gaze softens as it lands back on me. "In fact, if we could cryogenically replicate you for the HR Manager post at the new resort, my life would be much easier, Skyla." Judging by the compliment he makes in spite of his bad mood, I'm guessing Logan realizes I'm still in a funk. Then he wraps up the meeting.

"Thanks for showing up, everyone, and for all your hard work. You know what you need to do before we reconvene?"

I glance at my to-do list. Perfectly staffing a new resort will not be easy. Though, I'm sure the Blingwood reputation and the Miami beach location will help tempt the cream-of-the-crop candidates, not to mention our great benefits and generous insurance package.

I look up and nod to Logan. It's doable, though I lack my usual enthusiasm for the task. The past few days, I haven't even been able to look at the 3D mock-ups of the resort without thinking of Drew.

Dismissed, everyone files out of the boardroom except Logan, who hangs back and perches his hip on the side of the table. He takes a muffin from the untouched plate and twists it around in his hands like he doesn't have the stomach to eat it.

"You okay?" he asks again.

"I'm fine. I think the location will really draw new starters and I already have a lot of interest flooding in from the ads I put out. Never know, I might even apply myself," I joke, but the idea of a fresh place does sound appealing.

He puts the muffin in front of me. "I'm not talking about work; I'm asking if you are all right."

"You mean..."

"I'm sorry you heard what he said. Drew didn't mean it. The family has been grinding his gears over some stuff with our Dad and... you got the brunt of it." His mouth tips down at the corners and I believe him. Logan *is* sorry I heard what his brother said. It probably makes working with me super awkward.

"Really, Mr. Blingwood. I'm fine." I stand and pile up my notebook and files into my arms. "Drew obviously meant what he said, even if he didn't intend for me to hear it. It's better he's honest. If you'll excuse me, resort 2.0 won't staff itself."

I walk away, leaving the muffin, since I can barely stomach air and go to my office, pulling down the blinds so I can be alone.

* * *

I'M ABOUT to close down my computer for the day when I receive an email:

To: Skyla Manning

From: Drew Blingwood

Subject: I'm sorry.

> I was a jerk. It was about me, not you. I was lashing out at Logan and… seeing my family, it triggers all kinds of crazy inside my head and…. You didn't deserve that. Can I come see you and explain?

• -

As apologies go, it seems like a good one. I'm desperate to know what got into him that night but his words still sting, so I decide to sleep on it. Maybe speak to Jessie first, though that probably won't help much since when I told her how much what he said hurt, she got it into her head that I'm falling in love with him. She thinks she's intuitive. I think she's delusional. Yet I couldn't wholeheartedly deny it either.

When I pass Sally at the reception desk on my way out, she asks me how *the other* Mr. Blingwood is, winking to emphasize her meaning. I'm clutching my phone, so I lift it to my ear and pretend to be on a call, which doesn't stop my face from warming as the other staff members stare at me.

For once, it'd be nice if the gossip mill was up-to-date and everyone knew already not to ask about my ill-fated casual "arrangement." I'm embarrassed and it's making my hands so clammy that I almost drop the file listing the jobs titles for the new resort that I am taking home to work on.

Then I get a text from Jessie:

> Meet at the cafeteria for dinner?

I REPLY INSTANTLY:

> Not hungry. You go eat and I'll see you later. I'm tired and there's a great position I want to apply for.

A new job at the resort?

> Of course.

Phew. I thought for a minute you might be thinking of leaving Santa Barbara. Get some rest, I'll see you tomorrow.

I DON'T RESPOND. Jessie thought I meant this resort and I feel terrible for misleading her, but I can't help wonder if maybe it is time to start over. After a bunch of public fails here and my latest heartbreak, this resort is getting smaller by the day. Even once Drew's new house is built, he'll still be just up the road—not far away at all, so it's going to stay small. And one day, he's going to find someone who isn't just "someone he's screwing," and that's going to be unbearable.

At home, after I've updated my resume, I email it to Logan and ask that I be considered for the HR Manager position at the new resort. I propose that I relocate as soon as there is a workable office space so I can more easily conduct interviews and oversee the hiring and training of the workforce. I could be on my way out of Santa Barbara to pastures new before the month is out. The thought fills me with dread, but I also feel like my hand has been forced. The more I think about it, the more I decide that relocating to the new resort is the only way I can still work for Blingwood Resorts without clinging onto the dead hope that Drew will one day want me in the same way I want him. Then, I close down my computer and try to look forward to my future—which is easier said than done.

* * *

I'M fresh out of the shower, wrapped in my robe and staring out of the window at the storm rolling in when someone beats on my door. I tie my robe tighter and my pulse thunders beneath my skin. When I open the door, Drew is standing there. He's wearing faded jeans and a soaking wet white T-shirt that coats his body like a second skin. Droplets of rain make his hair look jet black as they cling to the ends of his mussed-up hair.

"You didn't answer my email," he says. Dark shadows circle his eyes and his expression is pained.

"I wasn't sure how to reply," I admit. "Come in, you're soaked." I leave the door open and walk through to the tiny sitting room, grabbing a towel as I pass the bathroom and throwing it to him to catch.

"I made a mistake," he says, holding the towel in both hands, unmoving. His voice is rough, his expression on the verge of sheer exhaustion.

"Was it a mistake? You seemed pretty sure that I mean nothing to you other than a screw buddy."

He shrinks back. I should feel glad what I said hurt him, like he hurt me, but I don't feel better. Seeing him hurting makes my own hurt worse.

"Logan said you applied for a transfer."

"He shouldn't have told you that."

Drew shrugs and water drips from his hair down onto the tiles. "He thought he was helping. Are you leaving because of me? Because of what I said?"

"I applied for the transfer because a fresh start will do me good. Here, I've been hopping from one bad experience to another. I've made some bad choices, and bad decisions are made worse by a small community watching and witnessing each one."

"So, you're running?" Drew uses the towel to absorb the worst of the rain from his hair. I try not to stare at his abs as his T-shirt rides up.

Pride forces me to circumvent his point. "I'm starting over. The new resort is going to be award winning and it's a good career move, getting involved right from the start; it'll look great on my resume."

"You're not doing this for your resume. I thought you were happy here? Is it because you regret sleeping with me? I wouldn't blame you if you did. Taking your virginity and then saying what I did… it's unforgivable."

I ponder for a moment, remembering how I felt then. It'd felt special, like we were making love, even though the logical part of my brain knows that love never entered the equation. But I felt cherished and safe, and I wanted him to be the one.

"I have no regrets," I admit.

"Then why? I don't want you to go because of the way I have behaved."

"Everyone here knows something went on between you and me. My love life, or rather, lack of, seems to be public knowledge and it's embarrassing. I knew it was a mistake to get involved with another guy at the resort, but I did it anyway. That's not your fault." He's looking at me so intently, his eyes so filled with sorrow it's making my head hurt. "It'll be good for me. I want to start over in a place where people aren't judging me."

"People will judge you wherever you go. It's human nature. You have nothing to be embarrassed about. I—"

"You hurt me," I say, spitting out the truth like it's a bullet. He grimaces like my words hit their target but I feel no relief. "I was fully aware our relationship wasn't going anywhere. I didn't dupe myself into believing I was your next greatest love. It was time limited, I knew that, but the way you spoke about me, you made me sound like a stupid kid who was following you around like a lovesick puppy." My cheeks flame as I mentally relive watching Drew tell his brother I meant nothing to him and my anger spikes. "You came to me. I didn't chase you, and I certainly didn't ask for anything you didn't give freely. You made me feel like I was nothing. An embarrassment. You made me feel how Mike made me feel." His reaction to my words causes me to pause. Eyes full of self-loathing, he steps closer. "You are not the reason I applied to move resorts, so you can leave with a clear conscience."

"Yeah, I am the reason and my conscience is anything but clear." He throws the towel onto the table and drops onto the sofa, holding his head in his hands before looking up and saying, "I'm sorry I hurt you, I really, truly am. I was a dick. I don't know why I..." He shakes his head and his eyes lose focus. "My family wants me to celebrate the life of a man I caused to hate me. The guilt gets in the way of everything I do. Every time I feel something good, there's a feeling right behind it warning me that I don't deserve it, and then I do whatever it takes to screw it up."

His revelation takes me by surprise. I knew Drew was in a bad mood at the engagement party. I could tell from the moment he picked me up that he didn't want to be there, but I also got a strong sense of love between his family members.

The entire state of California has heard of the Blingwoods. I worked for his father briefly before Logan took over. He was a perfectly likable boss, but I had no dealings with him outside of work. Mr. Blingwood Senior had the look of a man who lived for his family. I can't imagine he was anything less than a stellar dad, but then, nobody knows what goes on behind closed doors.

"Families are complicated." I seat myself beside him and his hand grips my knee.

"My relationship with my father was difficult. The oldest son. Before I was even born, I was lined up to take over the family business. But Logan was always going to be better at it, he was passionate about the resort, and hung off my father's every word. Logan's opening the second resort so he can designate it as *his* personal contribution to the empire. I never gave a damn about any of it," he shakes his head bitterly, "and I just loved to tell my dad that, even though I knew it hurt him because I couldn't stand the responsibility he was shoveling on my shoulders. I resented it all."

When I glance down, I notice I've cupped his hand in mine. The thumb of his other hand rubs circles on my leg.

"I imagine it's a lot of pressure to be born into such expectations."

"Dad thought I was the prodigal son. He never took any of my dreams seriously. He laughed when I said I wanted out. It didn't occur to him I might choose a different path. Even when I got my degree and started working for an architecture company in the city, he said it would never last, but I dug my heels in and stuck it out. I couldn't stand the thought of him watching me fail, and so I cut all ties."

"I never saw you at the resort. Logan was around,

learning the ropes from your father, but he had a photograph of you all, right on his desk."

Drew shrugs. "For years, I ghosted him. I suppose the photograph was to keep up appearances. I stopped attending family gatherings, didn't seem like there was much point if we never saw eye to eye. I thought I was avoiding the arguments, but really, I was ostracizing myself."

"You got married and had a child. Callie knows the family, so…"

"When Callie was born, Mom would travel to New York to spend time with us. I thought things might have changed with my dad. I had my own business, an office in New York and London, but things were still difficult between us, and I realized it didn't matter what I achieved, Dad couldn't get past me choosing different to what he offered. As Callie got older, she'd spend time with my parents during the summer. Mostly Crystal arranged it all since I was always working. Years went by without us talking, until Dad showed up at Crystal's funeral."

A chill ripples down my spine. "What happened?"

"He told me my tantrum had to end. He still thought I was a kid acting out. He told me I was selfish, that Callie needed her family and I should move home. And if I didn't, then I'd disappoint Callie, just like I did him."

"That's a terrible thing for him to say."

Drew's gaze is fixed on the tile floor, it's like he is reliving their conversation. "I'd been drinking. Mom had put Callie to bed, and this resentment, this unending pain that I had been holding onto all through Crystal's chemo and treatments just released itself. I told him I was a terrible father because I had learned it from him. And then I told him I fucking hated him."

I squeeze his hand, trying to bring him back to now. "You didn't mean those things, and I bet he didn't either." I pull on his hand and he looks at me. "You can't go on feeling guilty. Families fight, but most of what is said in anger isn't sincere. Often times families get the chance to get over their differences. You and your dad would've made up in time."

Drew's throat bobs as he swallows. "What does it say about me, Skyla? I hurt my father right before he died." His shoulders drop and he's back to staring at the floor. "And it's not even like I learned from it, I treated you just as appallingly. You know Callie is still furious with me? She doesn't know what I did, but she knows I did something."

"Drew, you weren't the cause of your father's heart attack, you know that, don't you?"

He shrugs. "He died seventeen days after our fight. I was still stewing on it when Mom called. I'm a father, I know he was stewing on it too."

"He was upset, but I bet he was also so proud of you. You Blingwoods are not always so even tempered, maybe you get that from your father, but you're also passionate and driven —and he was too. You locked horns, but they would have untangled in time."

He smiles and takes my hand. "That's kind of you to say, but you don't know that."

"If you fought with Callie, you wouldn't want her to remember the fight, you'd want her to remember the good stuff, right?"

"Damn sure about that." He nods and his eyes travel up my body until they land on mine. "And what about you? Can you remember the good stuff? Can you forgive the bad?"

"Yes." My hand squeezes his.

The way he's looking at me has my heart aching.

"I care about you." He winces. "And it's making me crazy, because I am not in a place in my life where I can give you what you deserve."

The tormented look in his eyes is unbearable and I wish I

197

could absorb his pain and set him free. I start by sliding my leg over his until I am facing him. Straddling him.

Drew's eyes alight with fire.

"Skyla, I didn't come here to—"

"I'm not a kid. I'm a twenty-four-year-old woman who makes her own decisions." I loosen my robe and slide it from my shoulders until my chest is bare and his mouth pops open. "You came here to apologize, and this is me, accepting that apology." My mouth is suddenly on his and I grind myself against him, readying myself to take him, here and now. Drew stops me by holding my hips still.

"I can't give you a future," he admits.

"I'm not asking for one."

"If we're doing this, we're not doing it fast and frantic. I'm going to worship you how you deserve to be worshipped."

Drew stands, taking my weight and holding me against his waist. All possibility of my resisting him, any belief I held that I could restrain myself from wanting his touch is gone. I know that now. As long as he wants me, I want him—no matter how short that time may be. I couldn't turn him away even if I tried.

Addicted.

Drew Blingwood has become my addiction.

He carries me to the bedroom—my robe lost along the way—and lays me out on the bed. His shoes, jeans and his T-shirt are gone in an instant and he stands before me, gloriously naked. Neither of us move, drinking each other in until the anticipation is unbearable. It's the most vulnerable I have ever felt, every inch of me spread out before him, but I don't feel self-conscious because the way he is looking at me makes me feel adored, and the sheer size of his erection, tells me I'm sexy.

"You're so beautiful," he says, creeping forward until he is beside me on the bed.

"Touché, Blingwood," I reply and his lips land on mine, kissing me fully and deeply. Each stroke of his tongue is an assault on my senses. His erection hard against my hip as he kisses a trail down my neck, exciting me. He might not be able to offer me everything I want, but maybe the short time we have until I move will be enough. After all, don't people say it is better to have loved and lost than not to have loved at all. This moment, this deep intimacy, maybe it'll be enough to carry me through. Maybe the memories will be worth the pain when I leave this place. I can't focus on the regrets I may have down the line, because Drew's fingers and mouth are worshipping my body and I am quivering beneath his touch. When he sheaths himself and enters me, I am lost in his eyes. Dark and intense, I stare into them as he slowly commands the pace. Skin to skin, I'm gone. He's building a delicious, slippery friction that has me shaking from the force of it.

"So perfect. Are you going to come for me, sugar?"

The sound of his deep voice and the way he is looking at me, vibrates through his body directly to every erogenous zone. I try to answer but the tingling is taking over me. Drew's slow, deep, in and out motions take on a new rhythm, slowly rubbing at my resolve.

"That's my girl," he breathes. "I can feel you getting closer."

I thought we were over but I am grateful we're not. I cling to his shoulders, not breaking our connection. Drew's pupils dilate like they are taken over by pure lust and something even stronger. With every thrust we become closer, more deeply connected like he is leaving a part of himself embedded within me. His expression is intense. His body firm, strong and so commanding I am completely at his mercy.

"Nothing is sexier than watching you come apart for me."

"That's good because I can't hold on much longer," I

admit and he pauses, circling his hips, withdrawing just enough that my core clenches in protest.

"Not yet," Drew commands, pulling away and then pushing back in, but not enough to satisfy my aching. He kisses me, running the tip of his tongue inside of my mouth, tasting me then smiling like he likes my flavor.

"I need more. I'm so close," I pant from the brink of desperation.

"So eager," he replies, kissing my mouth, my jaw, my neck, the valley between my breasts and cupping each of my nipples inside his mouth. He seems content, not rushing a single second of his torment. His eyes are focused on mine, his body reactive to my pleasure. I want the moment, exactly as it is, to last forever and yet I want more.

"Please, Drew," I beg, lifting my hips and arching my back, trying to get relief while hovering on the edge of no return.

"Please what, baby?" His voice is gruff and I try to think clearly enough to answer. "Tell me what you need," he says, giving me just a fraction more and my eyes flutter at the promise.

"I need..."

He circles his hips again and my core spasms and my clit throbs.

"I need you. All of you."

"Fuck!" He growls. "You got it, sugar."

He plunges into me, sliding in hard against my wetness, filling me. He's rubbing back and forth over my clit with his body as he drives deeper, and I'm so ripe for his taking I am immediately clenching around him and spasming out of control. Between the blasts of ecstasy, I delight in watching Drew's reserve collapse as he loses all control.

"Fuck, baby, you feel so good. Too fucking good." His jaw clenches, his composure shatters and his expression turns animalistic. "Skyla," he calls my name and I think I call his.

I'm so close to him, mind and body, and nothing has ever felt so perfect or so real, watching Drew come apart inside me without ever taking his eyes off mine.

* * *

"IS THAT THE TIME? Drew, you've got to go. Your mom will be wondering where the hell you are and Callie will be awake soon," I hiss and try to untangle myself from Drew's limbs.

"Muhummm," he says sleepily and kisses my shoulder. "Five more minutes."

"Drew, we fell asleep. You better go. People will see you leaving my apartment, and your daughter will be wondering what the f—" He stops my whining with a kiss that steals the breath from my lungs. "I'm serious," I say as we break apart, but my voice sounds strange through my smile.

He leans up on the bed and grabs his phone from the pocket of his jeans, reading aloud the voice message he is about to send:

"'*Sorry I stayed out, Mom. I had some very important business to attend to with Skyla. Please tell Callie I left for work early and I'll talk to her when I come home.*' God, you make me feel sixteen again." He grins boyishly and I ruffle his hair.

"Whereas you make me feel like the responsible one."

Drew drops the phone on the mattress and grabs me around my waist, pressing his lips against the flesh of my breast.

"So that was how you were feeling as you came on my cock, responsible?"

I let out a shriek of giggles as he kisses the soft spot in the crook of my neck. "Okay, okay. So responsible might not be the correct word in that context."

"Might not?" He tickles me and I erupt with laughter.

"Okay, so I felt a complete loss of inhibitions."

"And...," he prompts.

"Wildly sexy."

"You are wildly sexy, and..."

I blow a stray tendril of sex hair out of my eyes and reply, "In need of more."

He catches my finger as it trails a path down his chest and replies, "Me too, baby. Me too."

* * *

LATER, Drew kisses me more than a dozen times as he tries to leave my apartment so I can get ready for work. I don't know if it is the relief from having shared his troubles or how good it feels to have made up, but he seems different today.

Lighter.

"Let me take you for breakfast?" he says.

"I'm starving. I know this great place on the outskirts of town. No one will know us there. They sell these incredible blueberry muffins with these amazing little..." I notice he's grinning at me and I stop talking. "They're pretty good," I say, bursting out laughing.

"They sound it. Hearing you gush about muffins, it makes me wish you talked about me like that." He's dressed in just his T-shirt that somehow dried on the floor of my bedroom and doesn't smell so much as even a tiny bit musty, and jeans that on any guy in a ten-mile radius would look entirely ordinary, yet on him, he looks like the clothes were made to fit perfectly against his hard chest and narrow waist.

Delicious.

"You could never compare to such heaven, I'm afraid."

He loops his arms around my waist and pulls me closer, nuzzling his mouth against my neck. "You sure? Because last night, you called out to God so often that I thought you'd mistaken me for him."

"And you yelled, 'Holy fucking Christ' so often that you're probably going to hell for blasphemy," I counter.

Drew's mouth twitches, amused. "An eternity burning in hell for one night with you? Totally worth it." He winks and my stomach butterflies. "I'll go grab a shower and a change of clothes and meet you back here?"

"Sounds heavenly," I reply and then glance at the clock, suddenly remembering I have an earlier start than usual with Jessie's employee appraisal and back-to-back interviews. "Shoot. I can't today. Rain check?"

He rests his hands on my hips and pokes out his lower lip, affronted. "You could call in sick. Your face looks a little..." his index finger strokes my jaw and it takes all my restraint not to purr like a kitten, "flushed. I think you may need bed rest." He nods. "Yes, you definitely need to go back to bed."

I laugh. "And get fired by your brother when he finds out I've been playing hooky? I'd better not. *Muffin To Go* can wait."

Drew kicks his toe at the floor. "I'll see you later, though?"

"You think Callie will know you didn't come home last night?"

He checks his watch then shakes his head. "I'll probably be back before she wakes. But if she figures it out, I think she'll be pleased we made up."

I chuckle and pull my robe tighter. "You're going to tell her we made up?"

"I think it's safe to say we're friends again. If you don't mind?"

"No, I don't mind." I shake my head. "It's just, I'll be leaving eventually. I don't know the date yet, but I'd hate for Callie to be disappointed...." He hasn't asked me to stay and I can't bring myself to spoil our happiness by assuming any of this means more than he said he wanted in the beginning.

"You're still taking the job at the new resort then?" he asks, and I nod.

"There's no reason for me to stay. I'll be needed there before the place even opens to help with training and... Logan can't not give me the position, I'm the best HR Manager he's got."

He twirls a lock of my hair around his finger, deep in thought. "It gives us just a few weeks to enjoy the heck out of each other."

I trail my finger down his neck, wondering if I can get my fill of him by then, like it's possible I will ever get enough.

Drew takes my hand and brings it to his lips, kissing the palm of my hand and then holding it in his while he pulls me in for a hug and breathes in my hair, then chuckles. "You smell like me, only better."

I lean up onto my toes to inhale him. "You smell like you need a shower." It's a lie. He smells like all my fantasies.

I wait for him to jibe me back but he doesn't. He wraps me tighter and tells me, "Pilates tonight. Highlight of my week. I'll pick you and Jessie up on the way, and then will you have dinner with me and Callie?"

"I'll be all red-faced and sweaty—"

Drew pulls me closer. "That's exactly how I like you. See you soon, gorgeous." Then he pats my ass as he leaves, shutting the door behind him and pulling on the handle to make sure it's closed.

And it takes me a full two minutes to remember what I was about to do next.

"HERE FOR OUR NINE O'CLOCK, and yes, I know I'm ten minutes late, but I accosted a delivery guy on the way in who had these for Skyla Manning, and I thought you'd want me to get them before Sally did," Jessie says as she enters my office, carrying a white box with a logo that makes me grin from ear to ear. "I can tell by your face I did good," Jessie adds then places the box on my desk.

"Muffins To Go," I say, stating the obvious since the box is clearly labeled.

"Is there a note?" she asks, and I lift the lid.

The muffins taste good, but nowhere near as good as you.

I tuck the note into my desk drawer.

"What does it say?" Jessie asks impatiently.

"Never mind that. Want one?" I push the box of four toward Jessie and she takes one. When I bite into mine, my eyes flutter shut and I chew through a smile.

"Mystery admirer?" she asks.

"Let's get our work formalities done and I'll tell you all about it after. Deal?"

"Okay, but you better tell me everything. Muffins, after what he said to you, is a really shitty apology."

"There's more to it than that. Now," I scroll the company computer, "Jessie Yates, exemplary member of the cleaning crew for two years. You started here right after you had Macy. How do you think it's all going?"

Jessie pulls a face. "You know I hate it when you get all professional."

"Needs must. Besides, we need to get this done since Betty gave her two weeks notice... and you're getting promoted to her job," I say casually, then slowly gaze up to see her mouth hang open—muffin and all.

"What?! I mean, I knew she was retiring, but me?"

I grin. "I've already spoken to Logan. You're our best

maid. You know this place like the back of your hand. It's time you joined management."

"Can housekeeping ever really be called management?"

"It is when it's the head of housekeeping, manager of staff."

"Hmm. I like it. Jessie Yates, Head of Housekeeping. It has a ring to it, don't you think?"

"It does." Her expression beams proudly. "I'll even get you a special badge."

* * *

AFTER WORK, once I've pulled myself into some heavy-duty Lycra, Jessie and I are standing outside our apartment when Drew rolls up. Beside him, Callie is leaning out the window whooping for "girl time." Drew orders her to give up the front seat for a grown up, and even though I protest that she doesn't have to, she jumps in the back beside Jessie and insists I take her seat.

"Hi," I say feeling like a twelve-year-old on a supervised date.

"Hello," he says, equally bashful.

Tonight's Pilates class is as strenuous as the first, only this time, Drew makes no effort to hide the fact he is watching me, and as we walk back to the car Callie whispers to me, "I'm so sorry. My Dad was checking out your butt again."

I try not to laugh. "I know. But he's going to make up for it by buying us dinner."

"Are you coming?" Callie asks Jessie.

"Can't tonight I'm afraid. Macy and I have a date with a bathtub."

"I could come help?" I offer.

"Oh honey, you don't need to do that. You kids go and

have fun and leave this old lady to celebrate her new job with her baby, which honestly sounds perfect to me."

"Macy's so sweet. I wish I had a little brother or sister," Callie says. "You know, soon I'll be old enough to babysit."

"Callie, you'll have a brand-new cousin in seven months once Dana and Logan have their child. But it'll be years before you're old enough to babysit," Drew replies as we seat ourselves in the car.

"A new cousin, that's nice," Jessie says, her smile not reaching her eyes. "You could come play with Macy sometime, and get some baby practice in," Jessie offers. Her voice sounds strained; with an underlying emotion I can't put my finger on.

"Thank-you, I'd love that," Callie replies. "I'll come by after school one day."

We drop Jessie off and then head back to the penthouse. I offer to go for a shower first, but Drew tells me to grab some things so I can shower at his place while we wait for dinner.

"You ordered in?" I say.

"Dad can't cook," Callie replies, and Drew looks sheepish.

"The restaurant is sending over food. I didn't know if you prefer steak or chicken so I ordered both, and a seafood dish." He shrugs, but I know the resort restaurant is Michelin star-rated and food there costs an arm and a leg.

When we get to the penthouse, Drew says, "You can use the master shower. It's the nicest." He points me in the direction of the master suite, as Callie is grabbing the dishes to set the table.

Drew's right. The bathroom in the penthouse is pretty much the plushest I have ever seen with an entire wall of jets overlooking a wall-to-ceiling window that faces the ocean. I take a couple of minutes smelling the shampoo bottles and shower gel and then wash myself with the ones that smell most like Drew.

"I thought I preferred you dirty, but baby, you're hot when you're clean too."

I jump at the sound of his voice and throw the shampoo bottle at him. "Shit! You scared me."

"Sorry," he says, sliding out of his clothes.

"What are you doing. Callie—"

"Callie has gone out to get Sprite. She'll be at least fifteen minutes."

"Fifteen minutes?" I laugh throatily. "Will that be long enough?"

"Baby, after spending the last hour watching you twist that hot body into all manner of Goddamn sexy positions, I think thirty seconds might do it."

He steps inside, his cock fully erect and enticing against the spray of the water.

"But first, I want to eat you up. I'm starving. And maybe if there's time, we can put the jets to good use as well."

CHAPTER 20

DREW

"*W*hy is your hair soaking wet?" Callie asks and my gaze mischievously meets Skyla's.

"There was a pressure issue in the shower. I had to go fix it."

"Should I run down and get someone from maintenance? Uncle Logan won't let us stay if we don't take care of the place."

"I fixed it up pretty good. No problem." The penthouse phone rings, and when I answer it the lobby man informs me that dinner is on its way up. Skyla sits at the table, gazing out to the ocean, her face still flushed from either her shower or coming apart on my tongue; I'm guessing the latter.

Once Callie and Skyla sit at the table, I serve dinner as they chat about music and the latest film they want to see at the movies. A strange feeling passes across my chest. Contentment? I don't know, but I like it.

I top off Skyla's wine glass three times and the atmosphere is light and fun. Skyla gets the giggles when Callie tells her about the time I had to do the dad race at her previous private school and got so competitive that I sulked for a week when I lost to one of the other dad's.

"In my defense, the guy was an Olympic athlete," I complain.

"Sure he was." Skyla laughs and pokes her little pink tongue out at me.

"Nah, he's right. Taylor Blythe, her dad was actually an Olympic medal winner. But Dad still hates to lose, which only made me and Mom laugh even more."

Callie goes quiet for a moment, twisting a tendril of her hair into the light, and then she says, "Dad, would you book me the haircut, please."

"Sure, kiddo. So long as you're sure you're ready?"

"Yeah. I think it's time." Then Callie smiles at Skyla and asks, "Do you think you could come with me? I don't want them to cut too much off."

Skyla nods and takes hold of a piece of Callie's hair. "You have beautiful hair, just like I've seen on pictures of your mother. How about we ask them to trim just an inch and you can decide how you like it before they take any more?"

"Good idea. And it'll give my dad time to adjust before I get it dyed blue."

My mouth pops open, and I'm about to warn her she better not when Skyla bursts out laughing, closely followed by Callie. "Just screwing with you, Dad."

I calm myself and then reply, "Maybe you can dye it over summer break, but I think your school would throw a fit if you showed up with blue hair."

We finish up dinner, and while I am loading the dishwasher Callie guides Skyla to the sofa and says, "Nanna, me,

Uncle Logan, Uncle Tate and Aunt Tabitha are going to go to the movie theater. I haven't seen *Top Gun* yet, but it was Grandpop's favorite. He and my dad had a disagreement, so I didn't see him much growing up, but I wonder if I watch the film, if I'll feel like I'm closer to him. What do you think?"

My chest starts to ache while I carry on loading the dishwasher and pretend like I'm not listening. But I can't hide from the truth, my feud with my late father affected Callie, no matter how much I try to pretend that she still got to have a relationship with him.

"I'm sure your family can tell you lots about him. I didn't see much of my mom growing up, but whenever anyone said something nice, it made me feel really good to know that thing about her."

"Yeah. I think my dad finds it difficult to talk about him. But I get that, I don't always want to talk about my mom, but it doesn't mean I'm not thinking about her."

I'm frozen. I didn't think Callie paid much attention to her absent Grandpa, and I especially didn't think she knew all that much about my falling out with him.

"You should come watch the movie with us. My dad won't come because he thinks Grandpa is still mad with him, but no one takes a grudge to the grave, do they?"

Skyla seems to think on this carefully, and I wonder if she is thinking about her own mother. "No. I don't think people stay angry forever. They can be hurt and still forgive a person."

Callie nods. "That's what I thought."

I'm wondering how she got to be so thoughtful, when I clatter the dishes noisily and she looks up. "Callie, you better go wash up for bed."

"But I want to stay up," she protests. "We never have guests."

She's right. I can't remember the last time we had someone that wasn't my mother over for dinner.

"Ten minutes," I compromise, then join them on the sofa. Callie pulls the throw blanket from the back of the sofa and switches the TV on to some random channel featuring teens who speak a language I don't understand, and the room falls silent of voices other than those on the television. Beneath the cover, Skyla's hand finds mine, and I find myself once again with a surprisingly contented feeling.

* * *

When I wake, Skyla is curled into the nook of my arm that's wrapped around her waist. Callie is softly snoring beside her, and outside the sky is so black I can't even see the ocean. I carefully untangle myself from Skyla and guide Callie into her bedroom, pulling the comforter over her and bidding her goodnight.

When I return to the living room, Skyla is awake.

"I didn't realize the time." She yawns. Then searches for her shoes. "I better go."

I don't want her to go.

"Stay. I mean, it's late and I can't leave Callie to walk you home." It's a ridiculous excuse since she really is only having to take the elevator and walk across the hotel grounds, but I can't stop myself from repeating, "Stay."

She glances back at the sofa.

"Stay with me, in my bed. All night," I clarify.

"But Callie," her voice waivers, raw in its sleepy state.

I take her hand and tug her toward the bedroom. "Just a grown-up sleepover."

She yawns again and sleepily pads in the direction I am pulling her. "I suppose I could be persuaded."

Inside the room, she stretches up to kiss me. Her eyes are

only partially open and she looks beat, so I unbutton her jeans and roll them down her thighs and pull them off, then I tug her T-shirt over her head. I search the drawers for my softest T-shirt, kissing each of her breasts goodnight as I pull it over her head. Then I swipe back the sheets of the bed. "In you go, sleeping beauty," I tell her and she follows my command. I slide in behind her and pull her close.

Skyla murmurs something indistinguishable, and then I whisper right back, "Sweet dreams, sweetheart."

* * *

BY THE TIME I WAKE, the bed is cold and Skyla is gone. I jump up to go look for her and notice her shoes and the bag she packed with a change of clothes is gone.

"Skyla went home?" Callie asks.

"Yeah," I reply, finding my phone at the wireless charger and swiping it to life.

"I hoped she'd stay," Callie complains, pulling a carton of orange juice from the fridge and pouring two glasses. Then she takes out her cereal and a bowl.

"Me too," I say but the words stick in my throat.

When I sit down at the table with my juice, I check my emails—one is from Skyla, sent at 5 a.m. this morning.

To: Drew Blingwood

From: Skyla Manning

Subject: Thank-you for a lovely evening.

You were sleeping so soundly and looked so adorable that I couldn't bear to wake you so I snuck out before Callie woke. XX

213

. . .

Two XX's. I know they're standard, mechanical digital kisses that don't mean shit, but they have me grinning like a damn fool. And that is when I begin to suspect I am in deep shit.

CHAPTER 21

SKYLA

"When were you going to tell me?!" Jessie hisses, storming into my office with a stack of toilet paper balanced beneath her arm.

"I only just had the paperwork confirmed."

Jessie plops herself down on the seat opposite my desk and five rolls of toilet paper roll across the marble. "Why? I thought you loved it here."

"I do love it here. But I feel like a fresh start might be good for me."

Jessie cocks her brow and a murderous expression falls on her delicate features. "This is about Mike, isn't it? Or Drew, is it about Drew because I thought that was all cleared up? If it's about the FedEx guy…."

I let out a strangled laugh. "I only accepted the phone number of the FedEx guy out of politeness. I never called him." My cheeks warm. "I wish I'd never mentioned to the cafeteria staff I did that. Gossip spreads like wildfire in this place!" The list she reeled off is the exact confirmation of why I should start over. After all when things end with Drew, it's going to take every ounce of my restraint not to beg him to reconsider our arrangement, and he has made it clear that is not what he signed up for. Sticking around, once our fling is over, is going to be impossible. "Maybe I need a change of scenery. A place where I don't have history with any guys. People think I'm blowing through the guys in this place—"

"Skyla, I need you to—" Mike walks into my office unannounced and stares from Jessie to me. "From the conversation I walked in on, I guess it really is true what they say. It's the quiet ones you have to watch." He chuckles and dumps a pile of papers on my desk.

"What do you want?" I glare while also holding my palm out to steady Jessie from tearing his head off.

"Wage projections. You'll either need to cut down on staff or pay them less at the new resort." He throws his hands in the air. "Don't care. Not my problem. You deal with it. Though, sounds like you've already been dealing with quite a lot, of cock—"

Jessie is up out of her chair while I try to get between her and Mike before all hell breaks loose. "How dare you slut shame my friend, you needle-dicked moron!" She lurches toward him, fists balled. Mike takes a step back and holds his hands out ready to defend himself.

My money is on Jessie.

I stand between them, arms outstretched and pray that one of them will back down.

"You can't speak to me this way. I'm a member of management. You're going to be in trouble for this," Mike says to Jessie.

Little does he know that Jessie is also now a "member of management," as if that has anything to do with his complete lack of professionalism. As soon as that thought crosses my mind, Jessie mimics his entire sentence in a baby voice. "You're a *member*, all right. Go penetrate yourself with one of your little Spock dolls."

"They are not dolls!" He narrows his eyes and taps his index finger on his chin as he thinks. Then, hit by realization, he points said finger at Jessie. "It was you, wasn't it?!"

I look at Jessie, confused. She's smirking like whatever *it* was, was her.

"You put Admiral James T. Kirk in the men's urinal, face down!" Mike accuses.

Jessie grins. "Prove it, limp dick!"

Mike gasps. "You subscribed my email address to *erectile dysfunction* newsletters, didn't you?"

I bite my lip to hide my nervous smile. It sounds like something Jessie might do.

"You'd better have proof if you're going to make such accusations, Mike. And for the record, Jessie is a new member of management, she got promoted," I reply, intervening.

Mike turns to me, so angry his cheeks are red. "You're the HR Manager, and you know she's guilty as hell of... of... damaging personal property, misusing work email addresses, crass language." He throws his hands on his hips pathetically. "I want her fired for this."

To my left, Jessie is scratching her chin with her middle finger. To my right, Mike looks like he is about to sponta-neously combust.

I sigh. "And I want calorie-free cupcakes, Mike, but that isn't gonna happen either. You're not entirely innocent in this scenario—bursting into my office and verbally shaming me. It's probably best, don't you think, to go back to your own office and forget all about this unpleasantness."

"Skyla, you know what she did. She's been pranking me, messing with my stuff! The IT guy thinks I have," he lowers his voice to a whisper, *"erectile dysfunction!"* Saying the phrase seems to only make him angrier. "I want her fired."

I recall all the times I had the opportunity to have him fired but resisted, and anger flares in my gut. No way he's getting my friend fired.

"Let me make a few things clear to you, Mike, about your own conduct. First, you violated 6.1 of the Blingwood Resort company policy regarding privacy: knock before entering. Second, you violated 9.4 of the ethics code of conduct: Employees should respect coworkers, customers and other stakeholders—which includes character shaming. Third," I say, ticking off my fingers, "Code 9.5: managers must not abuse their position—by irresponsibly delegating your own work to other employees, AKA me. Are we on four or five now?"

Jessie interjects, "That would be four!"

"Section 4.09: Company property is not to be used for personal purposes. I know and have proof you've been selling geek war items on eBay during work hours and using company packaging, and then there's policy 14.07: adhering to strict standards of professionalism at all times. Was it professional curiosity that had you removing a colleague's skirt in the closet? Shall I continue?"

Without even looking at her, I can feel the heat of Jessie's grin lighting up with pride.

"Better go, Mike. Before you get tattled on," Jessie sings in a tone that I mostly recognize as pungent sarcasm.

"You're a bitch, you know that, Jessie," he spits back, while backing toward the door. "And you," he diverts his glare to me, "you're the office mattress, and you don't even put out!"

"Not for you, I don't. But guess what? I do for the right guy. Get out of my office and take *your* work with you, because I am not hiring less people than is required for the job, and I won't offer less pay than the going rate. Do the math and take the figures to Logan!" I hiss. And while Mike takes that as his cue to leave, Jessie bends down and throws a roll of toilet paper at his head.

"The nerve of that guy. I'd like to—"

"It's fine," I reassure her. "I don't care what he thinks. I'm just grossed out, I almost went there." I return to my seat and Jessie follows, sitting opposite me at my desk, grinning her face off. "Did you really do all that stuff?"

"Are you asking as Skyla Manning, BFF for life, or as Skyla Manning, HR Manager?"

My smile replaces any semblance of professionalism.

"Okay, I might have accidentally dropped something once or twice, but he deserved it. But the funniest thing is, I replaced the photo of his sister with a picture of Chewbacca and he hasn't even noticed!"

Involuntary laughter rolls through me until tears are streaming down my face. "The resemblance is uncanny, right?!"

"It is!" Our chuckles ramp up to belly laughs. When we're both breathing normally, her face turns serious and she says, "You're not a slut—not that there is anything wrong with satisfying your sexual needs with whomever you choose, however you choose."

"I know," I reply, looking away.

"Skyla, look at me." I do as she says. It's impossible to believe that even with her fun and vibrant personality, and her striking blue eyes and perfect, shiny blonde hair, she was left pregnant and single and has since chosen not to date. Jessie leans forward, and takes ahold of my hand that rests on the desk. "I mean it. You don't have to start over. The only person who has a negative opinion about you is Mike, and his brain is pathetically immature and underdeveloped. Macy has more brain cells than him."

"She is super smart."

"I know, right?! And so are you. You haven't done a single thing wrong, so why are you transferring?"

"I'll still see you—"

"You better!"

"I will and you can bring Macy to stay with me. This thing with me and Drew is only temporary while we get it out of our systems. And then I'll be so busy getting the staff up and running at the new resort. I can't trust anyone else to do it, not like I can. And I owe Logan that. He promoted me even though I only had assistant experience, and he put his trust in me. As you know, a resort is only as good as its employees—"

"And you found the best—bar Mike. You don't need to go anywhere or prove anything."

"I know. Who knows, maybe one day I'll ask to transfer back, but for now, this seems like a good decision." And also, because I know that when things end with Drew, it will hurt. Getting over him is not going to be easy.

"Think on it some more. You still have time."

"I'm interviewing this afternoon for my replacement here. Whoever gets the job will need time to learn the ropes before I go."

"Maybe you can send the new person to the new resort if you change your mind?"

"Maybe," I reply, absentminded. "We'll see."

"Maybe it'll work out with Drew?"

"No. He's made it clear this thing between us is temporary. I don't want to overstay my welcome."

"So, you're into him?"

I nod. "I tried not to be, but it's getting harder not to care about him and Callie."

"Have you told him how you feel?"

"And have him freak out and run for the hills? No."

"What if he didn't freak out?"

"Oh, he'd freak out. Trust me, we've gone down that road already. And that's okay. I knew what I was getting myself into and I agreed to it wholeheartedly. The timing of the new start is perfect. It'll provide a clear exit to our arrangement and manage everyone's expectations. Callie is becoming fond of me, but I hope her knowing I am transitory will prepare her. I'm *temporary*. It's in everyone's best interests."

"Including yours?"

"Including mine," I reply, inserting more enthusiasm into my voice than my heart feels comfortable with.

* * *

LATER THAT WEEK, I'm going over the numbers with Logan in his office.

"So you see, with the addition of another restaurant, the beach kiosk, sailing center, and the expanded club house, the new resort won't be like-for-like. We'll need a much bigger staffing budget or else it won't work. We can't pay people less or expect them to work harder."

Logan stops staring at the projections on the screen and turns to face me. "I know, I already explained this to Mike."

"Oh. He sent back the paperwork with the same budget projections as we have here."

"Did he, now? Guess he couldn't be bothered to do his damn job." Logan bolts to standing. "Skyla, you finish up for the day. Seems like you already did more than your fair share of the work. I'm going to talk to Mike." Logan snatches up his papers and leaves the room, while I wonder what the hell I am going to do with the rest of the afternoon off.

CHAPTER 22

DREW

allie:

Hey Dad. I'll be home late. Going to the salon
with Skyla.

I GOT the message an hour ago and have been sitting in my
car, outside the salon, watching Skyla holding Callie's hand.

Every time Callie stands and twirls in front of the mirror,
she sits back down and the stylist starts trimming again.
She's gone from hair that reaches her hips, to elbow length,
and though I am impressed, I am also starting to worry she
might freak out after this is all done.

When I see them heading to pay, I get out of the car and
rush inside.

My Amex card poised in my hand, I reach across the counter and say, "I'll pay."

"What are you doing here? No, you won't. It's my treat," Skyla says, and only then do I truly drink her in.

"Your hair. It's..." Softer looking, lighter, smells like coconut and vanilla, even from two steps away. "You look..." *Mesmerizing, beautiful, sophisticated, stunning.* "It's..." *alluring, fascinating, gorgeous...* "I mean, you... lovely," I settle on, since I seem to have lost the skill of sentence structure.

Skyla grins. "Thank-you. But the showstopper is..." She gestures her hand to Callie who steps forward.

"Wow. Callie, baby. You look so grown up."

"I'm not a baby, Dad. The stylist gave me a teen style. And now I look at least a year older."

"Oh." I turn back to Skyla and my smile widens. "A year older. Should I search for a fake ID?"

"I think you're safe." Skyla winks and my heart thumps in my chest. "We were about to go get milkshakes to celebrate. If that's okay with you?"

"Sure. Where are we going?"

"*We* are going to the place across the street. *You* can go back to stalking us from your car," Callie says.

I lower my voice and say to Skyla, "I got busted?"

"Oh, yeah. Someone was pretty peeved to see her daddy watching from the car." She holds her hand over her mouth and adds, "I thought it was sweet."

"I am very sweet." I wink and Skyla giggles.

"Urgh. Fine, you can come. But try not to be weird, Dad."

I mouth the word, *weird*, and thumb my chest then follow my ladies across the street, strangely glad to be a part of their day. We order milkshakes and I stare in wonder as Callie's hair swooshes over her shoulder and she shines so brightly it's like the treatment went all the way to her soul. She looks bone-deep happy. Untethered by the weight of loss and sadness that I am used to seeing her try to hide. I suppose it's been a gradual healing, but today she's blooming like a fresh rose in summer with no indication of how harsh the winter has been.

"Mom always said, a haircut isn't just a haircut. It's a rebirth. It washes out the old and spawns a brand-new person." She runs her fingers through her hair and adds, "I think she was right. I feel so… rejuvenated."

My hand itches to creep to Callie's but she's sitting so confidently, that the action, for the first time, feels redundant. "Remember what the therapist said, 'grief comes in waves but make sure to enjoy the good days.'"

"Today is a good day," Callie confirms.

Skyla runs her fingers through her own hair. "I think your mom was right. You took a big step today, and I bet she's super proud of you, just like your dad is."

"What about you? Do you like your new style? I love it, and my dad can't stop staring at you so I think it's *obvious* he likes it." She rolls her eyes at me, and Skyla laughs.

"You remind me of me at your age," Skyla tells Callie. "I was always thoroughly and affectionately embarrassed by everything my dad did. But you know, as weird as your dad is," I pout, affronted, and Skyla winks at me good-naturedly, "I think you hit the jackpot."

The compliment takes me by surprise, but I'm even more flabbergasted when Callie agrees, "I know I did." And then Callie reaches across and squeezes my hand for a second before sucking the last sips of her milkshake through the straw.

I'm hit by a deep feeling of sheer, overwhelming happiness. It's energizing, and I immediately want to capitalize on the moment before anything can change or dull the urgency. "We should celebrate. Let's go out for dinner."

"Dad, I can't. I'm going to Nanna's. She's teaching me piano. I did tell you."

"Oh. Shoot. Yeah, I remember. Another time, then?" Penciling in a date suddenly feels urgent so I add, "Tomorrow then. Or the next night."

"You should take Skyla out for dinner. She had a kick-ass day at work and deserves a treat too."

I ignore the cussing and glance at Skyla whose cheeks have flushed deliciously. "It was nothing."

"It was something, Dad. There's this guy she hates at work, and she stood up to him," Callie says.

"Oh?"

Even though she shrugs, I can tell she's feeling proud of herself. "Is this a certain someone that I'm aware of? Do I need to go kick his ass?"

She nods, then shakes her head. But her smile is all the confirmation I need that she's okay—she's better than okay.

"Good for you! This definitely calls for a celebration. Let's drop Callie off and then I'll take you to dinner. Callie can join us tomorrow night." And even though I've made plans, and a follow-up date, it doesn't seem enough. If she's relocating to Miami in a few weeks, I'm going to need to make sure I don't waste any of the time I get with her. "And obviously there's our regular Tuesday Pilates."

"Dad, you're joining our class?" Callie sounds elated, and since I can't admit I only like to go so I can admire Skyla's butt, I find myself agreeing.

"I can't wait to see you in Lycra," Skyla says, throwing me a heated gaze.

"I can wear regular workout gear, can't I?" It'd be hard to hide a stiffy beneath Lycra. I'd probably get arrested.

Skyla shakes her head. "Oh no. You're going to need the whole thing if you are to make the most of the workout.

Belly top. Tight, tight, fabric. You want to be able to see the work you are doing."

My expression must be horrified because Skyla lets out a loud, long giggle that Callie matches. "She's screwing with you Dad; you can wear whatever you want."

I let out a held breath. "Good. Loose clothes are definitely preferable."

CHAPTER 23

SKYLA

*W*e stumble on a place in the next town. Finding it by sheer chance, Drew explains, "I forgot this place was here. Mom and Dad used to bring us when there was something worth celebrating." He looks unsure, nervous, and I'm not sure if it's cause by being alone with me or visiting a place that means something to him. Either way, we've been driving out of town for a half an hour and the place looks charming, set back from the road with rustic, wooden cladding.

"Looks good to me," I reply, noncommittally.

"I think you'll like it, but as I say, it's not award winning or anything."

He turns left and I reassure him, "I'm not exactly used to award winning food. If they sell fries, I'll be quite content."

Drew smiles at me, his eyes lingering for a beat too long and my heart completely overreacts.

"I think fries will be available. Maybe I can even throw in an ice cream, if you're a good girl."

Momentarily, he clamps his teeth down onto his lower lip and shakes his head.

"What?" I ask.

He pulls the car into a space and switches off the engine, cocking a brow at me. "Good girl." He shakes his head again.

"What? I'm always a good girl, or didn't you notice?" My voice sounds sultry. Seductive.

Drew's eyes darken and he sighs. "I noticed all right. You're going to be the death of me."

"There's loads of life left in you yet. What is it they say, you're only as young as the woman you're feeling."

His hand reaches across and cups mine. "Twenty-four. You know, at your age, I became a father. I started my own business that same year." For a moment, I wonder if he thinks me lacking but his deep brown eyes fix on mine with a curious, interested stare. "You're more mature than I was at your age. The head of a department at a prestigious resort, hell, you're probably more mature than I am now. It's impressive. You are impressive." Drew nods, genuinely looking awestruck by me. And aroused.

It takes me a moment to respond. An unfamiliar sense of pride pulses through me and it's not until my cheeks begin to ache that I realize I am grinning my damn face off. "Thank-you. I've done all right, haven't I?"

"Better than all right. Skyla, everyone at Blingwood adores you. I even had some guy called Doug warn me that I better not let you down this time. He also asked me if I like bingo." He chuckles. "I can honestly say I've never been so fearful."

I chuckle. "Fearful? Over Doug's threats or going to bingo?"

He laughs too and the conversation feels so easy, here

with Drew, as dusk falls, sitting in his car, talking. "Bingo, obviously. I could totally take that dude if I had to." His jaw tenses. "But I don't want to hurt you again."

"You won't," I say much too quickly. I'm already trying to mentally prepare myself for when our temporary agreement ends. But I'm a binger. I eat the second and third slice of cake and deal with the indigestion after. I watch an entire season of my favorite show, and then go cold turkey waiting a year for the next one. This is like that. Some things are too good to pass up in the moment, and spending time with Drew is one of them. "I'm not naive. This is temporary, right? I know that." My voice is so light, it doesn't even sound like mine as I assure him that I've got this. His expression is still serious and the way he's watching me too closely is making me feel nervous that he's having second thoughts.

"You're an amazing woman."

Adrenaline pulses beneath my skin. He leans forward and pushes my hair back, cupping the back of my neck, gently pulling me toward him until his lips graze mine. Drew kisses me achingly slowly, dipping his tongue and stroking it against mine. My whole body warms and reacts. Too soon he pulls away, and his forehead rests against mine. "I wish I could offer you everything you desire."

I wish you could too.

"Right now, I desire fries. And maybe ice cream, *if I'm a good enough girl.*" I pull away and wink at him and he grins.

"Who am I to stand between a woman and her heart's desire." He gets out and before I have even collected my purse from the floor of the car, Drew is there, opening the door and holding out his hand, taking mine in his.

It's just dinner, I remind myself. It's to say thank-you for taking Callie to get her haircut and to celebrate another step forward for us both, but I can't help buying into the feeling that it is so much more.

* * *

THE RESTAURANT IS AN INFORMAL PLACE, a wooden building in an isolated spot overlooking the ocean. We sit on the deck at a table for two, lit by oversized storm candles. We order seafood with a side of fries, Drew picks out the wine, and being midweek, the restaurant is not at capacity. In fact in our little corner, it's like we have the entire place to ourselves. Or maybe it's that I can't take my eyes off Drew for long enough to notice other diners.

"Did you have a good time with Callie today?" he asks.

"We had a great time. She's an amazing kid. I could tell she was nervous; her hand squeezed mine so hard I almost lost a finger when the stylist made the first cut, and she told Nadia four times not to get scissor happy. But I think once she committed, Callie took it in her stride, only checking with me a couple of times that the hair falling to the floor wasn't too much."

Drew nods and temples his fingers as he leans into me. "She adores you."

I adore her too. She's like my little sidekick and her sense of humor is off the charts. But I worry she likes me too much for someone who is passing through her life. "Should I remind her that I'll be leaving? I don't want her to feel blindsided when I go, like I suddenly abandoned her."

He frowns. "I have noticed she seems rather taken with you. Leave it to me. I'll speak to her. She'll be disappointed, but I'm sure she'll understand." He fiddles with his napkin, looking decidedly unsure.

"She's adorable. When I think what she's been through…."

"It's been tough on her. She doesn't know much about me and Crystal as a couple. We split when she was young and we shared custody, taking alternate weeks. It was only when I had her full-time in the aftermath of her mother's death that I truly realized what I'd been missing out on."

"Why did you and Crystal break up?"

"I..."

"You don't have to tell me. I didn't mean to pry."

"No," he says. "I want to tell you. But I don't want you to think I'm an asshole." He tops off both our glasses while he thinks. "I already told you my dad wanted me to be involved with the resort." I nod. "He inherited the resort from his father. Of course, back then it was much smaller. Dad rebuilt it, added to it, made it into something better. Something you'd be proud to say you developed." His dad did a great job. The Blingwood Resort is renowned. It's unrivaled luxury.

"I can see that he'd be proud of it and want to hand it to his children," I add.

"Logan ate, slept, and breathed the place. He still does. I think that's why the second resort is so important to him. To further build on what Dad did, but create his own identity as well."

"But you took a different path."

"Yes. He was angry when I said I wanted something different. And when Dad told me my dream wasn't an option, I dug my heels in like we Blingwood's do, studied hard and graduated top of my architecture class, but that wasn't enough to prove to my dad I was serious, so I started my own company. And then I worked until it was the best, and somewhere in all that, I met Crystal and we had Callie. I wasn't a good husband. I was so single-minded to prove my father wrong, that I worked too hard and wasn't around when it mattered. Back then, Crystal was making a name for herself and her own business, so it was easy not to notice the cracks in our relationship. But eventually, the foundations started to crumble and Crystal gave me an ultimatum, cut back on work or cut back on her. I chose work over her. I won best new and up and coming architect in New York. Suddenly I was busier than ever, and I realized I had to hire more people if I was going to grow the brand like I wanted to. So, in a way, it worked out. My marriage ending enabled me to work on my business, and then growing my company gave me the time to devote to our new shared custody arrangement. I tried hard at working my business life around Callie." He sighs. "At least, I like to think that's how it was. I had to hire a nanny, and I wonder now, looking back on it how present I really was." Drew stops talking and for a moment, it's like he's trapped inside his own head, his expression punishing.

I slide my hand across the table, placing it over his and he looks up. "You were present. Take it from someone who knows absent parenting. You did your best. And then when you didn't think that was enough, you made changes. You brought Callie here, and you're revolving your entire life around her needs. Give yourself a break. She's a healthy, well-adjusted kid—as much as any kid is."

Drew's head tips to the side, still unsure. He turns my hand in his until it is palm up and he idly strokes it with his other hand. "I was there every other week, and then suddenly Crystal wasn't, and I was doing it on my own. It felt like I was treading water. Spinning too many plates, waiting for them all to come crashing down, but I couldn't give in. I couldn't ask for help from my family—my pride wouldn't allow it." He stares down at my palm, holding it carefully like it might break. "Then my dad died. I'd spent my entire adulthood trying to prove to him I could do everything on my own terms, to show him. And suddenly none of it mattered anymore because he wasn't there to witness it and give me his approval. And that's what it took for me to realize I'd been going about everything all wrong. What mattered was having a stable enough income to provide for my daughter and to be present in her life. And I'd been functioning solely to serve my own ego."

Drew slowly lifts his head to mine. "I'm sorry. I seem to have mistaken our date for a therapy session."

"Drew, nobody goes through life perfectly, making zero mistakes. Sounds to me like you realized you were spread too thin and you acted accordingly—"

"You mean, I was stubborn, wrecked my relationship with my father, worked too much, and maybe realized in the nick of time to save my relationship with my daughter—though that remains to be seen."

I turn my hand over and squeeze his. "No. I mean you're human. You're running a multi-million dollar company, and you're the best in the business. You're raising an incredible young woman and putting her first."

His lips twitch and his gaze darkens. "I really want to kiss you right now."

My own lips tip up in response. "I want to let you."

"Stand up."

"Here?" I glance around. The place is quiet with just one server attending to a couple at the other end of the deck.

Drew stands and walks around the table, pulling me to standing. He stoops his head while I tilt my chin up to him. His arms wrap around my waist, pulling me in tightly until there is no part of us separate. My heart goes wild and all I feel is the perfection of the moment running through us like a current.

The sound of a throat clearing has us breaking the kiss and chuckling like naughty teenagers.

"Can I get anyone dessert?"

We both laugh again.

"I'll take the check, please," Drew says. "And a tub of your finest ice cream to go."

CHAPTER 24

DREW

By the time I have Skyla back at her place, I am raging with desire.

"Thank-you for a perfect evening," she says over her shoulder, walking inside.

My chest reacts by clenching painfully. I'm not ready to say goodbye yet. I still want more. She turns to face me and pouts as she takes me in.

I'm leaning against the doorframe, waiting for an invitation and so eager, I'll beg for a goodnight kiss if I have to.

"You coming in?" she asks, and I don't wait to be asked a second time.

The second the door is closed, I pull her to me and run my fingers into her silky hair that's the color of spun gold. "I'm glad you had a nice evening."

"The evening is not over yet," she replies, leaning forward and pressing her soft, fleshy body against my own hard exterior. Her throat bobs as she feels how hard I am against her lower belly and she looks up at me through thick, dark lashes then bites down on her lip. It's such a sexy gesture, my cock becomes throttled in my pants.

"You still want the ice cream you insisted we take from the restaurant?" She cocks her head and a growl forces its way past my lips.

"I could definitely be tempted by something sweet. Should I get a spoon?"

She takes a step back and holds the tub in her hands higher, out of my reach. Her grin is a mischievous mix of nerves and sheer bravado, and I like it so much a bead of pride spills from my cock.

"Drew, to be clear, I am asking if you want to eat this ice cream from my body. No spoon required."

"Yes!" I lift her in one swoop, straight up and over my shoulder. I've taken the tub from her hand and am pinning her with my other hand by her ass as I take long strides into her bedroom. Thankfully it's not far to go before I am able to unbutton her dress and splay her out on the bed before me. By the time I have peeled off my own clothes and popped the lid of the ice cream, I am seriously wondering why I have never involved food in the bedroom before. Two of life's pleasures, combined for double the pleasure. "This was a great idea."

My erection is engorged to the point of pain and ready to explode, but it'll have to wait until I've eaten. With two fingers, I scoop out a generous helping of the softened ice cream. "You ready?"

"God, yes," she replies.

Skyla's back arches and she hisses as I smear the sweetened cream over her hard, pebbled nipples. When my mouth cups her breast, she pushes forward, offering me more. The taste is so sweet, the texture beneath divine. "My sweet, sweet, sugar." I take another two fingers of the dessert and lower my body down the bed until I have perfect access to her core. "Now for the most decadent of tastes. You don't need sweetening, sweetheart, but what my woman wants, she gets." Her back bucks from the mattress as I rub my cool fingers over her bundle of nerves and she almost comes right there, but I'm not ready for her to come yet. I want to enjoy this for a while longer, so I use my other hand to hold her down against the bed. "Not so fast, Miss Manning. A man should not be rushed when he is enjoying his meal."

"I—" she starts, but is silenced as my tongue rims her delicate bud. "Oh fuck. I think—"

I pull away and she gasps. "No thinking. No coming yet either." My cool breath blows against her sensitive spot and my eyes light as it plumps.

"Please…."

"Not yet, sugar."

I resume my torment, swirling my tongue, then pumping my fingers, only to retreat right as she approaches the peak. I do this a few times; the power it affords me has my cock threatening to burst, but the payoff of watching Skyla come apart more violently than ever will be worth our patience.

Building her back up, I know she can't take much more, so I suck and circle my tongue, pump her with my fingers, bending them in just the right way to hit the sweet spot that's been hidden from everyone but me. I slow the pace, then start the ascent all over again and her body stiffens. Her legs kick out like she's possessed and her fingers grab onto my hair. I can almost feel the tension from her body as it oscillates from losing control entirely, to keeping some type of composure, and it's making my cock ready to combust.

"Please. God, please. Drew. I need… I need… I need you. Now!"

I'm tempted to make her beg some more. The sound is a

bolt of pleasure, but the need to bury myself deep inside her is taking over my frayed will power.

"Thank God," she pants as my cock drives into her all the way to the hilt.

"You can thank God if you like, but it's me who is about to make you come."

I thrust once, twice, three times, so desperate am I to shoot my load and fill her up, but I push aside the craving and focus on her face.

"You're making me so hot. Drew... I'm going to... come," she pants as she reaches orgasm.

The slippery friction is the perfect blend of heat and pressure as I continue to pump her flesh. Watching her eyes flutter and her mouth pop open, I push my thumb in the pint of ice cream, then slide it into her mouth and watch her eyes come alive as she sucks.

"My baby wants ice cream she fucking gets ice cream."

The pull of her mouth and the draw of her clenching pussy milking me is too much. Intense sensation has my balls spasming and threatening to explode.

"Baby, you're going to make me—"

"God, I am going to—"

We cling to each other like we are the only humans on earth and this is the only purpose for our existence. There is nothing else. Just Skyla and me, riding out wave upon wave of pleasure. She fists my hair, my hands grip the flesh of her ass to lever myself to her and keep up the rhythm until we are both slick with sweat and coming loud and hard, and it's sweet perfection.

Crashes and waves turn to sweet ripples. Every drip of power becomes spent and my head drops between her breasts. Nuzzled inside such beauty, there is no better place. Skyla's clenches still, her breathing steadies, and when I look up into her eyes, my heart stops beating.

She's mesmerizingly flawless. "Perfection. You are incredible." I lean up to kiss the top of her head and lick my lips enjoying the salt that follows the sweetness.

She chuckles lightly, and with me still inside her, it sends a rippling tingle back into my cock that has me readying to go again. *Will I ever be satiated?* It's hard to imagine.

"That was epic. Who knew burning calories while enjoying dessert could be such fun."

"Fun is one word for it." Though I have a million others, but the burning feeling—from the endorphins probably—is love. I loved it. "Baby, I don't think I'll ever be able to eat dessert any other way. You've ruined other desserts for me now."

"Then I am at your disposal any time you desire something sweet."

"I'm holding you to that."

"Please hold it against me often." She grins wickedly. I could stay here forever, looking at her, inside of her, enjoying her. The thought is thrilling and terrifying all at the same time. She's more woman than I was prepared to experience. More than I expected and yet somehow not enough. I need more. One or even many tastes will never be enough.

And so, with renewed vigor, I take her mouth with mine and prepare for seconds, shelving all thoughts of my new addiction and focusing on my next big hit.

* * *

"You look aberrantly happy," Logan says the following Monday, mirthlessly scrunching his face like smiling is a crime.

It takes conscious effort to relax my cheeks and pull my mouth into a straight line, but then I decide, fuck it, I'm happy and I'm letting it show. "So, life's good right now. Shoot me."

Logan rolls his eyes and walks over to the window where he puts his hands on his hips. When something catches his interest, he moves closer, pulling apart the blinds so he can see better. "Damn it!"

I follow his gaze and see Dana leaving the spa through the side exit near the sauna.

"What's the problem?"

"Nothing. She..." He turns away from the window and returns to seat himself at his desk, busying himself by punching his finger down on his computer mouse five times.

"She's not supposed to be using the sauna while pregnant?" I guess.

There's a tick in Logan's jaw. He looks royally pissed until something through the open door of his office catches his attention and he forces an easy smile onto his face.

"Hi, favorite niece."

"Hi!" Callie responds, waltzing in, dumping herself down on the leather couch and slinging her feet up on the arm rest. "Guess what?"

Logan raises his eyebrows in anticipation of groundbreaking news.

"Ben Bartlett got a dog! They're not waiting for the pups from the new litter to be old enough. His mom went to see Nanna and now they've got a two-year old Pug-Zu named Tilly."

"A Pug-Zu?" Logan asks, and I throw Callie a warning look for two reasons. One, I already know where this conversation is going, and two, she knows the answer is no.

"It's a Pug and a Shih tzu mix. A Pug-Zu!"

"A Shih tzu cross Pug. Interesting. Some might call it a Shit-Pug," Logan mutters, his mood not entirely recovered from seeing Dana make yet another crap choice.

"Ha! A Shit-Pug, I have got to tell Ben. He'll think it's hilarious and no one can tell us off for cussing because it's just a phrase to describe a combination of dog breeds."

"You ready?" I ask Callie to swiftly move the conversation along. She's grinning at Logan like he told the best damn joke in the world.

"To go get a dog of our own? Hell, yeah, I am!"

I ignore the mild cuss and focus on the more important problem. "No, Callie, and we've had this discussion." It's like talking to a brick wall.

"Where are you going?" Logan asks.

"We're going to see the new house. The walls are up and the roof is on. There's still no kitchen installed but Dad says it'll be done before we move in next month. I want to pick my room before this one gets first dibs," she replies, motioning her thumb in my direction.

"You already know which room is yours. Two master suites, you chose the east one. You helped me design the entire building," I deadpan.

"Yeah, but it might look different in real life, and I'm reserving the right to switch rooms if I like yours better."

I shrug. The fact that Callie is invested in the new property enough to be excited to pick a room has me uncaring which bedroom I take—hell, I'd sleep on the porch if it put a smile on her face. Still, I can't help remind her, "Both the masters are mirror images of each other. Same footprint, same en suite master baths and walk-ins. The only discernible difference between the two rooms is that one will capture the sunrise and the other will catch the sunset."

Callie nods. There's a contemplative look on her face that has me bracing myself for what's she's going to say next. "I might choose the room nearest the outside door so it's easier to let the dog out to go potty."

"Not getting a dog, Callie. Allergies," I assert, again.

"How are your allergies? Haven't seen them flare up in like, twenty years?" Logan questions annoyingly and I throw him a screw-you glare.

"That's because I stay well away from anything with fur," I remind him.

"Nanna says you drank coconut juice once when you were a kid on vacation and now you think everything is going to set it off. It's all in your head, Dad."

"My allergy is real, Callie. Just as real as Uncle Logan's allergy to soy."

"Except my allergy is actually serious, whereas yours is a ploy to avoid anything you don't want to do." Logan folds his arms over his chest. "You know there's no scientific link between dogs and coconuts, right? If the kid wants a dog, get her a dog. I'll even pay for its upkeep."

Logan and Callie share a look and I hiss at them both. "No dog. End of discussion. Let's go!" I gesture to the door and Callie stands, throwing her backpack over her shoulder.

"Tomorrow I'm going over to Ben's with Nanna to see how Tilly is settling in. You could go sit with the puppies while we're gone. Two minutes with them, and I swear you'll change your mind..." She's got that pleading look in her eyes that makes me want to give her the world but I'm standing firm. Dogs, while cute, live on average a decade, and that's if they don't go and get run over, drown, eat something poisonous or be unlucky and end up with some incurable disease. I brought Callie to my hometown to ensure her happiness, I'm not risking another loss.

"No," I reply.

"Fine. But when I go off to college and you wind up a lonely old man, don't say I didn't warn you."

"Honey, you don't need to worry. By the time you go to college, I'm going to be in need of the peace and quiet. I'll be the happiest *lonely old man* on the planet. Let's go!"

I hold the door open and tell Logan we'll see him later, but his mind seems far away as he stares in the direction of the window, probably wondering what the hell he is going to do with his fiancée.

I lead Callie through the corridors, taking the route past Skyla's office before I even think of going a different way.

"Skyla!" Callie's face lights up the minute she sees her locking the door to her office. "You finished work?"

Skyla's wearing a knee-length red skirt with a floaty blouse that perfectly emphasizes her breasts that not very long ago, I was licking ice cream from.

"Yeah. I'm going to hit the pool and eat, maybe grab an ice cream after, if you'd like to join me?" Skyla asks, pulling her mouth into a rueful smile.

"We're going to see the new house and then after we're going through a drive-thru. Come with us!"

"Oh, I…" She looks at me like she thinks she's infringing, but I'm excited to show Skyla the house, so I wrap my arm over her shoulder and say, "That's settled." And since Skyla puts up no fight at all, I lead them both outside to the car.

* * *

"So, THIS WILL BE MY ROOM." Callie waves her hand around the empty shell of a space. "It's going to get the sunrise every morning. My bed will go here…," Callie continues, but I'm too busy staring at Skyla to pay much attention. I hadn't realized how much I wanted her to like the house until I notice the impressed look on her face that has me bursting with pride.

We follow Callie to the room that will be mine, and Callie tells her all about the sunsets and how when we first viewed the land, the sky was a brilliant orange. Suddenly I can envision the room with perfect clarity, and Skyla is in it, laying back on the bed as the room is flooded with the warm effervescent rays of a setting sun.

"You listening, Dad?" Callie asks.

No. I'm too busy thinking with my cock.

"Sorry, honey. I was miles away. What were you saying?"

I loop an arm around Skyla's waist and check, "You like it?"

"The house has a homey feel even with the modern design. When it's decorated, it'll be incredible. I love it," she replies through seductive lips and electricity runs through me.

"I said," Callie says loudly, over her shoulder as she's leading us out to the concrete and mahogany spiral staircase that overlooks the entry hall and gesturing to the guest suite, "this is our next chapter. Our new home. And Skyla can stay over all the time since we've got plenty of spare rooms."

While Callie is out of earshot, I examine Skyla's face. Her smile has gone and in its place is a look of concern.

Skyla lowers her voice to me. "Didn't you tell her I'm leaving? Callie seems to think I'm going to be around in this next chapter of yours."

"I didn't get around to it yet," I reply, self-consciously rubbing the back of my neck as her eyes complete a search of mine. I don't like seeing the smile gone from her face, so I grin and hope it's catching. "That's still two weeks away. I could mention it now, but the mood is so good, I don't want to spoil it. I'll do it. I will. Leave it to me."

Skyla nods, her mouth pulled into a barely there smile.

Callie stops walking and stares back at us. I casually drop my hand from Skyla's waist and step away.

"The kitchen will be through here. We're going to have cabinetry all the way along this wall and a great big island that will seat eight. Of course, Dad will probably need to learn to cook if we are going to have you over for dinner."

Then she turns to me with a face I'm coming to recognize and I brace waiting for it… "I also thought of another reason why it's important we have a dog. For security."

And before I can say a thing, the traitor I've been sleeping with pipes up. "Oh, I think she's right. All this house, you'll need security." Skyla joyfully waggles her brows.

"There's a fifteen-thousand-dollar home security system getting installed," I inform them both. "I think that will protect us better than one of the mongrel pups you've got your eye on."

"They're not mongrels!" Callie hisses. "Pixie is a great Lab."

"Pixie?" I deadpan. "Mom let you name one?"

"What a beautiful name," Skyla adds, a cute grin pulling her lips up at the edges.

"She's so smart. Pixie can sit and stand, and walk, and…"

"I can't believe she let you name one." I'm going to need to have a talk with my mother.

"They need names, Dad. How else will they know who they are. Identity is important."

"Callie," I sigh, exasperated. "For the last time—"

"I know. Allergies. Urgh! Dad, you're such a grouch! "

"It's a serious—"

"You are a bit of a grouch," Skyla interjects.

"Oh, really?" I move closer and whisper in her ear, "I don't remember you calling me a grouch last night." The length of her neck pinkens deliciously and I have the sudden urge to run my tongue along it.

"We'll keep working on him," Callie says, wandering out through the gap where the floor to ceiling bifold doors will go.

"You can keep working on me, if you like," I whisper, trailing behind Skyla as she follows Callie outside.

"That completes the tour of the house. Do you like it?" Callie asks Skyla.

"I love it. You and your dad thought of everything. And just look at that view." She gestures her hand toward the sea. "I can just see you guys hosting parties at the weekends or out on the water enjoying some sailing or surfing. You're going to love it here."

"It is a cool house. What are you doing tomorrow? We're going to the theater. You should come, Skyla. It's just a movie and some food. No one will mind. Nanna said we should keep Grandpop's memorial informal—he'd want it like that—and our family already loves you." Callie's grinning persuasively, her hands clamped together pleadingly.

"I already told you, Cal. I'm not going. I've got to work," I say.

"Please go, Dad. It won't feel right if you're not there and it'll be even more fun if Skyla comes too."

I shift uncomfortably. It won't feel right if I am there.

Sensing she is not getting an answer yet, Callie suggests, "I'm going to go check out the beach. Maybe Skyla can talk some sense into you while I'm gone and you'll decide to go after all."

We watch as Callie wanders through the grounds to get to the private stretch of beach.

"She's right, you know. You should go," Skyla says from beside me.

I turn to face her. Her smile is weighed down by concern.

"I... It's complicated."

She takes a hold of both my hands. "Families are complicated. You should still go."

"It's not that I don't want to, but it feels disingenuous to mark his anniversary when we never recovered from our final argument. I don't even know if he'd want me there. Not that it matters..."

"It matters," she says, her brown eyes pinning me as though in a choke hold. "You're carrying all this regret and anger inside you. He's gone. Don't you think it's time you put aside your argument and let bygones be bygones."

I let go of her hands and take a piece of her hair, running it through my fingers. God, she looks so beautiful as the sun sets behind her. It's as though this light is cast just for her, to somehow emphasize her goodness inside and out.

"You don't understand. You believe the best in people. But my relationship with my father was—"

"Complicated. You already said that. Tell me a relationship that isn't complicated. There aren't any. But you're punishing yourself, excluding yourself from joining in with a grief that belongs to you all. You are allowed to mourn him, even if you didn't behave well or particularly like him when he died, just like he was allowed to love you, even though he didn't like your decisions."

"This isn't—"

"I love my mother. Even though I hate her for leaving me, I love her."

"Would you go to her funeral?"

"Yes," she says instantly. "I never really thought about it before, but I would. Because someone wise once told me that parents aren't perfect. They make mistakes like we do. Our job is to try not to make the same mistakes they did."

I run my finger up her neck and along her jaw, resisting the urge to kiss her.

"Wise?" I ask, remembering how I told her that.

She nods.

"You make it sound easy."

"That's because you've spent so long overcomplicating it. It's just an old movie and a meal with your family—whom you love, and an opportunity to talk about the good times." Her expression falters and it makes me want to kiss her even more, to remove the sad look on her face. "There were good times, right?"

I nod, watching Callie collecting shells as she slowly heads back toward us. "So many good times. Great times. Somehow, they make how it all ended even more unbearable."

"Then try to focus on the good memories and not what happened after. Give your father and yourself a free pass. Like starting over how you would have if he were still here."

"Okay, I'll go. But only if you come with us."

"Me?" She looks unsure. "I don't know if—"

"Come on. I'm going to need another maladaptive human to even the numbers. Someone else there who didn't have a perfect relationship with both parents. It'll make me feel more normal."

"You think I'm maladaptive?"

"No!" I almost shout. "Skyla, you're perfectly rounded despite having been through so much. I didn't mean it like that. You're… you turned out great. In fact, you give me hope that it's possible." She smiles sweetly. God, I really want to kiss her. "And you have a perfectly rounded ass that will easily distract me if it all becomes too much." Her cheeks raise and she does an adorable snort-giggle.

"Okay, I'll come. But not because you need me. You've got this."

"Then why?"

"Because I like it when you check out my ass."

She winks and I am a goner. I wrap my arms around her, pulling her up and into me, and I kiss her.

"If you two have finished making out, I think I'd like to get some dinner now. Before you both ruin my appetite forever," Callie hisses through her grin and we break apart like naughty school kids. As we walk back to the car, my hand finds Skyla's, and when I look at Callie, she nods approvingly.

Cat's out of the bag now.

What the hell are you doing, Drew?

* * *

I WALK Skyla to her apartment, leaving Callie sitting in the car so she can take her ever-so-important update from the kid with the Shit Pug on FaceTime. She's got the window down and is doing a fine job of multitasking by watching me and Skyla while also gushing over dogs.

Skyla and I loiter at her doorway, me suddenly not wanting to say goodbye.

"I'll see you tomorrow?" I say, trying to keep my voice casual and not let the mixture of nerves at where we are going and excitement to see her again, bowl me over like a screwed up, love-struck fool.

"If you're sure you want me there. If you change your mind—"

"I won't."

"Then it's settled." She fumbles with her keys and finally opens the door. She's looking at my mouth but then suddenly, something catches her attention over my shoulder and she calls out, "Oh. Hi, Betty."

I turn and see the crazy lady who keeps talking about pussy behind me.

"You better go. Callie's waiting."

"Okay. See you soon." I reluctantly turn and walk away and hear Skyla's door quietly close behind me. Part of me is pissed I didn't get a goodnight kiss now that we have an audience, but the other part is unable to remove the smile from my face from a near perfect day.

"You look better," Betty says, stopping to rest between me and my car.

"Thank-you," I reply, unsure whether it is a compliment or not.

"Didn't I tell you, all you needed was pussy to put a smile on your face." She elbows me in the ribs, and I'm dying inside hoping to God my daughter is not understanding this old crazy lady.

"Good luck with that. Dad wouldn't agree to a cat, he won't even let me have a dog!" Callie moans and the old lady turns around to greet my daughter.

"Hmm. If you don't got a cat, must be the love of a good woman that's got your smile all big like it is."

I wipe the smile from my face.

"We better go. Have a good night, Betty," I say and scurry to the driver's side of the car.

Love of a good woman!
That's not what this is.
She doesn't... I don't...
Oh crap!

CHAPTER 25

SKYLA

"*I* should probably wear jeans. Or a skirt. Or yoga pants. Or maybe I should wear black, as a mark of respect. Or perhaps color since it should be informal, a celebration and… *argh*! I don't know but I don't want to get it wrong," I complain to Jessie, who is still wearing her maid's uniform, flicking through the latest edition of some celebrity magazine. "What does one wear to a memorial movie dinner?"

She lowers the magazine enough that I can see her blue eyes. "Why are you even going? You've got a friends with benefits thing going on. That doesn't usually entail spending time with his family or his kid."

I bite my lip sheepishly, knowing she's right. "He asked me to go. Callie wanted me there too. Do you think I should back out?" Even as I suggest it, I know I can't. I've committed, and Drew asked me to go. There's no way I would cancel now and let them both down.

Jessie sits up cross-legged and studies me. "You're in love with him, aren't you? No way you'd endure a family memorial for a guy you hardly know unless you're in—"

"Don't say it again, Jessie."

She puts the magazine down. "You are, aren't you?!" I turn away, busying myself in the drawers of my closet, hunting beneath piles of shirts like it contains the answer to global warming. "You love him."

I crash down to the floor, my hand clutching an old bra that was buried at the bottom. "I forgot I had this one." I fold it cup on cup, wondering if it's too old to keep.

"Put down the freakin' bra. You love Drew Blingwood. You do! It's written all over your face."

"No. I..."

"Does he know?"

"I don't think so."

"You think he feels the same way?"

I shake my head and stare at the pink satin, deciding it's too frayed to keep. "He's very determined in his plan to stay single. We're just..." I don't even know what we are anymore. "Callie knows something is going on between us. Logan does too. Hell, his whole family and the entire resort probably know. But there's a planned end to it. He's telling Callie I have to leave for work in two weeks so she doesn't get her hopes up."

I dare to look at Jessie. Her beautiful face is all scrunched with worry. "What are you going to do?"

"I'm going to go to the memorial. Then I'm going to..." I throw the bra at the trash can but it misses by a mile. "I can't tell him how I feel. He'll go heading for the hills. Maybe I should break it off, save myself the extended heartbreak."

"He might feel the same way. You've been spending a lot of time together. Dinners. Visiting his place. Time with his daughter… He could definitely love you. He'd be an idiot not to."

I try to keep the emotion from my voice. "No. He's been clear from the beginning. It's me who's the idiot for allowing myself to fall so damn hard. Maybe just enjoying it while it lasts will be enough. He'll be moving from the resort and then it's going to fizzle out and feel like it's July 5th. Over. I'll be okay."

"What if independence from each other isn't what you need? What if telling him that you want more makes him realize that's what he needs too? Maybe he'll confess his love for you. Beg you to stay. I mean, it happens, right?"

"It won't."

"Wear your black skinny jeans and your silk shirt that's the color of sunflowers. You'll look hot and it makes your eyes pop."

"You think?"

"Yeah, even I get hard for you in that shirt."

I chuckle. "You want me to operate on that imaginary penis of yours?"

"Nah, I'm going to need it so I can fuck Tate Blingwood in the ass." She reopens the magazine she has been holding. "He's been filming some futuristic movie in Hawaii where all the women wear skintight silver leotards. I bet he banged every single one of them." She's got a thoroughly disgusted look on her face.

"Why do you care who he bangs?"

"I don't give a damn what that douchebag does. It's Logan I feel sorry for. Tate being an attention whore is making the press curious about Logan and his Z-list fiancée."

"What happened now?"

She lifts the front page of the magazine to reveal a photograph of Dana patting a non-existent bump on her almost skeletal frame. Behind her, Logan's chin rests on her shoulder as he cradles his pregnant fiancée. The headline reads: "Dana Gee on being an heiress, marrying the man of her dreams, and how "eating clean" has her blooming through pregnancy."

"What's wrong with that?"

"Eating clean? I needed two trash bags to clear out the pizza boxes and vodka bottles from the penthouse, and I know it wasn't Logan since I caught him sleeping on the couch in his office."

"Maybe it wasn't her drinking the vodka. Did she have friends over?"

"Nope. I checked with Simon from security and he said there've been no parties since she announced the pregnancy."

"We shouldn't judge. Who knows what is going on." I think back to the engagement party, and while that night wasn't great for me, Logan didn't look all that happy at his own party. "Now that you mention it, I think Logan has been struggling with Dana. Seems like she's going off the rails."

"Off the rails? She's got a baby in her. She needs to take damn good care of herself. You can't be pulling this shit pregnant."

"Does Logan know?"

"I didn't have the heart to mention it. He's got eyebags you could carry your groceries in right now. Poor guy. You think he'll be at the memorial?"

"I expect so. I think they're all going."

"Tate going?"

And there it is again, Jessie mentioning Tate. "I think so. You want me to get his number for you, since you're so interested?"

"Yuk. No! I'm going to take Macy to visit my mother—she's out of toilet paper and I acquired some that will help her out."

I slip into my jeans and pull my yellow shirt over my

head, pretending I didn't hear Jessie admit to stealing hotel supplies.

"How do I look?"

"Like Drew Blingwood is the dumbest fuck on the planet."

* * *

"Dana didn't make it, then?" I say casually to Drew as we walk out of the cinema.

His tone is indifferent. "No. She wasn't feeling well, according to Logan."

"You don't believe she's sick?"

"More like, I don't think she gives enough of a crap to support Logan." He glances in his brother's direction, watching as Tate and Logan walk Callie across the parking lot in the direction of the restaurant. "If there were photographers, she would be here."

I toy with telling him what Jessie told me, but since it's already an emotional day I decide not to stir the pot. Besides, maybe Jessie was wrong. Maybe the alcohol belonged to someone else. Maybe it wasn't Dana's. *And*, it's none of my business.

"You okay?" Drew asks, taking my hand in his as we follow Callie and the rest of his family across the street to the restaurant.

"I was about to ask you the same thing," I say. He sat beside me throughout the film, and I couldn't resist the urge to keep looking at him. He went through the entire spectrum of emotions. His lips would move in time to the words on screen, but no sound came out and when Goose died, I couldn't tell if he was going to erupt with anger or cry—and not because Goose was floating in the sea, his best friend holding him, but something beneath, telling me he was not okay. I took Drew's hand, wrapped it in mine and squeezed tightly, and though he squeezed back, it was as if he were a million miles away.

"I'm okay, I think. Oddly, that felt cathartic. Like he was there." He shakes his head. "That sounds dumb, right. Like watching a film erases nearly two decades of animosity."

"No, it doesn't sound dumb. It's a sign you're processing. Gaining perspective."

"I kind of feel like I am. But now it's you I feel sorry for. A meal with my family. It's a good thing you're not driving because you'll need a drink to get through it." He winks. No matter how many times I see him wink, it still gives me flutters every time.

"We're both going to be fine, I'm your wingman." I smile, pushing my nerves deep beneath the flutters in my gut.

"You say that now, but when Tate and Tabs start arguing and Mom gets it into her head that we are an item, the shit is going to go down."

"If there's any sign of that happening maybe I'll drag you to the bathroom to avoid it."

He wraps his arm over my shoulder and pulls me close as we cross the road. "Hell yeah. I have definitely not lost that loving feeling for you."

Drew kisses my temple as Callie calls back over her shoulder, "Hurry up you two!"

And that's when the car veers around the corner much too quickly and her tiny little body is thrown up into the air.

CHAPTER 26

DREW

I run but my legs don't seem to respond and it takes forever to get to her.

She's on the ground, her limbs splayed out in hard angles.

The driver is out of the car and I punch the motherfucker in the face as I barge past him to get to my daughter. Logan is already on his phone calling the ambulance, Tate is beside Callie, I'm wringing my hands like a useless prick begging the Gods, pleading with Jesus Christ himself to make sure Callie is okay.

She's so still.

"Callie."

"Baby, talk to me. Open your eyes."

I'm crouching at her side, water pouring down my face saying her name over and over.

"She's going to be okay, Drew," Tate says.

I think I hear sirens but maybe it's the ringing in my ears

as the one thing I care most about in the whole world lies broken on the ground.

I wasn't with her.

I wasn't guiding her across the street. I wasn't present when it mattered. I assumed my family had her.

She should have been able to depend on me.

What was I doing while she was crossing the damn street alone?

Flirting with my fuck buddy.

Logan pulls me away. "Drew, you have to move back so the paramedics can help her."

Bone-deep shock and anger settles into my soul and everything goes black.

* * *

"She'll be out of surgery soon," Mom says pacing the corridor but she doesn't know that, she's guessing. They rushed Callie into surgery hours ago.

Internal bleeding.

My instincts urge me to go straight to the police station, find the guy who was driving the car, and thrash him until his insides are bleeding. His outsides too. Until he is nothing more than a bloody mess.

But the truth is, there's someone closer to home who deserves that punishment more.

Me.

"She's going to be fine," my sister says. It's the third time she's said it in as many minutes and I don't know if she's trying to persuade me or herself.

"The driver came around the corner like he was on a racing track. I'm going to hire the best lawyers. See that the imbecile doesn't set foot outside of a jail for the rest of his sorry life," Logan says, pacing, fists balled.

"The police have him. He's going to pay," Tate says, though I'm not sure if he's speaking to me. I'm trapped inside my own head, all that's going on around me is just noise and none of it matters until I know if my baby is okay.

My body is wound so tight I don't notice the hand squeezing my knee until I look down and see it shaking with tension.

When I look at Skyla, her face is sheet white. Her big brown eyes are shimmering, looking at me like she wants to help me. Or hell, maybe she wants me to help her. Maybe she feels as guilty as I do.

The pain in her eyes is unbearable.

I look away.

Then I stand and join my mother pacing.

"People that reckless shouldn't be allowed cars," Mom says.

"I should have been walking beside Callie, then this never would've happened."

"No, man. She was right behind me. I was chatting with Tabs. This is my fault," Logan says.

"I should've waited. She was spying on you two." Tate nods his head to me and Skyla. "But the car was going too fast. Must have been hitting fifty. The dude driving the car is to blame."

"No. I'm her father. I should never have let go of her hand."

"Drew, she's twelve years old. You can't hold her hand every day for the rest of her life. She was crossing safely. If the driver wasn't speeding—"

"Leave it, Tabitha!" I hiss. "I know he was driving too fast. I know. But I still should've been there to save her."

Mom tries to comfort me by wrapping her arms around me but I'm too agitated to remain still. The comfort she offers feels at odds with what I deserve. I shrug her off and move until I am standing at the window that faces the parking lot. The blue sky from earlier is now a dark, angry red as the sun sets and I wonder how I ever thought it was beautiful.

"Drew, I know it's been a terrible shock but your family —" Skyla's voice is warm, caring, touching. I can't bear it.

"You should go home. It's been a long day…" I can't finish the sentence. Hell, I can't even look at her.

"I don't mind staying—"

"Skyla. Go. There's nothing you can do for anyone here."

I don't even need to turn around to know what I said hurt her. The image is etched in my mind. Her full lips turning down at the edges by the knowledge that I let her down.

But she should know the truth: I let people down.

I let her down. I let Callie down. I let my father down. The list keeps going.

"I'll go then. If that's what you want…."

My voice sounds so cold it barely sounds like my own. "It is."

The silence makes me want to scream as I imagine a life without Callie.

Just a kid, her whole life ahead of her, the unfairness is driving me crazy. Yet somehow, even though it feels impossible, the earth keeps turning while we await news. Dusk has turned dark and the sky turns black. A bunch of stars shine brightly and I think about my father.

If you're up there. If I ever meant anything at all to you, save her. Take me, I don't care, but save Callie.

* * *

"She'll be at home now," Mom says from behind me awhile later.

I imagine Skyla, laying on her queen bed in her tiny apartment, worrying.

"She's better off at home."

"It's okay to lean on others," Mom replies, like leaning on anyone is going to make any of this better.

"Skyla's better off without me. If I had been focused on doing my job as a father then maybe none of this would—"

"You were doing your job as a father!" Mom's voice is so steely, so certain, it has me spinning around to check if she's serious.

"Callie got hit by a car, yards away from me!"

"Callie got hit by a speeding car that no one saw coming."

"I guess we'll never know if I had been closer, then maybe I could have pushed her out of the way, but that didn't happen because I was too busy thinking about when I was next going to put my dick in my fuck buddy!"

Mom flinches. "You can pretend all you like that Skyla means nothing to you, but we all saw it, Drew. I saw it. You care about her, and from the way she was looking at you, supporting you today, the way she was silently praying for your daughter, the way she walked out of here fighting tears because you're too much of a coward to admit you need her, she cares about you too." Mom's expression is as strained as I have ever seen. The lines on her face are deepened by her turmoil, like she aged twenty years right before my eyes.

I look away. I know she's only saying it because she cares, but right now, her love is making me feel worse. "She's better off without me," I mutter.

* * *

I'm SITTING on one of the plastic chairs scrolling through my phone looking at pictures of Callie when the doctor comes out. "Mr. Blingwood," he says and Tate, Logan, and I all stand.

The doctor somehow knows to approach me. He smiles and my fists clench. If he's giving me bad news and he has the audacity to push an expression onto his face that is anything other than destroyed, I'm going to kill him.

I brace myself.

"It's good news. Your daughter is one tough cookie."

"Good news?" I question. "You're going to have to give me more than that. How'd the operation go? She survived, yes? Tell me she survived."

He smiles again, only this time I feel more able to trust it.

"She survived. She's in recovery. You can see her in a bit. The nurses are with her and she's doing fine."

I don't catch anything else he says. I'm down on my knees crying like a baby, thanking him, thanking God, thanking the nurse who walks by and even the janitor. And then I look for Skyla, but she's not fucking here because I told her to leave.

CHAPTER 27

SKYLA

> Callie's okay. Fractured leg, broken rib, ruptured spleen, but she's awake and giving her old man shit—which I personally think is deserved.

> Hope you're okay?

A text from Logan. My boss. *Not Drew.*

"I HAVEN'T HEARD from him since it happened," I tell Jessie in the cafeteria five days later. "Okay, so he probably saw the flowers, chocolates, and the iTunes gift card I took into the hospital. Probably thinks I overstepped since whatever we had is obviously over. Callie was sleeping and the nurse informed me she made Drew go home to shower since he was stinking the place up, but I've had no contact. Not even a text. It's done." I blink away tears, crying will do me no good whatsoever. It's his decision and it's done. And it hurts like I had my heart amputated. But I'm glad of the pain, it reminds me it happened, that I loved him and also that he didn't love me back.

"He had a trauma. If that happened to Macy, I'd... he's shutting down, give him time."

"Jess, I know you're trying to help, I do, but he made it clear that we had no future from the get-go. The accident sped the ending. He doesn't want me in his life, and that's okay." I stand and take ahold of the plate with my untouched food. "I'm going to be late for my lunchtime walk. I'll see you later."

The sunshine blinds me the second I step out of the cafe. With my mood this bleak, the sun has no business shining so brightly. I rush to the pound, searching for Drew the entire way, even though I know he'll be at the hospital. I've seen Logan twice this week and he's given me updates about Callie, not to mention that Callie has texted me a dozen times. But nothing from Drew.

"You came!" Drew's mom, Cassandra, says from the porch of the pound. She's wearing a red T-shirt with the slogan: *You can't buy love, but you can rescue it.* Beside her are two dogs, their leashes already attached.

"Of course," I reply. "I come every day at lunch. Though normally one of your assistants hands me a dog to walk." A rather zealous sausage dog jumps up at me and I put as much enthusiasm as I can into greeting him.

"I know you do. I thought I'd join you today, if you don't mind?" I nod and she hands me the leash of the sausage dog. "You take Sammy and I'll handle Dobby." We set off toward the park and nerves flutter in my gut.

Why is Cassandra walking with me?

"Is everything okay? Is Callie..."

"She's fine." Cassandra's hand gently presses against mine. "Logan updated you, didn't he?"

"Yes. I've seen him twice. Last I heard, Callie was on crutches, pain meds, and antibiotics but hoping to go home soon."

"Callie no longer needs the pain meds and should be discharged later today. She was ecstatic you paid her a visit. It's a shame she was sleeping, Callie would have liked to have seen you." Cassandra speaks casually enough, her eyes trained on the path ahead, but there's a somber undertone to her voice. "It would have done Drew good to see you too. He's been hulking up the place like a bee with no honey."

"I thought it better not to hang around…. After the way things were left with Drew, I wondered if I might be over-stepping in visiting. He made it pretty clear at the hospital that he didn't want me around. But I had to go and see she was okay. I didn't want Callie to think I don't care, because I do, I really honestly do." I'm babbling and tears are prickling my eyes. "I'm sorry. I don't know why I'm so—"

Cassandra's hand grips my arm and she pulls me to a stop. "Skyla, darling, you're upset because you love them and they were hurt. And so were you. It's fine to label how you're feeling. My eldest son thinks if he tucks his feelings away, then he won't get hurt. He thinks that if he tells himself he doesn't have feelings for you, then it will become true." Her grip on my arm turns into a gentle, soothing rub. "He's a stubborn fool, just like his father was." She lets go of my arm and gestures for me to follow the trail. "Drew thought he lost her. His world almost came crashing down and he blamed himself. One day soon he's going to realize genuine, real feelings like love are not able to be switched off like a light."

"He doesn't…" I shake my head. "Cassandra, Drew and I, we weren't dating. Not really. He doesn't love me."

"Oh?" She sounds confused. "Callie said you were going

out for dinner and visiting the penthouse and the new house. She said you went to the salon with her. And I know he invited you to the engagement party."

"Well, yes. But it wasn't—" His mom's eyebrow is cocked, her eyes pinned on mine.

Please God, don't make me have to explain I was only ever a sex buddy to her son.

"Sounds a lot like dating to me," she supplies. "I think my son loves you, but he won't admit it, not even to himself. See, he blames himself for his father's death. Doesn't matter how many times I tell him, or his siblings tell him that nobody was to blame—Drew hates himself for not making up with his father sooner, and he's become stuck. He's stopped taking risks."

"Mrs. Blingwood—"

"Cassandra."

"Cassandra, I appreciate you trying to make me feel better, but I really think you have it wrong. We established some rules right from the start. See, I'm moving to the new resort. We never planned—"

"He planned to play it safe. You planned an exit strategy, both of you are miserable."

"I'm not miserable," I say with an audible pout. "Okay, I'm a little peeved. He's so stubborn and I don't want to have to persuade someone to be with me. That isn't how love is supposed to work."

"Drew's always been stubborn. Perhaps it's because he's the oldest child. He'd set all the rules and then go crazy when everyone else broke them. He knew his father wanted him to take over the business, and Drew surprised all of us when he chose something else. He might have told you a little about how that went down."

I nod, remembering Drew explaining how it destroyed his relationship with his father.

"Drew's sense of personal responsibility for everyone else will be his downfall. He thinks the happiness of others is entirely dependent on the decisions he makes and he blames himself when things go badly—it's part of the reason we were all so surprised when he followed his heart into a career he loved. But maybe that's why he's no longer so willing to follow his heart, he's scared it'll go wrong again."

"But that's stupid. He's got a huge heart and when he lets people inside it's…" *Magical.*

"His father was just as stubborn. He treated the alternate choice Drew made as a personal slight. I tried to intervene but it got me nowhere. It wasn't until the night of Crystal's wake that I thought they were going to make up. But then, would you believe it, the fight became not about Drew's line of business, but about where he should raise his daughter. Drew felt attacked."

"But he did move back home, like his father wanted."

"Yes. But, like most things, Drew had to think it was his idea." She winks.

"Makes sense, he likes to be in control."

We round the corner and I see the pound rescue center ahead.

"Drew has held onto a letter his father wrote him, and for the past year he's been too afraid to open it. He's worried it'll confirm all the things he thinks his father thought about him and so he's choosing not to find out. I have no idea what Peter wrote on that sheet of paper. Emotions were high after their argument. He wrote it on the morning of our departure and left it for Drew to find. I'd like to think Peter wouldn't have written anything bad—he knew how much Drew was hurting, but the truth is, I don't know. But it's time Drew realized, no one is responsible for another person's death, just like they can't guarantee another's happiness. That comes from within." She shakes her head. "Drew walks around with the weight of the world on his shoulders. He believes it's his job to hold everything up and he hasn't yet learned to share the burden. But don't give up on him, he'll figure it out eventually."

"I don't think there's much left to hold onto," I admit.

"What are you doing later?" she asks. "Callie is getting discharged and she'd like it if you were there to welcome her when she gets back to the penthouse."

I shake my head. "I don't think Drew would approve. Besides, I have a ton of laundry to take care of. I'll be at the laundromat half the night. But I will come see her once she's settled."

"You mean you'll come see her when you know Drew isn't there?"

I half chuckle, half nod. "Drew wants space."

Cassandra takes the leash I offer and pulls the dogs in the direction of the pound. "Okay. But remember, don't give up yet."

* * *

LATER THAT NIGHT, I am eating a pint of ice cream and watching *Sex and the City* reruns when I get an email:

To: Skyla Manning

From: Sue Manning

Subject: Please hear me out

I DELETE THE EMAIL.

CHAPTER 28

DREW

"That's it, watch the plant. Almost there—"

"Dad! I got this. Stop barking orders and relax. If I can navigate a tiny hospital room filled with equipment and machines, I can navigate our penthouse," Callie hisses.

"I'm trying to help. I can get you a wheelchair if it's easier? I know the nurse said the crutches would suffice, but if you're worried about hitting your cast I'll get you one."

She lowers herself down on the couch while I drop her backpack on the counter.

"I don't need a wheelchair. I need you to step back and give me some space. Ever since the accident, you've barely left my side." She pulls her phone out of her back pocket and scrolls it with her index finger. "That's weird. Skyla still hasn't replied to my message. Is she okay?"

There's a little furrow between her brows that causes my heart to ache.

"Yeah, she's probably working late."

"Urgh," Callie grunts, still looking at her phone.

"What is it?" I rush to her side.

"Nothing."

"Callie…"

"Dana. She messaged me. She wonders if I'd rather not be a bridesmaid since my leg's all bashed up and the crutches might make me look weird in the photos."

"What the—"

"It's fine, Dad. I don't even want to be in her stupid wedding anyway. Uncle Logan's only marrying her because of the baby."

"He cares about her…," I start to say, but I'm too pissed to be sympathetic. "I'll talk to him."

"No. Don't. He's got enough going on." She puts her phone away. "Tell me what's going on with you and Skyla. Her last message was a while ago but she said she couldn't come see me tonight. Did you break up with her?"

A sigh pushes past my lips. "Cal, you know Skyla and I weren't serious. We were getting to know one another and I'm sorry if this disappoints you but we're not dating."

She cocks her brow at me, her face deadly serious. "You were getting close, though."

"Just as friends." I can't bring myself to explain the ins and outs of adult, platonic yet sexual relationships, so I keep it simple. "We're not together."

"But why? She was at the memorial dinner. You've been staring at her butt and mouth and you kissed her…" She pulls a disgusted face. "You've been looking at her like you want to eat her."

I shrug. No way I can deny that. "We never planned to embark on a relationship. We were hanging out, as close friends."

"What, and now you're suddenly *not* hanging out as close friends? Why?"

"Grown-up relationships are complicated."

"Complicated!" Callie stands, her crutches clanking together as she tries to put them in position. I reach out to help but she already has her hands on the grips. "Dad, I don't need your help." She takes a step away. "I thought you liked her!"

I do like her.

"Callie, I'm focusing on you. You had a serious accident. We're moving soon and Skyla got this great new job at the second resort and... it wasn't meant to be."

She narrows her eyes on me. "You scared her away and now she's leaving us?"

Yes.

"No. She was never *with* us."

Callie stares at the ceiling and blinks away the threat of tears which breaks my heart. "I don't get it. You like her, she likes you. I thought we were going to be a real family."

"We are a real family. Me, you, your nanna. You've got a bunch of near-crazy uncles and an aunt."

She pins me with a stare. "Yeah. But I thought Skyla was gonna become one of us. I wanted you to be happy."

My throat tightens. "I am happy. I'm happy when you're happy."

"I know you are, Dad. It's a lot of pressure, that's all."

"What is?"

"Your happiness being dependent on mine. I want you to be happy outside of me, not for us to end up co-dependent and dysfunctional. You need to stop using your role as my father to shield you from getting hurt." She smiles a watery smile that's like a punch to my gut.

Is that what I'm doing?

"When did you get so smart?"

"Dad, you've had me in therapy since Mom died. I picked up a thing or two. So did you. You're the best dad, but you need to work on your other relationships and let people in."

"No, I—"

"Where's my beautiful grandbaby?" Mom walks in, carrying something that looks suspiciously like a dog in her arms. "Look who I brought to see you."

Today, Mom's T-shirt reads: *Keep calm and get a dog.*

Callie's face lights up by a fraction. "You brought Pixie!" She turns to me. "Dad, Pixie's the dog I've been telling you about. Nanna thinks she's about three months old."

I can't even bring myself to be angry with my mom for bringing the puppy, not when it makes Callie smile.

"I'm going to video call Ben. He's going to be so stoked when he sees her here."

"Yeah. Good idea. Call Ben. Like you haven't spent the entire past few days at the hospital on the phone with him."

"Chill, Dad. It's good to have friends. Maybe when you work that out, you can go apologize to Skyla and stop being so grumpy."

"I'm going to go get ice cream," I huff.

Mom smiles widely. "Good idea, son. Would you stop at the laundromat while you're out? I dropped my scarf and I'm wondering if someone found it."

"You think someone turned it in to the lost and found?"

Mom takes a beat too long to answer and I wonder what she's up to. "It's not at reception, so they told me to check storage at the laundromat. If it's too much trouble, I can always do it my—"

"It's fine. I'll go down to the laundromat and then go get ice cream."

CHAPTER 29

SKYLA

*A*midst the quiet routine of my life, muscle memory, perhaps, enables me to remember to continue breathing even though my body feels tethered beneath water.

Filling my day, putting one foot in front of the other, eating, and taking care of my daily tasks at work are so ingrained in me, I do them on autopilot without really experiencing any of the moments.

It's my same pre-Drew life, but it feels different. Worse.

The humming of the dryer almost has me falling asleep on the bench of the onsite laundromat.

Things are moving forward, like appointing my soon-to-be replacement and my dad calling me to say that he and his new girlfriend are checking into the resort and she can't wait to meet me, while other things, like the constant ache in my chest, stay the same.

I try to remember when I last had a full night's sleep. Lately all my nights seem broken and I lay in bed in turmoil over what I should do. I miss him. I miss Callie. And I wonder what my mother wrote in her email to me.

But Drew's silence hurts the most and it couldn't be louder.

He doesn't want me.

He never did, not long-term at least.

Just like my mom.

The bell above the door rings and I look up over the industrial-sized machines and I see him. Like I manifested him from my thoughts.

"You... I didn't know you'd be in here." He *tsks* loudly and shakes his head which annoys me more than it should.

"Just a woman with laundry to do." My tone is deceptively mild considering the angry current vibrating beneath my skin like a rising tide.

He approaches cautiously, his sneakers light on the terra-cotta tile.

"I've been meaning to come find you. I was waiting for Callie to get settled, and well, I've been trying to think of what to say to you."

"How to officially break off our arrangement, you mean? Don't bother, your silence was loud and clear."

His head dips to the side and I know that's exactly what he's about to do.

"It's been five days. I only know that Callie is okay thanks to your brother." My voice hitches with unreserved anger. "I deserved a conversation. A text. A call. An email. Something. I was there that night too. I deserved *something.*"

He cusses beneath his breath and nods. "I'm not trying to hurt you. What happened... the car..." He shudders, and even though I am angry with him, I want to go to him, absorb some of his pain—and it sucks because I want to hate him. I want to yell at him and tell him I never want to see him again, but it's hard to be angry with someone who believes they are doing what is best for their daughter, who you also love.

"Get it over with, then. Give me the thanks-but-no-thanks speech."

There's a slight bob to his head. His hair is in complete disarray. His normal closely shaved jaw has a five-day scruff and there are dark circles beneath his eyes.

"Skyla." He steps forward. "I never meant to take it so far. We agreed to a little fun, but then I let Callie get dragged into it. I should have known from the start I was being reckless—"

"Reckless?"

"I knew Callie'd get attached to you, she adored you from the second she met you."

"But you weren't attached to me?" I stare at him, boldly waiting for him to tell me no. That I wasn't enough.

"Our time together was the best I can remember, but it can't continue. I took my eye off the ball and Callie almost died."

"Drew, your daughter had a terrible accident. That is no one's fault except the driver of the car that was speeding. If you're ending things between us because you're not into me, then say it. Don't sugarcoat it with your responsibility. There are single dads across the entire world living their lives, having relationships, and still being amazing fathers. Hell, even my dad has managed to meet someone, and I never thought that would happen. This isn't about anyone except me and you." Drew is shaking his head and I already know there is nothing I can say, but still there are things I want to get off my chest. "Did you ever feel anything for me?"

"Of course, I did. Skyla, you're amazing."

"But not amazing enough."

"You can't rely on me to make you happy. I will let you down."

I look away. "You already did. I might have known you

didn't want anything serious, but you're the one who made plans with me outside the bedroom, you kept reeling me in, making it more. You've been a jerk," I shake my head with disgust, "but I've been a complete fool."

"You're right. I'm worse than a jerk. I'm sorry."

Drew turns to walk away and, as though he has a hold on my heart, I feel my heart tearing.

"Didn't you love me at all?" I call after him, sounding desperate, pathetic; like I have no pride at all, but a part of me still clings to the hope that I meant something to him.

He pauses, but he doesn't turn around. "I'm sorry."

CHAPTER 30

DREW

"*W*here's the ice cream?" Callie asks.

"Huh?"

"Dad, you went out for ice cream and Nanna's scarf and came back looking about fifty years older."

"Thanks, kid. I can always rely on you to cheer me up."

I'm so tired, it takes no effort to slide down onto the carpet beside Callie, watching as she rattles one of her childhood bears in front of Pixie's little face that's the color of a red sky. The pup hops about, growling at the bear playfully.

"What is it?" I ask.

Mom studies the pup. "We didn't see the mother or father; she was left tied to the post out front, all flea bitten and hungry. But she looks to me like she's got some Great Dane in her, maybe some Labrador. She's going to be big, just look at her paws."

"We'll say she's a Great Lab," Callie suggests.

"Is it even old enough to be away from its mother?" I ask Mom.

"Yep. She's had all her vaccinations. I've got some posts prepared to go up on my socials," Mom replies.

I cock a brow at her. "Socials?" My mother knows about as much about social media as I know about making people happy. Absolutely nothing.

Mom smiles, but it's barely there. Nothing like the kind of grin you get from her when she is genuinely happy. She looks... concerned. She waves her hand at Callie. "Your daughter has been teaching me how to set up groups and pages. The community response has been nothing short of amazing. Thanks to Callie, I'm growing my pool of dog walkers. People want to come and volunteer at the center. I even have a waiting list of people to vet who want to adopt their own little fur balls." Mom bends to stroke Pixie but her eyes stay trained on me. "Are you okay? You look tired."

I run my hands through my hair. I can't remember the last time I had a good night's sleep.

Oh, yeah, I do. It was when I had Skyla beside me.

"I'm fine, Mom. It's been a difficult few days." I watch Callie, her plastered calf sprawled out before her, playing with the little dog. She's smiling but I can tell she's holding something back.

"You need some Tylenol?" I ask Callie.

"Nah. I'm good. It doesn't hurt too bad." Callie turns to her Nanna, her eyes glassy. "You will make sure Pixie gets a good home? I can't bear to think of her not getting enough walks or treats when she does something good."

"It'll be the best home I can find, I promise," Mom replies but Callie doesn't look reassured. And it's too much to bear. Hurting people, feeling utterly miserable deep inside, I can't stand it.

"She'll have the best home in town," I say, and before I

have given it any thought at all, before I have recalled all the reasons I said we couldn't have a dog, words are spilling out my mouth. "Tomorrow, we'll go get her a bed and a bowl for her food. And we'll walk her every day. Every day. We're not going to be those types of pet owners who only do the good stuff when they're babies. If we're making a commitment, we're seeing it through. Right through to the end. We'll need to register her with a vet. Dogs need good health care, and you'll have to search up some obedience classes too. We're both going to need to know how to turn her into the guard dog you promised she'll be. Though looking at her, I can't imagine she's even capable of scaring a possum away."

Callie's mouth is wide open, her face frozen with shock. She blinks twice and then her cheeks slowly rise up. "We can keep her?"

"What about your allergies?" Mom asks, her tone suspicious.

I take a deep breath in. "No sneezing or wheezing. I guess I outgrew them?"

"Mmm. How wonderful." Mom's tone changes to sarcastic. "A sudden healing. What a blessing." Her eyes pin me with disdain. "You know a dog isn't a distraction?"

"What?" I blow off her assumption. "We've been thinking about getting a dog for ages." Mom's scrutiny is unbearable, so I divert my gaze to Callie. "Look how happy she is."

Callie gasps, grinning until every part of her face is lifted by about an inch. "Daddy!" Callie shrieks and for the first time since the accident, my heart fills with something that's almost close to happiness, until she says, "I can't wait to tell Skyla!" And without even looking at Mom, I can read the I-told-you-so look on her face. Then, as though someone pulled the plug, a little bit of my happiness seeps out. A drip at first, followed by a flood as I recall the sound of her choked voice.

"Didn't you love me at all?"
Yes, I loved her.
How could I not?

* * *

"YOU KNOW pets aren't allowed at the resort?" Logan asks, lifting Pixie to pet her before putting her back down on the puppy mat.

"Feel free to walk in like you own the place," I counter, glancing up from my blueprints.

"I *do* own the place."

"Yeah, well you want to enforce the no dog rule, you take it up with Callie. Pixie is her dog," I say smugly. There is no way he's going to tell his adored niece she can't have the dog.

"Pixie?" It's Logan's turn to be smug.

"Yeah, Pixie. Callie named her."

He chuckles. "I guessed. You're going to look very manly calling Pixie, while walking the—what is it?"

"It's a Great Lab. What are you doing here? I've got work to do," I say, throwing my pen down. I've been staring at these plans all day and have yet to make a single mark on the paper.

"I came to check on you. Mom thinks you're 'struggling.'"

"Mom thinks too much. She should switch it off already, she'll drive herself crazy overthinking my behavior."

"Oh, and what behavior is that?" Logan pulls out a chair and sits opposite me. Folding one knee over the other like he has no intention of going anywhere for a while. He squares his eyes on me and I immediately feel vexed. "Could it have anything to do with my HR Manager who is walking about the place with a face as sorry as yours?"

"Before you start coming over here, giving me crap, maybe you should get your own shit in order. Do you know your girlfriend texted Callie and asked her if she wanted to miss being a bridesmaid since her leg is all out of whack and it might look bad in the photos?"

His nose scrunches. "What? No, I didn't know that." He pulls out his phone but I interrupt before he makes the call.

"Leave it. Callie doesn't want to do it now anyway. She's got it in her head that the marriage is a sham for the baby anyway."

"How'd she get that idea?"

"Intuition? Overhearing a dozen conversations where Dana is acting out and forming her own conclusion? I don't know, but tell me she hasn't hit the nail on the head."

Logan heaves a sigh. "I don't want my unconventional relationship damaging Callie's outlook on relationships. Poor kid, like she hasn't got enough with your warped idea of relationships to deal with. Where is she?"

"With Mom. House check on Bloody Ben and his new dog." My voice drips with sarcasm. "They're apparently going to be mutt mates and have already found training classes to attend *together*." She's growing up too fast, and I don't like it one bit. Though, the way I feel since I stopped seeing Skyla, I don't like much of anything—including small talk with my brother. "I didn't want Callie to go with Mom today—she just had surgery—but my opinion apparently counts for shit these days. Mom and Callie said they'll be gone an hour, two tops."

"Callie will be fine, she's with Mom." He tilts his head. "But Ben? I don't like the sound of him."

"Me either. Ben. A boy. It's like she's trying to age me by ten years each and every day." I inhale deeply and blow out a sigh to try offset the pending coronary issues. "She says he's a friend."

"What is she, twelve now. You remember being twelve?"

"Not helping, Logan."

"Fine. I'll shut up." He shakes his head and looks around. "So, you broke up with Skyla and made it good with Callie by getting a dog to distract her? Genius."

"Fuck off, man. Callie wanted a dog long before I broke things off with Skyla. She was talking my damned ear off about getting a dog. You know how she is."

"Oh, yeah? You, going back on everything you said after a little wearing down—that's never happened. Like how you never once let me use your Sega, even though I begged. Even when I broke my arm fetching your ball out of the tree in the backyard—"

"You kicked the ball up there in the first place!"

"You still never once gave in. *Stubborn bastard.* I spent all summer watching you play that game and you never once let me have a turn."

"You took the Sega to summer camp while I was sweeping the leaves from the driveway—among many other chores you never had to do because you were too much of a baby!"

"Hey! I wasn't the baby. Tate's the youngest boy. Dad made you do chores because he trusted you. I had to earn his trust, painstakingly, over *years*. You had it from the moment you were born."

"Until I screwed it up, you mean?"

Logan leans onto his elbows on the desk. "You didn't screw it up. You made a decision, you stuck to it, and eventually," Logan's lips turn up into a smirk, "a decade later, Dad accepted it."

I chuckle. Put so simply, that about sums it up. "I miss the stubborn old fucker," I say.

"Me too. You remember that time on the boat, when I landed the perfect cannonball right on Tate's head and he almost drowned. Dad slept in the bunk with all us boys and we stayed awake all night reliving it over and over again."

"I remember Dad losing his shit at me for allowing you to jump off the boat while Tate was in the water with Dad practicing his front crawl."

Logan's lip curls up. "I remember him wrapping us up in the comforter so tight we could barely breathe, and telling us that he couldn't bear it if anything happened to us. That his fear influenced everything he did, and I remember him telling you how sorry he was for shouting at you."

"I'd forgotten that part," I say, feeling my throat tighten. How did I remember the sound of his voice yelling at me with such vivid clarity without remembering the comfort that came soon after? "I can still see the absolute terror in Dad's face as you landed feet first on Tate's head. It felt like hours waiting for him to resurface while Dad dove down, over and over again looking for him."

An uneasy silence fills the room.

"He was a good dad," I say, finally. "Stubborn as shit with a temper to match, but still a good dad."

"The best," Logan agrees. "Did you read his letter?"

I shake my head. "Water under the bridge. I forgive him. I don't need to read about how angry he felt when he penned what he wrote."

"What if the words aren't angry?"

I close my eyes. It's not like I haven't considered it might be my dream letter. It might contain everything I needed to hear my whole life. But it also might suck, and as parting words go, that would be unbearable.

"I'll read it when I'm ready."

"Okay, but maybe it'll help. You've been going through some stuff. After Crystal died, and then Dad, you seem angry at the world. You've been better since you came here and I thought you seemed happy with Skyla but... what happened between you two?"

I lean back and loll my head against the back of the chair, a weight falling over me.

"Skyla was great, but it'd never have worked. She's too young. I'm too set in my ways. She needs someone younger, someone who doesn't have all the baggage I do. And I need…"

I need her.

"I call bullshit on all of that."

"It's not as easy as calling bullshit. Callie will be broken if it doesn't work out. She already lost her mother. You won't get it until your own kid is here."

Logan shrugs. "Callie's more resilient than you give her credit for… but if you're too chicken to find out, then it's no skin off my back."

I shake my head. I'm not chicken.

"She'll be gone in a couple of days anyway. She's training her replacement as we speak and I've decided to send her early to get the new offices set up. She looks so miserable right now that the change of scenery will probably do her some good."

"You're shitting me?"

Logan shakes his head. "Nope. I need someone I trust to oversee the IT installation and allocating staff digs. There's a ton of work to do and I'll need to be here since the wedding is only two days away and I promised Dana I'd take a week off to go on honeymoon. The new woman Skyla hired is great, so at least that's something but Skyla will be missed. If I had my way I'd keep her here but she seems to have made her mind up, and it's not like I can trust Mike to go set up the new resort."

"That guy's a dick. I'm glad he's not going to the new resort with Skyla," I reply closing my eyes as a tension headache sets in.

"Mike's weird. He's got a framed photo of Chewbacca on

his desk." Logan rolls his eyes then continues, "Anyway, I'm just saying, if you want to make things right, then you better do something. Skyla is moving to the new resort, and pretty soon you'll have no reason to run into her again."

I sit up, opening one eye to look at him. "She coming to your wedding on Saturday?"

"Hasn't RSVP'd."

I nod feeling disappointed. "I thought she'd go." I was hoping I'd see her there—even if she hates me too much to look at me. "Are *you* going to your wedding on Saturday?" I ask seriously.

Logan nods. "I'm not backing out. Dana is hard work and I don't always like her, but I won't leave her to do this alone. Our baby needs two parents."

I don't say the obvious: that one parent will do, so long as it is a good one.

"Dana will get her priorities straight once the baby is actually here. She's been running herself low on making arrangements for the wedding."

"Bridezilla?"

He nods. "She's more focused on the wedding than she is the baby. Barely even talks about the pregnancy. Sometimes it feels like I'm talking to myself."

"Talking to Skyla wasn't like that. I felt like I had every bit of her attention. And when she spoke, there wasn't any sound in the world I'd rather hear." I find myself smiling and it doesn't go unnoticed by Logan.

"Tell me again why you and she *can't* be together?"

I blink slowly. "Tell me again why you and Dana *should* be together?"

"You know why. The baby."

"So we are in agreement, then. My kid deserves to come first too, Logan."

CHAPTER 31

SKYLA

*T*he day after I get the text to say they have checked into the hotel, I take Dad and his new girlfriend to Le Bateau for an early lunch. I prewarn them that I have a meeting with Logan after and so I'll need to head straight back to the office after we've eaten.

I'm wearing a floral tea dress, and with the warmth of the sun I can feel its rays through the fabric, though it doesn't stop the icy chill of heartbreak.

"Skyla." Dad scoops me up in a hug so tight it takes me back to my childhood, when he would pick me up right from the steps of the boarding school and for those first moments, I would feel complete. When he lets go, it's reminiscent of getting dropped right back off for the next semester.

He introduces me to Claire, and I hold out my hand to shake hers as she leans in to hug me. We both laugh and then complete a half-handed shake/one-armed hug.

"I've heard so much about you," she says.

"You too," I say, having no idea who she is other than my Dad's girlfriend and wondering how we will fill an entire hour if this is our best effort at small talk.

The server takes us to our table and then brings us a pitcher of ice water and three glasses. Claire remarks how cold the water is and I complement her comment by pointing out the condensation threatening to drip on her dress as she brings her water glass to her mouth.

"You don't seem yourself," Dad says.

Dad noticing catches me off guard and I try to keep the exhaustion from my voice. "I'm fine. Work has been busy, I'm tired. How has your vacation been going so far?"

"Your dad took me fishing which is funny since we met on the ocean, and it's the first place we went as soon as we got back on dry land." She looks adoringly at my father and he looks fondly right back at her.

It's the first time I've seen my dad since the holidays. He looks like he's gained a few pounds and looks better for it. His beard is freshly trimmed and the frames of his glasses are more modern than his usual style. But more obvious than any of the small signs of a man content in a relationship, he looks happy.

We eat three courses, well, Dad and Claire eat three courses. I push food around my plate, still feeling the tension in my gut that hasn't left since my conversation with Drew.

When Claire goes to the bathroom, I say, "You look happy."

Dad smiles at me. "I'm the happiest I've been in a long time."

"Claire seems lovely," I reply, and she does, there's nothing to dislike about her. Perhaps it might be easier not to feel so in a funk with my own love life if everyone else's is going terribly, but here I am, witnessing second chance love in full HD surround sound. It doesn't diminish how glad I am that my dad is in love, rather it makes me wonder what is so wrong with me.

"What's wrong, honey?" he asks.

I'm not sure where to begin, but find myself blurting, "I received an email from Mom."

Dad takes off his glasses and uses a napkin to wipe the lenses before putting them back on. "What did she say?"

"I deleted the email."

Dad's throat bobs with his swallow. "Probably for the best."

"But then I got curious and dug it out of the trash. She's asked to see me."

The crease between his brow deepens. "I see. And do you want to see her?"

"I don't know if I can forgive her, and I don't want to hurt you by meeting up with her but also, I feel like I need answers."

Claire comes back and Dad hands over his card to pay the bill. "You mind if I meet you back at the hotel? I'd like to take a walk with Skyla, if you don't mind?"

She smiles warmly. "I don't mind at all. You two have a lot to catch up on. I'll see you both later." She hugs me goodbye and this time it's less awkward.

"After you." Dad gestures and we walk along the sand, the gentle breeze flapping his shirt about in the wind. "I wasn't a good father to you."

"What? Dad, you did the best you could and—"

"Skyla, I worked away at sea three months at a time. I wasn't there for you like a father should be."

It's funny, I remember him being away and I remember begging him to come home, but mostly I remember the excitement building as I would count down the days before I saw him. "That was your job."

His mouth is a straight line until he talks. "It was easier

being away. You looked so much like her. I felt like such a fool when she left, and I spent a long time being angry and I didn't want you to see me like that. I didn't want to hurt you, but I think I managed that anyway."

"I don't understand."

"Your mom left me, but she didn't leave you."

"Dad, she left and then I never saw her again. She might have left your relationship, but she also left me behind."

Dad shakes his head. "She left me. I told her to never come back."

"Yeah, but she could've come back to see me or taken me with her. People say all the time, 'I never want to see you again,' but they don't mean it. Parents come back for the children they love."

"She came back."

I stop walking. This is the first time I've ever heard that my mom came back.

"When?"

A sudden blast of wind makes a chill run down my spine.

"A few times."

A few times.

"I don't remember that. A few times when?"

"You were living with Aunt Penny, remember?"

"Yeah. After Mom left, we moved out of the house when you had to go back to work. So, I stayed with Aunt Penny and then you arranged for me to go to boarding school." I gasp as realization seeps into my bones. "To keep me hidden from her?"

"No." My dad shakes his head. "I was angry and she was living with that guy and I didn't want you around him, and I couldn't trust your mom to make the right decisions for you and so I—"

"You put me in boarding school without ever asking what

I wanted, so I wouldn't know any different and I would stop asking to see her."

"No! Skyla, I needed to work and your mother, she tried a couple of times and then we barely heard from her again. If she really wanted to see you, she would have fought. I did what I did because—"

"You didn't give either of us a chance to find out. You've kept this from me for years!"

"I didn't want her to hurt you!"

"Are you sure, Dad? Or were you making sure she suffered like you did?"

His thick brows join in the middle as he frowns. "No. She signed over her rights awarding me full custody. She didn't fight for you."

Hurt covers me like a shadow.

"You didn't fight for me either! You didn't fight for me to have both my parents in my life and you didn't fight for me to know the truth or have a say in what happened to me."

"You were a kid," Dad says, though from his expression, I can tell he knows it's a cop out.

"All those birthdays and Christmases you chose not to tell me, you were lying to me. You were covering your own ass and you were letting me believe she walked away. You let me down like she did."

It's a cruel parting sentiment but I can't help it. I have yearned for my mother my whole life. Wondered where she was and what I did that was so bad she walked away, when in truth, maybe she might have stuck around if my dad could put his feelings to one side and accommodate her in our lives for my sake.

People walk by us on the beach, families, a couple holding hands. It's all too much. Today, this week, my whole life. And in a moment devoid of clarity, I want to blame my dad for everything that is missing in my life, even though I know that's unfair.

Dad opens his mouth to speak but I don't hang around to listen. I turn my back on him and run in the opposite direction until my lungs are heaving, my legs are shaking and then I keep walking until the sun is setting in the sky.

And suddenly, I'm standing outside a bar that's blaring angry-sounding punk music that matches my mood, and I push my way past the line to the front. The whole building is crammed full of people, yet I've never felt more alone. So I do what other people do when they're feeling alone, I go get a drink.

CHAPTER 32

DREW

$\mathcal{L}$ogan:

Long shot, but is Skyla with you?

THE MERE MENTION of her name has a need stirring inside me that is becoming impossible to push aside.

No. Why? She okay?

> We had a three o'clock and she hasn't turned up. Don't worry, she's probably at home packing and forgot about our meeting. She leaves tomorrow. Are you still coming to the wedding rehearsal dinner tonight?

Tomorrow?

My stomach clenches and I run to the bathroom.

> No, I'm not coming to the rehearsal. I think I've got a stomach flu. Mom's taking Callie, though. I'll see you tomorrow.

I put my phone away and try not to feel bad for flaking out. Nobody needs me at a wedding rehearsal and honestly, I can't face it. The past few days have been hell and I've almost broken my vow to leave Skyla alone more than a dozen times.

But Logan's text has me rocked. I knew she was leaving imminently. I shouldn't be shocked, but here I am feeling… devastated.

I won't ever see her infectious smile light up ever again.

It's not like Skyla to miss work and even though I try to ignore my concerns, the temptation to use Logan's text as an excuse to contact her is overwhelming. I dial her number and listen to her sweet voice telling me to leave a message after the tone. Then I hang up and dial her again. Straight to voicemail again. By the third time of listening to her message, my throat has closed up and I can barely swallow.

My gut stirs and not because I lied and said I have the stomach flu.

I feel overwhelmingly like I should go check on her. Then I remind myself that she won't want to see me anyway.

Instead, I force myself to stay home with the dog while Tate and my sister escort Mom and Callie to the wedding rehearsal. The late afternoon drags on to midnight and my thoughts swing back and forth from Skyla and how much I miss her to what Callie said—that I use my role as her father to shield myself from moving forward.

Is that what I'm doing?

I didn't think so but here, by myself, with nothing but time to think, I suddenly wonder if that is what I've been doing. Even Skyla said it, "there are single dad's everywhere embarking on relationships, living happy lives." What is it that's stopping me asking Skyla to love me?

I'm terrified I won't be enough.

The letter that's been burning a hole in my head since it arrived in the mailbox of my apartment in New York is folded in the back pocket of my jeans. Every time I try to open it, I pause.

I can't do it.

Pixie whines and sniffs the carpet where she pooped five minutes ago.

"Oh, hell. No, you don't!" I scoop her up and grab her leash as I propel us both to the waiting elevator. The doorman of my penthouse chuckles as I pass with the puppy outstretched in my hands until I am able to deposit her on the patch of grass beneath a palm tree outside the foyer of the penthouse.

"This is why I didn't want a dog," I tell Pixie as she squats. "You are kind of adorable, though."

Outside, the sky is black and there's a chill in the air. Callie is staying overnight at Mom's since Logan persuaded

Callie to be a bridesmaid after all. So, Callie will wake up there and there'll be a team of stylists to make over Tabs, Mom, and Callie. Dana will be sleeping in her own penthouse apartment to keep with tradition in not seeing the groom before the wedding. Tomorrow, Tate, Logan, and I will get ready at Logan's penthouse, but no matter how hard I try to talk him out of marrying Dana, I can't persuade Logan otherwise.

Damn fool.

If only he and Dana had something like me and Skyla did, he'd stand a chance of happiness.

I stop myself from thinking the thought and focus on all the reasons I was sure it wouldn't work.

The age gap.

Sure, Skyla's younger than I am, but she's not immature.

Callie.

I've barely had so much as a text from Callie all night. We moved to be closer to family, and it's gone better than I dared to even hope. Accident aside, she's making friends and integrating into life here perfectly. She's happy. And she loves Skyla.

As the clock creeps closer to midnight and the end of Skyla's last day at the resort, I worry. Tonight will be like last night, tossing and turning, thinking of Skyla with no clue how to make everyone happy.

Skyla.

God, I miss her so damn much.

I thought I could stick to my rules. I thought I could ignore her pull but this pain in my chest isn't going away.

I pull out my phone, tempted to try calling her but decide not to.

I don't want her to go. I need her back and it's something I must tell her in person. Not that I even deserve another chance but I'm too weak not to beg for one.

I bag up what Pixie has left, deposit it in the trash outside the penthouse, and pull Pixie in the direction of Skyla's apartment. I try to plan what to say, expecting that she will refuse to even let me inside of her apartment. My resolve starts to kick in and I decide, even if it takes me going back and forth to Miami to prove to her that I am committed to her, I'll do it. I just need to show her that I am worth taking a chance on.

And suddenly, I believe I can be a better man. For her, I can be anything.

As I round the corner, I see someone else who has every right to hate me.

"Jessie. Is that you?"

She's wearing pajamas, her face is pale. "Drew, thank God! I was just coming to see you. Is Skyla with you?"

"No. I haven't seen her since…" I broke her heart. "In a while. What happened?"

"Skyla's dad called me. She and he had… a disagreement about her mother. I've checked with everyone at the resort and no one has seen her since this morning. She's been gone all day and we were supposed to get together for our goodbye drinks tonight at the beach bar. There's no way Skyla wouldn't show up without a text or a call—or sending a fruit basket and an apology card," she says sarcastically, but I can hear the real worry in her voice. "This isn't like her."

Sweat clings to the back of my neck. I've felt at odds all evening with her missing her appointment with Logan. I put it down to me missing her and making up an excuse just to contact her but Jessie's right, not showing up to work or to meet with her best friend with no word is not like Skyla.

"What do you mean, she hasn't come home? Where could she be?"

"She. Hasn't. Fucking. Come. Home. Doofus!" Jessie is waggling her finger at me. "She's never just gone off before.

Her Dad said they had a huge fight and she was in a state. He's worried sick about her and so am I."

My cell is still in my hand so I lift it and begin calling. Her sweet voice asks me to leave a message and so I leave her a rambling plea to call me.

"Straight to voicemail?"

I nod.

"She ran off from Le Bateau. You know it?"

I nod again.

"Get your car. We need to find her!"

* * *

WE DRIVE in the direction of the restaurant, but it's long since closed by the time we get there, and the streets are almost empty from the usual late night drinkers leaving bars.

"What happened with her dad?" I ask, driving around aimlessly looking for any sight of Skyla.

"He screwed up bad. Much like you did," Jessie replies, anger boiling off her.

"I know I fucked up. I'm a dick."

"Yes, you are." She pets the puppy on her lap and then talks directly to Pixie. "You're not a dick, though. You're super cute. Absolutely adorable in fact. My Macy would love you!" She kisses the dog, then looks at me side eye. Her eyes narrowly sour then she looks sweetly at Pixie. "You're not a complete loser, not like your owner. You'd never stomp on someone's heart, would you, baby?"

"I was worried I'd ruin it with Skyla so I..."

"You shot it down. Good one—that way you get to hurt absolutely everyone."

Our eyes lock with fury. "I know, okay! No need to make me feel worse than I already do."

"I disagree. I think there is every need because had you

not ghosted her, then she might have been better able to take the news about her mother."

Jessie fires off a ton of deserved insults and I take them like I'm her personal, willing target. The pain of each low blow helps to remind me why it's so important I find her.

I love her.

And knowing she is hurting is crushing me.

I take a left along the beach road and follow it all the way down. The more time that passes, the bigger the ball of tension in my gut becomes. The sky is lit by stars and I say a silent prayer that we find her soon and that she is okay. Then I think of my dad and know if he is up there, he'll be looking down, wanting us both to be okay. He was that type of guy. So I say a silent prayer to him too.

"She's got to be here somewhere. What state was she in? You don't think she'd…"

"She was upset. She's had the shittiest of weeks to end all shitty weeks. But she's a strong woman, so she'll be okay. We need to find her. Walking the streets pissed and upset in the middle of the night is not how I want to think of her."

"Me either," I reply. "And, for the record, I am sorry I hurt her. I'm going to make it up to her."

"As you should be! Skyla Manning is the kindest, sweetest person I know. Any guy would be lucky to have her and then you go and woo her—twice I might add—and make her care about you only to piss all over it. Do you think she doesn't know you love your daughter? Do you think she doesn't know you put her before any other relationship in the entire world? You could have made it work if you wanted to, but you're stupid and blind. Too dumb to see what's right in front of you."

"Really," I hiss. "And what exactly is it I'm missing?"

I don't have to look at Jessie to know she's rolling her eyes hard at me right now. "She loves you, you idiot. And you love her too. You've been in town eight weeks, chasing her around, finding excuses to see her, but when the going gets tough you split."

She loves me too?

"What did you say?"

Jessie screw her face up like she doesn't want to say what she's about to say, "She loves you."

"She loves me," I repeat in utter disbelief.

"Not that you deserve her, the way you have been behaving."

She's right but still, I can't stop the hope from blooming inside my chest.

"I messed up but I want to fix it. I miss her! I love her," I say. I feel stressed, worried and the only thing that's going to make me feel better is holding Skyla in my arms. "Where's your kid?" I ask, turning down a road I already drove down but slowing the car so I can check the benches that line the beach.

Jessie's head lurches in my direction and I realize I probably shouldn't have asked. "She's with Betty. I didn't just leave her by herself. What do you take me for?"

I nod. "I'm sorry, I wasn't suggesting that she was alone. I'm not exactly father of the year."

"You're a good father. You'd be better if you created an actual life and didn't just exist, but you can work on that."

"You sound like Callie," I reply.

"Callie's a smart girl."

"She is."

"I'm guessing she gets her brains from her mother," Jesse says with a sarcastic grin.

"Thanks," I reply. "Wait, is that her?" I hit the brakes and leap from the car. "Stay here."

"Like hell, I am," Jessie replies and we're both rushing to Skyla's side. She's sitting on a bench watching the sea roll in.

"Where have you been?" Jessie calls thrusting Pixie in my arms and then wrapping her arms around Skyla. I hold myself back even though I'm desperate to hold her; Skyla probably doesn't want to see me. I hurt her and it was unforgiveable.

"I've been in the bar but the bartender told me it was time to go home and I realized, I don't have a home. I don't have a family either, not a real one." She lets out a little sob and then looks up and it shreds my heart to see her tearstained cheeks. "What are you doing here?" she asks me, wiping her face. Her glossy eyes widen, lingering on mine. I try to convey through a close-lipped smile that I am sorry—so fucking sorry—and as though she understands the expression, she tries to reassure me. "I'm fine. You don't need to worry about me. I needed a minute. It's been a strange day." Then she notices Pixie in my arms and then glances at Jessie. "Where did you get the puppy? Jess, if you stole it…."

Jessie and I both chuckle. "It's mine, well, Callie's actually. Come on, let's get you home."

* * *

"Skyla is tucked in and sleeping. She was asleep before her head hit the pillow. I'll stay with her," I tell Jessie, who is walking out of Skyla's bedroom.

Jessie hands me the dog. "I need to get back to Macy and let Betty get some sleep." She takes a step toward the door and I feel slightly safer.

"You're a good friend," I say. She dropped everything tonight to go find her friend, and where was I? Not even on the call list because I hurt her.

"Skyla's the good friend. I just showed up like she deserves."

Jessie's right. Skyla deserves that. I'd lay money on every

person at this resort being willing to get out of their nice warm beds to look for Skyla in an instant if it were needed— and then I thank God it wasn't necessary, she's safe. I let her down. I want to be someone she can rely on.

"Thank-you," I say. "I'm glad you came to me for help."

"I was checking if she was with you, not coming to you because we needed you. I am a good friend. You're a Blingwood and a shitty boyfriend." She squares me with a stare that has me wondering if she might punch me in the nose. Then she sighs, "But, you were shitting your pants back there looking for her."

"You're right," I admit. "I broke up with her to avoid hurting her, but the thought of any harm coming to her, I don't think I would have survived it." I remember being at the hospital, praying for Callie to be okay, and an hour ago I was going through similar emotions worrying about Skyla.

"You love her. Which means you can do better. Figure your shit out, Blingwood, and be the man she deserves." She looks at her watch. "Her suitcases are packed and her flight is midday tomorrow. Clock is ticking, Blingwood, what are you going to do?"

Fuck. I don't have long. "I'm going to fix it," I reply.

"You better. I've got to go. I'm on the early shift and everything's got to be 'peachy' perfect for tomorrow night's wedding of the year." She performs a huge eyeroll and then walks out the door, calling over her shoulder, "Tell her to call me when she wakes up and don't screw it up this time, Blingwood!"

I find a bowl of water for Pixie and then start to list all the ways I can make it up to Skyla.

CHAPTER 33

SKYLA

*M*y eyelids are heavy, like I slept in my mascara and my mouth tastes like a skunk kicked my tongue out and took up residence. When I open my eyes, I'm relieved to see I'm in my own bed, but I forgot to close the curtains and bright white light streams into the room.

"How'd you sleep?" The voice is male and as comfortingly familiar as the deep woody scent that accompanies it. "You want some water?" Suddenly he's there beside me, holding a glass.

What I want is Listerine and about a gallon of it!

"What are you doing here?" My head is foggy. I remember crying and then... "Did Jessie steal a dog?"

"You were upset and a little drunk."

I immediately check beneath the covers. I'm still wearing yesterday's tea dress, sans my shoes.

"Your shoes are by the door. Your purse is on the counter. I put your phone on the charger over there." He points to my phone and then sits at the end of my bed still holding the glass of water. He seems sheepishly guilty. "I texted your dad from your phone. I know I shouldn't have, but when I put your phone on the charger, the screen lit up and he was calling. I didn't want it to wake you, but I also didn't want to make him suffer by not knowing if you were safe. You should probably change your password from 1234. I hope you don't mind me doing that, he was worried. I said you are okay, safe at least," he shrugs, "and that you'll call him later."

I nod. It feels kind of nice that he's taken care of that for now.

"We didn't…" I'm more confident in my statement than my voice sounds.

I don't feel like we slept together and after a night with Drew Blingwood, I can always *feel* it for a few days afterward.

"No." His hand pats my calf over the top of the comforter. "I'll get the shower running for you and then I'll find you some breakfast. Just got to put Pixie outside to go to the bathroom first."

He scoops up a tiny, adorable little puppy and parts of last night come back to me.

"Is Jessie furious?" I ask.

Drew nods. "Yes. But not with you, with me, and probably your dad too. She asked me to tell you to call her."

"Drew," I say, trying not to get used to the sound of his name on my lips. "What are you doing here? You told me it was over."

"I did. I'm an idiot, in case you didn't realize. Jessie and I were driving around looking for you and…" He shakes his head and when his eyes meet mine, they're filled with pain. "We were worried about you."

The good girl in me immediately feels bad for making people worry.

"What happened with your dad?" Drew asks, and I put the pieces of my jumbled thoughts into words.

"My mom emailed me. My dad thought she was out of our lives but she wants to see me. She wanted to see me before, when I was younger, but he kept it from me."

"And now you're mad at him?"

"I *was* mad at him," I reply. "But now I think he was doing what he thought was best for me."

"Are you going to see her?"

"I don't know. It makes a difference knowing she tried to stay in contact. But, she didn't try all that hard, considering she gave up her rights to me. Even if she regretted it, she could have hired a lawyer to fight to see me. I've thought about looking her up on social media all these years. She must have thought about it too."

"But you didn't reach out to her?"

I shake my head and laugh bitterly. "I was scared she'd reject me and I didn't want to upset my dad. All these years, I've felt like I wasn't enough. That she didn't love me. Knowing she wanted to see me and that she tried—even if it was just a couple of times—matters. Even if I decided not to see her or if my dad or the court said no, I'd have at least known she loved me. I see you with Callie, and you'd sacrifice anything for her, give anything. I never felt like my mom or my dad would go to those lengths." I look up at the ceiling to stave off the hurt that's trying to overpower me. "I've spent my whole life trying to be a good girl because I was scared people would leave me otherwise. But it doesn't matter, does it? You can't force people to stay in your life— they have to want you enough. I want better than that. I deserve people who stick by me during the rough and the smooth times, and I've had enough of settling for scraps. I deserve complete and unconditional love."

Drew's hand takes a hold of mine and squeezes gently.

When I dare to meet his eyes, he is piercing me with an intense gaze that has my heart thumping against the inside of my chest. "Skyla, you selflessly give so much and rarely ask for anything in return; you're everything that's right with the world."

"Doing that hasn't served me so well."

"You're loved. So, fucking loved. And not just by everyone here at the resort, though it's pretty powerful, the feelings folks here have for you. I literally get stopped in the street by people asking about you, and I do mean everyone. You said last night that you don't have a home, that you don't have family. Not all family is tied by blood. You have family. Everyone here is your family. I am your family. Callie is your family. You are our family now. Your dad was terrified at the thought of losing you last night. Maybe your mom didn't fight as hard as she could have out of love for you."

I'm swept up in everything he just said. It sounded like a declaration but I don't dare hope. He's a good guy and maybe he's trying to make me feel better after I lost my damn mind yesterday.

"Could your mom have stopped fighting for you if she believed you'd be better off with your dad." He shrugs.

My mom was young when she left, so maybe he's right? Though I don't know her at all to know if that was part of her reasoning.

His thumb catches my chin as I look away and he says, enunciating every syllable, "You are loved. You hear me?" I nod. "Some of us have got to work on making sure you can never doubt that fact, but change is afoot," he adds rather mysteriously.

Drew leaves the room and I pick up my phone, reading the messages and then listening to the voicemails. The first text is from Callie with a picture of their new puppy, asking me if we can meet up soon. I reply quickly, telling her that I am sorry I waited so long to reply, to have fun at the wedding, and that I'll call her later. The other text messages and voicemails come from my dad, worried at first, frantic by the third message and crying by the fourth, asking me, no begging me to forgive him. Then the voicemail changes to Jessie's, and after a string of expletives she tells me to call her immediately because she loves me and wants to know I'm okay. After that it's Drew. "Skyla, where are you. Call me. I'm worried. I love you, baby. I love you. I love you. I love you. Call me as soon as you get this."

I listen to it two more times to make sure I heard right.

Drew Blingwood said he loves me.

I feel like I went to sleep last night with barely a soul who cared about me and I woke up in a parallel universe where everyone took Ecstasy and now all of a sudden the world is all psychedelic flowers, love hearts and rainbows.

"Shower's ready for you. You've got ten minutes until your breakfast is here," Drew calls and I get up mechanically and undress for the shower. But first, where the hell is the toothpaste and Listerine to kill whatever died in my mouth?

* * *

ONCE I'VE THOROUGHLY SANITIZED my mouth, I step beneath the jets. The water is the perfect temperature and feels good as it pours over me, cleansing my thumping, dehydrated brain and making me feel almost whole again. Then I dry and throw on some yoga pants and a T-shirt and am met by the smell of freshly baked muffins as I enter the living area off the bedroom.

On the counter is breakfast. I sit and Drew places a fresh coffee in a to-go cup before me. "Where did you get all this?" I ask, surprised. I don't have a kitchen so he didn't cook it here.

"I had it flown in from Italy," he replies seriously through a wide smile.

"What?"

"Okay, if you're going to grill me, I'll tell you the truth. I gave a kid riding his bike around the block fifty bucks to go to the restaurant and pick it up. But if the pup could fly, and I could bear to leave you, I'd have gone to the ends of the earth to serve you the breakfast you deserve."

"Tell me who you are and what you have done with Drew Blingwood," I say warily, narrowing my eyes on him.

He bends down, picks up Pixie, and tells me, "I'm a new man. A reformed character."

"You don't need to change, and you didn't need to pick up breakfast for me. I'm fine. I'm sorry you got drawn into what happened yesterday…." I'm still not sure how he found me or why people were looking for me. "I didn't mean to worry anyone. I would have come home if I realized—"

"Skyla. I was coming to find you anyway. I… I've been doing some thinking and I… I made a mistake. The biggest mistake of my life. I shut you out. I told you to go when I wanted you to stay. I need you in my life. Now, I know I'm going to have to prove to you I'm worth it. I haven't acted the way you deserve and I'm sorry—"

"Drew. You told me it was over."

He puts the dog down and takes my hand. "I know. I'm going to have to catch you up, because I've been pouring over this all night and I'm a little further ahead. I love you. My daughter loves you. You are quite simply, perfect, and even though I might never be considered perfect, I'm going to work on it. You are perfect for me. I have been an idiot. I do not deserve you, but when I thought something had happened to you last night, I realized I can't trudge through another day without begging you to be by my side. My life has been the best version of itself since I met you. I don't know how I didn't see it sooner... Pixie, don't eat that!" He bends and picks the dog back up and I look at him absolutely stupefied.

"Drew, you said you didn't have space for me." I'm leaning into him, hanging off his every word. He's promising me everything I want, yet I can't bring myself to believe that this could be real.

"Baby, I'm making space for you. I am fucking empty without you. I'm barren without you beside me. I apparently have space for a dog, too." He holds Pixie up to demonstrate and kisses her, then pulls a disgusted, comical face. "She does not kiss anywhere near as nice as you. But if you don't want to kiss me for a while, then I'll make do. Because, Skyla Manning, I am going to prove to you I am worthy of your love—"

"Drew. What changed? I went on a bender at a bar and came back to see you, a reformed whatever this is."

He stops short, puts Pixie back down and puts the palms of his hands on my shoulders. "Because, my life isn't the same without you in it. It is worse, so much worse. I've been trying to realize the exact moment it all changed, but I can't pinpoint it other than the first time I laid eyes on you at the pool. I didn't think I needed anyone other than my daughter to be happy. But I do. I've never felt this way before and it scares the shit out of me. I need you, Skyla. In the laundromat, you asked if I felt anything for you at all and it killed me to stay silent. I wanted to tell you I love you, but I was too damn scared to admit it because if I admitted to you that I love you, then I had to admit it to myself. And once I admitted it to myself, I knew that I stood the chance of losing everything because you can't come back from feelings like that. When love goes wrong, it destroys you and I didn't think I could go through that again."

I shake my head, confused.

"And now you think you could risk loving again? Even though it could fail and hurt you?"

"Baby, it can't hurt more than it does right now. I haven't stopped thinking about you since I first laid eyes on you, and the past week without you has been hell. Unless you don't feel the same?" His gaze searches mine like he's desperate for a sign, something to cling to and I smile a small, reassuring smile.

I love him and pretending otherwise is impossible.

Buoyed by my reassurance he leans down and takes my hand in his. "I am serious about you. I've never been more serious about anything. I love you and I really think we can make a go at this."

It's everything I have wanted to hear my whole life, but it's overwhelming.

He blinks and I watch the color drain from his face.

"You're not sure. I blew it, I know, but if you give me a chance, I can prove how much I care. All I'm asking for is a chance."

"Drew, I'll be leaving soon."

"Then don't leave. Jump in with both feet and stay here with me. Move in with me and Callie. You can pick the furniture, and I'll get you whatever you need so that it feels like home. The timing is perfect. We can make it work." His voice is pleading and I so badly want to step into the fantasy he is imagining for us that my bones ache from holding back. "Make us your home?"

"What happens when you change your mind?"

"I won't," he says too quickly.

"But what if you do? You feel this way now, but after Callie's accident, you withdrew. You couldn't get away from me soon enough."

"I know I hurt you. I was in shock or, fuck, I don't know. Terrified is probably a better way to describe how I was starting to feel about you and combined with being in a hospital for Callie, I was beyond rational thought. I've also been thinking a lot about my father and how I've always felt like I let him down. The world was getting smaller, and the people in my life bigger, and I freaked out."

"But you're not freaked out anymore?"

He takes a deep breath. "I am petrified. But I can't live another day without telling you how I feel and asking you to take a chance on a life with me."

"I'm scared too," I admit. "I've spent so long telling myself not to have feelings for you that none of this feels possible. I've got the chance for a fresh start. A new place with new people who barely know anything about me. It reminds me of how I felt when I arrived at the boarding school. You're offering everything and yet I'm terrified to trust the feeling because losing this time around feels bigger. I don't think I'd survive it."

"Don't be afraid, baby. You've got nothing to lose. I'm all in and my gut is telling me we are going to make it. What does your gut tell you?"

I puff out a strangled chuckle. "My heart is aching and I'm already tiring of trying to resist you."

"Then don't resist." He pulls something out of his back pocket and puts it on the counter. "The last year I have been so torn up about what my father might have written in this letter that I haven't been able to see any of the good in my life. I was stuck. But here with you now, I'm not afraid of what it says because I am a work in progress and I am trying to be a better man. What the contents of this letter makes me feel is insignificant when compared to how I will feel if you decide you never want to see me again."

"And if you get spooked again?"

"I'll never shut you out. Not worth it."

"I think you should read the letter," I reply, and a feeling of dread settles in my solar plexus.

"Now?" he asks, looking nervous.

"You'll never move forward completely until you know what it says."

Drew nods and tears the envelope. "Nothing's going to change how I feel about you," he says, and God, I hope he's right.

CHAPTER 34

DREW

J pull the sheet of paper from the envelope, immediately recognizing my father's childlike, scrawling handwriting. The only sound is Pixie, snoring lightly by my feet.

I clear my throat, ready to read my father's thoughts aloud, when Skyla's delicate hand lands on mine. "You don't have to read it." Her deep brown eyes glisten in the sun soaked room. "I want to be with you. If what is written in that letter is going to hurt you, if it's going to change you, or change things between us, then I don't want you to read it."

The one hundred pounds of pent-up tension that's been sitting on my chest suddenly evaporates, leaving me feeling lighter, energized. New.

"Really? You'll give us a chance?"

She nods, her cheeks pinken with her smile but I know she's just trying to save me the heartache. There's unfinished business in this letter and I won't let it get in the way of my future with Skyla.

"You won't regret it. I won't let you ever regret it, not even for one second." I wrap my arms around her, and still clutching the piece of paper, lift her from the stool at the counter, twirling her around. Skyla brings her mouth down to mine and the slight pressure of her kiss has electricity zinging through my body. "I love you," I say, breaking the kiss before initiating another one. She fits so perfectly against me, flawless. Every dip and curve of her body is unequaled, unrivaled utopia.

We break for air and my mouth travels to the apex of her neck, then down along her collar bone and she lets out a tantalizing groan. I'm suddenly thinking of all the ways I can make her moan some more, and then realize, we have exponential potential for a lifetime of these kinds of moments. This perfect bliss. It doesn't have to end; it can actually last forever. All it takes is time and a leap of faith.

"Damn!" I say, coming back down to reality. I lower Skyla onto her feet and then check my watch.

"What is it?" Her voice quivers with fear and I kiss the breath out of her to reassure her.

"It's Logan's wedding tonight." I lift my father's letter until it's between us. "My family. Callie. They're expecting me there. And I don't want the contents of this letter to hold me back from moving forward anymore. I need to read it and make peace with whatever it says."

And then it happens again—the paper suddenly feels like it weighs a hundred pounds. Skyla gave me the perfect excuse to fold it away and to never look at it. And I want to do that. Putting this letter away and never reading it means I never have to find out how my father felt about me right before he died. But the other half of me, the part that feels brave and strengthened by the woman beside me, feels like it's time I found out.

"I need to be present for the people I love, and that includes you. Reading this won't change the way I feel about you, but it might change the way you feel about me." And that right there, I realize, is the sole reason now for my trepidation. I look in her eyes, so innocent and pure, I wonder what I am asking of her to take a risk on a guy like me. "Promise you won't hear me read this and realize what a mistake you're making?" It's a feeble plea, and a promise I shouldn't ask her to make.

She strokes my jaw, tilting my chin using her thumb and forefinger until her eyes meet mine. "There is nothing anyone could write or say about you that would scare me away because I know the real you. I know you're grumpy and bossy and self-sacrificing. But I also know you are kind, and generous, passionate and that you love so deeply it makes you fearful and act a little crazy. Your heart is big and pure, and I'm trusting you to take care of mine."

The relief is a wave cascading over me.

"You won't regret it. I believe in us," I reply, resting my forehead against hers. She smells so good I drink her in. When I lean back, I watch her gently sweep her lower lip with her tongue and it makes my balls throb.

"I really want to fuck you right now."

She smiles seductively and the hand that doesn't clutch the letter reaches around and squeezes her peach of an ass.

Will touching her ever get old? I doubt it.

"Scratch that. I don't want to fuck you. I want to make love to you. I want to cherish every inch of your body and intimately reacquaint myself with every part of you." My thumb is running circles on her hip, my dick hardening at the thought, but my head is telling me there are things I need to do first. "I read this damn letter, we go to the damn wedding, and then after it's all done, you come back to the penthouse with me and I spend the entire night making you come. Deal?"

She shakes her head. "I didn't RSVP to the wedding. But I am down with the rest of your plan."

"I don't care if you didn't RSVP, neither will the organizers. It's a quarter of a million dollar wedding. I'm sure they can find an extra chair and a plate of food. If they can't, you can sit on my knee and I'll feed you from my plate."

She giggles and it's the best sound in the entire world. "Okay, I'll come to the wedding. But I need to see my dad before he checks out. I don't want to hate on him for what's happened because I know he's not a bad person. I'll make him understand that one day, I would like to see my mom and get some answers."

"You're incredible."

"So are you." Her eyes glance down at the sheet of paper I'm still holding and she smiles. "I'm here for you."

"Okay. Here goes. Just a note from my dead dad. It won't be so bad, will it?"

"Doesn't matter if he wrote the absolute worst, Drew. I know the truth. You're a good son, a great father, and an excellent lover." She grins deviously and my cock strains in my pants.

"You know what?"

She raises her brows.

"I'm going to be an even better husband someday."

"Is that so?"

"Oh, yeah. I'm going to learn your body like I'm studying for the exam of my life and then when you're ready I am going to marry the fuck out of you."

"Well, you already got an A from me."

I look at her seriously. "Only an A? Baby, you mistook me for God himself."

"It's the O's I've been most focused on." She smiles ruefully.

I rub my thumb over her bottom lip. "You make me so happy."

I lead Skyla to the sofa and gesture for her to sit and then I seat myself beside her and hold the letter out so she can see it too.

"Son," I start and suddenly I can hear his voice, smell the faint scent of his Saturday night cigar, and feel the warmth of the fire we used to light in the living room. *"Things have gotten out of hand."* I turn to face Skyla and she looks at me encouragingly. *"I suppose, if I look back to when it all started, it was when you were born. My son. My first born. You came into this world with the force of an earthquake. The gusto of a hurricane. Three weeks early, I've never been so scared in my entire life. Of course, your mother was calm and collected like always. She held my hand and told me everything would work out, but I was still shitting my pants and praying to the stars you'd both be okay. And you were. A fine, seven-pound boy with a pair of lungs that could outperform a choir. I loved you instantly, but I guess you know the strength of that love, since you had a child yourself—and what a fine father you have become.*

You grew fast, your siblings following in quick succession. It was like I only had to look at your mother and suddenly another child was on its way, but you were always special to me, because it was the moment you were born that I fully understood the meaning of love and sacrifice and what some might call the ultimate sin, pride.

You were just a small boy who I paraded through the resort like a trophy. Like you already got me first place in the race. I told everyone you were my protégé, you were so like me in every way. Everyone said so. You used to hang off my every word and follow me everywhere.

I didn't see it coming.

315

When Logan chose to play football and Tate began acting, you joined the school council and petitioned for better changing facilities and a new auditorium for the performers. I see now that was the infancy of your passion for design and your enduring love for your family, and not, as I had thought at the time, a clear sign you were to become a leader of something your grandfather and I had built. You see, I had a vision of what you were to become: A better version of me.

The night you told me you were changing majors, I was so damn angry—I felt like such a fool. I'd spent the afternoon telling a reporter you were all set to one day take over.

Didn't I know my son at all? I was wrong to take that out on you. I worried you were making a mistake, but worse I was angered that you didn't want to be like me.

Of course, your mother, in her everlasting patience told me not to be so damn stupid, that you were strong and smart and were making the right decisions for you. Of course it took me too long to see it, pride will make a man go blind.

Son, I am sorry to say you are like me, and not just the good parts. You inherited my stubbornness and single-mindedness. When you get your head stuck on an idea, there's little that will change your mind. And now, I don't want you to be so much like me after all. I work too damn much and your old man has gotten stuck in his ways. I want more for you.

You've built an impressive business. You're award winning, but you were always a winner to me anyway.

My biggest fear for you is that you forget to make a life.

We let the years go by.

I let the years go by, and now, when you are at your lowest, and your daughter has lost her mother, I can't guide you, because we have lost our way.

I lost my way.

But not all things stay lost, and I don't want to waste any more time.

Son, I think it's time you came home, but if you decide to stay and run your empire in New York with Callie, then I support your decision.

I'm proud of you and I love you.
Dad

"YOU OKAY?" Skyla says from beside me.

I'm unsure if I finished reading the letter a minute or an hour ago.

"He was proud of me?" I check.

She nods and her hands tighten around mine. "He loved you."

"I've been putting off reading that letter for over a year because I was certain... I was so sure it'd be a list of everything that's wrong with me, everything I failed at." I don't know whether to cry or fist punch the air, but I settle on grinning because it's relief that overwhelms me most. "He didn't hate me when he died."

"He didn't. Your father loved you," she says again. "And even without reading the letter or doing as he outright told you, it's like he's guided you to this moment. You have made a life for yourself. You have a good future."

"Baby, I'm so sorry. Being so unavailable, I lost my way, too, just like my Dad. I was scared of screwing things up but I'm not afraid anymore."

She puts the letter on the side table, then retakes my hands in hers. "So, we're doing this. You and me? Because I understand if you need some time to process. Your life has been on hold, but now you can finally move forward."

"What?" I pull my hands from her grip and wrap my arms around her waist, pulling her onto my lap so she's facing me and there's no chance of her going anywhere. "Baby, it's done. I don't need time, my sole focus is not fucking up this chance you're giving me. That is how I am moving forward now, with you. Skyla, you don't understand, I am a man standing at the starting line of the race, and I've already won, because here you are beside me, but if I make a mistake, I lose everything."

"You're not going to lose me. You're the first man I ever loved, my first, that should tell you something."

"I don't know how I got lucky enough to be your first but I'm going to do everything to be worthy of being your last." She starts to rock against me through the fabric of our clothes. "I love the way you move," I grab her ass and squeeze, "and these cheeks had me at hello."

She grins proudly and then her lips crash against mine. I drink in the sweet taste of her, devouring her. The intensity of my feelings for her swells in my chest like a raging fire. When I pull back, her dark brown eyes gleam with desire. "You make me feel like I could conquer the world."

"Well, you already conquered my heart," she admits. "I can't wait to see what's next."

Skyla lets out a moan as I kiss her neck and my cock immediately hardens.

Bang. Bang. Bang.

I ignore the door being beat off its hinges. Skyla feels so perfect, nothing can be as important as this moment, right now.

Bang. Bang. Bang.

Skyla stops writhing.

No!

"I better go see who it is," she says and I loop my fingers around her wrists.

"No, baby. Stay. We've got to consummate our relationship." Her hand slips from mine as she gets off the sofa and I have to stop myself from pouting like a child.

"I can't wait to consummate our relationship," Skyla

breathes. "Coming!" *Bang. Bang. Bang.* "Hang on," she calls, picking up Pixie who is now yapping.

She barely has the door unlocked when Jessie bursts in.

"There are photographers everywhere. Where is your phone? I've been trying to call you!" Jessie—AKA cock-blocker—looks from Skyla to me and I raise my hand up to say hi. "No need to guess why you haven't been answering your phone either." She rolls her eyes but doesn't look too pissed. "It's good you're here. You better go find Logan and tell him. It's Dana. She's gone AWOL and the world's press is here to report on it!"

CHAPTER 35

SKYLA

*I*t's a funny thing, to be so blissfully, bone-deep happy, while witnessing a person you care about being hurt so cruelly. Today should be the happiest day of Logan's entire life, instead it's like he got kicked in the balls.

After racing to Logan's penthouse, we pushed passed dozens of photographers until we reach security, who let me, Drew, Pixie, and Jessie through right in time to find Logan about to hit a bottle of Macallan straight from the neck.

"Sally was just in here and told me. Dana's gone?" Logan says, glancing around at all of us.

Jessie steps forward. "She's gone all right. I looked everywhere for her. Simon on security saw her getting in an Uber with her suitcases about an hour ago."

I gaze at Drew for the hundredth time, wondering if Logan's fiancée walking out on him has in anyway rocked his belief in happy ever afters, but his hand barely leaves mine. While Logan leaves a voicemail on Dana's cell, begging her to call him, Drew holds me close and whispers that he loves me. I'm not sure if he needs to say it or, in the face of witnessing such despair, he knows I need to hear it.

"Dana's not answering. Where has she gone?" Logan pushes his thumb on the screen of his cell to dial a different number and then lifts it to his ear. "Where's the jet?" He runs his other hand through his hair, his face contorting with pain. "Who authorized that?" Then he lowers himself on the couch, pins the phone against his ear and shoulder and unscrews the lid from the Scottish whisky.

"I'm guessing she's skipped town on the private jet, then," Jessie whispers, bending down to pick up the puppy and stroking her head.

"The wedding is supposed to start in a couple of hours and the place is crawling with reporters." Drew pulls out his phone, presses the screen and then lifts it to his ear. "Tate? Get your ass over to Mom's. Lay low, there are paps here and your face will only make them crazier. We'll come over once the fuss has died down, and tell Callie not to worry. Logan, Skyla, and I are all fine."

There's a crash against the wall and Logan's cell phone splinters into pieces on the marble floor. "She's gone. She's pregnant and taken the private jet and she's left me."

"I can't believe she left. She's been promoting your relationship like it's a billion-dollar business. Did you guys have an argument?" Drew asks.

I let go of Drew's hand and seat myself at the table, away from the center of the open plan living area while Jessie paces; she's as mad as I ever seen her. It's a strange vision since I wasn't sure she cared for the Blingwoods all that much.

"No argument. In fact, things have been going okay. Dana's been frustrated with me, yes. She wanted full press coverage of the wedding, and I put my foot down and said no, but she seemed to be coming around to my reasons." He sighs and his whole body sags. "She's cut back on drinking and she's been insatiable in the bedroom, pregnancy hormones, I guess," Logan replies. "I thought she was happy. Well, as happy as Dana gets. I don't understand why she didn't come to me."

Jessie harrumphs loudly.

"She said marrying me was all she ever wanted, well, that and to sign a deal with Versace." Logan takes a swig of the whisky and his face is stone, as though he is numb to everything.

"What are you going to do? Do you want me to tell everyone the wedding is off?" Drew says, taking the bottle from Logan, having a small sip, and casually putting it on the table out of his reach.

We all glance at one another uneasily. Telling everyone the wedding is off will send the reporters into a frenzy .

A long sigh leaves Logan's lips. "My guy at the airport said she's flying to New York. My best guess is she had second thoughts, made up with her father, and is going to his hotel in the city." His fists ball. "We only did the rehearsal last night and there was no indication that she didn't plan on going through with it." Logan shakes his head, then stares at the floor in a state of shock. "The reporters are going to eat this up. If Jessie hadn't discovered Dana gone, the first I would have known about it would have been while I was standing at the altar waiting for a bride who had no intention of showing up!"

"That bitch did a real number on you," Jessie hisses and all of us turn our heads to her. If Jessie was closer and she didn't have Pixie in her arms, I'd nudge her with my foot to remind her to keep her own foot out of her mouth. Logan is still our boss, and now probably isn't the time to piss him off.

"What Jessie probably means is that pregnancy hormones

can make people do crazy things and well, maybe—" I say trying to cover for my friend's insensitivity.

"No. I *mean* she did a real number on you," Jessie says, squaring Logan right in the eyes.

"What do you know that you're not telling me?" His voice is so detached, it hardly even sounds like him.

"I wasn't going to mention it, because it is fifty shades of crazy, but you need to know the truth."

"What is it? What did she do?" Logan demands, standing up. Drew is beside him, and I stand too, moving to Jessie's side.

"I was down to clear out Dana's suite this morning. Dana always leaves a pigsty to tidy. I let myself in as usual, opened the windows to clear out the stench of weed, and she was in bed snoring her head off. By the door were all her suitcases already packed. So, I started in the bathroom to give sleeping beauty a chance to wake up. She wasn't expecting me so early, and she slept right through my service. But she must have known I saw what I saw, because I rage-cleaned the shit out of the bathroom before I left. Later, when I came back hoping she'd be awake so I could finish up, she was gone, but she'd left the wedding dress, so I knew she wasn't waiting around to get caught."

Logan's eyes tighten on her. "Get caught for what?"

"The half a dozen used pregnancy tests on the counter."

"Jessie, it's no secret that Dana's pregnant," Drew says.

The tension in the room is thick as soup and I'm not sure Jessie's revelations are helping.

"A half a dozen *negative* pregnancy tests," Jessie clarifies.

Logan's eyes widen. "You sure they were hers?" He inhales deeply, then answers his own question. "Of course, they were hers. Her followers on social media tripled when she announced the engagement, and went tenfold after she dropped the pregnancy bombshell. For once, she had something to post that people were interested in." He sits back down, then immediately stands. "She wasn't pregnant. You're right, she really did a number on me." Logan grabs the Macallan and takes a long draw. "She was, however, trying to *get* pregnant and when that didn't work... she was going to leave me standing at the altar, humiliated in front of the world's press." He shakes his head. Drew rubs his brother's shoulder and is about to say something when his cell starts ringing. "Tate... Yeah, sure, I'll look." Drew stares at Logan and his voice is low as he says, "Tate said his publicist called. You should see Dana's Instagram."

All of us pull out our cell phones, Logan skims the screen of Drew's over his shoulder, and suddenly there is a collective sigh.

On the screen, with red-rimmed eyes and an expression that'd make the devil himself look innocent and hurt, is a photograph of Dana Gee looking right into the camera. Behind her I can still see the airplane seats, suggesting she took the selfie while still on the plane. Her post reads: *The Great Escape: How losing my baby helped me find my power.*

I skim the post and am horrified with the depths she has gone to.

The whole world thought I had everything, but really I was trapped in a one-sided relationship based on toxic masculinity and pernicious power plays.

It reads like a drunken rant. Dana listing how she was a supportive partner to an abusive, power-hungry monster.

When I look up at Logan, the color has drained right out of his face.

"She's going to ruin me. I didn't give her a baby and I wouldn't get involved with her publicity and now she's looking for another way to squeeze five minutes of fame out of me and my family. It'll hurt Tate too, and all of you."

"No. She..." My voice trails off. I have no words to defend

her and I don't want to. I've worked for Logan for three years and I know deep in my bones that every word Dana has put out into the world are lies from a spoiled girl with daddy issues.

"That no good, lying bitch!" Jessie spits.

"Maybe it was…" My voice trails off. I can't defend her by suggesting her account was hacked. Everyone in the room knows Dana has done this but I can't figure out why.

"Jessie's right. Dana wasn't pregnant. She's duped me and lied all this time." Logan paces, clearly trying to sort out what the hell Dana was up to. "I was breaking up with her. The night she told me she was pregnant, I was breaking up with her." He goes to the window and stares down at the reporters. "Dana was going to have me wait at the altar for her, only for her not to show. But why? Why would she humiliate me like that?"

"To boost her profile," Jessie says. "Being attached to a Blingwood was pretty much the only thing that made her interesting."

Logan takes Drew's phone from him and scans Dana's post. "Follow my socials for a serialized breakdown of my relationship with Hollywood sweetheart's older brother."

He shakes his head and his laugh is filled with pain. Then he turns to Jessie, his face as humble as I've ever witnessed. "Thank-you, Jessie, for your honesty on all counts. She was out to trap me, and when trapping me didn't work, she wanted to humiliate me to further her own popularity. Judging from the time she posted this nonsense, Dana must have listened to her voicemails and knew I wouldn't be waiting at the altar, and so now she's changed the narrative, again—telling her followers I was abusive and that she lost a baby that was never there in the first place." His face is white. Sickened. "This could ruin me. Who wants to vacation at a resort owned by a man like she describes?" He goes back to

325

scrolling the screen of Drew's phone. "The comments are already panning me and my business."

"No one is going to believe her. Logan, you're a good man," Drew says, his voice full of conviction, but the silence that follows is weighted with alarm.

In an ideal world, Drew's sentiment would be undeniable. Truth should trump lie. Benefit of doubt should be applied, yet everyone knows in reality, social media and popular opinion rule over fact.

"Then, we change the narrative," I say. "Jessie, did you take any photos of the cleanup of Dana's room with all the negative pregnancy tests?"

Jessie smirks. "Sure did. No way I was risking the bitch denying it."

"The reporters are here by invitation, right?"

Logan shakes his head. "There was not supposed to be any members of the press reporting on the wedding. I vetoed any mention of it. So of course, Dana no doubt tipped them off. She wanted publicity. I wanted a quiet, low-key affair. The date of the wedding wasn't publicized, so I'm sure she was the one to alert them to come today." He closes his eyes in a long blink.

"Then let's play this out two ways. First, we get the reporters. Jessie, call Simon on security and have his team complete a sweep to rid the premises of all reporters." I swipe my cell to life. "I'll email the pictures of the negative tests to Dana right now, tell her that if she doesn't delete her Insta post and if she publishes any further nonsense, then we'll push your side—the truth: there was no baby. You could bring a lawsuit, there'll be no medical evidence she was ever pregnant. I doubt she'll want the world knowing she faked a pregnancy for celebrity status. And second, let's spread the word that there never was a wedding planned today. If there is no wedding and Dana's lies are deleted, then what have the paps got to report?"

"The first part could work, though it boils my blood that you might be forced to take legal action to defend yourself, but the press will never believe there was no wedding. The place is decorated up like a fondant cake," Jessie says. "Unless... there is a wedding, just not Logan and Dana's. It'd be a shame to let such an expensive wedding go to waste..." Jessie's eyes widen to me and Drew and my heart almost stops.

"I mean, it could work," Drew says, with a panty-dropping smile.

CHAPTER 36

DREW

"You ready for the wedding of the year?" I ask Callie, who looks beautiful and about five years older with her shorter hair piled up on her head. In her hand is a jewel encrusted dog leash with Pixie attached at the bottom. Her nails are a deep pink and I smell perfume. "Is that makeup on your face?"

"Relax, Dad. It's a wedding. People wear makeup."

"I'm fine," I breathe. "But you're not old enough for makeup."

"I'm twelve not two. Relax," she says again. "Where's Skyla?"

"She had some last-minute stuff to arrange. Seeing her father before he checks out, changes in guests, that sort of thing. She'll be here."

She nods. "You look good, Dad."

I'm wearing a suit, and despite the sun setting over the

ocean, it feels about a hundred degrees and there is not so much as a whiff of a breeze.

"Please take your seats; the bride will be here soon," the pastor calls and a bunch of the hotel staff, some still in uniforms since they had no time to change, stop chattering and find seats for themselves since the seating plan no longer applies.

Callie leads me to a set of wooden chairs that face the altar. There is not a reporter in sight, though there is the barely audible sound of drones, fitted with high-tech zoom-in cameras buzzing overhead. Hopefully, the now fading light will deem any photographs they manage to take of my family unusable. Still, Logan shifts uncomfortably and it's no wonder, he has had the very worst of days—but I know, with our family's support, he's going to be just fine.

"Dana took her Instagram post down," Logan whispers beside me.

"Good," I reply. "It'll blow over, so long as she heeds the warning of legal action."

"People won't forget," he says.

"People aren't interested in Dana and her fake-ass life-style. They'll see through all that shit. Keep doing you and you'll be fine."

Logan's gaze skims the place. "No way I am getting involved with all this shit again. Not ever."

I clap him on the back. "You didn't meet the right woman," I tell him. "When you meet her, there won't be so much as an ounce of doubt in your mind."

Logan clears his throat distastefully. "Sounds to me like you owe me the hundred bucks I bet you."

I look at him questioningly.

"I bet you you'd be dating a woman of Callie's choosing before the year was out."

I take out my wallet and hand him five twenties. "Got to

say, for once it feels good that you were right. Your time will come too, brother."

"Just 'cuz you got all lit up by love, no way I'm making the same mistake."

"Lit up by love? You made up with Skyla?" Callie's expression is one of sheer joy. I'd forgotten in all the commotion that I'd never said anything to her about my apology to Skyla.

"We're trying things out," I say, unable to keep the grin from my face.

"Daddy! That's amazing." Callie throws her arms around me and somehow, it makes my utter joy even bigger. Better.

"Guess you're not so different from the old man, after all," Logan says. "Stubborn fuckers, both of you, but you also know when it's time to make things right."

"I'm done being stubborn. From now on if it feels good, I'm doing it."

"I'm just glad I don't have to lose my HR Manager. Did Skyla let the new girl know she'll train here but work at the new resort?"

"She's on it," I say through a smile. "There's nothing getting in our way from here on out."

"It's getting late," Mom says from behind us. "Where is the bride? I can't wait to see what she is wearing. Poor love had to find something in a flash."

"I'm pretty sure she would have worn a trash bag to marry the love of her life at a quarter-million-dollar wedding," Logan deadpans.

"You salty?" I ask him.

"Nah. Quarter of a million well spent if it gets Dana out of my life."

"And are you okay with not being a dad yet? I know you were looking forward to it."

"It is what it is," Logan replies coldly.

"You'll be a father one day."

"Half a dozen tests and a lot of action, maybe I'm barren." Logan says it jovially, like it's no skin off his back, but beneath it there's a hurt in his eyes that's not lost on me.

"Those Blingwood swimmers will be in good order. It's in the genes, but if they're not, then you have other options. Crystal's friend used this clinic in New York that suck the best swimmers right out the sample and inserted them—"

"I am not having kids. I'm done, Drew. Leave it. I'm showing my face for the service, and then I'm getting back to my office. My career has been distracted by bullshit long enough."

"Okay, man. I'll leave it, for now, but only because you've had an absolute shit of a day. But take it from someone who has been there, cutting yourself off isn't worth it. Keep living your life one day at a time. You're going to be fine."

Logan nods but I can tell he's digging his heels in. He's hurting badly right now but I know he'll be fine. Eventually.

The music starts and we all turn to see Skyla almost sprint up the aisle. "Phew. That was close," she says, darting into the row of seats to join our family.

"I saved you a seat," I say, patting the chair beside me. As she scurries past Logan and high fives Callie to get to the other side of me, I give her ass a little squeeze then bite my fist. "That ass gets me every time."

"Later." She winks.

"Is the bride all set?" Mom asks between our shoulders.

"She is," Skyla replies. "She looks fabulous!" Skyla looks back at Mom and then along our little row of chairs. "Where're Tate and Tabitha?"

"Tate was called into work, and since it was no longer his brother's wedding he couldn't really get out of it. And Tabs decided to catch the private flight with him." Mom looks around. "You think there are enough guests to make it look authentically planned?"

"There's almost the entire resort workforce here. I told Dana's half of the attendees that she'd been spammed and there is no wedding. They believe Dana and Logan getting married today was all a hoax and they've checked out. A few from your side of the family have hung around to watch a stranger get married and to catch up. And I put a post-up on the Blingwood business page to announce that Logan had fully funded the wedding of their dreams to two, loyal staff members." Skyla grins widely. "We changed the narrative. Logan sounds adorably sweet. Dana has reposted on Insta to say that her account got hacked, which reconciles with the accounts of Dana's guests, and since the wedding was paid for via the business account, there's no evidence it was ever for anyone else."

"A job well done, baby." I flick a lock of her hair out the way and kiss her cheek. "You look beautiful."

"Thank-you."

I catch the hand that rests in her lap, and stroke her ring finger. "It could have been us standing up there."

Her gaze pins me to the spot. "When we get married, I want Callie to have the chance to fully wrap her head around it. We couldn't drop a last-minute wedding on her."

"I'd marry you in a flash. I love you, and I can't wait to make you my wife."

"Please rise for the bride," the pastor orders.

Skyla takes out her phone and begins recording. Doug's entire face lights up as the music changes, and Sally begins dancing her way up the aisle to Bruno Mars' "Marry You."

CHAPTER 37

SKYLA

I stretch my toes out on the finest cotton sheets with a gloriously high thread count and without even opening my eyes, I know I am in Drew's bed, still naked and aching from an entire night of feeling cherished. The scent of his musky shampoo clings to the pillow, but when I stretch my foot farther I don't feel him.

The room is brightly lit by the sun's rays streaming through the floor to ceiling windows but there are no sounds, no sight of Drew in the bedroom and the en suite door is open with no sign of him in there either.

"Drew," I quietly call out even though Callie went back to her Nanna's house with Pixie last night.

The door flies open and suddenly Drew stands before me clutching two coffee cups. I lick my lips. Even dressed in sweats and a T-shirt, he looks divine.

"Where have you been?"

"I went to get muffins and coffee, and I thought I better check on Logan."

He comes and joins me on the bed, and I sit up, pulling the sheet to cover my nakedness and take the coffee he hands me.

"How's Logan?" I ask.

Drew shrugs. "Surviving, I guess. I found him at the office. He's throwing himself into work. I suppose he needs the distraction."

"Poor guy. He'll be okay, though. We'll look out for him. Dana will probably announce a miscarriage any day now and concoct some story about how she's devoting her life to Buddhism and kale." I roll my eyes, still annoyed by her shitty treatment of Logan. "I think the right person will come out on top. The coverage in the news of the Blingwood staff wedding has been incredible, and it's going a long way to improve Logan's image following Dana's lies. Sally is ecstatic, she and Doug got a free wedding. In fact, they should be touching down in the Bahamas any moment now. I can't wait for her to start posting on her socials how incredible her free honeymoon is. Real, honest coverage that shows the world what a good, kind family you have."

Drew's hand clutches mine above the covers. "I want to thank you for everything you did yesterday. You were amazing."

"You already thanked me." I raise my brows at him, remembering his mouth, heavy between my thighs and my hands almost ripping his hair from the roots. "You thanked me quite a lot of times, if I remember right, *God.*" I chuckle, embarrassed that I somehow wind up calling him God each time we make love—though his touch is rather heavenly, so the term of endearment is kind of fitting.

"I mean it, Sky. Your actions yesterday helped my family so much. Since Tate went A-list, reporters have been obsessed with getting a story about all of us. They even covered Crystal's death. This could have been the end for

Logan's company. I feel like I owe you more than a handful of orgasms and coffee."

"And muffins, don't forget the muffins."

He grins and replies, "They're on the counter. You want me to go get them?"

"First let's work up an appetite," I say grabbing his shirt in my fist and pulling him closer.

Drew chuckles deeply. "You're insatiable. I created a monster," he replies with a devious smile.

My face becomes flush. He's right, lately I want him all the time. "That reminds me, Jenny handed her notice effective immediately."

"Why does my mentioning you coming remind you of my brother's assistant handing her notice in? I mean, it'll screw Logan up with how busy he is, but seriously, I'm offended." He's still grinning so I know he isn't offended in the slightest, so I continue.

"She broke up with Mike—"

"You're not going back to that douche bag, I'll kill him first."

I snort rather indelicately. The idea of going anywhere near Mike is laughable after falling so damn deeply for Drew. "Of course I'm not, silly. But she said something that got me thinking."

"Oh yeah, what did she say?"

"She said Mike wasn't fulfilling her needs."

"Not surprised. I doubt he could fill a thimble. So?" He shrugs.

"She wasn't satisfied." I emphasize my words but then spit it out. "She told me, she was quitting because she broke up with Mike, and then she told me that they only made out. It never went further because... he couldn't...." I raise my brows up again, urging him not to make me say it.

"He couldn't get it up?" Drew coughs to cover his laugh.

"So, he was an asshole to you, telling you that you were to blame for his problems—which you weren't, by the way, because I'm hard for you, baby, *all the time*. But the truth is that the reason he couldn't hit the mark is because his own equipment is faulty. I'm not surprised. That dude has a chip on his shoulder, it's nothing to do with anyone else, and certainly not your fault."

"Mike and I tried to have sex that one time but it didn't work. I always thought it was because of me. That he didn't find me attractive, that maybe if I was thinner, or did my hair a different way or... something else. But if he couldn't get hard for her, then it proves it the problem lies with him, not me."

Drew puts both our coffees on the bedside table. Then he takes my hand. "Baby, the problem was always with him. You're fucking gorgeous. I'm rock solid right now just looking at you." He presses my hand against his crotch and he is indeed hard. Then he puts my hand on his heart. "Never believe you are anything less than perfect. I mean it, Skyla. You've changed everything for me. My daughter loves you. I love you." His smile has my insides melting and my skin vibrating. "There's something I want to ask you."

"Oh." My heart gallops.

"I already checked with Callie, and she is stoked, but she'll understand if you want to wait."

My heart is racing, anticipation and excitement has my body rigidly still, but beneath the surface, an electrical current of excitement is gaining momentum.

Drew's expression is a desperate combination of hope and fear as he searches mine for a glimmer of courage. He swallows hard and exhales slowly, his voice heavy with emotion. "The house is almost finished and ready for us to move into. I can't imagine a life where I move out of this penthouse and don't see you every day. In fact, I hate the thought of not seeing you every day. I know we're dating now, and we need to plan stuff together, but I want more. There are no guarantees in this life, I know that, but I also know we can push the odds in our favor. So…" Nervousness radiates from him, making him look adorable. "I'm so nervous I'm sweating." He takes a deep breath. "Move in with us?"

"I…" I was sure he was going to propose and a laugh escapes my throat at my overexcitement. "Move in with you? That's a big step, are you sure?"

He's grinning his face off, nodding at the same time. It's catching and I start to nod too.

"I'd love to move in with you and Callie."

I throw my arms around him and immediately seek out his mouth but he pulls back, tucking his arms behind his back. I stare at him curiously for a beat.

"Thank God you said yes to moving in, because it'd really suck for my wife to live somewhere else."

Drew's smile shrinks from something like a combination of nerves and uncertainty. He holds his hands out before us and I see a small, black box made of embossed leather. When he flips the lid open with his thumb, there is an enormous, perfectly circular diamond sitting proudly in its middle. The band is white gold and the stone is secured by a cluster of smaller stones. It throws colorful rays of light out in every direction and has my heart threatening to burst from my chest.

"It's so big," I whisper, awestruck.

"It's not the first time I've heard you say that," he replies devilishly.

I flush and shift on the bed, staring in wonder at the beautiful promise in his hands.

"Marry me, Skyla. I don't want to waste another moment

hesitating and living in the past. Say yes and let's dive into our futures together?"

Sheer excitement and joy fill me until I feel close to bursting. I fling my arms around his broad shoulders and his gaze turns heated as the comforter falls away and his eyes lock on my nakedness. My heart races at the swell of desire between us. Without saying a word, I know he wants me and it sends a thrill through my veins. We make quick work of removing his clothes, and in no time at all he's as gloriously naked as I am.

"Condom. Now," I pant and he pulls one from the drawer, sheathing himself in moments. I've never taken the time to admire him like this before, but his erection is impressive. Silky, girthy and long, my heart goes wild, my body trembles with need.

"Hungry little Goddess this morning," he says, smirking.

"You have no idea," I reply. I want him so much it's blurring my vision and making me dizzy. At this point, I'm scared I'll go into cardiac arrest before I get to feel him inside me.

I've been missing this all my adult life, this connection and closeness to a partner, but I have no regrets. Since the first time he ogled my ass, Drew has made me feel so beautiful, desired, and loved, I can't imagine there is anything superior to the way I feel about him. I tug his head down and lick his lower lip. "I want you."

He pants as he kisses my neck. "I'm going to go real slow." His finger trails over my breast. "See, I made you a promise that I'm going to worship and learn every inch of you. Each and every time will be better than the last." He lowers me down on the bed. "Stronger." His fingers travel down across my navel. "More intense." He skims my cleft. "See, I didn't know you honored me with your first time. It was too rough; I was too quick...."

"I liked it." I breathe, my knees starting to shake.

"Oh, but baby, there is so much more to enjoy."

His finger dips inside of me and I resist bucking against him, allowing him to take charge. Drew's eyes rove across my body as though seeing it for the first time and my body reacts like it is responding to him anew. Goosebumps prickle my skin, and when his mouth meets my core Drew holds me so I don't jerk off the bed.

"So wet for me, baby." Desire fires off inside me as he works me and I start to whimper and rock my hips. "Good God. Drew!" I mewl nonsensically as I shatter into a million pieces.

"Good girl," he replies. "You come so hard for me." And by the time he is easing inside me, I am already feeling the onset of my next orgasm. "So perfect. Beautiful." He goes slow. So achingly slow and gentle, giving me a little at a time, while looking deep into my eyes, communicating loudly and without uncertainty that what we have is more than just lust or sex. The connection we have built is so deep, it is in my DNA.

"Drew!" I gasp as he fills me. Our bodies couldn't be closer.

"It turns me on when you say my name. No one has ever said my name like you do. No one has ever looked at me like you do, like you see all of me. Guess that makes you my first too."

He leans down to kiss me, rocking so gently against me, I might pass out with need. Every nerve ending is on fire. My core is aching for release. His mouth is hot on mine. Heat burns at my core and my legs start to scissor, so I grasp his shoulders to anchor myself as the need to come apart rises.

"Sugar, I'm going to..." His eyes squeeze shut then open. He's watching me like I am the most beautiful person in the world, and it's throwing gasoline on the fire already tearing through me. For a second he breaks eye contact and I follow his gaze as he looks down at our entwined bodies. He circles his hips, then pumps while I grind myself against him with total abandon.

We unravel together, clinging to one another as though we are anchoring each to the other. Drew lets out a primal growl, while I hiss for the Lord to have mercy and other nonsensical pleas that ultimately end with fireworks and explosions. And all the while, I wonder how I suddenly became so utterly, blissfully, and perfectly satisfied.

By the time I become aware of my body again, and our breathing is slow, steady, ins and outs, and with Drew still inside me, completing our union, I realize, this is my life now, and I couldn't be happier.

Then Drew turns to me and says, "Is that a yes, then? You'll marry me?"

"Yes," I breathe. "God, yes!"

EPILOGUE

DREW

A FEW MONTHS LATER

"*P*ut the sun lotion down and take your hands off my butt, Mr. Blingwood," Skyla says over her shoulder from the sun lounger as I rub in the lotion, taking care to pull her bottoms aside so her sweet ass doesn't burn.

"I like to be thorough, Mrs. Blingwood," I reply, skimming an extra circle, loving the way her skin plumps beneath my palm.

She rolls over onto her back and pulls the magazine she has been reading off the side table. "Oh, you're thorough, Mr. Blingwood. Very thorough, indeed." A smile pulls her mouth up at the corners. I trail my finger down her thigh as I remember just how thorough I was with her last night and twice this morning.

"Mr. and Mrs. Blingwood, can I get you anything to

drink?" the server asks as he collects our empty glasses. We order drinks and then he reminds us, "Couples Pilates in thirty minutes. Will you be attending?"

I smirk at Skyla but answer the server. "Depends if my butt is going to get stared at. Sometimes, I feel like I'm a piece of meat in there."

Skyla rolls up the magazine and it skims my ear as she playfully swats me. "I do not stare at your butt." She hisses *butt* like it's a dirty word and I love how she's so easily flustered. "Not the whole time."

I cock a brow at her. She was checking out my ass and she knows it. Then I turn back to the server. "Sir, is there a CCTV camera that could verify whether my privacy was indeed violated?"

Skyla is laughing and shaking her head while the poor server looks torn whether he should take us seriously or not.

"I'll get drinks," he says finally deciding our debate is one he doesn't wish to involve himself in and leaving us to bicker.

"You were so checking out my ass."

She shakes her head, giggling, and then attempts to swat me with the magazine again, but this time I catch it and pull her closer, the temptation to kiss her is overwhelming.

"You have a one-track mind," she says, her gaze heating. Her lips, full and inviting, are dangerously close to my own.

"Now you're my wife, it's a condition I must learn to endure." She pushes her lips against mine and I reach my arms around her to pull her over to share my sun lounger. Her swimsuit, still wet from her earlier swim presses against my chest as I deepen the kiss. "We really should get you out of these wet clothes."

Her grin turns coy. "Oh? Is it time to go back to the room?"

"I believe so. I'm feeling lightheaded and I'm not sure if

it's sunstroke or my boner that's causing it. I'm guessing the latter."

"Maybe we should go back to our room and I can fix that for you."

I nod but we're interrupted. The server has returned and he hands me a bowl with some ice. "For your eye, *señor.*"

At my curious stare, he nods at my temple and my fingers automatically probe the skin where I took a stray knee to the head last night as Skyla came apart on my tongue.

I find myself smirking, as I remember the moment in all its glory.

"It's fine," I reply. "It was an accident." I'm grinning so hard the poor server has no clue whether I am a battered husband or a clumsy fool. Either way, I don't care. It's worth a bruise. Skyla's come face has become my single most favorite vision. It's priceless.

When he's gone, I tell Skyla, "I love it when you lose control."

She reaches out and strokes my temple and I admire the wedding ring on her finger that signals she's mine. "I'm sorry. Does it hurt much?"

"Nope. Doesn't hurt at all. You can give me another one on the other side later if you like?"

Skyla playfully pushes me with the palm of her hand and replies, "You're crazy."

"I'm crazy for you, sugar."

She giggles even though I haven't told a joke and, seeing her so blissfully happy, it creates a stirring in my chest. This is my life now. I've become one of those people who have it all.

"Mrs. Blingwood," I say, purely because I like how the name sounds on my tongue.

"Yes, Mr. Blingwood," Skyla replies, bending to retrieve

the magazine that has fallen on the ground. "It's going to take me some time to get used to being called Mrs. Blingwood."

I catch her hand in mine and stroke it with my thumb. "Mrs. Blingwood," I repeat. "You wear the name well."

"Three days and you haven't stopped calling me that." She sighs a smile. "It was a beautiful wedding."

"The best I ever went to," I reply.

"You heard from Callie yet today?"

"Yes. She, Mom, and Pixie have been out walking with the other rescues. They're taking Logan lunch later so she said she'll video call us after they've eaten."

Skyla smiles. "She's growing up so fast. How's Logan?"

I squeeze her hand. Skyla wanted to wait to get married so we didn't rub our bliss in Logan's face following his lucky escape from Dana, but I knew he wouldn't mind.

"Logan's fine. I think he's glad we eloped with Callie and he swears he's never going near another wedding, but he was happy for us. He loves you."

"Jessie texted me and said another of Logan's PA's walked out. That's three that have left now. He's always been so nice to work with, but lately he's so unhappy it's spilling into his work." She grabs her phone from her purse and swipes the screen, cussing beneath her breath. "Just checking my emails. Another employment agency refuses to send him any more replacements. If he keeps this up, he'll end up with no staff."

"I don't know what's gotten into him. Are there any other agencies he can get a PA from?"

"I sent an SOS out last night. Another agency I sometimes use is trying to fill the position. I hope he plays nice." She looks uncertain and worried for him.

"When we get back from the honeymoon, I'll talk to him. I'm sure he'll be fine once the press stops publishing gossip pieces speculating why he and Dana broke up. Don't worry. This is our honeymoon, no more checking emails."

Skyla nods and then puts down her phone and holds up the magazine. "This one claims Dana had a miscarriage and Logan blames himself for being a workaholic. They're making out like Dana is a saint and Logan was cold and distant. The lies are so annoying, I don't know how he can stand it. I thought once Dana stopped posting her lies on social media the fuss would die down, but the silence is increasing speculation."

I shrug. "Fuck what they say. Everyone knows what they print in those rags and online is total bullshit."

Skyla's gaze saddens and she puts the magazine in her beach bag. "Still, it's affecting him. He's so stressed with the new resort and picking up his life. I worry about him."

"I do too, but he's strong. Besides, he texted me earlier. He ran into Betty, and guess what she said to him?"

She shakes her head. "She didn't say—"

"Yep. Came right out and told him, 'What you need is pussy!'"

We both start howling with laughter, then Skyla says, "Well, when Betty has an epiphany, she's usually right."

"She certainly nailed it when she said it to me." I wink and her skin flushes.

"Betty's the best! I'm so glad she's staying close by now she's retired. She's like family to me and Jessie."

"Talking of family, you heard from your mom?"

"Only by phone since we met for lunch before the wedding. We agreed we'd arrange something when I come home. We're still taking our relationship slow."

"I'm so proud of you, baby."

Skyla raises a brow. "How so?"

"Your capacity to love. To forgive. It took real guts to reach out to your mom and start the conversation. I spent almost a year avoiding getting answers from my old man's letter, and years prior to that avoiding the discussion entirely. You decided to see what she had to say, and even though you didn't like all of it, you forgave her."

Her thumb starts running circles on the back of my hand and she smiles. "I guess, going through that with you taught me a lesson. No good can come from delaying things. I was ready to get answers, so I decided I had two choices. Meet her while I still had the chance or decide I wasn't going to forgive her and learn how to move forward. I'm glad I decided to see her. It helps that I was in the right mental space and I had the support of friends and family to fall back on in case it didn't go well." Her gaze meets mine and I'm hit with another feeling of sheer love and amazement. "My mom was young when she had me and she made mistakes she regrets. My dad made mistakes too, but I'm glad he apologized. I'll be okay. I turned out fine—"

"You turned out better than fine."

Her eyes lazily flick to mine. "You turned out pretty great yourself."

"That's because you agreed to marry me and live with me and Callie. My life has never been better and I'm going to make sure it stays that way."

Skyla leans over to kiss my shoulder but I swoop down and snatch her lips with mine, deepening the kiss with my tongue. "Perfection."

She sits up and takes a sip of her cocktail. "I can't promise it'll stay perfect."

"Oh," I reply, pushing myself up to a seated position. "What makes you say that?"

"Well, I might have agreed that we'll do something, and it's something you might not enjoy."

I crack my neck and roll my shoulders. "Baby, if it's with you, there isn't anything I can't face."

Skyla looks unsure enough that it piques my interest. "What am I in for?"

"I might have agreed we would go on a double date with Sally and Doug."

"Oh." I try to keep my expression neutral. "That's okay, baby. I can tolerate anything for you."

"We're off to couples bingo," she adds, and to her credit she looks as unsure as I feel.

"Couples bingo?" She nods, then I lurch across and pull her legs up and over my waist, tickling her until she squeals with laughter.

I'm so in the moment, skin against skin, Skyla writhing beneath me with uncontrollable laughter spilling from her beautiful lips, that it's not until I hear someone clearing their throat loudly that I stop teasing her and we both compose ourselves and turn toward the sound.

"*Señor?*"

I turn my head over my shoulder and see the server is back. "Pilates is starting if you would like to join in?"

I turn back to Skyla and lick my lips. Forty minutes of watching her bend her gorgeous body into positions that make my balls ache....

"You want to do couples Pilates in the gym or you want to go back to our suite and do me?" I whisper.

"You. Definitely you," she breathes, and it's all the encouragement I need.

"Sir, my wife has a headache. I'm taking her back to our room and putting her to bed. Thank-you."

"Yes, *señor*," the server replies.

I pick Skyla up and she reaches out her hand and quickly scoops up her purse. I take long strides in the direction of our room when her phone chimes, so she pulls it out and swipes the screen. Both of us are in the habit of checking our messages in case Callie needs us, though it's doubtful since she's with my mother while we are on our honeymoon.

"Shit," Skyla hisses and I freeze.

"What is it?"

"It's from Jessie. Logan's new assistant arrived early."

I relax. "It's good he has a new assistant. Stop worrying." I kiss the tip of her button nose.

"Guess what she's wearing?"

An image of Skyla in her work clothes flashes through my head and I start striding to our luxury suite. "Don't care. Whatever she's wearing, no way she looks as hot as my woman in her work clothes, her Pilates gear," I salivate and slide my finger under her strap, "or her swimsuit that's one flick of my finger from coming loose."

Skyla bites her lip to hide her smile then her expression turns momentarily serious. "His new assistant showed up in a full-on wedding dress. She's taken the job with Logan, despite its terrible reputation, because she ditched some guy at the altar and needs some place to lie low."

"Oh, crap!" I hiss, imagining my brother, who was dumped on his wedding day, face to face with a runaway bride.

"You think you should call him and see if he's okay?"

"Nope. I think I should take my wife back to the honeymoon suite and make sweet love to her. Logan will be fine." As I get to the door of our room, I flick my finger against the little bow holding her top together. "Let's get you out of this wet swimsuit." And by the time the door has swung shut behind us, I am halfway to having her gloriously naked.

"I love you," she hisses as I suck her pebbling breasts and maneuver my hands to her waist to lower her feet to the floor. "Baby, I'm going to love the heck out of you."

"Yes please," she replies breathless, as my hand cups her breast and my lips graze her neck.

A stray, recurring thought that's been running through my mind pops up again and I unleash it in my next sentence. "I want to put a baby in you." I brace myself for her reaction, and soften the blow by inserting my finger into her moist folds. Skyla leans into my hand, swaying against where she needs pressure. I increase the rhythm and she grips my shoulder with one hand and uses her other to push down my shorts until she has me gripped at the shaft. "I mean it, Skyla. I'd love to see you swollen with my child. Have a house full of perfect little Skyla and Drew's, and I'd love it if it was soon."

Her breathing becomes labored, her body trembling. "God, I'm going to—" I lean back to watch her face giddy from her orgasmic high while her muscles greedily squeeze my fingers. I brace her weight until her knees regain their strength and stare into her perfect brown eyes that are lit on fire from her orgasm.

"Is that a yes?" I ask, realizing how much I want this with her. "I'll take care of you, I promise. For the rest of your life, I will take care of your every need. Let's grow our family."

I pull her into me by her waist until her breasts are pushed against my chest and she is looking up into my eyes.

"You're serious?"

I nod. "I've never been more serious in my life."

"I thought your family was complete?"

"Not when it comes to you. You'll make an amazing mother. You already mother Callie as though she is your own, and she's always saying how she'd love to have siblings. What are we waiting for?"

Her lips tip up at the edges making her cheeks adorably plump. "You're right. We should start right away." My finger travels back to her sex and Skyla licks her lips in anticipation.

We're grinning like fools. She's nodding and I am nodding right along with her. Everything until now has been a serendipitous surprise, but since the wedding it feels like in every choice we're choosing each other. We are choosing forever. And it couldn't feel more perfect or more meant to be.

"I don't care how long it takes, how many times we have to do it, even if we have to stay up all night, every night. It's a sacrifice I'm willing to make," I tell her.

Her nod turns serious. "You're right. Put a baby in me, Blingwood. I'm ready!"

CLICK HERE TO grab Logan's story and discover how the jilted Blingwood brother reacts when his new assistant turns out to be a runaway bride.

BOOK 2 – CHASING THE WRONG BRIDE

SIGN up to my newsletter to be alerted about new releases and sales.

PLEASE CAN I ask for your support by leaving a review. I read every single one and nothing makes me happier than seeing your feedback

THE END

ACKNOWLEDGMENTS

To one of my favorite humans in the entire world, Randie Creamer. You edit and polish like a MF but better than that, I get to call you my friend. Thank you!

To Kari from Kari March Designs, thank you for a cover more beautiful than I imagined.

To the wonderfully smart, funny, and kind Ellen Montoya. I love you! Thank you for trusting me with your time.

To Christina Gamboa, I love your fantastic sense of humor and your appreciation—*cough* addiction—of spicy books! Thank you for all your help and guidance.

To the beautiful soul that is Ana Rita Clemente. I love our chats, your sweet way with words and your massive heart. Thank you!

To Sandi (A.K.A Book Dragon Heart. Please check her out on TikTok for spicy book reviews and titillating book chat!). You light up my screen! I adore watching you and I love seeing you in my DM's. Thank you for all your support in making this book its best version!

To my readers, thank you, thank you, thank you! Your support means everything to me and I appreciate your grace in taking a chance on little old me. No one has better readers than I do. Fact!

ALSO BY EMILY JAMES

The Blingwood Billionaires series

Book 1 –Sorry. Not Sorry

Book 2 – Chasing the Wrong Bride

Book 3 – Catch a Falling Star

The Love in Short series

Book 1—Operation My Fake Girlfriend

Book 2—Sexy With Attitude Too

Book 3—You Only Love Once

Book 4—Leaving Out Love

The Power of Ten series

Book 1—Ten Dates

Book 2—Ten Dares

Book 3—Ten Lies

ABOUT THE AUTHOR

Emily James is a British author who lives on the south coast of England. She loves to travel and enjoys nothing more than a great romance story with a heart-of-gold hero. On the rare occasions that she hasn't got her nose in a book, Emily likes to keep her heart full by spending time with her bonkers yet beautiful family and friends.

Facebook
  Goodreads
  Amazon
  Newsletter